A MARCH
TO REMEMBER

D1007678

Books by Anna Loan-Wilsey

A LACK OF TEMPERANCE

ANYTHING BUT CIVIL

A SENSE OF ENTITLEMENT

A DECEPTIVE HOMECOMING

A MARCH TO REMEMBER

Published by Kensington Publishing Corporation

Praise for Anna Loan-Wilsey
and her Hattie Davish Mysteries!

A LACK OF TEMPERANCE

"Ms. Loan-Wilsey writes with vivid imagery that immediately brings to life the late nineteenth century in this engrossing and thoroughly enjoyable tale. Miss Hattie Davish is a force to be reckoned with, and I'm eagerly awaiting more of her adventures." —Kate Kingsbury

"Fans of historical mysteries should be delighted with this debut."
—*Mystery Scene*

"*A Lack of Temperance* shows no lack of a fresh setting, spunky amateur detective, fascinating characters and intriguing mystery. Anna Loan-Wilsey has a real talent for pulling the reader into a past world of both charm and chaos. Heroine Hattie and her typewriter certainly travel well! I can't wait to read her next adventure." —Karen Harper

"This historical cozy debut showcases the author's superb research. Readers will be fascinated . . . this is a warm beginning."
—*Library Journal*

"Eureka Springs is usually a peaceful spa resort, but when Hattie Davish arrives with her typewriter she finds the town in uproar. Temperance ladies are attacking saloons and her new employer is missing. This is a fast-paced and fascinating read, peopled with feisty females, giving us a glimpse of how far women were actually prepared to go for the cause." —Rhys Bowen

ANYTHING BUT CIVIL

"Loan-Wilsey combines meticulous research with sturdy characters."
—*Publishers Weekly*

A SENSE OF ENTITLEMENT

"Thoroughly entertaining . . . well researched and plotted, this fast-paced historical mystery delivers." —*RT Book Reviews*

Please turn the page for more praise for Anna Loan-Wilsey.

A DECEPTIVE HOMECOMING

"Poignant backstory, historical color and expert pacing distinguish this mystery, the best yet in Loan-Wilsey's 19th-century cozy series."—*Publishers Weekly*

"Once you pick up one Davish mystery, you'll be running to get another."—*Suspense Magazine*

A MARCH
TO REMEMBER

ANNA LOAN-WILSEY

KENSINGTON BOOKS
www.kensingtonbooks.com

KENSINGTON BOOKS are published by

Kensington Publishing Corp.
119 West 40th Street
New York, NY 10018

All Kensington titles, imprints, and distributed lines are available at special quantity discounts for bulk purchases for sales promotion, premiums, fundraising, educational, or institutional use.

Special book excerpts or customized printings can also be created to fit specific needs. For details, write or phone the office of the Kensington Sales Manager: Kensington Publishing Corp., 119 West 40th Street, New York, NY 10018. Attn. Sales Department. Phone: 1-800-221-2647.

Kensington and the K logo Reg. U.S. Pat. & TM Off.

eISBN-13: 978-1-61773-729-9
eISBN-10: 1-61773-729-1
First Kensington Electronic Edition: October 2016

ISBN-13: 978-1-61773-728-2
ISBN-10: 1-61773-728-3
First Kensington Trade Paperback Printing: October 2016

10 9 8 7 6 5 4 3 2 1

Printed in the United States of America

To all those who love Hattie as much as I do

ACKNOWLEDGMENTS

I would like to thank Benjamin F. Alexander, professor of American history at New York City College of Technology, for his kind help and his invaluable book: *Coxey's Army: Popular Protest in the Gilded Age.* I relied heavily on his research for authenticity, accuracy, and detail, and any errors are mine alone.

I would also like to thank Sarah Wilson, dog expert, for her aid in finding the perfect breed for Spencer, and to Mindy Groff, from The Carriage Museum of America, for her useful suggestions to my inquiries.

To Kristine Mills and Judy York at Kensington: I'm thrilled, yet again, at how well you captured in your cover art the Washington, D.C., that Hattie would have known.

To my fans and family to whom Hattie has become as much a part of your lives as mine, I couldn't have done any of this without you.

At his best, man is the noblest of all animals;
separated from law and justice he is the worst.

—ARISTOTLE

It's the action, not the fruit of the action, that's important.
You have to do the right thing. . . . You may never
know what results come from your action.
But if you do nothing, there will be no result.

—GANDHI

Chapter 1

O n any other day I would have been honored, humbled,
even excited to be here. So why did I have to come today?
I wondered. Yet I knew why. Because Sir Arthur had suggested I
go, and one always did as Sir Arthur suggested.

Determined to make the best of it, I willed my stomach to
settle, brushed imaginary lint from my sleeve, and followed the
senator's wife up the path. And yet, as I ascended the steps beneath the towering white columns and stared at the stained
glass Tiffany fan light above the door, I still couldn't help but
wish I were somewhere else. I glanced at the watch pinned to
my dress. The watch pin, a small spray of bluebells, had been a
gift. I sighed. It was barely eleven o'clock.

"After you, Miss Davish," Mrs. Smith, the matronly wife of
the senator, said, smiling.

Upon first meeting the Smiths, I wondered how they
could tolerate one another: Mrs. Smith was always smiling, and
her husband could only be described as a curmudgeon. But after
living as a guest in their home for several weeks, I'd learned they
complemented each other: She smiled because he wouldn't, she

was gracious because he wasn't, and she did or said what was necessary because he couldn't. In return, he gave her a beautiful home, a prominent place in Washington's society, and the freedom to do almost anything she wanted.

"Are you ready?" Mrs. Smith said, noticing my hesitation.

I nodded, adjusted my new hat, a pink straw with a bell-shaped crown and wide brim turned up in front and embellished with ostrich feathers, and stepped through the open front door of the White House.

"Oh, my!" I said out loud despite myself. I hadn't stepped farther than the vestibule and the opulence surrounding me rivaled even the grandest "cottages" I'd visited in Newport.

We crossed the multicolored mosaic floor tiles and stopped to join the other admirers of the famous floor-to-ceiling Tiffany stained-glass screens. Topaz, ruby, and amethyst jewels were set into the glass alongside four eagles and a shield with the initials U.S.

Even as Mrs. Smith moved on, I lingered a bit longer.

"Coming, Miss Davish?" Mrs. Smith said, her smile never leaving her face.

"Of course."

In the grand East Room, a banquet hall nearly eighty feet long with floor-to-ceiling windows, ornate glass chandeliers with prominent clusters of globe lights, and silver ceiling wallpaper, installed by Louis Tiffany to resemble Pompeiian mosaics, we joined the receiving line. I was much relieved when I saw most of the women in attendance were working women like me: maids, clerks, and shopgirls wearing their Sunday clothes, the best they owned. Mixed among them were a few politicians' wives wearing bored expressions and merchants' wives holding their heads high while staring around them with wide, awestruck eyes. The din in the immense room, which the thick Brussels carpet did little to diminish, was testimony to the excitement around me. Mrs. Cleveland's weekly Saturday receptions, in which she encouraged the attendance of working women who couldn't attend on the weekdays, were well known during President Cleveland's first term. But until Sir Arthur mentioned it, I hadn't realized she still hosted them.

Maybe this will be fun after all, I thought. It might even distract me until one o'clock. I glanced at my watch again. And then something the two ladies ahead of me said caught my ear.

"Washington, invaded? I don't believe it," the lady with a sailor hat adorned with loops of rose velvet said.

"It's true," said her companion, wearing a toque from several seasons ago. "Colonel Clay himself mentioned an imminent invasion when he addressed his battalions the other day. Supposedly he's dedicated forty-two thousand of his National Guard troops if the police can't handle the marchers when they approach on May Day."

"But I thought the marchers were peaceful?" the woman in the sailor hat said.

"An army of possibly tens of thousands of disgruntled, unemployed men who've marched for three months, wearing rags for clothes, and who haven't had a decent bath or meal in three months? What do you think?" Before they could say more, their turn had come to greet the First Lady.

They must mean Coxey's Army.

These men who, after walking all the way from Ohio, were camped outside of the city waiting until May Day to march to the Capitol to promote awareness of the dire straits much of the country suffered from. They had been a topic of discussion for months, as every day a new article in the newspaper described their progress, their triumphs, and their setbacks. Along with thousands of others across the country, I'd been avidly following their every step. I was thrilled to learn I'd be in Washington when the marchers arrived and was counting down the days. Only three days to go. But did the government really think they were a threat? Like the lady in the fashionable sailor hat, I couldn't believe it.

The two women I'd overheard, after shaking hands and speaking with Mrs. Cleveland, walked away giggling with excitement, all thoughts of violence and Coxey's Army gone from their heads. *So why am I still thinking about it?* I wondered, absentmindedly taking a step forward. My wondering was interrupted when a melodic voice spoke to my companion. "So nice to see you again, Mrs. Smith. I pray all is well with you and Senator Smith?"

It was Frances Cleveland, the President's wife. Her black hair was adorned with rose quartz combs that matched her fashionable deep rose, pleated, dotted Swiss and satin dress. Two inches taller than me, she was a lovely, yet commanding, presence. Mrs. Cleveland had entered the White House an inexperienced bride of a president three decades older than she. Now, at twenty-eight, the same age as me, she reigned over the reception with warmth and regal grace.

"Very well, thank you," Mrs. Smith said. "May I present Miss Hattie Davish, secretary to Sir Arthur Windom-Greene, an American history scholar visiting us from Richmond?"

I had seen her image on advertisements, trade cards, and objects as diverse as sewing kits and cigar boxes. It hadn't prepared me for the bright intelligence in her dark blue eyes as she turned to me.

"I'm pleased to make your acquaintance, Miss Davish." Mrs. Cleveland held out her hand. I hesitated only a moment before shaking it. I was grateful to be wearing gloves; they easily hid the calluses on my fingertips.

"I'm honored to meet you, ma'am."

"The President and I met Sir Arthur last week. The President thoroughly enjoyed Sir Arthur's book on Appomattox."

I should've known Sir Arthur would've met the President. Was there no one he didn't know?

"You must have been quite a help, Miss Davish. Sir Arthur mentioned you," the First Lady said.

"He did?" I was astounded that Sir Arthur would mention

me at all, let alone to the President of the United States. And then I was mortified that I'd said it out loud. "I mean, that was kind of you to remember." She smiled, taking my bad manners in stride, being as gracious as her reputation purported her to be.

"Enjoy yourself, ladies," she said before turning and greeting the shopgirl behind me. "Good morning. What is your name, my dear?"

"I must apologize, Mrs. Smith," I said, as soon as we couldn't be overheard by the First Lady. "I have no excuse for my ill manners."

"I have to admit, I didn't suspect you as the type to be bedazzled by celebrity and lose your head. But not to worry, Miss Davish." The senator's wife smiled kindly. "Mrs. Cleveland won't think another thing of it."

After what I'd done, I wasn't about to correct Mrs. Smith. Let her think I was overwhelmed by meeting Mrs. Cleveland when, in fact, it was Sir Arthur's comment that had staggered me. I couldn't wait to tell Walter. I glanced at my watch again.

"Shall we have tea?" Mrs. Smith said, indicating the buffet table laden with roll sandwiches, crumpets, pickled eggs, baked tomatoes, strawberries in cream, cookies, cakes, and ices.

"Yes, please." As I followed her across the room, I overheard snippets from conversations of all kinds.

"No, no, Mrs. Hawley. I've already tried speaking with my husband about it. He won't change his vote."

"Don't you adore Mrs. Cleveland's dress? She's always so fashionable. I wish I could wear such bright colors. Who do you think made it: Lottie Barton, Madame Stauffer, or House of Worth?"

"These tarts remind me. Did you hear that the Hortons' cook resigned on the eve of Lenora's coming-out party?"

"If you haven't been to the Corcoran Gallery yet, Orpha, you mustn't miss it."

"What do you think Ada and the Minsky girls would say if

they saw us now? I bet they wouldn't believe it, us having tea and cake with Mrs. Cleveland in the White House!"

"Oh, you'll have to read it. It's called *The Prisoner of Zenda* by Anthony Hope. I was up all last night. I couldn't put it down."

"Did you see that stained glass screen? That must be worth a fortune."

"Did you know that Mrs. Grady, the lady who runs my boardinghouse, spent a year at Wells College when Frankie was a student there?" I cringed, having read in the paper that Mrs. Cleveland didn't like the nickname Frankie.

"Oh, Mildred, dear. So good to see you. When is the Washington Wives Club meeting next?" This was directed at Mrs. Smith, who paused to join their conversation.

"May I introduce Miss Davish," Mrs. Smith said to a group of elderly ladies, who all acknowledged me with a nod before quickly forgetting I was there.

"Excuse me," I said, as we hadn't reached the refreshment table yet. Mrs. Smith smiled and dismissed me with a wave.

Once at the buffet table, I accepted a cup of black coffee and added to my plate a slice of rhubarb pie, a strawberry shortcake, and a slice of silver cake with icing. As I made my way back toward Mrs. Smith, I heard more comments about Coxey's approaching army of marching men that seemed discordant with the occasion.

"Supposedly federal agents have been secretly planted among them since Allegheny City."

"Really? I had no idea," was the reply.

Neither had I, I thought. I'd never heard anything before about the Secret Service agents among Coxey's men.

"At the very least, we're in for a riot. Why else would the Marines stationed in the Navy Yard go through close-quarter riot drills?"

A woman gasped.

"Surely there won't be bloodshed? American soldiers using bayonets on American citizens in Washington City? It's unthinkable."

"Why else would General Ordway arm his men with bayonets?"

I took a bite of my rhubarb pie and moved away from this disturbing conversation. With plate and cup still in hand, I navigated my way past a group of girls who, based on their hats and gloves, were most likely maids or shopgirls.

"And did you see the row of ruby beads on her skirt? I heard they were a gift from the Viceroy of India," one of the girls said.

I finally took a place near Mrs. Smith, who acknowledged me with a smile but continued on in her conversation. I took a sip of my coffee, admired the Boston fern nearby, a large, lush specimen of the plant, and finished the shortcake before looking at my watch again. I listened to the women chatter on about a recent visit to an orphanage the Washington Wives Club had sponsored as I nibbled on my silver cake for a few more minutes, my impatience growing. When they turned to discussing the prehistoric look of the alligators at the National Zoo's Carnivora House, I glanced at my watch again. Twelve o'clock. I couldn't stand to stay any longer.

"Excuse me, but I must go now, Mrs. Smith. Thank you for bringing me."

"Already?" Mrs. Smith said, barely turning to look at me.

"Yes, I'm afraid so." Which was an unabashed lie. I couldn't wait to leave.

"Very well. Glad you enjoyed yourself." She immediately returned to the conversation I'd interrupted and never noticed my departure.

As fast as decorum allowed, I shuffled through the crowd of

women until I was in the Entrance Hall again. As I approached the door, two men crossed my path as they headed toward a back staircase.

"And the Treasury Department has deployed dozens of additional revolvers and carbines to its security men," one man read from a notebook as they walked.

"But why the Treasury Department?" the other asked.

"The march route is going right past there, isn't it? They're a rabble of desperate, unemployed men. Who's to say the Treasury isn't their real target? Who's to say that after the marchers fail to gain the Capitol steps that someone doesn't yell, 'Here is the United States Treasury filled with money, while our families are starving'?" The second man nodded, agreeing with this logic. "If nothing else, we should not regard the invasion of Coxey's Army as a joke."

As I watched the men turn the corner, their conversation too faint to hear, I paused in concern. It was one thing to have women idly gossip about bloodshed and violence; it was another to hear men who ran the government confirm some of the rumors were true.

Through the daily newspaper accounts, I had the impression that Coxey and his men were peaceful, Christian men; I wouldn't have concerned myself with a band of ruffians. But these comments gave me reason to pause. Were Coxey and his followers really intent on marching into the city, regardless of the cost? Were they willing to lay down their lives for their cause? Would the government kill unarmed Americans to prevent Coxey's message from being heard?

I hope not! Then I glanced at my watch again and banished all concerns of the marchers from my mind as I stepped back into the sunshine. I had a train to meet!

CHAPTER 2

"I believe in bettering the condition of the workingman!" The shouting accosted me the moment I emerged from the White House. A clean-shaven young man in a dusty brown derby, standing in the carriageway beneath the columns, punched his fist into his open palm with each word to accentuate his point. Several women, still arriving for the reception, quickly shied away and gave him a wide berth. I stood my ground, sympathetic to his message, but not wanting to get any closer.

"That can't be done by talk," he yelled as two large policemen dashed past me. They confronted the fist-pounding young man, insisting he leave. He refused to budge.

"There's only one way to do it, only one way of waking up the 'soulless capitalists' who own Washington," the young man shouted, as the two policemen grabbed him by the arms and began dragging him away. "By blowing up the whole damned works, the Capitol, the White House, Congress, everything."

Could the city be in real danger after all? I wondered. Why

would he be so careless as to reveal his plans to the White House police beforehand?

Putting my back to the anarchist, still spouting his plans for the destruction of the city, I hastened on my way, annoyed to have been delayed. *His rhetoric isn't helping anyone,* I thought. With my foot in midair above the top step, my progress was again hampered when a hand gripped my shoulder.

"Let go of me," I said, yanking my shoulder away.

"Miss Davish!" a man's sharp voice exclaimed as I nearly lost my footing on the stairs. He grabbed hold of my arm and pulled me back. My feet firmly on the ground, I pulled out of his grip and stared the man in the face.

"Mr. Morris?"

"I didn't mean to startle you."

"You didn't." I sounded more peevish than I would've liked. Annoyed both at myself for overreacting and at him for presuming to grip my shoulder, I said sternly, "What do you want, Mr. Morris?"

"I . . . I . . ." he stammered. "I'm finished here and thought I'd walk back with you."

He being Senator Smith's confidential clerk and private secretary, I knew better than to ask what business took Claude Morris to the White House. I admit, though, I was curious. Since the day Sir Arthur and I came to Washington as guests of Senator Meriwether Lewis Smith, I'd been curious about what role Mr. Morris played in the senator's household. Similar to what I did for Sir Arthur, Mr. Morris performed the basic duties of stenographer and typist, saw to the senator's correspondence and schedule and any other general tasks the senator might require. But that's where my knowledge of what he did ended. I'd only been in Washington for a couple of weeks, but Claude Morris appeared to do far more for his employer than simply the duties of a private secretary. (Of course, the same could be said for me.) Mr. Morris appeared to be the senator's liaison between other members of Congress, his font of knowledge regarding all things political, his adviser, as well as, dare I say, his spy.

Claude Morris was a pleasant-looking man, with keen eyes, a long, thick, well-trimmed mustache, and a few fawn curls swept back high on his forehead. He wore the same tailored dark suit and derby hat that seemed the uniform of men of his class and position. He was always ready with a shy smile for any of the ladies, including me, but was slightly pompous when given the chance to speak at any length. Yet I was still surprised that he'd grabbed my shoulder. I hadn't thought his presumption went that far.

"Thank you, but I'm not going back right away. I'm meeting someone at the train station."

"I'll escort you there, then."

"Thank you, Mr. Morris, but I'm quite used to walking about on my own." I tried in vain to keep my annoyance out of my voice.

"Yes, I've heard about your outlandish habit of wandering about the city in the early-morning hours. Risky, if you ask me." I didn't ask. "You may be unaware, though, that these are unusual days. Already men of unknown quality have made their way from Coxey's camp into the city. We are preparing, even as we speak, for the eventuality of the army as a whole attempting to approach the Capitol. Simply put, with that Populism-spouting, Theosophy-touting rabble heading our way soon, it's not safe for a woman to be rambling about on her own."

"I'm walking to the train station, Mr. Morris. I'm not rambling about."

"But you must've heard that man threatening to blow up the White House and the Capitol just now?"

"Of course, Mr. Morris. And the police have him well in hand."

"Well, if you won't let me escort you, mind that you don't

stray from Pennsylvania Avenue until you get there. No short-cuts toward B Street, particularly not between Pennsylvania and Ohio. We wouldn't want you to inadvertently find yourself in Murder Bay, now, would we? I don't think the senator or your Sir Arthur would like to hear that, even in the day, you were mistaken for, shall we say, 'a fallen woman'?"

Murder Bay? I'd never heard of it and said so.

"Maybe you've heard it referred to as 'Hooker's Division' after that general's habit of sending his troops there to let off some steam?"

Now, *that* rang a bell. In my research for Sir Arthur, a prominent Civil War historian, I'd read about the time when General Hooker and his men had quartered inside the city. I'd come across that name before, "Hooker's Division," but had only read hints of the scandalous behavior being concentrated in that part of the city. I'd had no idea it was nearby.

"I may have. What is it?"

Claude Morris was more than enthusiastic in his description of a neighborhood notorious for its gambling, brothels, and crime. I was amused as he attempted to impart the depravity of the area while using language suitable for a lady's ear, such as "young men out for misadventure," "odoriferous alleys in need of civic attention," and "misguided girls who walk the streets at night." Curious, I was an attentive audience. I wasn't surprised the city had such a neighborhood; most larger cities do, whether we ladies are supposed to know about them or not. What did surprise me, if I understood correctly from the directions that Mr. Morris made me promise to follow, was that it was merely blocks away from where we stood. I had no intention of wandering into the den of criminals, but it made me bristle to have this man, several years younger than me, dictate how I was to traverse the city.

As Mr. Morris finished, he tilted his head in anticipation of my response. I silently counted backward from ten in French.

"Thank you, Mr. Morris," I said calmly. "I will heed your warning and make mine a direct route to the station. Good day!" *How easily you lie, Hattie Davish!* I admonished myself. Yet I felt strangely at ease with my deception.

He smiled, satisfied he'd done his good deed for the day, tipped his hat, and headed down the steps to the circle drive. I waited and watched him until he crossed the street and entered Lafayette Square, a tree-lined public park north of the White House. When he passed the statue of Andrew Jackson astride his rearing horse and turned toward the Smith home, Mr. Morris disappeared from view beneath the trees. I then skipped down the stairs and headed down Pennsylvania Avenue in search of a shortcut through the so-called Murder Bay.

Is that what a fallen woman looks like?

I'd ignored Claude Morris's advice, a circuitous route from Fifteenth to B Street NW, cutting across the Mall at Fourteenth to B Street SW and then back up Sixth to the train station, and instead took the more direct route down Pennsylvania Avenue to the station. I admit I cut down Fourteenth Street, which crossed Ohio Avenue, in direct defiance of Mr. Morris's advice, as the man was too presumptuous toward me. In my mind, we were on the same social and economic level. On the whole, we held the same position for our respective employers, equals, if I may be so bold, and I was not obliged to take his advice. Of course, he saw it differently. Since the day I'd arrived, he'd taken on the role of brotherly protector, which I neither asked for nor was in need of. And as the days wore on, his condescension had worn thin. Without offending our host, Senator Smith, or my employer, Sir Arthur, I'd managed to defy almost every direc- tive, command, and "piece of advice" Claude Morris bestowed upon me.

But I'd also strolled down Fourteenth because I was curi- ous. It was past noon and the street was noisy and bustling with buggy and wagon traffic, as men in dark suits and derby hats, with papers, books, or satchels tucked beneath their arms, rushed about. I even spied other women: two elderly ladies wearing bonnets and taking turns carrying a pampered Boston terrier and a young woman pulling a toy wagon stacked with Bibles. Hence I saw no danger in my being mistaken for a resident of this questionable neighborhood nor of having my reputation damaged by finding myself strolling its broad avenue on my way to the train station. Even about my person I had so little of value, unless a thief valued the ostrich feathers in my hat or my new watch pin, that I wouldn't be a likely target. So I took the shortcut for the chance of getting a glimpse of a gambling house or a bagnio.

Would I even be able to detect from the building front what depravities occurred within? I doubted signs swayed above doors with peeling red paint, reading BAWDY HOUSE or GAMBLING DEN, so no mistake could be made. Criminal activity such as this, mere blocks from where Frances Cleveland kissed her children good night, wasn't going to announce its presence blatantly, I was certain. So how would I know?

I glanced at each structure casually as to not bring attention to myself and was surprised to find several buildings, some covering entire blocks, that did indeed announce their purpose: Andrew J. Joice & Co. Carriage Factory, E. E. Jackson & Co. Lumberyard, Pettit & Dripps's Eagle Iron Works, all seemingly respectable. Even the National Theatre was housed on the corners of Fourteenth and Pennsylvania Avenue, mere blocks from where Mr. Morris claimed was a "veritable den of depravity." Was Claude Morris, at this moment, laughing at my expense? I had read the term Hooker's Division, but knowing little of what the term meant, he could have invented the whole thing and I'd be none the wiser.

And then I saw her.

Half a block down on C Street, a woman wearing only a

white muslin chemise and drawers, with her long blond hair loose about her shoulders, sat on a small second-floor balcony enjoying the warm sun. Compelled by morbid curiosity, I turned onto C Street in order to walk beneath her. She had a brown tabby cat in her lap, which she stroked methodically, and her face was partially obscured by the copy of *Godey's Magazine and Lady's Book* raised in her hand. Her feet were propped up on the railing, with the back of her legs all the way to her knee clearly visible to all who chanced by. I covered my eyes, embarrassed to witness such a manner of undress, only to peek through a crack in my gloved fingers and stare at this woman, so different and yet not. Standing below her, I felt at once both inferior to and almost envious of this woman, who was more free to do as she pleased than I could ever dream. When was the last time I was unrestrained by a corset or had leisure time enough to read a magazine in the middle of the day? And yet, I pitied her. She would never fit into society. She had to cater to the whims of men's desires. She would never have a family and children. She would never . . . Was I so different? Despite my distaste for her livelihood, who was I to pity her?

"But for the grace of God . . ." I whispered to myself.

As an orphaned girl, if not for my father's foresight in directing me toward a respectable vocation and the patronage of Sir Arthur, I could've found myself in this woman's position. I shuddered at the horror of the thought even as I peeked at her again. I then diverted my eyes properly and walked brusquely past. In doing so, I nearly bumped into a fair-haired man about my age in a well-creased slate fedora, approaching the front door of that same unremarkable, unmarked building. Understandably distracted, he mumbled, "Excuse me," and tipped his hat, all without giving me a glance. His eyes were focused elsewhere.

Maybe the girl on the balcony was the "swaying sign" I'd imagined.

I continued on my way, with exceedingly slow steps, until I stopped in the darkened doorway of a tenement building, unable to take my eyes away. I'd be ashamed of indulging my curiosity later, but for now nothing was more compelling, more shocking, than the scene before me.

The man tapped on the door, which flew open immediately. A broad, middle-aged woman with unnaturally blond hair that could only have been the result of dye treatment, a round face, and small eyes that never looked at any one thing for long, stepped out and deliberately closed the door behind her. Unlike the girl above them on the balcony, she was dressed respectably, and expensively, in a beige silk tea gown.

Was she too a fallen woman or could this be what they called a madam? Or were there other functions for women within a brothel I didn't know about? I was woefully ignorant about these things.

The couple immediately began a heated discussion, the woman speaking through tears, but I was too far away to discern a word. The man pressed the woman's shoulder. The woman nodded—reluctantly, it seemed to me—and I expected them to disappear inside. Instead, the man surprised me by pulling out a small notebook and pencil. How often had I done the same to jot down a note or add an item to an ever-growing list?

The man wrote something down, looked up, and with a nod from the woman, jotted down something else. Who was this man? What could he possibly want to know about the life and worries of a fallen woman? Was he a policeman? Was that why the woman was upset? But no, their conversation was not confrontational, the opposite of what I'd assume: he was patting her shoulder gently, shaking his head in consolation, and offering her his handkerchief. These two knew each other and were on friendly terms. But then what were they discussing?

The girl on the balcony leaned over, her bosom in danger of exposure, and called to the man. He smiled and waved. He shouted something I couldn't hear as the blaring of a train whistle jarred me from my enthrallment. Walter! I instantly felt the pull of the excitement and anticipation of seeing the man I loved. Within minutes, I would be back in Walter's embrace. Without a second thought to the couple in the doorway, I barely kept myself from running all the way to the train station.

CHAPTER 3

With his top hat, tailored suit, well-trimmed mustache, and teeth sparkling in the midday sun, Walter was as handsome as I'd ever seen him. It took my breath away to see how his blue eyes tracked my every movement and how his smile never left his face from the moment he caught sight of me waiting in the crowd.

"Hattie!" he shouted as he leaned out of the window.

I waved and he pulled back from the window, disappearing into the shadow of the carriage. Within moments he was standing in the open doorway, before the train had come to a complete stop. He didn't wait. Even when the brakes hissed and the steam screamed as the train came to a halt, Walter was leaping down the steps and off the train. We each wound our way through the waiting crowd on the platform and into each other's arms.

"Hattie," he whispered in my ear, sending chills tingling throughout my whole body.

I clung to him for a moment before propriety brought me to my senses. He gently kissed my cheek before letting me step back. He still held my hand in his. We were jostled by the arriving passengers, porters pushing trunks and luggage.

When a man's case thumped Walter in the back, so hard in the man's desire to be free of the crowd that Walter's hat almost fell off, he said, "Let's get out of here!"

I wrapped my arm tightly around his, he placed his hand on top of mine, and we scurried past the rush and ramble until we found a quiet spot behind a tower of stacked luggage. Walter pulled me to him again.

"Oh, how I've missed you. It's been too long." I couldn't agree more.

Walter and I had spent the previous summer together in Newport, parting not long after I'd returned from a short visit to my hometown of St. Joseph, Missouri; he back to Eureka Springs where he was one of the prominent town doctors and me to Richmond with Sir Arthur and his wife, Lady Phillippa. Although we had written on a regular basis, this was our first meeting since. The year had been filled with predictable work as I helped Sir Arthur on his latest research project and consequent manuscript. I couldn't count how many days I'd spent typing and taking dictation while I waited patiently for Walter's next letter.

Walter took a deep breath and sighed. "Let's walk," he said, suddenly uncharacteristically solemn.

I nodded, afraid my voice would betray the sudden anxiety that clutched at my heart. Something was wrong.

"I've heard there's a lovely botanical garden not far from here," he said, trying in vain to sound calm. "I know you would like that. Let's go there."

Normally so easygoing, why was Walter suddenly tense? Bones in his jaw protruded slightly as he clamped down on his teeth, his skin was pallid, and beads of perspiration glistened on his brow. I looked about me, trying to distract myself from Walter's uncharacteristic mood. A brougham, with an elaborate

monogram of *MLS* painted in gold leaf on the door, was parked
nearby. A man, pulling off his gloves, stood waiting for the driver
to open the door. I stared at him for a moment, struck by his resemblance to our host, Senator Smith. And then, as the driver
reached to open the door, the man jabbed the poor driver in
the back with his black umbrella, fuming for having to wait.
Embarrassed to have witnessed such boorish behavior, I
looked back at Walter, hoping to find a change. It was a mistake. His face was drawn, and when he noticed me looking at
him, he struggled to offer me a limp smile.

Oh, Walter, what has happened?

I walked beside him, wordlessly guiding him toward one of
my favorite places in all of the city, while my stomach clenched
and breathing became a chore. Walter, an exceptional physician,
a compliment I never thought I'd give any doctor, didn't take
long to notice I was struggling to keep my composure.

"Is there something wrong? Are you ill?"

"I could ask you the same thing," I said, my laugh sounding feeble even to my own ears.

Walter's smile was as feeble as my laugh, not at all like the
grin he'd given me moments ago from the train. What had
happened in those few moments? Had he recovered from his
joy of seeing me and sobered to the reality of our situation?
Had he received bad news and hesitated to tell me? Was he
due to leave for a tour of Europe and wished not to go? Had
his mother changed her mind?

Walter took a deep breath, and I feared the worst. "You
like the watch pin I sent you then?" He pointed to the gift
pinned to my dress.

"You know I do." He was doing everything to avoid saying
what must be said. "Please tell me. I can't take the anticipation
anymore."

I put my hand to my chest, nearly gasping for breath. My
corset suddenly felt too tight. I'd been so excited to see him

and now, if he didn't speak soon, I feared I would run away and not come back.

"Indulge me a few more minutes? Is the garden far?"

"No, look." Unable to say more, I pointed toward the towering circular conservatory, the sun glinting off the hundreds of glass panels on its dome, a few blocks away. He patted my hand and we strode in silence until we passed a police station with a sign on the door that read FE, FI, FO, FIGHT, WE SMELL THE BLOOD OF A COXEYITE.

"What's that all about?" Walter said. My heart beating too hard to answer, I led him quickly past. The last thing I needed to worry about was the threat of Coxey's Army.

When we arrived, he began scouring the outdoor gardens, looking about him nervously, until he spied the spot where he was to tell me the crushing news. He took my hands in his and led me to the marble wall that encircled the famous Bartholdi Fountain, in the shadow of the ornate, thirty-foot-tall cast-iron sculpture including reptiles, seashells, tritons, and three classical female figures holding a large basin encircled with a dozen lamps. The mist from the cascading water cooled my flushed face. He sat. I didn't. A flash of concern passed over his face. He patted the spot next to him.

"Please, Hattie, don't make this harder than it has to be." And there it was. Confirmation that he'd traveled all this way to tell me face-to-face that he'd bent to the wishes of his mother and was engaged to someone else, that he was dying, that . . . that for whatever reason, I'd never see him again. "Will you sit?"

The smell of the water mixed with the scent of the nearby rose garden filled the air as a brilliant red cardinal alighted and then disappeared into an arborvitae hedge nearby. At any other time, I would have inhaled the sweet scents deeply. Now I could barely breathe.

"No, I'll stand."

"Very well," he said, the words forced from his lips. "After what you've been through, it's only fitting I should do this properly." He inched to the edge of the wall and took my hands in his. With his soft skin against mine, I had to look away. "At least I won't have to get my knees dirty." He chuckled.

Knees dirty? Was he planning to beg my forgiveness for leading me astray? For elevating my hopes, only to dash them when I had so gallantly fought against such a bitter end?

"Just say what you have to say." I could taste the bitterness in my mouth.

"Dearest Hattie, will you not even look at me?"

"No." Tears welling in my eyes slowly dripped down my face. With both of my hands in his, I had no way of brushing them aside as I wanted to.

Suddenly Walter was on his feet, his hands cradling my face, staring into my eyes. "This isn't at all what I wanted. Oh, Hattie, my God, why are you crying? Please, if I've been wrong . . . Oh God. How could I be so wrong?" He took several steps away and turned from me. We stood in silence for a moment as I drew my courage to speak.

"I'm sorry, Walter. I didn't mean to break down." Not taking the time to find my handkerchief in my bag, I wiped my tears with the back of my hand. "Please, say what you came to say. I'll be fine."

He swiveled around to stare at me and then the smile I so adored widened across his face. He took one step, and I was wrapped in his arms as he kissed my eyes and my cheeks where my tears mingled with his kisses.

"And here I thought for a moment . . . oh, how could I have ever doubted you?"

"Doubted me? Oh, Walter, what are you talking about?"

With his face mere inches from mine he said, "I love you, Miss Hattie Davish. Will you do me the honor of becoming my wife?"

Waves of shock and disbelief rippled through my body so

that I couldn't feel my feet or hands and as quickly were replaced by overwhelming relief, happiness, and joy. My head swam and tears blurred my vision. How could I have misread his nervousness for rejection, his hesitation for having to relay tragic news? Walter loved me. I knew he did. Why was I so quick to believe he'd given up?

It didn't matter now, I realized, as he stared at me in anticipation of my answer.

"Well? Will you have me, Hattie?"

What else could I say? "Yes, my dearest Walter. Yes!"

He swept me into his arms, and swung me in a circle like a whirligig. We both laughed in relief and joy. The disapproving stares of a middle-aged couple strolling by brought me back to myself, and Walter put me back on my feet. Still clutching each other's hands, we sat simultaneously on the fountain wall and leaned in, neither wanting to be farther apart than we must.

"So your mother gave you her blessing after all?"

"Yes, though I won't go into the details of our last meeting. Suffice to say, she will not stand in our way and will welcome you into her home." That was as much as I could expect from the woman who was disappointed in her aspirations to find her son a wealthy, socially suitable wife.

"I know both Father and Mother would've adored you." I only wished I'd had the chance to introduce them to this wonderful man. "Though Mother, having raised me to be a 'good Catholic girl,' wanted me to marry a 'nice Catholic boy.' So despite having married a Protestant herself, she would've tried to convert you."

"She wouldn't need to."

"What do you mean?"

"I spent our time away wisely, dearest Hattie. I know how much your faith means to you, and I know you would never ask it of me, so I did it for you."

"You converted?"

He nodded.

"Yes, now I too believe in One Holy Catholic and Apostolic Church."

"Oh, Walter." I was so full of joy that I couldn't say more.

"But what about Sir Arthur?" Walter said. "Will he give us his blessing, despite losing you as his secretary?"

"Oh!" I gasped, my hand flying to cover my mouth.

"You did mention this inevitability to him, didn't you?"

I was mortified to have to admit I had never mentioned the possibility, let alone the inevitability, to Sir Arthur that I might marry and leave his employ. I loved Walter, but I had never committed to the idea that we would someday marry. After his mother's rejection of me in Newport, it seemed too much of a dream, like I was setting myself up for a terrible disappointment. And yet when Walter had written to tell me he was coming to Washington and had news he wanted to discuss, I'd immediately hoped for a proposal. So why hadn't I broached the subject with Sir Arthur? He'd been so good to me, I couldn't imagine marrying and leaving him without his well wishes. Was that why? Did I doubt he would wish me well? Would he concern himself only with the loss of a trusted servant? Or had the appropriate moment simply not presented itself? I hoped it was the latter but feared it was the former.

"I haven't spoken to him about it."

"Not at all?" Walter's eyes widened in surprise.

I wanted to tell him I'd done it, that I hadn't feared what Sir Arthur would say, that I hadn't doubted there would ever be a need to discuss it. I'd found avoiding the truth and sometimes outright lying had come easier and easier to me, ever since I'd gotten caught up in crime and murder, but I couldn't, wouldn't lie to this man.

"Not at all." Walter silently contemplated this revelation.

"Then we must speak to him as soon as possible, mustn't we?"

"Yes." I was relieved not to be chastised for my lapse. "In

fact, I have to meet him at the Capitol in an hour. Maybe I can speak with him then."

"Oh, no, I've arranged to have a late luncheon with my sister. As one of my biggest allies in this world, she has a right to know the happy news first. She lives in Dupont Circle. Do you have time to at least come and meet Sarah?"

Walter's sister, Sarah, Mrs. Daniel Clayworth, was several years old than her brother but, unlike Walter, had made her mother proud in her choice of a spouse. Sarah had married a wealthy banker from the state of Missouri who was now serving his third term as a United States congressman, and the couple was entrenched in Washington's high society. Walter adored his sister, writing of her often in his letters, but with Sarah having lived first in St. Louis and then in Washington, they saw each other rarely. Needless to say, I hadn't yet met her.

"I'm so sorry, Walter." I glanced at the watch pinned to my dress, his gift to me. "You'll have to go without me. Sir Arthur wants me to cover the Senate's session this afternoon. Dupont Circle is a bit far, and I can't risk being late. You know how Sir Arthur is about punctuality." I tried to keep the relief from my voice. After the fiasco of meeting Walter's mother, I was none too eager to meet the sister. "I am sorry."

"Don't be. Of course, I'm disappointed, but you have to do what you need to do."

"Can we see each other tonight?"

"I have a better idea," Walter said, brightening. "I've never been to a session of Congress. Maybe I can meet you there. And I'll bring Sarah, if she can join us, so you two can get acquainted."

"This afternoon?"

"Nervous?" he asked, though he hadn't needed to. He could easily tell I was nervous.

"Yes, I am."

"Don't be. She's eager to meet you and will love you as

much as I do." I nodded, praying she would love me even half as much. It would be an improvement over Mrs. Grice. I said as much. Walter laughed, his head tilting back, his Adam's apple prominent.

Oh, to kiss him right there. Blood rushed to my cheeks at the thought. I glanced at my lap to compose myself before he noticed.

"You're right. No one could love you as much as I do." And with that he put his arms around my shoulders, pulling me the few inches toward him that separated us, and kissed me with all the abandon and joy of a man in love. And the world melted away.

CHAPTER 4

My trousseau!
After a reluctant parting with Walter, I walked about for a few minutes to calm myself before meeting Sir Arthur for the Senate session. As I passed Hutchinson's Ladies' Furnishings on Pennsylvania Avenue, the window dressing caught my eye. Bolt after bolt of lace, draped across bars suspended high from the ceiling, flowed down and across the floor like waterfalls, with individual silk flowers of every color scattered and "floating" among them. And then it hit me. My trousseau. I didn't have a trousseau.

Unlike some girls who had years of linens and underclothes delicately sewn and stored in a hope chest, waiting for the groom to come along, I had not spent a single moment contemplating what I would need if I were ever to marry. But I was now engaged (I still couldn't believe it!) and, as I admired the lovely lace in the window, realized I was terribly underequipped. I pulled my notebook and pencil out of my chatelaine bag and jotted down the minimum I needed to properly furnish myself.

1. a reception dress
2. walking dress
3. suit dress
4. three day dresses
5. two housedresses
6. three nightgowns
7. three petticoats
8. two chemises
9. three pairs of drawers
10. six handkerchiefs
11. three corsets
12. two dozen pairs of plain stockings
13. a tablecloth
14. a set of towels

I still had a little time before meeting Sir Arthur, so I stepped in and, after explaining my predicament, found an enthusiastic shopgirl to help me. She looked at my list and within minutes pulled everything I needed from the glass cases and wooden shelves lining the walls of the store. Not having anticipated the extra expense, I stood firm when she suggested adding more drawers, chemises, and nightgowns to my order. The only extravagance I allowed myself was to add embroidery to the petticoats and exquisite French lace to the nightdresses. As the shopgirl took my address to have my packages delivered, a gasp behind me made me glance up. Two women in shirtwaists and skirts, their heads bent toward one another, whispered while staring and pointing at something at the door. I followed their gaze, and my mouth opened agape. Standing just inside, in a crimson evening gown covered with flounces of alternating yellow and lavender lace, was the "fallen woman" I'd seen sunning herself on the balcony of the bawdy house this morning.

I couldn't decide what was more astonishing, that she had

the audacity to come in a respectable shop, which was, to be fair, mere blocks away from the establishment where the girl worked, that she was wearing an evening gown in the early afternoon, or that I'd seen this same girl twice in one day.

Either way, close your mouth, Davish, I chided myself, *and stop staring.* She might be what she was, but that didn't give me cause to act less than respectable.

As I clamped my jaw shut and looked slightly away, though keeping the girl in my sights, she glanced about her as if not certain how to proceed. Immediately a matronly woman, in a simple but well-tailored black dress, most likely a senior member of the staff, approached and whispered something to the girl.

"No, I will not leave," the girl said with a harsh twang, defiantly loud.

"If you don't go quietly, you will be forcibly removed," the matron said.

"I'm going to be respectable very soon and you'll regret treating me like this."

"That's all very well. But please leave." When the girl in the garish dress didn't move, the matron waved her hand to a man in the cap and uniform of a guard, who immediately approached. "Mr. Homer, would you please escort this 'girl' from the store and see that she doesn't return?"

"My pleasure, ma'am," the guard said, gripping the girl's arm.

"Let go of me!" The flounces on the girl's dress flapped as she struggled to free herself from the guard's hold.

"Mr. Homer?" the matron said. And with that the guard opened the door with one hand and proceeded to drag the girl outside with the other.

"You can't treat me like this!" she shouted. "You don't know who I know. My man is powerful in this city. Just you wait until I tell him what you've done."

And then the door closed behind her and all was quiet in

the store once more. The matron wiped her hands on her skirt, turned her back on the door, and returned to the accessories counter.

"I have to admit," the shopgirl helping me said, as she finished writing my address and then leaned over the counter, "I've never seen one of 'them' before."

If only I could say the same thing.

"Sir, may I have a word?"

Sir Arthur checked his watch. A slight frown inched across his face. "Later perhaps, Hattie. There isn't time now. The session is soon to begin."

"Yes, but—"

"Here's your gallery pass."

Sir Arthur handed me a small piece of paper with an etching of the Capitol and the United States Senate Chamber across the top. Next to the typewritten word *ADMIT, Sir Arthur Windom-Greene and friends* was handwritten. It was signed *Meriwether Lewis Smith, U.S. Senator.* After ordering my trousseau, I had met Sir Arthur at the Smith home on Lafayette Square. I'd accompanied him on the ride to the Capitol, a massive white stone building dominated by a towering central dome flanked by two wings, in silence. Equally overwhelmed by the imposing presence of the iconic seat of America's government and the daunting task of broaching the subject of my engagement with my employer, I'd said nothing during the entire ride. Now waiting outside the Senate Chamber, I drew up my courage to speak.

"And you have your map of the Senate floor so you know who is who?" I showed him the 53rd Congress's *Official Congressional Directory* that Claude Morris had given me, with its map of numbered desks and list of the senators' names who sat at each desk.

"Yes, sir. But—"

"Ah, Smith. Is it time?" Sir Arthur said, cutting off anything I was about to say, when he saw our host, Senator Smith, approaching.

The senator, a solid older man with a thick gray mustache, standing several inches shorter than Sir Arthur, nodded while looking up at me through his spectacles. The intensity in his eyes and the perpetual scowl on his face remained unchanged.

"Sir Arthur." The senator acknowledged him with the slightest bow of his bald head. "Why is Miss Davish here?"

"She is going to record the session for me," Sir Arthur said. "Shouldn't we go in?"

"Quite right," Senator Smith said, wrinkling his nose in obvious distaste at my presence. And he continued to scowl as a young, handsome man with thick brown hair and a beard smiled at the senator as he passed.

"Fine day, eh, Meriwether?" the man said, in an obvious Southern drawl.

"Go to Hell, Abbott," Senator Smith sneered under his breath. The young man laughed as he headed down the hall to the Senate Chamber.

Before Sir Arthur could question the senator about the incident, Senator Smith said, "Ah, Chester," to a man of similar height, build, and sullen countenance as the senator making his way across the floor toward us. He too had a bald pate but a crescent of thick black hair encircled his crown. Sir Arthur glanced at his watch again.

"Chester, I don't think you've met our houseguest," Senator Smith said.

"No, I haven't," the new arrival said.

"Chester, this is Sir Arthur Windom-Greene. He's a renowned historian staying with us while he conducts his latest research. Sir Arthur, this is my son, Chester Smith."

As Sir Arthur shook hands with the newly arrived man, I ignored the senator's snub of not introducing me and studied the new arrival. I had seen him before. He was the man I'd watched at the train station jab his carriage driver in the back with his umbrella for his presumed lack of haste. At the time, his resemblance to our host had struck me and now I knew why. My first impression was not improved upon as he began a discussion with the men without even looking at me in acknowledgment.

"Can you believe that counsel for Boss McKane filed an appeal today at the Supreme Court?" Chester said. "Do you think they'll consider it, Father?"

"I should say not," Senator Smith said, taking off his spectacles and wiping them with a handkerchief.

"Anyone associated with Tammany Hall, any politician at all, for that matter, caught defrauding the voters deserves to be in prison," Sir Arthur said.

Did Chester Smith wince? If he had, the look was gone as quickly as it came.

"Shall we go?" Sir Arthur said, less of a question than a command. The men turned their backs on me. As was expected, I followed.

"This is where I leave you," the senator said when we arrived at the gallery doors. "Must go and take my seat now."

"Right." Sir Arthur, not hesitating a minute more, stepped through. Chester followed and I came in behind, relinquishing my pass to the attendant. "There's the ladies' gallery, Hattie." Sir Arthur pointed to the other side of the room. "I'll meet you here when it's over."

"Yes, sir," I said, turning to make my way past the rows of gallery seats.

As the chamber was built with the acoustics of a theater, I heard Chester ask quietly, "Who is your lovely companion, Sir Arthur?"

"Pardon me, Mr. Smith, but I've been remiss in not introducing you. Hattie," Sir Arthur said, beckoning me back.

"Chester Smith, this is Miss Hattie Davish."

"Miss Davish, how charming," Chester said, bowing his head, the distracted look in his eye not matching the smile on his face. "And how do you come to be here today?"

"Miss Davish is my private assistant and secretary," Sir Arthur said, again pulling out his pocket watch.

"Oh, I see." Chester Smith purposely glanced down at the chamber floor where the senators were gathering. "Shall we find our seats, Sir Arthur?" He avoided looking at me again.

"By all means." The two men set off down the aisle.

Unperturbed by the senator's son's cool reception, I navigated my way across to the ladies' gallery. Armed with my pencil and notepaper, I settled myself in the front row next to a group of women all wearing National American Woman Suffrage Association stickpins. As the men below were still standing about in clusters whispering, I took the time to look around me. The chamber was a large rectangular room, at least 100 feet long and almost that wide, with second-story public galleries on each of the four sides, all crowded by now, all painted in hues of gold and white. Below where I sat, the senators' individual wooden desks, some dating back to the Old Senate Chamber almost a half-century ago, were arranged on a tiered semicircular platform facing a raised rostrum. Above me, beautifully illuminated by the sun rays streaming through, was a skylight made of iron and glass panels painted in the symbols of the Union, the army, the navy, and the medical arts.

There he is again!

As my eyes rested on the press gallery, directly above the desk of the president pro tempore on the raised rostrum, I instantly recognized the man I'd seen outside the bawdy house this morning. Craning his neck as if to find a particular person in the adjacent gallery, he smirked when he spied who he'd been looking for. He left his spot, shoving his way through the crush of journalists crammed together in his row, and headed down the aisle. He reached the gallery where Chester Smith and Sir Arthur sat and headed straight up toward them, taking two stairs at a time. I expected him to be greeted by Chester Smith, but Sir Arthur patted the man on the back. To my dismay, the two men shook hands. How could Sir Arthur know such a man? Could he know what that man was doing this morning? I doubted it. When Sir Arthur, by his gestures, introduced Chester Smith, the reporter wagged his finger toward the scowling senator's son. The two men obviously knew each other as well.

Whack! "The Senate will come to order."

The sound of the gavel interrupted my ponderings and alerted me to my purpose for being here. Immediately I was poised with pencil and notepad to record every word, my attention absorbed by the men below. And after the chaplain led the prayer and the Pledge of Allegiance was recited by all, the topic of the day's debate was soon evident and much to my surprise.

"Mr. President?" Senator Smith said, wiping his spectacles.

"The senator from Virginia," Senator Isham Harris, the president pro tempore, said, acknowledging Smith.

"Mr. President, I would like to begin by reminding my esteemed colleagues of the 1882 Act to Regulate the Use of the Capitol Grounds." He flipped open a large book of statutes. "As it states:

'Whereas the Capitol Grounds have been formed to subserve the quiet and dignity of the Capitol of the United States, and to prevent the occurrence near it of such disturbances as are incident to the ordinary use of public streets and places: Therefore, the following statute for the regulation of the public use of said grounds is hereby enacted.'

"I list only those parts of sections of which my friends who support Mr. Coxey and his followers should take heed." He read again.

" *'That it is forbidden to make any harangue or oration, or utter loud, threatening, or abusive language. That it is forbidden to parade, stand or move in processions or assemblages, or display any flag, banner, or device designed or adapted to bring into public notice any party, organization or movement. That it shall be the duty of all policemen having authority to make arrests in the District of Columbia to be watchful for offences against this act and to arrest and bring before the proper tribunal those who shall offend against it.'* "

With this, Senator Smith ceded the floor. Several senators spoke for over an hour, arguing back and forth, adding to an earlier debate on whether Coxey's March constituted a legitimate way of petitioning the government for the redress of grievances, until one rotund senator spoke, all the while rubbing his protruding belly.

"As my colleague from Virginia said, Mr. President, there should be no debate. These lawbreakers should be arrested the moment one of them utters a word on Capitol grounds."

"Hogwash!" cried the young Southern man who had infuriated Senator Smith earlier. I looked at my map of the Senate floor. It was Clarence Abbott, the Populist junior senator from North Carolina.

Did Senator Smith dislike him because he was a Populist? Or was there something more between them?

"Mr. President?" a tall, sturdy, clean-shaven man said as he rose.

"The senator from Nebraska," President Pro Tempore Harris said, ignoring Senator Abbott's comment and acknowledging Senator William Allen, a fellow Populist.

"I once said that this march on Washington was 'absurd and useless,' that it was 'the work of a man who, if not a knave, is crazy and who does not represent any of the principles of our party.' And that may still ring true. But I must object and am dismayed by the buildup of military and police forces in our fair city for the purpose of repelling the Coxeyites."

So it was true. The rumors I had overheard at the White House weren't idle gossip after all.

"And the suggestion of the senator from Virginia to use the Capitol Grounds Act to stop them, I ask, is it American?" Allen said. "Is it right to deny to such men the privilege of not only entering the District of Columbia and the city of Washington, but to enter these galleries, if they see fit to enter them?"

Senator Allen gestured to the galleries above him with a sweep of his arm, eliciting a few sharp gasps and cries of "No!" from those seated above him.

"Are American citizens coming here for a lawful purpose to be met at the confines of the capital of their nation by hired soldiery, by a police force, and kept out of the city and beaten into submission if they persist in coming?"

This elicited both boos and shouts of approval from Allen's fellow senators. Immediately Senator Hawley, a Republican from Connecticut, rose to oppose him.

"Now, sir," Hawley declared, "it is a matter of common sense that the behavior of multitudes around this Capitol and these squares here should be carefully regulated by laws and rules. And if there be any patriotism in the misguided company of men near here, or the others who are coming, there are men in this Senate who could address them and satisfy them, I am sure, if they are Americans and have any respect for their country. And may I add that the speech given by the gentleman from Nebraska, though roughly received here, as it should be, would have been received with tumultuous applause in a meeting of anarchists, having as it did the bacteria and bacilli of anarchy!"

A large uproar followed, both on the floor and in the galleries above, as men shouted and waved their arms in objection to Senator Hawley's words.

"That's absurd!"

"Boooooo!"

"Hissssss!"

"Preposterous!"

Whack! Whack! Whack!

As Senator Harris hit the gavel several times trying to restore order, I stole a moment to glance at the press gallery. There the men were feverishly writing, trying to capture the words and mood for their articles. The reporter I'd seen at the bawdy house this morning was among them again. Absentmindedly he unwrapped something and popped it in his mouth. From the mastication of his jaw, I guessed he was chewing gum. He suddenly looked up and stared across the chamber toward me. I immediately looked down and engrossed myself in my own work. Could he sense I was staring at him? Could he have recognized me from this morning? What if he told Sir Arthur?

That's preposterous, I thought, echoing the shouts from below. He was too distracted to notice me outside the bawdy house. Wasn't he?

CHAPTER 5

"There's Coxey!" someone shouted.

A rush of men, clerks and journalists I recognized from the press gallery and visitors alike, pushed past Sir Arthur, Chester Smith, and me as we left the galleries at the end of the session. The man from the bawdy house wasn't among them. One man's unexpected pause to tie the loose laces on his shoe forced three others to slip and stumble on the marble floor as they attempted to navigate around the bent figure, one grabbing Sir Arthur's arm for support, another bumping into Chester Smith.

"Hey!" Chester said, shoving the man away, into the path of the stragglers.

In a chaos of flying hats, waving arms, and curses, men tumbled into a heap. But nothing deterred them. Untangling themselves and collecting their fallen hats, they gained their feet and hurried away.

"I say," Sir Arthur said, brushing his sleeve. "What was that about?"

"General Coxey appears to be in the corridor, sir," I said as calmly as I could, inwardly sharing the crowd's enthusiasm.

"Oh, well then, we must meet this Coxey. Care to join the spectacle, Mr. Smith?" Sir Arthur said. Chester yawned, but my heart fluttered with excitement. I couldn't wait.

"Very well."

We three headed toward the congregation of reporters, pages, and clerks surrounding the famous man and waving scraps of paper in the air. Coxey was signing autographs. For all the descriptions of "revolutionary" and "crank" and "crazy" and "cerebrum of Christ," the man I'd followed in the newspaper for months was slighter of build than I'd imagined, wore a tidy, light-brown mustache, wire-rimmed spectacles, and a well-tailored dark gray suit. To my relief and satisfaction, I would have more easily mistaken him for a senior government clerk than a maniacal leader of an invading army of miscreants.

"What brings you to the Capitol?" someone was asking when Sir Arthur led the way into the crowd.

"I seek permission to speak from the Capitol steps. I first attempted to gain it from the office of the police superintendent. Major Moore asked me if it was my idea to make a speech from the east front of the Capitol, and I told him yes. He told me I can't do that, that the law prohibits it. When I asked him if there is any law against making a speech on the streets, again he said the law prohibits that too."

As autograph seekers flapped their papers as close to Coxey's face as possible, the journalists were jotting down his every word. Although I would have preferred an autograph, I too took down what he said. Sir Arthur didn't ask it of me, but I knew he'd expect a copy of the man's comments later.

"But that's what we propose to attempt," Coxey said. "It's a constitutional right!" A few cheers rose from the crowd. To emphasize his point, he said it again. "I claim it under the Constitution."

"But what brings you to the Capitol today?" someone asked again.

"Only Vice President Stevenson or Speaker Crisp can suspend the law."

"And did they?" a reporter asked.

"The chief representative of the Democratic Party in Congress has refused to grant these rights to the American people," Coxey said of Speaker Crisp's refusal to help. "I'm still trying to locate the Vice President."

"What do you think of Congress using the 1882 Capitol Grounds Act to stop you?" someone asked. I craned my neck to see the speaker. The man from the bawdy house, pad and pencil in hand, had joined the crowd around Coxey.

"We will keep off the grass around the Capitol," Coxey replied. "Of course, I appreciate as well as anyone else the fact that the preservation of the grass around the Capitol is of more importance than saving thousands from starvation." Both guffaws and gasps followed Coxey's verbal jab.

"Will you resort to violence to make your point? Does the city have something to fear from you and that army of thousands suffering from starvation on the city's border? I overheard one of your zealots claiming he'd blow up the Capitol."

Was he referring to the same man who had proclaimed his violent intentions at the White House or to someone new? I wondered.

Distant steps could be heard echoing down the corridor as everyone hushed and strained to hear Coxey's reply. The fate of the city could depend on it. Coxey straightened his shoulders and took a big breath.

"We come in peace to lay our grievances at the doors of our national legislature and ask them in the name of Him whose banners we bear, in the name of Him who pleads for the poor and the oppressed, that they should heed the voice of despair and distress, that they should consider the conditions of the starving unemployed of our land, and enact such laws as will give them employment, bring happier conditions to the people, and the smile of contentment to our citizens."

Audible sighs of relief rose from the crowd, my own included. And then dozens of voices began at once.

"Who are these men of violence who claim to speak for the Commonweal of Christ?"

"How can you guarantee peace when your men are suffering so?"

"Amen and thanks be to Him whom we praise."

Ignoring all questions and comments, Coxey excused himself and proceeded to push through the crowd.

"Sir Arthur Windom-Greene." Sir Arthur introduced himself as he stepped in front of General Coxey and halted his advance. "And this is Mr. Chester Smith."

"Pleased to meet you," Coxey said.

"It was my secretary, Miss Davish here, who made me aware of your extraordinary trek from Ohio," Sir Arthur said, pointing to me. "Hattie has been an avid follower, I can assure you."

"And supporter too, I hope, Miss Davish?" General Coxey said. I smiled.

Knowing better than to voice any opinion in regard to politics, I ignored his question and said, "I'm most pleased to meet you in person, Mr. Coxey. Is Mr. Browne with you?" Marshal Carl Browne was second only to General Jacob Coxey in status in the Commonweal of Christ, the name they called themselves, and was the man who intrigued me the most.

"No, he is at the camp. But if you'd like to meet him, come visit us tomorrow or Monday. You are more than welcome. You too, Sir Windom-Greene and Mr. Smith. Bring as many friends as you like." I looked to Sir Arthur, silently praying he would accept the invitation.

"I believe I'll take you up on that," Sir Arthur said, always wanting to be in the thick of any historical event. "And I will bring friends. Senator Smith, for one, will relish the opportunity."

"Good," Coxey said, as he took his leave. "And I hope to see you again on the Capitol steps!"

"Father's not going to like this," Chester Smith said, frowning as he watched Coxey disappear through the crowd.

"Nonsense," Sir Arthur said. "Such a curiosity as this shouldn't be missed."

"I hope you're right, Sir Arthur," Chester said, shaking his head in doubt.

I hope so too, I thought, too excited to worry about the repercussions Chester had implied.

"Hattie!"

I turned at the sound of my name. Walter was ascending the steps with a tall blond woman on his arm who had Walter's sparkling blue eyes and brilliant white teeth. She was laughing.

"Excuse me a moment, sir?" I said. Sir Arthur, deep in conversation discussing the relative strength of the British pound with Chester Smith as we waited outside for the senator to rejoin us, nodded slightly.

"I must say this city does agree with me, like a sunflower on a warm summer's day. I didn't know what to expect when we arrived, but it's been marvelous, Walter, simply marvelous. I was saying to Mildred the other . . ." She stopped mid-sentence when I skipped down the flight of stairs to meet them and she saw me for the first time.

"Oh, darling boy," she said, without taking her eyes off me, "who is this charming creature?"

Walter pulled away gently from the woman who could only be his sister and came to my side, taking my arm. "Who we came to meet," he said, smiling at me.

"Oh?"

"Hattie, this is my sister, Mrs. Sarah Clayworth, and this, Sister dear, is Miss Hattie Davish, my intended."

Sarah had reached out to offer her hand but let it float in midair the minute she heard Walter's last words. Only the caw of a crow and the plodding *clomp, clomp* of the horses in the street filled the silence between us. I braced myself for the coldness that would sweep over Walter's sister now. As if I were the object of an employer's displeasure, I kept my professional composure and maintained eye contact. If I were to marry Walter, I would have to stay strong as his wife, even if his family disapproved. Instead, I felt a rush of air as Walter's sister threw her arms about me. She smelled of lilies of the valley and face powder. I stood there dumbfounded and wasn't sure if I should embrace her in return. As she didn't seem inclined to let go, I lightly set my hand on the woman's back. Her peacock blue dress was made of the softest silk.

"I'm so pleased!" she said, releasing me. She placed one hand on my shoulder and another on Walter's. "Yes, very pleased indeed. You are most welcome to the family."

"Thank you, Mrs. Clayworth," I said, still stunned by my reception. How could the daughter be so different from the mother? Obviously his sister was more like Walter than I'd expected.

"Do call me Sarah and I'll call you Hattie. We are soon to be sisters, are we not?"

"Yes, I suppose we are." Walter smiled at my shyness but knew I had not been expecting such a warm reception.

"So you aren't cross with me for not telling you about the engagement, Sarah?" Walter said.

"Cross? Why would I be cross? You told me you were coming to visit and you had a surprise. I wouldn't have wanted you to spoil the surprise now, would I?"

So Walter hadn't told her about our engagement after all. Wasn't that why he'd had luncheon with her instead of accompanying me? Was he, like me in speaking with Sir Arthur, unsure how to broach the subject? Or was it simply to surprise her, as she thought? But what else hadn't he told her? Did she know I worked for a living? That I was an orphan? My hopes that Sarah was different from her mother were premature if she knew nothing about me.

"Shall we join the others?" Walter said.

"Yes, there's Daniel." Sarah picked up her skirts slightly and proceeded up the stairs.

Walter and I followed. In the few minutes we'd been talking, Senator Smith had rejoined his son, Chester, and Sir Arthur, as had the reporter from the press gallery. Chester scowled as the reporter laughed at a joke I couldn't hear.

Who is that man? I wondered yet again.

A tall, barrel-chested man I'd never seen before was also among the growing party. As soon as she reached the new arrival, Sarah wrapped both hands around his arm and pulled him in our direction. He rolled his wide-set brown eyes, but an indulgent smile spread across his clean-shaven face. Walter stretched out his arm toward the man who could only be Daniel Clayworth, and the two men heartily shook hands.

"Good to see you again, Walter," Daniel said. "Sarah says you were recently in St. Louis. I trust your mother is well?"

"You know our mother. She's as sharp as a thistle and as strong as a prairie wind," Sarah answered before Walter had the chance.

"And your journey?"

"A bit long but routine," Walter said.

"Happen to catch a Browns' ball game while you were in

St. Louis? I haven't seen them play since they moved to the New Sportsman's Park."

"Enough small talk, boys," Sarah said, turning herself and Daniel slightly to face me. "This, Daniel, is Miss Hattie Davish." Daniel tipped his head slightly.

"Pleased to meet you, Miss Davish," he said. The smile on his face was refreshing among the somber Smiths.

"And this, my dear Hattie, is Congressman Daniel Clayworth," Walter added, "my esteemed brother-in-law."

"Nice to meet you, Congressman," I said.

"Nonsense, Hattie, you must call him Daniel," Sarah insisted. Her husband glanced at her in surprise. Sarah recognized his questioning gaze. Walter and I locked eyes in the instant before Sarah leaned forward and said, "Darling, Miss Davish is—"

"Daniel, have you met Sir Arthur Windom-Greene yet?" Walter said, cutting off his sister before she could reveal our secret. This was not how I would have Sir Arthur learn of our engagement. Sarah would have ample time on the ride home to Dupont Circle to inform her husband of her brother's news.

"I have," Daniel said, as Walter led him toward the group of men.

"Nice to see you again, Dr. Grice," Sir Arthur said, extending his hand to Walter when the two men approached. "Gentlemen, may I introduce Dr. Walter Grice, a good man to have on your side if ever you're in a tight spot."

Sir Arthur smiled broadly as he lightheartedly referred to the Christmas we all had spent in Illinois when Walter and I helped clear Sir Arthur's name of murder.

After the round of introductions, Sarah's husband joined the men's discussion. Walter made his excuses and returned to us.

"Walter, you cut me off." His sister pouted. "I was about to tell Daniel—"

"I know what you were about to do," Walter said under his

breath. "This is not the time nor the place to reveal such things publicly."

"Oh," Sarah said, looking about her guiltily. "Yes, of course, how indiscreet of me. Forgive me, Miss Davish."

"Of course. Thank you for understanding," I said.

"You may tell Daniel later, at home, but certain parties here need to be told formally, if you understand me," Walter said.

"You haven't told Sir Arthur yet?" Sarah said, more astute than I would've given her credit.

"What haven't you told me yet?" Sir Arthur said. I nearly jumped as Sir Arthur with the reporter joined our group. "Something concerning you, Hattie?"

"Yes, sir," I said. "Something that has only recently come up."

"Well?" Sir Arthur stared at me in slight impatience.

"It's a personal matter, sir. May we speak of it in private?"

"Of course, but first, some introductions are in order. Dr. Grice?" Sir Arthur said.

"Sir Arthur Windom-Greene, please meet my sister, Mrs. Daniel Clayworth," Walter said.

"Delighted. And this," Sir Arthur said, indicating the man I'd seen at the bawdy house, "is Simeon Harper, a—shall we say—colleague of mine. He's a journalist who's been marching with Coxey since that dime museum business in Allegheny City."

The episode had filled all the newspapers. The proprietor of a dime museum invited Coxey and his men to be one of the exhibits for a week. Coxey had declined, declaring, "We will have no dime museum freaks in this aggregation." When three members of the Commonweal accepted the dime museum owner's invitation, Coxey expelled all three men forever from the army.

"Coxey's Army!" Sarah declared. "I have followed the newspapers' accounts since the man stepped foot out of his front door in Ohio. You must tell us some of your personal stories."

Yes, Mr. Harper, do. Tell us why you were interviewing a fallen woman on the doorstep of a bawdy house this morning.

Of course, I never said such a thing and felt ashamed even after I thought it. And, in fact, I was as eager as Sarah to hear the stories of his adventures with the Coxeyites. But my curiosity had been piqued. Did Sir Arthur know his colleague was in Hooker's Division this morning? What would he think if he did? And why was Mr. Harper, journalist or not, associating with a woman like that, especially since he was supposedly reporting on Coxey's Army? Did Coxey's Army have a connection with the bagnio? If only I could ask such a question.

"Of course, Mrs. Clayworth," Mr. Harper was saying as he unwrapped a piece of Wrigley's chewing gum. "And who is this lovely lady?" Again I'd been left out of the introductions. This time I wasn't offended; I was uneasy. Whether I was more uneasy being caught ruminating on such thoughts by the very man I was thinking about or as the object of that man's regard, I wasn't sure.

"Miss Davish is my personal secretary," Sir Arthur said.

"Ah, I've heard about you," Mr. Harper said, popping the chewing gum into his mouth.

He had? First Mrs. Cleveland and now this journalist. Why was Sir Arthur mentioning me to his acquaintances?

Before I could consider the reasons further, Sir Arthur said, "Now, Harper, after that heated discussion in the Senate, you must tell us something we don't know about Coxey and his band of misfit men."

"What would you like to know?"

"Is it true Carl Browne was once a journalist, like you?" Sir Arthur asked.

"Indeed, among other things. Unlike Coxey, who is a respected businessman, Browne has had a questionable career as a journalist, a political agitator, a patent medicine salesman, a carnival barker, a sketch artist, and a painter."

"The man's a charlatan," Senator Smith grumbled.

"What would *you* like to know?" the journalist said, leaning in toward me. I could smell the spearmint on his breath. If our engagement had been public knowledge, Walter would've put his arm around me or confronted Mr. Harper for the lingering look he was now giving me. Regardless, Walter took an almost imperceptible step closer.

My mind raced through the dozens of questions I had about the marchers, but with the man so close, I said the first thing that popped into my head. "Since you were there, do you believe the rumors that the Secret Service has had agents among Coxey's men at least since Allegheny City?"

"My, my, Sir Arthur, you told me your secretary had done a little investigative work for you in the past, but I had no idea she would be competing with me for a byline."

"What?" Sir Arthur said.

"Where did you hear said rumors, Miss Davish?" Mr. Harper's lascivious smile had been replaced by professional curiosity. I had truly overheard something that wasn't meant to be public knowledge.

"Is it true?"

"Yes, it is true. Now I only came across this information after a great deal of footwork and palm greasing. Tell me, Miss Davish, how did you come to know this?"

"You should attend Mrs. Cleveland's receptions, Mr. Harper," I said. "You'd be surprised by what the women of this city know."

"Here, here!" Sarah said, laughing. "You'd make a fine member of the Washington Wives Club, Hattie. You'll have to come to our next meeting. The women of this city will love you."

"But—?" Mr. Harper said, his brows knitted and his head tilted in puzzlement.

"Dinner awaits, gentlemen," Senator Smith pronounced, interrupting the journalist's question.

"About that conversation, sir?" I said, ignoring Mr. Harper's quizzical expression and the satisfied smirk on Walter's face. "The personal matter?"

"It will have to wait, Hattie," Sir Arthur said. Without another thought for me, he launched into a discussion on arranging a visit to Coxey's camp with Senator Smith as he descended the stairs.

CHAPTER 6

The city was resplendent. After taking our leave from everyone after the Senate session, Walter and I had a light dinner at Vorlander's near the Capitol, of soup with fried bread, riced potatoes, lettuce with mayonnaise dressing, and lemon pie. Afterward, as the sun set, we strolled slowly, very slowly, arm and arm back toward Senator Smith's home in Lafayette Square. Beginning at the Capitol, lit up like a glorious, ghostly beacon on its hill for all night travelers to guide themselves by, we passed the Botanical Gardens, its conservatory dark and filled with leaf-shaped shadows. We walked down Pennsylvania Avenue, the thriving thoroughfare lined with buildings of limestone, brick, granite, and wood, of heights commonly three to four but as tall as nine stories high, even at this hour resonant with the *clomp, clomp, clomp* of horses and *clickety-clack* of carriage wheels. We passed the four-story, narrow *Evening Star* newspaper building; the popular, six-story Palais Royal Department store with its mansard roof; a two-story dime museum, the paint peeling from its sign, closed for the night; and, one block from the President's House, the Willard. With its brick façade curving smoothly around the corner, the elegant hotel icon was known to have hosted every president since Franklin Pierce in 1853 and numerous other luminaries including Charles Dickens, Buffalo Bill, P. T. Barnum, Samuel Morse, Lord and Lady Napier, and the first Japanese delegation. Eventually we strolled past the imposing structures of the Treasury Building and the White House. I'd spent weeks in this city and never fully appreciated the magnificence of its architecture, the lushness of its parks, the simple majesty of its grand design. But then I hadn't been on the arm of the man I loved.

All too soon we had to say good night.

"Don't forget to talk to Sir Arthur," Walter whispered as I took the first step toward the Smiths' front door.

"I won't. Good night."

"Good night, my dearest Hattie." And then he muttered under his breath, "Ah, what the hell."

I turned, surprised by his language, not by what he'd said—I'd heard far worse from Sir Arthur every day—but by the fact that he had said it at all. Before I could ask what was wrong, he leaped up the stairs, wrapped me in his embrace, and kissed me ardently. I couldn't imagine anything ever being wrong again.

I could still feel the silky touch of Walter's lips on mine when I found Sir Arthur drinking coffee in the drawing room and chatting with Senator and Mrs. Smith. Although I knew him to have been invited to dine with the Smiths, Simeon Harper wasn't among them.

"Sir, may I—?"

"Here's my boy!" Mrs. Smith said, interrupting me. A brown, wavy-haired puppy with eager, intelligent eyes loped into the room, wagging its long tail. It scrambled into Mrs. Smith's arms and panted happily in her lap as it took in the room.

"Isn't he a good boy," Mrs. Smith said, hugging the dog to her chest. "This is my Chessie, Spencer. The Chesapeake Bay retriever I was telling you about, Sir Arthur." The dog, drool hanging from his jowls, jumped down to greet the men.

"Fine dog, Mrs. Smith. Just fine," Sir Arthur said, patting the dog firmly on its head. "Known to be more protective of their owners than other retrievers, you said?" Mrs. Smith nodded while Senator Smith stood to pour himself another drink, giving the dog a wide berth.

"I'm sorry, Miss Davish," Mrs. Smith said, smiling at her puppy. "You were saying?"

"I wondered if I could speak to you privately, sir?" I said.

"Of course," Sir Arthur said, heartily rubbing the dog's ears. "May we use your study, Smith?"

"Of course, of course," the senator said. "Second door on the left."

"By the way, how is your visit to Washington going, Miss Davish?" Mrs. Smith said without looking at me. She continued to smile at her dog. "Have you visited any of the sights yet?"

"As you know, I have been to the President's Executive Mansion, and the Capitol, of course. But that's all."

"You have a notebook, don't you?"

"Yes, of course." I always carried my notebook.

"Then write these down," Mrs. Smith said, as she patted her knee. Spencer gleefully loped across the room, into her lap again. "These shouldn't be missed."

I looked to Sir Arthur, who nodded indulgently. I got out my notebook and pencil from my bag and jotted down the list as she ticked them off her fingers.

1. Smithsonian Institution
2. Medical Museum
3. Corcoran Gallery
4. National Museum
5. Washington Monument
6. Ford's Theatre and the house where Lincoln died

7. Patent Office
8. Zoological Park
9. Naval Observatory
10. Agricultural Department

"Anything to add, Mr. Smith?" his wife said.

"No, no," the senator grumbled. He pulled his spectacles from his face, breathed on them until they fogged over, and wiped them with his handkerchief. "You've been quite thorough."

"Thank you, Mrs. Smith. I'll certainly try to visit as many as my time allows. Sir?" I said, reminding Sir Arthur of my request.

"Yes, if you'll excuse us," Sir Arthur said.

I followed him out of the room and down the hall in silence. Staring at his rigid back, I suddenly wondered how I was going to tell him I planned to marry Walter, and leave his service. *What if he doesn't approve? What if he doesn't give us his blessing? What if he dismisses me on the spot?*

"Like hell you will!" Sir Arthur had his hand on the study room door when a voice from within shouted. "Damn you, Harper! Why can't you leave it alone?"

"Hey, I'm a reporter. And you, my friend, are news. So answer the question, Chester. Did you or did you not—?"

"You disgust me, Harper."

"I'm just doing my job, Chester."

"Why the hell did Father let you in his house in the first place?"

"Because he's a friend of mine," Sir Arthur said, swinging the door open.

"Then *you* answer his question," Chester Smith sneered as he pushed past Sir Arthur. "Get out of my way," he barked as he passed me.

I watched as he stomped down the hall and then flung himself, two steps at a time, up the stairs. I turned back toward

Sir Arthur and Simeon Harper when I heard Mr. Harper say, "But, Arthur, you don't expect me to let an opportunity like this go by, do you?"

"I'm asking you not to offend my host," Sir Arthur replied. Sir Arthur turned toward me when Mr. Harper indicated me with a nod of his head.

"Need something, Miss Davish?" Mr. Harper said, pulling a stick of chewing gum from his vest pocket.

"We'll talk later, Hattie. And I'd like those new pages first thing Monday morning," Sir Arthur said, closing the door.

"Of course," I said to the closed door. But I didn't leave. What had Chester Smith and Simeon Harper been arguing about? Why did Mr. Harper think Chester Smith was newsworthy? It wasn't simply because he was a senator's son. I leaned a bit toward the door to listen. Sir Arthur said something, but it wasn't clear. I pressed my ear to the door.

"He's been in self-imposed exile for months. This is the first chance I've had to question him," Simeon Harper was saying.

"It doesn't bloody matter," Sir Arthur said. "I'm his father's guest and you are mine. Don't embarrass me."

"Of course, it was never my intention to bring any of this upon you. Truly, I came tonight with a pure heart and good intentions. Nothing like this will happen again."

"See that it doesn't," Sir Arthur said.

"Aren't you even a bit curious, Arthur?"

"No. What Chester Smith does or did is none of my concern."

"Well, I'm going to tell you anyway. Maybe then you won't judge me so harshly."

I was curious what Chester Smith had done even if Sir Arthur wasn't and waited in anticipation. But it wasn't to be. Footsteps sounded in the hall as Claude Morris approached. I immediately backed away and heard no more.

"Can I be of some service, Miss Davish?" Mr. Morris called to me as I scurried away in the opposite direction.

Not unless you can tell me why Chester Smith is of such interest to a newspaper man, I thought, knowing the senator's secretary would never do any such thing.

Grrr . . . woof, woof, woof, woof! Grrr . . .

I awoke with a jerk. I was sitting at my desk and had fallen asleep at my typewriter. *What time is it?* I wondered. I pushed my chair back and glanced at the clock on the nightstand. It was one o'clock in the morning.

Despite the excitement of the previous day, Sunday morning had found me refreshed, relaxed, and almost giddy whenever thoughts of my engagement drifted into my mind. When Sir Arthur, despite being Anglican, had readily accepted the Smiths' invitation to join them for services at St. John's, a small, classical Episcopal church on Lafayette Square well known because every president since James Madison had worshiped there on some occasion, I had happily strolled the two blocks to St. Matthew's. Walter had been waiting. As always, the light streaming through the stained glass windows, the incense, and the rhythmic cadence of the Mass soothed me, enveloping me with peace. And to have Walter with me, celebrating Mass with me for the first time, I couldn't imagine feeling happier. And then we spent a most pleasant afternoon and evening together, strolling the Mall hand in hand, stealing kisses behind elm trees and basking in each other's company. When I'd finally bidden him good night, after several lingering embraces, my heart had been light and I'd felt more at peace than I had for a long time. What did I care if I'd have to spend the night on my unfinished typing?

Woof, woof, woof, woof, woof!

But why is Spencer barking? I thought.

I'd never been one for animals, never having had one as a

pet. I had grown to tolerate Mrs. Mayhew's cat, Bonaparte, while working for that lady in Newport last summer. The cat had a habit of stopping by my rooms whenever it was meal-time, and I never disappointed him, never having finished all the food that was prepared for me. I'd been more than happy to share. But Spencer was different. I liked Spencer. I had grown accustomed to the puppy, as Mrs. Smith was never without him, except at the dining table and social events. Even then I was as-sured he was getting spoiled eating gizzards and ham bones in the kitchen. But then the feeling grew to true fondness. De-spite seldom being able to interact with him, as the dog was al-most always on Mrs. Smith's lap, we nevertheless regarded one another with kindness and genuine friendship. When given the chance, Spencer always took the opportunity to prick up his ears and pant in excitement whenever I entered the room. And likewise, I always had a kind word, and if the opportunity arose, a good scratch behind his ears. Mrs. Smith commented every time how Spencer was never overtly friendly with strangers but had taken an instant liking to me.

But I'd never once heard Spencer bark like this. Still a puppy, his most valiant efforts resulted in more of a high-pitched whine than a deep growl or bark. But this, if I hadn't known better, sounded like it came from a much larger, more ferocious dog.

Woof, woof, woof, woof, woof!

"Shut that dog up," someone shouted.

Spencer, hampered by something or someone, yelped in distress and then gave a stifled growl before falling silent. Sud-denly the front door slammed, and the puppy began another round of barking. Mrs. Smith had mentioned that the breed was protective. Could she be in danger?

I pushed back from the desk, ignoring the ache in my neck, and went to the window, my second-floor room having a good view of the street. I was in time to see a man in a black fedora, his back to me, twirling a black umbrella, stroll away from the house and through the park toward Pennsylvania Avenue. I grabbed my shawl from the back of the chair and poked my head out of my door. Claude Morris stood in his dressing gown near the end of the hall. I pulled my shawl closed about my neck.

Before I could ask, Mr. Morris said, "Nothing to worry your pretty head about, Miss Davish. All's well. Just the silly dog barking."

"Mrs. Smith? Is she all right?"

"Of course." I bristled at his tone. He didn't say "silly woman," but it was implied. "You can go back to bed now, Miss Davish."

"I'm still working. But I will say good night to you, Mr. Morris."

"Yes, well, then, good night."

It took all I had not to slam my door. The nerve of that man to speak to me in that tone. Not even Sir Arthur spoke to me with such condescension. Grateful to have work to distill my anger (having falling asleep, I still hadn't finished typing the pages Sir Arthur expected in the morning), I sat back down in front of my typewriter. Before beginning again, I hesitated, fingers hovering over the keys, not dwelling on the audacity of Claude Morris, but wondering in earnest where on earth Chester Smith was going at this time of the night.

CHAPTER 7

After the pattering of rain late last night, a fresh, warm breeze and the scent of cut grass greeted me when I left the Smith home to hike. Sir Arthur's pages were neatly stacked on the desk Senator Smith had graciously relegated for Sir Arthur's use, waiting for him to arise. Despite having finished the typing in the early-morning hours, I woke before dawn rested. I'd dreamed of Walter inching to the edge of the Bartholdi Fountain, trying not to fall and get his knees dirty before he proposed. The image brought an irrepressible smile to my face. I was happy and relished the thought of a hike in the fresh air.

Wearing my storm rubbers, I strolled down Seventeenth Street with the intention of hiking through the Potomac Flats, an often muddy, marshy strip in and around the tidal reservoir, created by the dredging of the river west of the Washington Monument grounds. I'd been there several times, successfully finding new species of plants for my botanical collection including wormseed and smartweed.

As I'd done before, I stopped at the expansive Fish Commission's carp ponds on the corner of B Street and Seven-

teenth, in the shadow of the Washington Monument. I enjoyed lingering at the edge of the largest, studying the surface
for a glimpse of one of the gigantic fish that populated the
ponds. A light, cool breeze rippled across the water, obscuring
my view. I shivered and wrapped my arms around me. I stood
gazing across the pond, waiting for a fish to break the surface.

Splash! The early-morning silence was broken as a huge
specimen of carp leaped into the air and crashed back below
the water, sending circular waves where it had disappeared. I
clapped my approval, thrilled to have been a witness, but stopped
mid-clap when the sound of a fast-approaching carriage
caught my attention. The two-passenger trap careened along B
Street, the horse jerking his head about in protest at the speed.
The driver, as his neck scarf flew in the wind, blocking his vision as well as my view of his face, snapped the reins at the
poor animal again and again. The passenger, a hatless young
woman in a crimson evening gown covered with flounces of
alternating yellow and lavender lace that flapped with every
step of the protesting horse, held a large wine bottle in one
hand. As she tipped her head back to drink straight from the
bottle, a sleeve fell, revealing her bare shoulder. She propped
her foot on the dash, allowing her bare leg, all the way to her
knee, to be plainly seen. I was mortified and yet couldn't look
away.

Could there be more than one of those garish dresses? I
wondered. I doubted it.

When finished with her bottle, she sent it shattering to the
pavement, wiped her mouth with the back of her hand, and
cackled maniacally, urging the driver to drive faster and faster.
Walter was a notoriously reckless driver, but I'd never seen
anyone drive like this.

I was far enough away that I was in no danger, but I couldn't
say the same for the people in the trap. And as they attempted to
turn onto Seventeenth Street, my prediction horribly became

reality. They turned too sharply, missing the pavement of the street and hitting the curb instead. The trap tipped and, for a breathless moment or two, it was propelled along solely on two wheels. As the driver lost control of the horse, the trap jumped the curb, sped across the grass, and crashed against the cobblestones embanking the pond. And then the horse reared.

"Aaahhhh!!!!"

The woman screamed again when the horse bolted, flinging both man and woman through the air. Her scream was cut off when she plunged into the pond, quickly disappearing beneath the surface. I watched in horror as the runaway horse, dragging the trap behind it, galloped away down Seventeenth Street. I rushed over to the point where the driver and woman had gone in, and I held my breath waiting for them to resurface. The man, his back to me, immediately rocketed upward and gasped for breath before plunging beneath the water again. All was silent as the man's fedora floated over the ripples his splash had created.

What's happening? I wondered. *Why don't they surface?*

I had once been forcibly thrown into deep water and had struggled with all my strength to surface. But there were no new signs of a struggle, no more signs of the man or the woman trying to keep their heads above the water, to mar the calm.

Finally, a loud inhalation drew my attention along the shore ahead of me. The man, still facing away from me, was, thank goodness, crawling out of the pond about fifteen yards away. He must have swum all the way underwater. I cringed at the thought of having to navigate through the schools of giant carp.

"Sir!" I yelled. "Are you all right?"

Without turning to look back at me, he stood, staggered a bit, and then ran stumbling as fast as he could toward the Washington Monument.

"Don't leave!" I shouted at his retreating figure. "Your companion needs your help. Sir!" He never looked back and soon disappeared into the expansive Mall. I focused again on the water. The woman still had not surfaced.

She's going to die!

I glanced about and saw no one else. Before I could question what I was doing, I plunged into the water. It was shallow at the edge, and within a few forced steps, my skirt beneath the waist-high cold water clung to my legs, weighing me down.

What am I doing? I wondered as I slowly pushed forward through the water, now up to my chest. I can't swim. How am I going to help the drowning woman if I can't even swim? Holding out my arms for balance, I took another step.

Still several yards from where the woman had crashed into the water, something solid bumped into my waist and I froze. The water churned and shadows dashed about as hundreds of carp encircled me. Several rose to the surface, their gaping mouths inches from my sides.

"Help!" I screamed. The rush of swishing tails made waves as the startled fish darted around me. "Help! Help!" I closed my eyes and screamed again and again.

My eyes flew open at the rumble of carriage wheels. A rickety wagon with a banner on the side reading WORKING MEN WANT WORK NOT CHARITY was approaching the pond.

"Help!" I yelled again as they passed.

The driver turned his team toward me. As I waded back to dry land as fast as I could, two young, rough-looking men alighted. One was tall with unkempt, long, flaxen hair, a shaggy mustache, and clothes that needed more than a wash and a mending. He wasn't wearing a hat, yet his green eyes were bright and attentive. The other man, significantly shorter, wore a slightly misshapen brown derby, had unevenly cut curly brown hair, was in desperate need of a shave, and had the most peculiar nose that twisted to the side with a gnarled bump in the middle. Not the type of men I would've chosen to meet in this distressing time or at this early hour, but someone needed to help that woman.

"Oh my God. What happened? Are you all right, ma'am?" the taller of the two men said. "Your clothes are soaked." Suddenly self-conscious and shivering, I gratefully took the faded coat the shorter of the two men offered me and draped it over my shoulders. Luckily it was cleaner than it appeared and smelled only of dust.

"I'm fine. But there's been a terrible accident. A runaway horse crashed its trap into the pond embankment, plunging the passengers into the water. A woman is still down there. She never resurfaced."

"She must've hit her head. Go get the police!" the man yelled to the driver of the wagon.

As the wagon raced off to find the nearest police station, its banner flapping from the sheer speed of the horses, the tall man stripped off his stained, crinkled coat, throwing it heedlessly to the ground. He plucked off his boots, revealing several holes in his stockings, and waded into the water. He dove in and he too disappeared beneath the surface.

"Is he okay?" I asked, when it seemed an interminable time since the diver had resurfaced. His companion nodded.

"Don't worry, I've seen Billy swim three miles nonstop down the Chesapeake and Ohio Canal."

The man, Billy, resurfaced with a crash, splashing water about, gasping for breath. Before we on the shore could shout our questions, he plunged back into the deep. Again we waited, all hope for the woman fading fast. Finally, the man burst through the surface again. And yet again he was alone. One final time he bobbed about, catching his breath in one loud inhalation, and dove under again. This time when he resurfaced he shook his head.

"I can't find her," he yelled before swimming back to the shore.

"Want me to have a look?" his companion said.

"No, Jasper. It's no use."

"Strange for a woman to be out alone at this hour of the morning," Jasper said, and then regarding me, realized what he had said. "Oh, pardon me. I hope you didn't take offense."

"No offense taken. But in her case, you're mistaken."

"Oh?"

"She wasn't alone."

"What?" Billy said, his eyes boring into mine.

"She wasn't alone. When the carriage went in, a man was driving."

"You didn't say anything about a man," Billy said, again stripping off the coat he had put back on to keep warm.

"No, you misunderstand me. He didn't drown. He resurfaced over there." I pointed. "But when I called out to him, he ran away."

"That's despicable!" Billy said, spitting out the words. "How could he not at least try to save her?"

Jasper shook his head in disbelief. "What is this world coming to?"

We all turned at the sound of a carriage rumbling past. Another lone traveler in the early-morning hours. Billy pulled out a solid gold watch with *W. M.* engraved upon it.

Where did he get such an expensive watch? I wondered.

Did he steal it? Is it all that's left of a fortune misspent? I unconsciously took a slight step back. Luckily he had put away the watch and was busy wringing the water from his trouser leg and didn't notice. His companion, Jasper, did, though, and frowned.

"The police should be here soon. Hopefully they'll catch the vile snake and at least find some justice for her," Billy said.

Jasper, watching the carp rise to the surface, scoffed. "You're too idealistic, Billy. The police bring justice? Ha!"

"You're too cynical, Jasper Neely."

"Mark my words, Billy," Jasper Neely said. "It will never happen. If you leave finding justice to the police, you'll wait until the end of your days."

"At least they'll be able to get her out of there," Billy said.

The police? In my shock I hadn't given the command Billy had barked to his driver another thought. I'd set out this morning to hike and maybe collect some plant specimens. But now, flanked by two strangers, one drenched from his foray into the pond in search of a dead woman, the other decrying the police, the implications were beginning to set in.

Oh, no! Not again!

"Shouldn't we be getting back?" Jasper Neely said, after silently watching me pace as we waited for the arrival of the police. "The police don't need or want us here."

"You can go, but I'm staying here," Billy said.

"We don't know anything. Why stay?" was Jasper's reply.

"If you don't know anything, why are you so eager to go?"

"Okay, fine. I'll stay."

"*Un, deux, trois . . .*" I counted in French, as the two men argued, trying to keep myself calm.

I couldn't believe I was entangled in yet another police affair. I'd had no cause to be in contact with the police for over nine months. I'd begun to hope that I would never have to speak to a policeman ever again, that the unfortunate incidents I'd been party to were happily in the past. However understanding Walter was, he would not appreciate his future wife being continuously entangled in police business. From now on, the only dead bodies I anticipated seeing would be unfortunate loved ones passing away from sickness or "old age." I deplored being involved with another crime.

"*Quatre, cinq, six . . .* Oh!"

I nearly tripped on something. I picked it up.

"What's that you got there?" Billy said, approaching me. I showed him.

It was a lamp from the carriage, now mangled with its glass shattered on the ground, which must have snapped off as the horse dragged the trap away. I shuddered to think what would have happened had the horse, with the carriage still attached, fallen into the water.

"Where is the horse?" I said.

Could it still be wandering about with a shattered trap attached to it? Had it broken free? Was it even now nibbling on the green grass of the White House lawn? Or did it find its way home?

"We never saw it," Billy said. "I suspect a stray horse without a rider, especially one with part of a trap still attached to him, will not go unnoticed."

"So the police will find it?" I said.

"Yes, I'm sure it will be fine. Got spooked, obviously, but no harm done to it in the end."

Unlike the poor woman, I thought.

"Then they'll be able to figure out who the man who deserted the woman is," I said, "when they find his horse?"

"Assuming it was his horse, and he didn't hire the trap," Jasper Neely said. "Then maybe."

"Why maybe?" My family never owned a horse, living above my father's hat store as we did. When we wanted to go somewhere the train or stagecoach couldn't take us, my father hired a team and buggy. Otherwise we walked everywhere. So I was well accustomed to knowing which boots to buy that would hold up and be comfortable to hike in, but I knew nothing of owning, tending, or identifying a horse.

"I doubt he'll come forward looking for it," Billy said.

"But who would abandon a horse?" I said, the irony of my words apparent the moment I spoke them. Billy didn't miss it either.

"A man who would abandon a woman to her death," he said.

"But horses are valuable property."

"Yes, but if he's rich, he can afford to buy another, and if he's poor, he can't afford to claim it."

"But can't the police track down the owner?"

"Like I said, maybe," Jasper said.

"I see." I looked at the lamp again and noticed a small carriage bolt lying not far away on the ground.

What else is here? These things were indistinguishable from any number of carriages. But could I find something that could help the police identify the man who had run away?

Not finding any more pieces of the carriage in the direct path the carriage took, I began to survey the area, starting with the spot where the lamp lay and slowly circling outward.

"What are you doing?" Billy asked.

"Looking," I said.

"For what?"

"I don't know yet." Billy scratched his wet head but didn't take his eyes off me.

I found a piece of metal, which I had no idea its purpose, a few yards away but little else until I came to the area where the man had climbed back onto shore. Slightly embedded in the soil were two finely etched pearl dress buttons, with frayed black silk thread still attached. Could these have come from the man's shirt or vest? If so, these were the only evidence, the only link to the man who had abandoned this poor woman to her fate.

"Did you find something?" Billy shouted.

"Yes." I looked about and saw nothing more so I carried my find to where the men stood waiting.

"What is it?"

"Buttons." I held them out so they could examine them.

"They could've belonged to the man." Anyone could have lost them at any time, but it would be a great coincidence if someone else had lost them in the exact spot where the man had left the water. And I don't believe in such coincidences.

"Yes, they're definitely from a wealthy man's vest, but not much to go by," Billy said. "The only distinguishing marks are the geometric etchings. They would never prove who the man was, what he was doing here, or that he'd left a woman to drown."

"You're right," I said. "But I'll give them to the police just in case."

Jasper snorted in disgust. "Why? It won't do any good."

"It might," Billy said. "You never know what will bring justice to that poor woman."

I reflected back on all the murders and crimes I'd had the unfortunate opportunity to be a part of. There had been stranger and smaller things than these buttons that had brought about justice.

"You're right, Billy," I said. "You never know."

CHAPTER 8

"So you witnessed the horse bolt and the passengers go into the water?" the policeman said.

"No, when I arrived the horse and trap were long gone," Billy replied.

"The lady saw everything." Jasper Neely pointed to me. With a lap robe the police had given me wrapped about me, I'd been watching the two policemen in black rubber coats and rubber wading pants as they dragged a heavy fishing net along the bottom of the pond. So far they hadn't had any more luck finding the woman's body than Billy had.

"So you witnessed folks go into the water?" the policeman said to me.

"Yes."

"All right then, ma'am." He licked the end of his pencil and was poised to write what I said in his notebook. "Tell me everything you saw." So I did, from the reckless driver to the woman's shocking behavior, the horrible crash, the horse's escape, and the man's flight toward the Mall.

"So you got a good look at the man and the woman?"

"No. At first the man's face was obscured by his scarf blowing across it. The scarf must've blocked his sight as well. And then he had his back to me."

"And the woman?" the policeman said. I hesitated. I had a good idea who the woman was, but how could I admit that I knew her?

"I could identify the dress she was wearing," I said. "It was the strangest-colored ensemble, and she clearly had blond hair, since she wasn't wearing a hat."

"Did you get a look at her face?"

What was I to say? That she was too far away, which was true, but that I could guess what she looked like, having seen her twice before?

"Sir!" one of the men dredging the pond shouted, cutting off any answer from me. We all turned to see the policeman carrying the dead weight of a body in his arms. We rushed to the shore and met him as the policeman set the body on dry ground. It was covered from head to toe with green algae.

"Is she dead?" Billy asked, his eyes wide with interest. From the pallor of her skin and her complete stillness, it was hard to believe otherwise. The policeman in charge knelt beside her and placed his fingers on the woman's wrist as I'd seen Walter do countless times before. The policeman nodded.

"She's dead."

"May I?" I pointed to her dress wrapped high about her bare thighs. He nodded, and I pulled her skirt down to cover her weed-tangled legs.

"So, do you recognize the dress?" the policeman said.

"Yes, this is what the woman in the trap was wearing." The policeman nodded. I regarded the dress again and wondered what had possessed the woman to match crimson with yellow and lavender. Even without the added green of the algae, it was the most garish dress I'd ever seen.

"Do you know who she is?" I said, still kneeling beside her.

"Well, there doesn't seem to be anything on her to identify her by name, but at least we know where to find her kind. She's sure to be missed tonight."

"What do mean?" I asked.

"You're a lady, madam. This one"—he pointed to the dead woman at his feet—"is no lady, if you catch my meaning."

"It's still despicable," Billy said, spitting out the words. "The man with her didn't even attempt to help this fallen creature?"

"No, not at all."

"Like I said, despicable."

"Some men don't put too much value on the likes of her," the policeman said as he brushed back the hair and weeds from her face.

"It is her!" I exclaimed. I couldn't believe I'd said it out loud. "I know her," I said, glancing at the men, who were as surprised as I was.

"You do?" all three men said simultaneously.

"She came into Hutchinson's Ladies' Furnishings on Pennsylvania Avenue yesterday when I was shopping. She was wearing the same dress. You don't forget someone like that." I watched as they picked up the woman's body and carried it to the wagon.

"Hutchinson's, huh? Well, that's not too far from Hooker's Division. Thanks. We'll start there, though I can tell you I'm not looking forward to going door-to-door asking who's missing a whore. Pardon me," the policeman added when Billy glared at him.

"No need, officer," Billy said. "We too know this girl."

Jasper Neely was holding his hat in his hand and nodded. "It's Annie."

"Annie?" the policeman said.

"She's one of Lottie Fox's girls," Billy said.

"We just saw her last night," Jasper Neely said in disbelief.

"So you were at Lottie Fox's place last night, were you?" the policeman said.

This time I took a deliberate step back from Jasper Neely and Billy. I said nothing, but my reproach must have been evident on my face.

Billy said, looking at me, not the policeman, "It's not what you think."

Jasper Neely laughed. "Of course it's what she thinks."

"Okay, maybe we did enjoy the company of Lottie's ladies. But we wouldn't have been there at all if we weren't sent on Marshal Browne's business."

Marshal Browne? How could the co-leader of Coxey's Army have anything to do with this?

"You some of them Coxey's marchers?" the officer said. He glanced over at the wagon that had led him here. The driver nodded, pointing to the banner draped along its side.

"That's right," Jasper said. "We came into town last night to run some errands on behalf of the Commonweal. And enjoy the fruits of our labor."

"We went to Lottie's on Marshal Browne's behalf," Billy said, still addressing me. "She's a follower of the marshal's 'Christ's soul is in many of us' preaching and had something she wanted to give him."

"And what would that be?" the officer asked, chuckling. "Or can't you say in front of the lady?"

Jasper Neely pulled out a small purse. He opened it for the policeman to inspect.

"A donation," Billy said. "When you're starving, you can't reject any offer to feed your lot."

"How do I know this isn't stolen?" the policeman said.

"You can always ask Lottie Fox," Jasper Neely said. The policeman dismissed this with a wave of his hand.

"All right then. Did you happen to get a look at who this Annie was with last night?"

"No, she said hello, that's all," Jasper said. "We were otherwise occupied." The policeman chuckled and then blushed when he saw the disapproval on my face.

"Pretty happy she was, though," Billy added. "Said she had made it big."

"Rich customer, then," the officer concluded.

"That's what we thought."

"Could be anyone in this town."

"Not just anyone," I said. "Annie had mentioned a powerful man at the store, one who was going to make her respectable."

Had that powerful man been the driver who abandoned her? I wondered.

"That narrows it down a little bit," the policeman said skeptically. "Lots of rich and powerful men around here, if he was who he said he was. Lots of pretenders in this town too, you know."

"These might help." I held out the fancy pearl dress buttons. He looked at the small objects dubiously. "I found these where the man came ashore. If finding his horse doesn't help identify the man who did this, perhaps these will." I handed them to him.

"Thank you, ma'am," the policeman said. He pocketed the buttons, glanced around, and said, "I think we're finished here."

Before I could offer my name and my residence in case he wished to speak to me again, he strode away. He leaped onto the back of the patrol wagon, banged on the door to alert the driver, and drove away.

"Are you going to be all right?" Billy said. "You've had a shock. Not every day you see a dead body."

In a more appropriate time and place, I might've laughed. If only he knew how many dead bodies I'd seen of late and in far more horrific scenes than this one.

"Yes, thank you. I'm fine." I handed Jasper back his jacket.

"Then we'll bid you good day." Billy tipped his hatless head. Jasper Neely touched the brim of his hat. "May we meet again," Billy said.

I hope not, I thought, but didn't say as the two men climbed back into their wagon and drove away.

I stayed, alone, staring at the point where Annie had entered the water. A large carp skimmed the surface of the water, and I shuddered. I had no interest in the fish now. I was distressed by the poor woman's death, but I was equally troubled about the man. By recklessly driving the carriage and causing the horse to bolt and then leaving his companion to drown, he had indirectly caused her death.

"But who would do such a thing?" I whispered to myself.

Could the Coxeyites, Billy and Jasper Neely, be trusted? Did they truly not know who Annie was with? After all I'd heard about the marching men, I had no idea. And of course, Billy and Jasper Neely weren't the only ones to have been to Lottie Fox's establishment recently, or who knew Annie by name, including a journalist I knew. What would Sir Arthur do if his friend was involved? What would Sir Arthur think when he found out I had witnessed the whole thing?

Please let me get his blessing first, I thought, knowing how unlikely that would be.

CHAPTER 9

"Halt!"

After returning to the Smith house in Lafayette Square and changing into drier, more suitable clothes and shoes, I proceeded to the Treasury Building for my day's work.

After I had climbed the steps of the Treasury Building and crossed under the shadow of its towering granite columns, a large, burly policeman with a long, drooping mustache stepped in front of me, barring my way to the door.

"Halt," he shouted again, though we were only a few feet apart. I did as I was told, one foot on the top step. "State your business here."

He began tapping his club in the open palm of his left hand. I hesitated, staring at the club as it rose and fell into the man's hand.

"State your business," he repeated, taking a step closer.

"I'm expected," I said. "I'm researching miscellaneous Civil War records stored here. Here. I have a letter of introduction." I pulled out the letter Senator Smith had written so as to give me access to the *Index to Property Destroyed by Confederate Authorities and that which was Destroyed by the Enemy,* of which Sir Arthur had requested I make a copy.

The policeman, ignoring the letter I thrust out toward him, never took his eyes off me. "The Treasury is locked. No one from the public is to be admitted."

"Why?"

The man ignored my question. "Please leave the area."

"Will it be open tomorrow?"

"I must insist you leave the area now." He took a step closer while continuing to tap his club in his hand.

I didn't need to be told again. I scurried back down the stairs and took the corner quickly, only slowing when I was out of the policeman's sight. And then I saw another pacing along the eastern side of the building.

What's going on? I wondered. And then I remembered the conversation I'd overheard in the White House. Could they have locked the building because of Coxey's Army? I needed to know.

I approached the second policeman, who was younger than his counterpart and wasn't holding a club in his hand, hoping for better luck.

"Excuse me, ma'am, you'll have to leave the area," he said when I was fewer than ten feet away.

"Yes, I know. The brusque policeman at the front door informed me in no uncertain terms."

"Please leave."

"I will, I assure you. But I need to confirm the reason the Treasury is closed today, for my employer. Otherwise he'll think I'm being delinquent in performing my duties." I took a step forward. He said nothing, so I took a few steps more.

"Is it true the Treasury is locked due to the approach of Coxey's Army?"

"Yes, I can confirm that."

"But why today? The marchers aren't due to approach the Capitol until tomorrow."

"We are taking precautions. Many of Coxey's men are known to have already made their way into the city." I too knew this to be true. Besides Billy and Jasper, I'd met Mr. Coxey himself at the Capitol on Saturday. Who knew how many more Coxeyites wandered the streets?

"So it will be locked until the marchers are gone?"

"Most likely."

"Thank you, officer."

"You're welcome. Now if you please, ma'am?"

Not wanting to test the limits of his indulgence any longer, I smiled and deliberately walked back down the street.

Now what?

I had allotted myself all morning to copy the property index. I could hike, as my morning hike had been interrupted by the terrible accident. I could take the trolley to Dupont Circle and pay a call on Sarah and Walter. I should return to Lafayette Square and get instructions from Sir Arthur on how to proceed. But I did none of these: I hadn't worn the proper shoes for a hike, it was too early even for a future sister-in-law to visit, and I'd completed all the manuscript pages Sir Arthur had given me. Instead, I allowed my feet to take me down random streets. With my head full of questions about Annie and her mysterious companion, it wasn't a surprise that I soon found myself less than a block from Lottie Fox's establishment again.

And then I saw Chester Smith. He was skulking around the corner of Lottie Fox's building. What was he doing here? And in broad daylight? I had no idea these types of places were open for business at this time of day. He glanced about him furtively and then disappeared around the corner. Without a moment's thought, I followed after him.

I hurried to the point where he'd disappeared and discovered an alleyway that ran alongside the building, lined with whiskey barrels filled to the rim with torn linen, empty bottles, and rotten produce that attracted hundreds of flies. Chester was nowhere to be seen. I tiptoed the length of the alley, covering my nose with my handkerchief as I passed a particularly pungent waste barrel, overflowing with soiled newspaper, hairbrushes, combs, half-empty bottles of toothpowder, and dozens of rubber syringes, the purpose of which I didn't want to know. I crouched down as I passed each window until I came to the last window of the house. It was open. I halted and slowly raised my head until I peeked through snowy white Chantilly lace curtains, all that was between me and a den of iniquity. Two dimmed figures stood a few feet away.

"Ah, Mr. Smith," a woman's voice said from within. "So good to see you again. We've missed you these past months."

"Is Jenny here?" Chester Smith said.

I squinted to see what type of buttons Chester Smith wore on his vest. They looked to be pearl, but the light was too dim to be certain.

"Jenny is currently with another gentleman, sir. May I suggest perhaps another girl for your pleasure today?"

"What about Annie?"

I gasped and immediately covered my mouth, hoping no one heard me. Chester Smith knew Annie? Could he have been the man in the trap this morning? Was he the powerful man she'd bragged about? Had he come back to learn her fate? Had he come back to throw suspicion off himself by appearing not to know what had happened? But then wouldn't the woman have seen him here last night? Or had Annie met him somewhere else?

One of the figures glanced toward the window, and I ducked below the windowsill. I pressed my body as flat against the side of the building as I could. A line of small black ants that I hadn't noticed before made a trail from the ground to a slight hole in the clapboards a few inches from my cheek. Heavy footsteps approached the window. I didn't dare look up.

"Annie?" The woman's voice rose in pitch. "What do you want with Annie?"

"She comes . . . recommended," Chester said, his voice clearly coming from mere inches above my head. If he leaned out and looked down, he'd see me. I held my breath.

"Well, Annie is not here. She went out last night and never came home."

Home? That's the last thing I'd call a bawdy house, I thought.

"Too bad but not surprising, eh? Girls like these aren't the most reliable."

"Well, Mr. Smith, *my* girls are reliable," the woman declared. "It's not at all like Annie not to check in with me." The distress in her voice was undeniable.

So the woman, who I assumed was the madam, Lottie Fox, didn't know what had happened. Hadn't the police arrived yet?

"I guess Fanny will have to do," Chester said. "Assuming she's still here."

"Of course, Fanny would be delighted to—"

Bang! Bang! Bang!

"What the hell?" Chester said.

"Someone's at the front door," the woman said. "The police, by the sound of it."

To confirm her suspicions, a voice shouted, "Police! Open up, Lottie."

"I can't be found here," Chester said. His heavy footsteps stomped away from the window.

I counted to three before daring to peek through the window again—in time to see Chester fling open the back door.

Oh, no! He's going to see me here.

I glanced about in a panic for somewhere to hide. Finding nothing, I began to turn to flee when a large, fleshy hand covered my mouth. And then an arm swung around the front of my shoulders and impeded my escape. Was that spearmint I smelled?

As I struggled to free myself, desperately trying to open my mouth wide enough to bite my captor, a familiar voice whispered in my ear, "What are you doing here, Miss Davish?"

I turned, with the loosening of his grip upon me, into the face of Simeon Harper.

"I'll release you, but please, for all our sakes, be quiet."

Voices, the familiar baritone of the policeman who had questioned me this morning in particular, carried through the open window. I nodded my assent and he let go of me. I immediately stepped away from him, glancing about for a glimpse of Chester Smith. He was nowhere in sight.

Guessing my concern, Mr. Harper whispered, "Chester's not here. He took one look at me and thought he'd chance it with the police."

"He did?"

"No," he said, chuckling. "He took the other alleyway, simply by chance." In a rush, I let out the breath I'd been holding.

Un, deux, trois, I silently counted in French, trying to gain my composure.

As I did, I couldn't help but study the journalist, glancing first at the buttons on his vest. They were plain brown agate. Was he the man who had abandoned Annie in the carp pond this morning? Luckily I have had long practice keeping my emotions and my suspicions from showing on my face. Without that skill, I would have been dismissed from almost every position I've ever had.

"So what are you doing here?" Harper asked again.

"I could ask the same of you."

"I came here on a tip. I followed the police. Now hush a minute." He put his ear as close to the window as possible without being seen.

Assuming he was telling the truth and didn't know about the accident, who could've known to tell Harper? And then I remembered—Billy and Jasper. They knew Harper from the march. He'd camped outdoors with them for months. They would trust him. Jasper had voiced doubts that the police would investigate. Maybe he thought a reporter might do better.

"Jasper Neely told you, didn't he?" Simeon Harper jerked around to face me so fast he nearly stumbled.

"How in the hell—? Excuse my language, but damn! How did you know that?"

I ignored his question and said, "Where were you this morning?"

Simeon Harper looked sideways at me and then laughed heartily in a hushed voice, until the blood rose in my cheeks with embarrassment.

"I've heard about you, Miss Davish, but I never thought you'd aim your investigative eye toward me. I told Sir Arthur you'd make a top-notch journalist if he didn't have you otherwise employed."

Brushing aside the compliment and the fact that he hadn't answered my question, I said, "You've heard about me?"

"Of course I have. You were in the papers." Of course, a journalist of all people would have read the newspaper articles mentioning my involvement in the murder cases of several prominent people.

When will people forget? I wondered. Perhaps they never will. Then I'd have to use this to my advantage.

"Well, then," I said, "you didn't answer my question. Where were you this morning?"

"I see you're like a bulldog, never giving up. Yes, ma'am, you would've made a fine journalist." I raised my eyebrows as I continued to stare at him. He still was evading the question. "I give up!" He mockingly held up his hands. "But before I tell you, answer me this. Why do you want to know?"

"Because I know why the police are here."

"And you'll tell me what you know?"

"If you tell me where you were this morning."

"Deal." Harper held out his hand. I hesitated for a moment before shaking it.

"Oh, no, no, no!" a woman inside the building cried. I closed my eyes, trying to ward off the pain in her voice.

"What's going on in there?" Simeon Harper whispered, straining to see through the window without being caught.

"Let's walk. Neither one of us needs to be found here."

"You certainly shouldn't be." The journalist laughed before heading back along the alley.

I crouched down and followed, careful not to bump into the garbage barrels. Thankfully, I couldn't see Mr. Harper's reaction to the discarded rubber syringes he must've noticed as we passed. He glanced around the corner of the building, hoping to avoid the police, and waved me forward when the sidewalk was clear.

"My gig is this way," he said, and started to walk briskly down C Street. After walking in silence for several blocks, he said, "Well?"

"First answer my question. Where were you this morning?"

"I was in Coxey's camp. It is still the biggest story in town, you know. I spent the night there, one last time, and was there until after breakfast, what little there was of it. Jasper came back, insisting I make a call on Lottie. He said it would be worth my while. So I left. I stopped at the Treasury first to check something out, but it was closed. So then I came here. And you know the rest. Now what's going on in there?" He pointed back toward Lottie Fox's place.

"Why were you at the Treasury?"

"You don't give up, do you?" I waited in silence. When he realized I wasn't saying a word until he answered, he said, "I was there to follow up on a tip I got two days ago involving a certain bank I've long suspected was involved in fraudulent dealings during the whole gold depletion crisis last year."

"Gold depletion crisis?" I tried to keep current with the news, public affairs, and world events. I tried to read the newspapers whenever I had spare time. "Does that have anything to do with the Sherman Silver Purchase Act?"

"Yeah," he said, surprised. "What do you know about it?"

"That under the Sherman Purchase Act, the government purchased millions of ounces of silver. It was supposed to improve the economy by directly helping miners who were struggling due to an oversupply of silver, and indirectly by raising inflation and letting farmers pay off their debts."

"Yeah, but the problem was that the law required the Treasury to buy the silver with specially issued treasury notes that could be redeemed for either silver or gold."

"Why was that a problem?"

"Because almost everyone redeemed the treasury notes for gold."

"And the country almost became bankrupt?"

"And the country almost became bankrupt."

"So what are you investigating?"

"The tip mentioned the name of a bank, the National Bank of the Potomac. It piqued my interest because I've always suspected it of having insider information, knowing about the passing of the Sherman Purchase Act before it was even passed and then knowing about its repeal beforehand. Having such knowledge, it bought as many treasury notes as it could when silver was at its lowest and then exchanged them for gold."

"And you suspect they also knew when the gold reserves were growing dangerously low, but continued to exchange the notes for gold anyway?"

"Exactly."

"But is that illegal?"

"No, but it's scandalous, especially if the head of the bank is a relative of a member of Congress and he used congressional insight for profit. The Division of Notes, Coupons, and Currency should have a record of all the transactions. I hoped to look into it."

"But why? Didn't you say that Coxey's Army is the big story?"

"Sure it is. But after they march to the Capitol tomorrow, there won't be a story any more. I was hoping to get a jump on a new story—this bank scandal could've been just the thing. Or maybe you have something to tell me that is even better?"

"Yes, I believe so."

"I'm all ears, Miss Davish. All ears!"

"People underestimate the prostitutes of this city," Simeon Harper said as we plodded along. Unlike Walter, who drove with reckless abandon at breakneck speed, Mr. Harper handled his horse with casual inattention. And I was almost as much on edge as if Walter were driving. We trudged along so slowly, I could've walked faster.

"Most people ignore that they even exist," he said. "In fact, I'll be surprised if the police spend more than the time it takes to type the paperwork investigating this. They did inform Lottie of the girl's fate, but I think Jasper's right. That man, who fled the scene, won't be sought unless I bring the injustice of it to light."

As promised, I'd told Mr. Harper about the carriage accident I'd witnessed and about how the victim was one of Lottie Fox's girls. He'd insisted I show him the exact spot where Annie entered the water. So he'd assisted me into his gig, introduced me to Swift (named for Jonathan Swift and not the horse's inclination toward speed), who flicked his tail at a fly in acknowledgment and proceeded ever so slowly back to the carp ponds. When I told Mr. Harper, I'd watched his face carefully for any signs he knew this story already, that he was guilty of abandoning that poor "unfortunate woman." I saw nothing but honest surprise and professional interest. But I've known murderers to lie before. I had to ask.

"So several people can verify that you were at Coxey's camp and not with the dead woman this morning?"

"Lots of people."

"Thank goodness. I can't imagine what Sir Arthur would've thought if you were caught up in this business."

"You're right there. I certainly wouldn't be invited to dine again." He laughed. Both of us knew, after his confrontation with Chester Smith, Mr. Harper wasn't going to be dining at the Smith home ever again.

"But I saw you," I said, my conscience on Sir Arthur's behalf not yet clear.

"You're mistaken, Miss Davish," Simeon Harper said, misunderstanding me. "Truly, I wasn't there."

"No, I mean I saw you at the place where Annie . . . worked." I stammered at the thought of what she actually did to make her living.

"Of course you did." He flashed me a mock look of surprise before smirking. "You were there as well, remember? And you never did tell me what you were doing there."

"No, I mean I saw you there before. On Saturday." He raised an eyebrow. Before he could come to the wrong conclusion, I added, "I was walking to the depot. By chance I happened to see Annie sunning herself on a balcony as I passed. When I crossed the street, I saw you speaking to another . . . such woman in the doorway of the same house."

"Yes, you caught me. I'm a regular there." When my eyes widened, he added, "No, it's not what you think. I didn't know Annie. Well, maybe I've met her once or twice—I've met all Madam Fox's girls once or twice—but I do know Lottie Fox. It's like I was saying earlier—prostitutes are unappreciated, and that goes double for their madams. Lottie is one of my best sources. You'd be shocked to hear some of things she's told me over the past few months."

"Yes, I'm sure I would be," I said in all seriousness. He laughed.

"Things I eventually wrote for the paper," he said, chuckling at my misapprehension. He was enjoying my discomfort a bit as well.

"Oh," was all I could say.

"I met Lottie Fox while I was following Coxey's Army. Ever heard of the Veiled Lady?"

The Veiled Lady? Of course I had. This mystery woman, a marcher who wore a black veil, was one of the many intrigues of the Commonweal of Christ that kept me, and I dare say many women, reading every story that was printed about Coxey's Army. The Veiled Lady, as we knew her, had disappeared from the march as mysteriously as she had appeared.

"You know who the Veiled Lady is?" He nodded but said nothing more. "Well?" Like thousands of others, I was eager for news of her, who she was, why she was there, and what had happened to her. To prolong my anticipation, he retrieved a yellow-and-red packet of Wrigley's Spearmint pepsin gum from his vest pocket. He offered the packet of gum to me, pointing the green arrow on the wrapper toward me.

"No, thank you."

"Suit yourself." He pulled out a stick, slowly unwrapped it, and popped it into his mouth.

"Well?"

After chewing several times, Harper finally answered me. "Lottie Fox."

"Lottie Fox?" I couldn't believe it. "But the Veiled Lady was 'the Great Unknown's' wife. Are you saying that Lottie Fox is the wife of the Great Unknown?"

Coxey's Army was populated with many colorful characters: the Veiled Lady, of course; Abraham Lincoln Jenkins, an

Irishman known for eating four pounds of cheese at a sitting; "Weary Bill," a steamboat captain who perpetually looked exhausted driving the Army's signature panorama wagon; and Honoré Jaxon, clad in the traditional dress of the Métis, who claimed to represent American Indians while carrying only a blanket, a hatchet, and some cooking utensils, to name but a few. But most intriguing of all, besides Marshal Carl Browne, was "The Great Unknown," whose past, real name, and association with the Commonweal of Christ was an enigma. He was tall and handsome, had the bearing of a military man and a pronounced limp, and spoke passionately about the rise of the poor and the fall of the rich, bordering on anarchistic. After he joined the ranks of Coxey's Army, he became Carl Browne's assistant marshal and a regular feature in the newspapers.

"The veiled woman was not the Great Unknown's wife. She's one of the madams of C Street, hence the need for a veil. She's a devout follower of Marshal Browne and his odd brand of Theosophy, but Browne asked her to travel well ahead of the men. She tried to stay, wanting to hear Browne preach, by keeping her identity a secret. But Browne insisted, concerned the presence of a woman, let alone a madam, would call into question the morality of the marchers. I and a few others from Washington knew who she was, but the mystery was a better story than revealing her identity so we kept quiet. And then a third-rate hack writer from Allegheny City bragged that he was going to reveal her secret. So she left."

"Then why didn't he reveal her secret?"

"He did. He said she was the wife of the 'Great Unknown.'"

"Of course," I said, chuckling. "How else would I have thought I knew who she was?"

"When the Army got close enough to Washington, I made a point of talking to her on her own grounds as often as I could. She's been informative."

I was too embarrassed to even broach the subject of whether they met for more than professional reasons. Besides, as long as he had an alibi for this morning, it wasn't anyone's business but his own. And with that the silence stretched on as we plodded along block after block down Fifteenth Street, the Executive Mansion gardens on the right and the massive lumberyards on the left. I was relieved when we finally cut through the lush greenery of Washington Park and approached the carp ponds. I nearly leaped out of my seat.

"Okay, Miss Davish," the journalist said, pulling out a notepad and another stick of gum, "show me where Annie and this man went in."

CHAPTER 10

After giving Simeon Harper the details as I knew them, I
left him at the site of the accident. I had no desire to
spend any more time thinking about the poor dead woman or
the man who had abandoned her to her fate. Instead I focused
on the thrilling prospect of going to Coxey's Army camp later
and, more immediately, on meeting Walter as we'd planned.
Turning my back on the carp ponds, I strolled toward the Washington Monument, that famous landmark, an obelisk made of
marble towering 555 feet in the sky, looming larger and larger
as I approached. In height, it was second only to the Eiffel
Tower in France as the tallest structure in the world, and I was
going to the top of it. When I arrived, Walter was already
there.

"Extremely punctual as usual," Walter said, taking my hand
and kissing me on the cheek.

"I almost had to cancel. Sir Arthur wanted me to copy an
index of property destruction at the Treasury this morning."

"But we arranged this with him on Saturday after the Senate session. He was to give you the morning off."

"You forget who we are talking about. Sir Arthur wants what he wants, regardless of what he promised you."

"I can't wait until we're wed," Walter grumbled under his breath. "No Sir Arthur, or any other employers, to dictate what you do or don't do."

"No, just you," I teased. Walter smiled.

"And I will be the most lenient of masters." When my eyes widened at his choice of words, he leaned in close and kissed the tip of my nose. "Most lenient." I giggled despite myself. "But you're here now, despite Sir Arthur, and that's all that matters."

"I'm here thanks to Coxey's Army." When Walter raised a brow in question, I added, "What I heard on Saturday was true. The Treasury was locked due to concerns over the potential for rogue members of the Commonweal to storm the building. I wasn't allowed to enter."

"Thank you, Coxey!"

"You can thank the man in person this afternoon," I reminded him. Walter laughed.

"That I might."

He offered me his arm, and we headed to the base of the famous obelisk. When we inquired at the door, we were told we needed to wait for the next elevator. It would be another ten or fifteen minutes. We found a spot to wait among the other visitors and took in the view from the top of the knoll, the well-groomed lawns of the Executive Mansion gardens to our left, a large party picnicking on the grass, and the long, lush, wooded greenery of the Mall, its winding paths stretching out for blocks before us, dotted on both sides with grand redbrick museums and the white Capitol magnificent at the far end.

"Since you couldn't work, what have you been up to? Get in any hiking?"

"I did go hiking this morning, but I wish I hadn't." Walter's

head turned in my direction, concern clouding his countenance. He could tell from my face and tone of voice that I
wasn't teasing this time.

"Hattie, what happened?"

I retold the whole incident again.

"You saw the man resurface and run away?" I nodded.
"That's despicable!" I was surprised by his choice of words. It
was the same thing the man, Billy, had said. "What kind of
man would abandon a helpless woman to her death?"

It was a rhetorical question, so I remained silent as I stared
out across the Mall.

"It is bad enough you had to witness the accident, but to
be exposed to that type of woman in life and in death. . . ."

"You know I've seen worse," I reminded him. Should I tell
him that I'd twice been to the establishment where the dead
woman worked? I would, I decided, but said nothing yet.

He nodded slowly. "Yes, you have. I'm proud of how well
you are taking the whole affair." He took my hand, turned it
over, and put two fingers to my wrist. "Not even a rapid
pulse."

"It happened hours ago."

"Yes, but you do seem much calmer about it. Remember
how shocked you were when you found that man's body in
Grotto Spring?" How could I forget anything about my stay in
Eureka Springs? I'd found two dead bodies and had met Walter. It wasn't a trip easily forgotten. "Your heart raced for a
while."

"You're right. I am calmer. Since my visit to St. Joe and re-
solving my fears surrounding my father's death, I've found that
I'm not nearly as excitable. If I'd been told a few years ago I was
going to accompany Sir Arthur to Coxey's camp, I would've
been apprehensive. Now it sounds thrilling." Walter smiled.

"Next!" yelled the attendant near the elevator. "Next elevator
to the top."

We scuttled into the building, joining the other thrill seekers, and took our places in the elevator. When everyone was inside, the elevator doors clanked closed. With a low grinding noise and a jerk, it started its slow ascent.

"This should prove to be thrilling too. I've wanted to do this since they finished it ten years ago," I said. I sounded brave, but I was more than grateful that Walter and I stood arm in arm. My knees were a bit weak just thinking about being in an elevator for the ten-minute ascent. His closeness, like everything about Walter, made me feel safe while at the same time sending delicious chills through my body.

"And I've been wanting to do this since I saw you this morning." Walter kissed me, right in front of everyone. "I can't wait until you're my wife, Hattie," he whispered, his breath tickling my ear.

"Well, you'll have to, Dr. Grice. We don't even have Sir Arthur's blessing yet." Walter groaned his disapproval as the guide pointed out, through the metal bars of the elevator, a memorial stone from the state of Iowa set into the wall of the monument.

"Over 175 stone tablets are set into the interior walls of the monument," our guide said. "Most of the stones date from 1849 through 1855. Every state has its own stone, as do various cities and towns, foreign countries, fraternal and community organizations, and individual personages. The stones are made of marble, granite, limestone, sandstone, soapstone, and even jade. No two stones are alike. You will be able to see many of them before we reach the top."

"When will we reach the top?" a woman standing across from me said in a squeaky voice as she wiped tiny beads of perspiration from her brow with her handkerchief.

"In a few more minutes, ma'am. Trust me, the view will be worth the wait."

Walter glanced over at me, purposely allowing his eyes to roam across my body. I began to blush and then outright gasped in both shock and pleasure when he whispered, "The view will most definitely be worth the wait."

And the view from the top, miles and miles of wondrously miniaturized landscapes, was indeed worth the ten-minute elevator ride. We lingered for some time, in part enjoying the thrill of being over 500 feet high in the air, seeing the view once only a bird could see and in part dreading the long elevator ride back down. But soon it was time to leave; Sir Arthur would be expecting me. After the long descent, it felt good to have my feet on the ground again. I glanced once more at the monument soaring above me before taking Walter's hand and heading down the hill. We strolled over to Fifteenth Street, purposely avoiding the carp ponds, and caught the trolley. As we rode toward Lafayette Park, my excitement began to build. I'd enjoyed the peaceful time with Walter, but with the outing to Brightwood Riding Park, the current camp of Coxey's Army, imminent, the thrill of meeting Marshal Browne made my heart flutter. We arrived at Senator Smith's home with minutes to spare as everyone was gathering to go.

"Hattie!" Sarah, Walter's sister, called when she and her husband arrived moments after we did. As Daniel Clayworth and Walter shook hands, Sarah rushed across the room. "Isn't this exciting?" She grabbed and squeezed my hand to accentuate her point.

"It certainly is," I said, returning her enthusiasm.

"I can't believe we're going to meet Coxey and his men," she said, releasing me to clap her hands. "I can't imagine walking all the way from Ohio. I heard Mrs. Browne and Mrs. Coxey and their little baby will be there too. Can you imagine bringing your baby on a march?"

As Sarah chatted on, I half listened, forcing myself to double-check for my notebook and pencil in my bag. I shared Sarah's enthusiasm and could easily allow it to distract me, but Sir Arthur expected me to be prepared.

"Are we all here?" Sir Arthur said, pulling out his pocket watch. "We ought to be going."

"Chester!" Senator Smith yelled. "We're leaving without you!"

Spencer barked as Chester Smith came down the stairs.

"I can't believe you're bringing that dog to the camp," Senator Smith complained to his wife. Mildred Smith ignored him. "This isn't a place for women, let alone a dog."

"You need us there, dear," Mrs. Smith said, smiling and patting her husband on the cheek. "Remember, the contrast between the civilized and the ruffians?"

"Yes, well . . ." Senator Smith grumbled.

"I'm so glad you could join us, Dr. Grice," Mrs. Smith said, smiling. "Congressman Clayworth, Mrs. Clayworth, I'm always delighted to see you."

"If you could sign this before you leave," Claude Morris, the senator's aide, said, entering the hall from the study. He led the senator to the hall table where a pen and inkwell waited. He laid down the document he was carrying.

"Of course, of course, but make it quick," Senator Smith said, retreating to the table.

"Aren't you joining us, Mr. Morris?" Sarah asked. The man seemed surprised by the question.

"No, why would I?" His expression was at odds with his words. I understood his conflict. The only reason I was being allowed to go was because Sir Arthur needed me there in a professional capacity. Like me, Mr. Morris desperately wanted to go but had to hide that desire behind a façade of professional detachment. It is what we do.

"Because not every day do you get to visit the Commonweal of Christ," Sarah said. "You should come with us."

"I have work to do," he said, regret in his voice. He quickly turned his back and retrieved the now signed document.

"You could come if you want," Senator Smith said without conviction.

"Don't you need Mr. Morris to document the visit?" I said.

Sir Arthur was going simply out of curiosity and the desire to be able to say he'd been there. But it was obvious Senator Smith and Congressman Clayworth were attending for political reasons. The more I was around the senator, the more I learned he did nothing uncalculated, nothing but for its political significance. A trip to the camp of the Commonweal of Christ must have its benefits. So why not have it on record? Mr. Morris's eyes lit up with hope.

"That's an excellent idea," the senator said, taking off his spectacles and wiping them with a handkerchief. "Sorry, Morris, your work here will have to wait. You're going with us."

"What? Why don't we bring Cook and Pratt as well?" Chester sneered. His father scowled back.

"Very well, sir." Claude Morris tipped his head in acquiescence to the senator, ignored Chester, but to me he gave an almost imperceptible smile.

"Your hired vehicle is here, Senator," Pratt, the butler, announced.

We all spilled out onto the walk in front of the Smiths' house and headed to the hired excursion wagon. As we clambered aboard I counted our number—Mr. and Mrs. Smith, Mr. and Mrs. Clayworth, Chester Smith, Claude Morris, Sir Arthur, Walter, and me. Not counting Spencer snuggling in Mrs. Smith's arms, it made nine. It would be a tight fit for the hour's journey to Brightwood Riding Park. I couldn't help but remember the elevator ride with Walter to the top of the Washington Monument. I easily kept myself from blushing by focusing on the scowl on Chester Smith's face and the buttons on his vest. They were polished white horn buttons.

I hope this is worth the trip, I thought, Walter's words echoing in my mind. But with my enthusiasm dulled by the complaints of father and son, this time I wasn't so certain.

CHAPTER 11

"We're here!" Sarah said, with an excited clap.

"Donations for the marchers?" A thin man, covered in dust, said from his post at the gate. "Ten cents for the gents, ladies free."

"I will not!" Senator Smith said.

"The gall!" Chester mumbled.

"Here, this should cover it." Walter handed a silver dollar coin to the man. "You look like you're starving."

"We are," the man said simply as he stepped away from the gate to allow our excursion wagon to pass.

Brightwood Riding Park was a ten-acre fairground with a half-mile oval horse track, inside which had been erected an immense canvas wall encircling the camp that read HE IS ALIVE. Inside the canvas wall, the camp was a scattering of old wagons hung with battered tin pans and dishes; emaciated horses grazing; idle cook fires; two tents, one round, about sixteen feet in diameter, and a small square one, colorfully painted—presumably by Marshal Browne, a painter—and hundreds of haggard, undernourished men lounging about on the ground.

These men were only a small fraction of the millions of jobless men and women across the country who were facing starvation, some of whom chopped wood, broke rocks, and even resorted to prostitution in exchange for food for their families. That was why these men had come to Washington in the first place—to raise awareness of their predicament. I'd come, admiring and envious of the men who had the freedom to march in the name of their cause, to see the heroes I'd read about come to life. Instead I felt pity for their plight and gratitude and relief that I wasn't counted among them.

The men of our company alighted from the wagon without hesitation. I would have readily followed them but had to wait as the other women hesitated. Taken aback by the scene before them, Sarah and Mrs. Smith were less than enthusiastic in disembarking. Mrs. Smith clutched Spencer as her son helped her down. Sarah gave me a nervous smile before taking her husband's hand and stepping off. Walter offered his aid, which I took simply to have an excuse to hold his hand and not because I was concerned for my safety. These marchers were not revolutionaries or rioters, as some in the city feared. These men were weary and hungry, nothing more.

"Where's Coxey?" Senator Smith said to no one in particular.

"Simeon will know," Sir Arthur said, as we spied Simeon Harper approaching us from across the field.

"Welcome to the camp of the Commonweal of Christ!" Harper said, sweeping his hand across the view before us. "You wouldn't know it now, but yesterday was like a circus with Secretary of Agriculture Morton visiting as well as Senators Peffer, Allen, Dolph, Manderson, Frye, Coke, several congressmen, the entire Mexican legation, two members of the Chinese legation, the Japanese minister and his wife, and a seamlessly endless stream of gawkers. But as you can see, it's quiet today. Much better if you want to talk to the men, Sir Arthur."

Sir Arthur nodded in appreciation.

"Where's Coxey?" Senator Smith repeated.

"Well, there's the thing," Simeon said. "He's not here."

"What?" several people exclaimed simultaneously.

"Where is he?" the senator demanded.

"He went to the Capitol to try to gain an audience with Vice President Stevenson again in hopes Stevenson will give him permission to give his speech tomorrow from the Capitol steps."

Still no luck then, I thought.

"And the rumor is that the word is 'No,'" said a man who had sauntered up to our group. I turned to the speaker. With the most peculiarly twisted nose, I'd know him anywhere.

"Good afternoon, Mr. Neely," I said.

And then as I glimpsed the startled expressions on the faces about me, I wished I'd remained silent. Jasper Neely tipped his hat, but without another word or explanation, he sauntered away again. Walter questioned me with his gaze.

"I met the gentleman on my hike this morning," I said as explanation. Simeon Harper chuckled as Walter nodded knowingly.

"All right, then we'll speak to Browne," Senator Smith said.

"Well, there's the thing," Simeon said again.

"You're not telling us Browne isn't here either?" Senator Smith demanded.

"I'm afraid so. Rumor is he went into town to get his picture taken."

"This is preposterous!" Senator Smith said. "We came all the way out here and the man can't even show up?"

"Imagine what the men who marched from Ohio with him think of it," Simeon Harper said. "These men are starving while Coxey and Browne enjoy the fruits of the city."

"Well, something should be done about these Coxey and Browne tomfools," Chester said.

"I overheard a few men suggest lynching Browne when he finally shows. Is that what you had in mind, Mr. Smith?" Simeon Harper said. Chester's face reddened in anger and embarrassment, but he held his peace.

"We should still try to speak with some of the men," Sir Arthur said. "I'm not going to waste my afternoon waiting. Hattie." And with that he headed to the center of the camp with me right behind him.

Before we had reached the first tent, a commotion ensued back near our excursion wagon.

"He's got bread!" a waifish man, in obvious need of more than bread, shouted nearby.

A throng of men, who moments ago had appeared lethargic and hopeless, abruptly scrambled to their feet and raced past us. Sir Arthur held his ground as I stood behind him, hoping to avoid being shoved or trampled as the men rushed to get bread. Sir Arthur swiveled around to see what the fuss was all about. A mud-spattered wagon, upon which was painted a fantastic swirling of bright reds, yellows, and greens, had arrived. Driving was a man I knew could only be either Buffalo Bill, Daniel Boone, or more likely, Marshal Carl Browne. I'd never seen anyone like him. With a large, sturdy build, he sported a heavy mustache and a beard with two spirals. He wore a white sombrero tilted over his right eye and wore his hair to the shoulders. To my relief, a row of silver dollar buttons, shining in the late-afternoon sun, ornamented his fringed buckskin coat.

"Finally," Senator Smith grumbled as Sir Arthur and I returned to our group, which had gathered next to Browne's supply wagon.

In the commotion, Mrs. Smith's dog leaped from her arms,

and with ears and tongue flapping, sped past us into the center of the camp.

"Spencer! Spencer!" she cried after the puppy.

"Why on earth did you bring that damn dog here anyway?" Senator Smith demanded, loud enough to be heard above the din of the men shouting to Browne to pass down the bread.

"There he is," Mrs. Smith said, relieved.

The dog jogged back toward his owner, his tail wagging and his mouth full of a treasure. When he reached Mrs. Smith, he dropped the object in his mouth. Mrs. Smith picked up the dog, ignoring the offering it had brought. I knelt down. The heavy web strap was once part of a man's suspenders, the corroded buckle shiny and wet from the dog's slobber.

"Don't bother with it, Miss Davish," Mrs. Smith said. "Spencer is always scrounging up rubbish."

We all turned our attention back to Carl Browne, who had taken the opportunity of his lofty position to speak to the gathering. He told of his fruitless search for a new campsite.

"We don't know where we will stay tomorrow night. Perhaps we're going to camp in the Capitol grounds."

"Like hell they will," Chester Smith muttered under his breath. Senator Smith too was frowning.

Whether he heard Chester or not, Browne continued, "We're going to carry this thing through to the end. Haven't we done everything I said we would?"

"All except having a hundred thousand men to form the parade," someone shouted angrily from the crowd.

"I didn't say we'd have a hundred thousand men in line," Browne replied. "I said there would be a hundred thousand people with us in Washington. Death to usury!" He shouted as he alighted from the wagon.

As Marshal Browne approached our group, my conscience and curiosity were at odds. Despite his shout of "Death to usury!" I was disappointed Browne wasn't going to preach or give a sermon to the crowd. I knew we'd missed the Sunday sermon he'd given yesterday; I'd read about it in this morning's paper. But still I had hoped for something . . . unusual. Having followed Carl Browne and the rest of Coxey's marching army in the newspapers, I knew Marshal Browne to be notorious for his scandalous religion. He preached a unique form of Theosophy to which he'd converted Coxey when the two met at the World's Fair last year. So I felt slightly cheated not to hear Browne expound on his peculiar theory of reincarnation wherein all human souls, upon death, entered a reservoir, which he called a huge cauldron, which contained a mixture of all the souls that had gone before. According to Carl Browne, each child born was given a soul made from this mixture and was therefore a fractional reincarnation of all the souls who had died before his birth. Shockingly, this included the soul of Christ. He claimed he and Coxey had been reincarnated with exceptionally large quantities of Christ's soul. Moreover, he felt those who flocked to their standard had also been born with part of Christ's soul, and thus together, they would bring a large part of Christ's soul to bear on Washington for their cause. Hence the "He Is Alive" painted on the canvas wall and the name "The Commonweal of Christ," which Coxey and Browne had christened their band of marching men.

At least I won't have to go to confession to cleanse myself from hearing him preach, I thought.

Browne shook everyone's hand equally, mine included, and welcomed us. But then he made his excuses as he had much to do before the march to the Capitol in the morning. He encouraged us to walk around, mingle with the men, and hear their stories. Maybe then, he hoped, we'd understand better the plight of the unemployed worker and the cause behind this "petition in boots."

Senator Smith grumbled something under his breath about lack of respect, but then Claude Morris reminded him why they had come. "Quite right, Morris, let's mingle," the senator said.

We all spread out, me following Sir Arthur and Simeon Harper, Walter accompanying Sarah and Congressman Clayworth. Mr. Harper introduced Sir Arthur to several men he'd gotten to know over the course of his travels with the marchers. One man, once a butcher from Ohio, in the prime of his life, saw his wages cut in half every month until he had nothing left. His children survived only by working in the local mill while he marched. Another man, a blacksmith from Chicago, hadn't found work since January and had seen his wife weaken and die of starvation.

"I once heard this advice to the jobless," the blacksmith said. " 'Cheerfully and courageously do the best you can. Do not cry, commit suicide, or join Coxey's Army.' I couldn't fathom the first two, so here I am." He turned his head away as tears dripped down his cheeks.

Without being asked, I wrote down everything the men said, in shorthand, as though taking dictation, so as not to miss a word. I could easily imagine their stories being used in Sir Arthur's next book. Despite having read the accounts of these men in the newspapers, it was still inspiring to meet them in person and hear their plight spoken in their own words. Sir Arthur was speaking to a man who had lost his job in a steel plant in Coxey's hometown of Massillon, Ohio, days before the march began, when shouting drew our attention to a crowd surrounding Senator Smith. Mrs. Smith, Chester, and Claude Morris stood slightly behind the senator. Directly in front of him was the man with the misshapen nose, Jasper Neely, pumping his fist into the air.

"But don't you see?" Mr. Neely's shout rose above the din of the camp. "General Coxey's Good Roads project would put thousands of unemployed men back to work, building and repairing this great nation's roads." I'd read about Coxey's Good

Roads idea in the newspaper. It was the impetus behind the march, to convince Congress to fund it.

"That's Jasper Neely," Simeon Harper said to Sir Arthur. "He's a character. You won't want to miss this."

With Harper in the lead, Sir Arthur and I made our way over. We arrived as Walter, Sarah, and Daniel Clayworth joined the crowd as well.

"I don't think you quite appreciate our position, young man," Senator Smith was saying.

"I don't think that blockhead could understand anything," Chester said to his father behind his hand. "Or any of these half-wits, for that matter."

"You have a point, son," Senator Smith replied under his breath. "Who else but a simpleton would walk from Ohio to complain about not having a job? If they put that much effort into finding employment, they'd have nothing to complain about."

"Oh, I understand your position, Senator," Mr. Neely said, too far away to have overheard the derogatory exchange. "You will argue the program is too expensive."

"It is," Senator Smith said.

I sympathized with Mr. Neely's cause, the destitution of millions was undeniable, but his tactics reminded me too much of another, a labor reformer I'd met in Newport. Nothing good came of that man's judgmental lectures. And I couldn't see anything good coming from Mr. Neely's demands either. Why do men insist on haranguing others about their cause and then resort to violence when their message is dismissed or ignored? Even women, at times, resorted to such measures; Mrs. Trevelyan had been infamous for smashing barrels of whiskey with hatchets in her protest against intemperance.

Will Coxey's speech, if ignored, lead to the violent protest the government fears after all? I wondered.

"But don't you think it's too expensive for this country not to fund it?" someone shouted from the crowd.

"Now see, that's exactly my point," Neely said. "What costs more, the Good Roads project or allowing thousands of able-bodied men to languish in unemployment? Do you enjoy knowing their families starve because you won't fund the Good Roads project, Senator?"

"But see here, son," Senator Smith said.

As the argument continued, each man repeating his views without deviation, I grew disenchanted and glanced about me. And there she was. The woman I'd seen Simeon Harper speaking to Saturday morning—the madam, Lottie Fox. She was speaking with Carl Browne and a few others. Fascinated, I couldn't keep from staring at her as she moved away and mingled throughout the camp, speaking with many of the men, all who were more respectful to her than I expected. Not that I had any experience with women who made their living doing what she did, but I had expected her to have a different reception. But then again she was the "veiled lady" after all, traveling with the men at times. Perhaps it was only her "girls" who interested the men in . . . that way, as she was a known follower of Carl Browne's brand of religion.

Did she too think she had part of Christ's soul? I suppressed the desire to make the sign of the cross at the very thought of it.

She slowly made her way toward the crowd surrounding the senator and Jasper Neely. I wondered what the others would do. If I hadn't known who, or more precisely what, she was, I wouldn't have doubted her respectability for a moment. Hopefully no one else would have cause to either.

She gave a nod of recognition when Simeon Harper tipped his hat at her. She walked right up behind Jasper Neely and placed her hand on his shoulder.

"And furthermore—" he shouted, his fist in the air. Madam Fox leaned close and whispered in his ear. He nodded reluctantly and lowered his arm, but he still clenched his fists. "Never mind," he said. "We'll see you all tomorrow on the Capitol steps!"

The men from the camp cheered while the senator and Chester Smith frowned and grumbled incoherent protests.

"When Hell freezes over," Chester declared, unconcerned at being overheard. Jasper Neely, who had turned and was walking away, jerked his head in our direction, his lip curled in disgust. Madam Fox grabbed the man's arm in an attempt to keep him by her side, but Jasper shook her off without a glance, took several large steps, and was inches from Chester Smith's face before someone stronger than the madam grabbed his shoulder and stopped him.

"We'll see, won't we?" Jasper Neely said, sneering. "You hangdog, you scapegrace." The other women's mouths gaped open at hearing such insults. I didn't bat an eye. I'd heard my male employers, including Sir Arthur, use these and more.

"How dare you!" Chester Smith reared back his fist and punched Neely squarely in the face. Neely's head snapped back as he fell.

"Chester!" Senator and Mrs. Smith cried simultaneously. Spencer barked.

As they pulled their son back, men pushed past to gather around the fallen figure of Jasper Neely, who glared at Chester from the ground.

"I'll see you at the Capitol tomorrow, you son of a bitch, and there's nothing you can do about it," Neely said, blood streaming down his hand as he tried to stanch the flow from his nose. Lottie Fox knelt beside him and offered her handkerchief.

"There's something I can do about it, all right, you bastard," Chester said, shoving past his parents toward the fallen man. He raised his leg, intending to kick Neely, still prostrate on the ground. Simeon Harper leaped through the crowd, encircled Chester's throat with his arm, and yanked him backward.

Off-balance, Chester stumbled back, swearing vehemently under his breath.

"You've done enough damage already, don't you think?" Simeon Harper whispered into the man's ear but loud enough for those immediately around to hear.

"Let go of me, Harper," Chester growled.

"I'm not just referring to your assault on Jasper," the journalist continued calmly, as if he wasn't in imminent danger of finding himself on the ground bleeding. "I've been investigating other stories that might interest you. Ever heard the name the National Bank of the Potomac?"

Chester drove the heel of his boot into Harper's foot, causing the journalist to release his grip. "Don't ever touch me again."

"Harper, I forbid you to put this in the paper," Senator Smith said.

"Don't worry, Senator," Harper said, shaking his injured foot. "I wouldn't dream of it. But then again, I won't have to." He motioned with his arm to the crowd surrounding them. "Plenty of my colleagues here will do it for me." Several men in brown derbies were frantically scribbling in their notebooks.

Was that a chuckle? Was Simeon Harper enjoying this? As I glanced at Sir Arthur, with his arms crossed against his chest and a frown on his face, I wondered how the two men could be friends.

"It's time we leave," Mrs. Smith said sensibly, as Jasper Neely was helped up and led away.

"Yes, this was a fiasco," Senator Smith said.

"I can't imagine how it could've gone worse," Claude Morris muttered in agreement.

And then we heard the rumbling of another arriving carriage. We turned to the sound as a Grand Victoria made its way through the gates and pulled beside our excursion wagon.

A familiar, young, energetic man leaped out almost before the carriage had come to a stop. A collective groan escaped Chester, Claude Morris, and Daniel Clayworth. Even Mrs. Smith's smile faded briefly from her face.

"Abbott!" Senator Smith hissed.

"Well, gentlemen," Daniel Clayworth said. "It seems you were wrong. It just got a whole lot worse."

CHAPTER 12

"Well, hello, Meriwether. Hello, Daniel," Senator Abbott said, in his distinctly Southern drawl. "And who are these lovely ladies?" He touched the rim of his black planter hat and tipped his head slightly.

Mrs. Smith rewarded him with one of her ever-present smiles. Sarah, more reserved, acknowledged him with a slight, quickly fading grin. Daniel Clayworth nodded curtly and then, with his arm wrapped around his wife's shoulders, turned both of their backs as if something immensely more interesting were occurring on the vacant horse track. When the new arrival's gaze met mine, I simply regarded him with curiosity, glancing at his plain white ball vest buttons until he looked away. Walter, who had been attending to Mr. Neely's injuries, was suddenly at my side.

"Hello, Clarence," Senator Smith said. "Didn't expect to see you here."

"And why not? I voted in favor of the Good Roads initiative when it came up for a vote the first time. I've visited with

General Coxey and Marshal Browne on several occasions. I'm the Populist here. It's you who surprises me by your presence."

"Why? I'm not against labor or farmers."

"Really? Well, they will be most pleased to hear that."

"You know what I mean, Abbott."

"Yes, Meriwether. Unfortunately, I do know what you mean. As long as it doesn't cost this country a cent, you'll support anything."

"The senator is also here at the bequest of a famous historian," Claude Morris added, attempting to salvage Senator Smith's image. Senator Smith nodded appreciatively at his clerk.

"Well, that at least is commendable," Senator Abbott said. "History will be very interested in what happens here today and tomorrow."

"Yes, he is my houseguest, and it was he who was keen to meet this grand army face-to-face," Senator Smith said. "Ask Sir Arthur to join us, won't you, Morris?"

Claude Morris navigated through the marchers, lounging about eating their dinner of bread, to Sir Arthur, who was halfway across the camp in conversation with Marshal Browne. Sir Arthur excused himself and came over.

"Sir Arthur Windom-Greene, may I introduce you to Senator Clarence Abbott," Senator Smith said.

"Pleased to make your acquaintance, Sir Arthur," Senator Abbott said, thrusting out his hand.

"And I yours," Sir Arthur said. "I saw you at the Senate session on Saturday. Do you happen to be related to Major Maurice Abbott of the First Regiment, North Carolina Cavalry, Ninth Regiment Volunteers?"

Senator Abbott's eyes widened as he shifted his glance from Sir Arthur to Senator Smith. A smile broadened on his face. "Why yes, he was my granddaddy."

"Did your father serve as well, Senator?" Sir Arthur asked.

"Yes, he did," Abbott said, glancing over at Senator Smith to see his reaction. Smith was frowning. "He joined the Bethel Regiment at Camp Mangum in 'sixty-two."

"Your family saw some heavy fighting, Senator," Sir Arthur said. "And both were at Appomattox." It wasn't a question. Sir Arthur had written, with me as his assistant, one of the definitive texts on the battle and surrender at Appomattox.

"Yes, that's right, sir," Senator Abbott said, smiling at Senator Smith, who was grumbling beneath his breath.

Sir Arthur and Senator Abbott fell into an easy discussion about the War. Soon Simeon Harper joined them while Senator Smith and Claude Morris took the opportunity to distance themselves from the newly arrived senator from North Carolina. Not knowing if I was expected to take down what the men discussed, I took advantage of a momentary silence to ask.

"Sir?"

"Yes?" Sir Arthur and Senator Abbott said simultaneously. Sir Arthur glanced questioningly at the senator.

"Sorry. A Southern habit, I'm afraid."

"Yes, Hattie?" Sir Arthur said.

"Do you need my services?" I didn't want to spell out that I'd been taking down word for word what the senator had said.

"No, not now. Go see if you can find what happened to Browne."

"Yes, sir."

Only Sir Arthur wouldn't hesitate to send a woman alone on a quest wandering through an encampment of unwashed, unemployed, hungry, and most likely lonely men. I was thrilled at the prospect of talking further with Marshal Browne. I had so many questions to ask him, but I had no intention of going alone. I looked about for Walter.

Leaving Sir Arthur, Simeon Harper, and Senator Abbott to themselves, I quickly spied Walter sitting around a campfire with Sarah, Mrs. Smith, and the man I'd been sent to find, Carl Browne. Daniel Clayworth, Sarah's husband, was in an earnest conversation several yards away. I smiled when I heard him mention baseball and the St. Louis Browns again. Like Daniel, my father too was a fan of the Browns, though they were called the Brown Stockings then.

As I made my way over, I passed Senator Smith and Claude Morris as Chester rejoined them. Where had Chester been? I wondered, realizing I hadn't seen him for some time.

"What's he doing here?" Chester hissed as he glared toward the group I had just left. Whom was he referring to, Senator Abbott or Simeon Harper?

"Shut up or you'll draw attention," his father said.

"But I swear he's the one who spread the rumors about me last year. Father, he's the reason I had to leave town."

"Yes, and you should've stayed out of town, at least until after the election."

"But it isn't until November," Chester said.

"Exactly."

"Father!"

Suddenly Claude Morris noticed that I was near. "Sir, I don't think this is the time or place for such a private conversation."

"Quite so. Thank you, Morris."

"Yes," Chester said sarcastically, "thank you, Morris." Claude Morris frowned but said nothing. "There's Browne, Father. Let's get this over with, so we can go home."

Senator Smith nodded, and the three men started toward my own destination. I stepped quickly with my skirts up, in an attempt to avoid dragging my hem through the mud, horse dung, and other unspeakable filth, and arrived at the campfire moments before they did.

"Was it more pleasant to walk or ride in a canal boat?" Sarah was asking when I sat beside her. "Hattie!" She greeted me before her brother had a chance. "May I formally introduce Marshal Carl Browne? Marshal Browne, this is Miss Hattie Davish, my brother's fiancée." I blushed at having my engagement so blatantly announced among strangers.

Good thing Sir Arthur isn't here, I thought, wondering when I was ever going to get a chance to tell him.

Marshal Browne stood, flourished his sombrero, and bowed. I caught a glimpse of Madam Fox over his shoulder. She was watching us, her eyes focused on Browne. Was that sadness in her face or longing? A moment later, she turned her back and walked away.

"Pleased to formally meet you, Mr. Browne," I said. "We shook hands when you first arrived."

"And I'd repeat that pleasure again and again, charming lady," he said, smiling. As he sat back down, slapping his hat back on his head, he returned to the conversation I'd interrupted. "This revolutionary spirit of 'seventy-six is making the moneylenders tremble now. Congress takes two years to vote on anything, if left to itself. Twenty-millions of people are hungry and cannot wait two years to eat."

Several men around the fire nodded in approval. Chester groaned. The rest of us, wisely, remained silent. It was dangerous talk this man spouted.

"When is Mr. Coxey going to arrive?" Senator Smith asked.

"He's not. He and his daughter, Mamie, our Goddess of Peace, are spending the night in the city."

"What?" Senator Smith said. "The man personally invited us knowing he wasn't even going to be here?"

"The Great Unknown always camped with us," a man behind me mumbled.

The one-time leader of the Commonweal of Christ and friend of Carl Browne, the Great Unknown had been cast out of the group for contesting Browne's authority. A grand episode of tension and betrayal, it was one among many dramas reported in the newspapers that drove the appeal of the marchers' journey. I personally had sided with Marshal Browne, he being one of the founders of the march, but I missed the entertainment and mystery the Great Unknown provided.

"Pinkerton spy," Browne spat, referring to the Great Unknown.

"Do you think you'll gain what you seek tomorrow, Marshal Browne?" Sarah said.

"We are here like Grant before Richmond, and intend to fight it out on this line if it takes all summer and all winter," Browne said, smiling again.

"You are no Grant," Chester mumbled.

"Well, it's been nice to meet you, Mr. Browne, but it's time we were leaving," Mrs. Smith said, smiling as she stood. Walter, Sarah, and I rose as well at this pronouncement. I kept my disappointment from my face. I'd read about this man and his marchers for months and this was to be my opportunity to ask him the questions I'd longed to know. I'd even jotted down a list, just in case.

1. What was the real name of the Great Unknown?
2. Was Lottie Fox the veiled lady, as Simeon Harper claimed?
3. Did he or Coxey have any connection to or control over the other "armies" descending on Washington from California and other parts of the country?

4. How did he come up with the idea that he and
   Coxey had strong traces of the spirits of both Andrew
   Jackson and Jesus Christ?
5. Did he or Coxey come up with the name "the
   Commonweal of Christ"?
6. Why did he dress like Buffalo Bill?

"I'm disappointed but yes, my wife is right," the senator
conceded. "It's been interesting, Browne."

"Peace on earth. Good will toward men, but death to in-
terest on bonds," Browne said, reaching over and rumpling
Spencer's fur. The dog panted with delight. Senator Smith and
Chester both scowled, turned their backs, and stomped away.
Claude Morris scrambled to catch up.

The rest of us made our good-byes to Carl Browne and
headed toward the waiting excursion wagon. With my arm in
Walter's, we followed at a more leisurely pace, several yards behind Sarah and Mrs. Smith, clutching Spencer. Despite the
sting of disappointment, I was relieved to be leaving the noise
and filth of the camp. I glanced over toward Daniel Clayworth.
He was no longer speaking to the man he had been a moment
ago. Instead he was being addressed by a man with his back to
me. The man stood too close, forcing Daniel to step back several times.

"Who is Daniel talking to?" I asked Walter. "Do you think
he'll mind leaving with the rest of us?"

"I don't know who that is—one of his constituents, most
likely. I'm sure he won't mind."

Daniel was a congressman for Missouri. Most of the marchers
were from Ohio and Pennsylvania. According to the newspaper
accounts, several other groups or "armies" from all over the country were approaching Washington in hopes of joining Coxey
and his men at the Capitol: Fry's Army from Los Angeles, Kel-

ley's men from San Francisco reported to be held up in Iowa, two different groups marching from Boston, among others. And with the devastation of the economy leaving no part of the country unscathed, it wasn't surprising. Men from every corner wanted to answer Coxey's call. It was possible, then, that a man from Missouri could've joined somewhere along the way.

The man placed his hand on Daniel's shoulder. Daniel violently shrugged it off and turned on his heel. The man turned to watch Daniel's retreat.

I started in surprise. It was Billy, the man I'd met at the carp ponds this morning. Was that sadness or regret on his face? I watched him shake his head ruefully before walking in the opposite direction.

"Sarah, we're leaving," Daniel said. His face was red and he was obviously flustered.

"We're all leaving anyway," Sarah said, trying to soothe her husband, as she pointed to the Smiths already waiting at the excursion wagon. He nodded curtly.

Walter looked at me, having seen the recognition on my face. The question on his face was obvious. Who was the man who had flustered Daniel so?

"Besides Jasper Neely, he was the other man I met after the carriage accident at the carp pond," I whispered to Walter. "He was the one who attempted to rescue the drowning woman."

"What's he doing here?"

"Like Mr. Neely, he's a Coxeyite." I glanced about for Jasper Neely, but he was nowhere to be seen.

"But what could he have said to upset Daniel so?" Walter whispered back. I shook my head. I had no idea. As we approached, Sir Arthur and Simeon Harper joined us.

"Abbott gone back then?" Senator Smith asked.

"No," Sir Arthur said. "I believe he went over there." He pointed in the general direction of the tents. We all looked and spied Senator Abbott by the painted tent, standing in a group that included Jasper Neely, who was holding a white rag to his nose.

"Senator Abbott had some interesting things to say about you, Chester," Simeon Harper said, smirking. "I might have to follow up on some of them."

"You misbegotten . . ." Chester said, before he lunged for the journalist.

Harper tried to dodge the blow, but Chester's fist connected with Simeon Harper's cheek. Harper's head jerked to the side, staggering the journalist back a few steps. Sir Arthur and Claude Morris each grabbed one of Chester's arms and pulled the furious man back away from Harper.

"Chester!" Mrs. Smith said, placing herself in front of her son. "Again? What is wrong with you?" Spencer, pushing against Mrs. Smith's restraining embrace, growled and barked at Chester.

"Shut that stupid dog up or I will," Senator Smith said, pushing Mrs. Smith out of the way to get to his son. "If this gets into the papers—"

"Don't worry, it will," Harper said, interrupting Senator Smith. He accepted the handkerchief Sir Arthur offered and held it to his cheek.

"We will speak of this later, Harper," Senator Smith said. "But you . . ." He glared at his son. "If you cost me the election, I'll . . ." He was too enraged to finish. "Get in the wagon." Chester opened his mouth to object but thought better of it. Without another word, he climbed sullenly to the back of the excursion wagon.

"I must apologize for my son, Sir Arthur," Mrs. Smith said, her perpetual smile fading. She avoided looking at the journalist. "I do hope your visit to the camp wasn't marred by this."

"I am offended that my friend was treated so poorly, yes, but that is no reflection on you, dear lady. After you." Mrs.

Smith, carrying her agitated puppy, climbed into the carriage next to her son. Spencer growled quietly until her stroking of his fur calmed him.

"Simeon?" Sir Arthur said, gesturing toward the excursion wagon. Chester glared at the journalist, daring him to join us. "There is room."

"Thank you, but I'm staying here tonight," the journalist said. "Want to be there when they march out tomorrow. So I'll say good evening to you ladies." He tipped his brown crusher and attempted a smile. Instead he winced at the pain of it. "Sir Arthur."

"Looking forward to your account then, Harper," Sir Arthur said.

"Which reminds me." Harper pulled a folded part of a broadsheet newspaper from his vest pocket. "I brought this for you." He handed it to me.

I unfolded the newsprint, a copy of the *Evening Star* so recently printed, ink came off on my gloves. It read:

TRAGEDY AND MYSTERY

DEATH DROWNING AND DISGRACE IN THE
SHADOW OF THE WASHINGTON MONUMENT

Early this morning, the body of Annie Wilcox, a prostitute working in this city, was found after drowning in a carp pond in the Washington Monument parklands. Witnesses, two members of Coxey's Commonweal of Christ and the secretary of a reputable historical scholar visiting this city, claim Miss Wilcox and an unknown well-dressed man fell into the pond after their car-

riage was upset. The unidentified man was seen
fleeing the scene. Who could this man be? A
banker, a lawyer, a congressman?

I stopped reading and handed it Walter, who had been trying to read over my shoulder.

Oh, no! Mr. Harper wasn't supposed to mention me, let
alone Sir Arthur. I glanced over at Sir Arthur, having last words
with Harper before we left. *What will he think when he sees this?*

Walter handed the article back. "That's the last time I'd
trust him." I agreed.

But before I could confront him, Simeon Harper sauntered
away as the rest of us piled into the wagon without speaking or
looking at Chester, who with arms folded tightly against his
chest stared unblinking toward the camp. I followed his gaze to
where Senator Abbott and Jasper Neely were still talking.
Simeon Harper soon joined them. Whether he knew he was at
the root of what had happened or not, Senator Abbott, upon
noticing that our wagon was moving, smiled broadly and
waved.

"He's the devil," Chester muttered under his breath. Although I didn't know whom he meant, the journalist or the
politician, I knew which one I'd choose.

"Shush now," Mrs. Smith said, as if speaking to her dog.
"You're not such an angel yourself."

As we pulled away, I noticed Madam Fox and Carl Browne
join the little group. And then, to my surprise, Billy, the man
who had upset Daniel Clayworth, strolled over to the group
and was greeted heartily by Carl Browne.

Who is this Billy? I wondered. Champion of fallen women,
expert swimmer, marcher in Coxey's Army, someone to upset
Congressman Clayworth, owner of threadbare clothes and an
expensive watch. Dare I ask Sarah or Daniel to learn more?

As the driver swatted the horses and the excursion wagon pulled away, I watched the discussion in the small, friendly group grow animated. Despite the confrontations, the accusations, the cursing, and the declarations I had heard today, I'd bet (and I'm not a betting person) a month's wages that we were missing the most significant conversation of the day.

CHAPTER 13

"Sir, may I have a word?"

The return trip from Brightwood Riding Park had been solemn and silent. No one had spoken for the entire trip back. When we arrived, Chester and Senator Smith disembarked from the excursion wagon and went into the house without saying a single word. Claude Morris, unsure what protocol to follow, tipped his hat and then scurried in behind his employer. Mrs. Smith and Sir Arthur, equally embarrassed by their discourtesy, properly bid Walter, Sarah, and Daniel Clayworth good night. I longed for Walter to kiss me good night, but without Sir Arthur's knowledge of our engagement, I knew it was inappropriate. As it was, when Walter kissed my hand, Sir Arthur's eyebrows raised. Was that disapproval or surprise I saw in his eyes? Sir Arthur, Mrs. Smith, and I had watched as Walter and the Clayworths climbed into the Victoria they had waiting and drove away before heading into the house. I had to speak to Sir Arthur about Walter and me. So again I took the opportunity to ask.

"Not tonight, Hattie," Sir Arthur said. "We'll discuss the index you copied today in the morning."

"Of course," I said. But not of course. In the excitement of the day, I hadn't told Sir Arthur I'd been unable to copy the index for him. I hadn't told him the Treasury had been closed. I hadn't even told him about the accident I had witnessed. I hadn't shown him the newspaper article mentioning both of us.

What's wrong with me? I wondered. The thought of being so distracted and unprofessional bothered me. Granted, getting engaged one day and witnessing a drowning two days later was far from routine.

"Buck up, Davish. You have a job to do," I chided myself out loud as I climbed the stairs to my room. I would explain everything to Sir Arthur in the morning.

"What's that, you say?"

I turned to see Claude Morris coming up the stairs behind me. Mrs. Smith was kind enough to give me a second-floor room. The only drawback was its relatively close proximity to Claude Morris's room. He always seemed to manage to be coming or going at the same time as me.

"Nothing, Mr. Morris. I was simply reminding myself of something."

"Talking to yourself, Miss Davish? You'd better not let Sir Arthur catch you doing that. Sure sign of a deranged mind."

I'd met patients in the State Lunatic Asylum last year in St. Joe. Many of them had muttered to themselves. I had forgotten to tell Sir Arthur about the Treasury, but I certainly wasn't deranged.

"As always, your advice is unnecessary, Mr. Morris," I said, trying to be polite but not truly succeeding.

"Going to the march tomorrow?" His change in topic was a pleasant surprise.

"Yes, I wouldn't miss it for the world."

"Me neither. The senator is promised to be among those who will turn Coxey away. It should be quite the moment, and there's sure to be a great number of reporters and photographers there to capture it."

As always, Claude Morris wasn't thinking of himself or his own amusement. He was thinking about how the march would improve Senator Smith's chances of being reelected in November.

"Yes, quite the moment. Maybe they'll even let Coxey speak," I said, as we approached my door.

"Not a chance." Claude chuckled condescendingly. I wouldn't have been surprised if he'd patted my head. "Good night, Miss Davish."

"Mr. Morris."

I waited for him to reach his door before I opened mine and slipped in. With no work to do, I prepared for bed early. But I wasn't to get an early night. Every attempt to close my eyes brought images of this morning's accident. I'd been able to put it out of my mind at Coxey's camp, but now in the quiet and dark of my room, I could think of nothing else.

Why did that man leave the woman to her death? After an hour of struggling over this question, I rose, grabbed the notebook and pencil from my bag hanging on the chair, and made a quick list.

1. He was mentally shocked by the incident and was unaware of his actions.
2. He was running to get help.
3. He was unaware that the woman hadn't resurfaced.
4. He was frightened to be found there.
5. He had planned to do this and intentionally killed her.

The last statement came to me unbidden. Could he have caused the crash intentionally, purposefully inciting the horse to buck and rear? But how could he have known they would be thrown from the carriage? Or that she would drown in the pond? Did he know that she couldn't swim? No, I saw the entire crash and couldn't believe it was orchestrated. Most likely, number four was closest to the truth. It was well known and acceptable that men visited women of her kind. What wasn't acceptable was being found with a dead woman of her kind after you are thrown from a carriage into a carp pond yards away from the Washington Monument in the early-morning hours.

So who was he? He was too well dressed to be an unemployed marcher from Coxey's Army coming into the city for a night of debauchery, unless he was Coxey himself. The likelihood of that was next to nil, considering this city was filled with many other possible candidates of well-dressed politicians, lawyers, bankers, and government officials, any of which could be the powerful man Annie mentioned at the ladies' furnishing store. And what about the pearl buttons? They too indicated someone with extra money to spend. Yet I hadn't seen the like of them on any man all day.

I might never learn who he was. But what about the woman? I knew her name was Annie Wilcox and that she worked for Madam Fox. But why was she in that carriage with that particular man? I couldn't imagine any woman choosing to sell herself for money. Perhaps she hoped to escape her fate, even for a few hours. Perhaps, as she herself believed, her companion this morning promised to take her away from that life.

And now she's dead.

I tried to banish the images I had of her being flung from the trap and smashing into the water, and then of her lying dead on the shore covered with algae. Instead I concentrated on the first time I'd seen her, sunning herself on the balcony. She'd been reading, enjoying the warmth of the sun, and petting her cat. And she wasn't much younger than me.

She could have been me, I thought.

A shudder ran through my whole body as I envisioned myself in her place, an orphan with no other family to support me, lounging in my undergarments outside for all to see. If not for my father buying my typewriter before he died, thus providing me with a means to make a living, *that truly could've been me.*

Unable to shake off this haunting thought, I pulled a dressing gown around me and headed downstairs to the library. If only I had the index to copy. Work always kept the dark thoughts at bay. Tonight the best I could hope for was a distracting novel.

"What kind of idiot are you?" I heard Senator Smith say as I approached the library.

"How was I to know that Abbott would be there?" Chester replied.

"I'm not talking about Abbott. I'm talking about Harper," his father said.

"I'm not worried about Harper."

"That's why you're an idiot. Harper is a dangerous man." Had the senator seen the article? Did he too suspect Chester?

"Then why did you invite him to dinner? Why were you friendly with him at the camp?" Chester sneered.

"This is why you should never go into politics, my boy. Never."

"You didn't answer my question, Father."

"You wouldn't need the answer if you understood politics. Besides, he's a friend of Sir Arthur. Sir Arthur is a powerful ally and contributor. It would do me no good to alienate him by snubbing his friend, no matter how much I loathe the man. So what does Harper know?"

"Harper doesn't know anything, Father. How could he?"

Doesn't know anything about what? Annie Wilcox's death or something else?

The journalist had threatened to investigate something he'd heard from Senator Abbott that related to Chester. There had also been several comments about Chester's reappearance in Washington endangering the senator's chances in the next election. And of course, like me, Simeon Harper had seen Chester at Lottie Fox's establishment. So what had the son done that could tarnish the father?

"He said he was investigating something you'd be interested in. You don't think he's learned something?"

"I'll look into it," Chester conceded with a sigh. "I'll take care of it."

"See that you do."

What did that mean? I remembered other threats I'd overheard in the past. Could Chester be planning to harm Simeon Harper before he could learn more?

That's enough of that, Davish! I chided myself silently. I was yet again letting my imagination rule my head instead of my reason.

"By the way, why did you come back? I told you to stay away until after the election."

"For the march, of course."

Creeeeeak!

I turned at the sound of the parlor door closing deliberately slowly. If I hadn't been near I would never have heard it.

Now that was not my imagination.

I dashed across the hall to the parlor door and put my ear to it. I heard nothing through the thick oak pocket door. I grabbed the handle and slowly slid it open. *Creeeeeeak.* I winced at the noise but for no reason. No one was in sight. Someone else had overheard the conversation in the library and didn't want to be discovered eavesdropping. But who?

"Well, I'm off to bed," Chester said. "Good night, Father."

Before Chester could discover me in the hall, I slipped inside the parlor and slid the door closed behind me. The pocket doors between the parlor and the drawing room were wide-open. Both rooms were empty. Whoever had been in there was gone. To avoid running into Chester in the main hall, I crossed the parlor into the drawing room, bumping into a side table in the dark. The sweet fragrance of lilacs and lavender filled the air as a vase on the table teetered for an interminable moment until I could steady it. I took a deep breath, appreciating the floral scents as well as calming my nerves, before treading more cautiously across the drawing room toward the faint flickering light shining beneath the small door at the back of the room. I groped for the doorknob and, upon opening the door, found myself in a dimly lit hall near the servants' stairs. I'd followed the same route the unknown person must have taken.

But they would be undeterred by the dark, being more familiar with the house than I was. I'd never catch up. But did I want to? The more I considered my situation, the more I realized I was the one acting suspiciously. I needed to get back to my room.

Leery of meeting anyone, I ascended the back stairs, one step at a time, holding my breath to listen for signs of someone else's breathing or footsteps that would warn me of their presence. When I'd heard nothing for several steps, I climbed the stairs as fast as I could, arriving almost at my bedroom door. As I opened my door, the creaking of a floorboard made me turn. Shadows, from the streetlamp shining through the window-panes at the end of the hall, streamed across the floor. A flicker of darkness crossed the shadows and then was gone. I waited a few moments, but all was silent except the distant ticking of a clock. I let out a sigh as I closed my bedroom door behind me.

"Stop being so jumpy, Davish," I admonished myself as I climbed into bed and pulled the coverlet up to my chin. "And you forgot to get a book."

Despite my brave words, I only halfheartedly lamented not being able to get a book; no amount of reading was going to help me to sleep tonight.

CHAPTER 14

Who was that?

As I stepped outside and quietly closed the door behind me, I noticed movement in the park across the street. After last night's episode in the dark, I'd continued to admonish myself for conjuring suspicion out of nothing until I'd fallen into a restless sleep. And yet here I was again, suspecting every shadow, every flash of motion, to be harboring secrets. But this time, someone *was* hiding in the shadows of the park.

I loved Lafayette Square. With its statues, its towering old trees, and quaint townhouses of redbrick and painted yellow limestone encircling it, it was a peaceful place at any time of the day. Even when dozens of people strolled through or reposed in the park, the large trees offering welcome shade on the odd day when the afternoon became unseasonably warm, it was a lovely place to be. But now, it being barely dawn, was my favorite time of all. Before another living soul stirred, with the exception of a few songbirds, the park was almost magical. I'd taken my daily morning hike at almost the same time every morning and hadn't yet seen a street vendor pushing his cart, a government clerk rushing to start his day, or a nanny attempting to soothe a colicky infant with fresh air. The only person I'd ever seen was the sleepy-eyed policeman who walked past the house while patrolling his beat.

So who was that, slinking from tree to tree?

I stepped onto the brick sidewalk and strolled toward the President's House, looking straight ahead but my eyes alert to any movement. Sure enough, when I left the square and began crossing Pennsylvania Avenue, I detected motion out of the corner of my eye. I dashed behind the nearest tree and peered around. A figure emerged and stepped cautiously into the open street.

It was Jasper Neely, the man with the crooked nose whom I'd met at the scene of the carriage accident. The same man who had had an altercation with Chester Smith yesterday at Coxey's camp.

What was he doing here at this hour?

My heart skipped a beat when he headed straight for the house I had left moments ago. As I watched, my eyes riveted to the house, a curtain from Senator Smith's upstairs landing window moved. Only the hint of the hand showed as the white lace curtain was pulled back slightly and dropped closed again.

Who else was awake at this hour? Not Sir Arthur, who made it a point never to rise before nine o'clock. And from my days in the Smith house, no one besides the kitchen staff and housemaid ever rose before seven and none of them had cause to be at that window at this hour. So who could it be? Chester? Senator Smith?

Anyone, I told myself.

Jasper Neely, with his countenance clouded with concern, glanced left, and then right, before approaching the house. Before his hand touched the knocker, the door opened, barely wide enough to allow him in. With the distance between us and the dim light, I couldn't see who had opened the door. Mr. Neely slipped in, disappearing quickly as the door closed behind him. I leaned against the tree, alternating my attention from the front door to the upstairs window, speculating about what Jasper Neely's early-morning visit could mean. Did he have business with the senator, with Chester, or with someone else? Either way, the day of the march had finally arrived, and it must have something to do with that. But what? Senator Smith was a well-known opponent of Coxey and his Populist ideas. They had nothing in common. I continued to stare at the house as I puzzled it out.

Had Coxey sent Neely to apologize to Chester in hopes of enlisting Senator Smith's help in gaining Coxey the Capitol steps? It was a farfetched idea, his helping Coxey, being such a great departure from the senator's normal stance on labor issues. But it would explain why Chester or the senator agreed to meet Neely in such a clandestine way. Even as I considered this possibility, I shook my head in dismissal. Neither Coxey nor Neely would ever believe a simple apology would change the senator's mind. Or were they desperate enough to try anyway? Or did someone other than Chester or the senator open the door?

As birds began waking, their calls and trills filling the park with song, I grew impatient with speculating and determined to embark on my preplanned hike. Yet before I left the shelter of the trees, the door opened again, and Jasper Neely slipped out as he had slipped in. The door closed behind him. I still couldn't tell who was behind it. Unlike before, Jasper Neely wore a smug grin on his face and skipped lightly down the steps. He strolled along the sidewalk toward H Street, whistling "The Cat Came Back," a popular song about an unwanted cat that wouldn't go away. When he was out of sight, I hurried back toward the house and stepped inside. I dashed methodically through each and every downstairs room. They were all empty. No one was about. Then who had met with Jasper Neely?

Whoever it was hadn't wanted to be seen and had promptly taken one of the staircases.

I sighed in frustration. I was to stay in the dark about this as well. First the circumstances surrounding Annie the fallen woman's death, the connection between Daniel Clayworth and the man I knew only as Billy, and now this.

Serves you right for being so nosy, I told myself. It didn't make me feel any better.

As I headed back toward the door, a maid, a slight girl with carroty hair, came through the servant's door, up from the kitchen.

"I don't know how you do it, Miss Davish," she said, "getting up at this hour when you don't have to."

"It's the best part of the day," I said. "By the way, you didn't happen to see a stranger in the house a few moments ago? He has a distinctively bent nose."

The maid stared at me as if I'd sprouted wings. "No, miss. The senator never allows any callers before two o'clock."

"Right. Of course."

The maid headed down the hall to start the morning fires but glanced back twice more at me with a suspicious eye before disappearing into the drawing room. I headed back outside, watching the park for any other unusual activity, but all was peaceful; only the birds clamored about in the warm, gentle breeze and soft glow of sunrise. As I headed toward my destination for the second time that morning, I had more to ponder than what plant specimens I might collect. Whoever let Jasper Neely into the house did so without the maid knowing. But who? And why?

After catching the trolley near St. John's Church, I rode it to its terminal end, disembarking at Rock Creek Park, a federally managed twelve-mile-long park stretching from the Potomac River to the Maryland border. I happily hiked along Rock Creek, following the park trail for several miles. Although Senator Smith's home was right on Lafayette Square, it was still in the city. Here I was able to stroll through woodlands, passing orchards, pastures, fields, gardens, and working mills. More than once I startled squirrels as they foraged on the ground. As the rising sun stippled through the trees and reflected on the slowly moving water, the smell of blossoms, decaying leaves, and fresh damp soil filled my lungs. I scoured the ground, the riverbanks, and the forested hillsides rising on either side of the river for new specimens for my plant collection. Despite my triumph in finding several new species, including American golden saxifrage, mountain laurel, white wood aster, and pink azalea, I couldn't shake the implication of Jasper Neely's predawn visit. My hike was meant to soothe my thoughts, as it had always in the past, but not today. And then, while I was on my tiptoes, stretching to reach the lowest branch of a chestnut oak, another first for my collection, I heard the pounding of a horse's hooves behind me. Before I could react, a rider, wearing a black fedora, similar to the one I'd seen on the driver of the carriage that had crashed, raced his horse, foam clinging to the corners of its mouth, recklessly close to me on the trail. I lurched forward to avoid being trampled and fell to my knees. The horse and rider were a quarter of a mile away before I stood, brushed the dirt and grass from my skirt, and tucked a stray curl back under my hat. I collected the branch I'd sought, but I no longer appreciated my treasure.

Was that him? I stared at the distant rider.

I knew it wasn't the carriage driver from yesterday's fatal accident; this man was much taller, but the thought was enough to send my thoughts further into turmoil. Why was I so upset? Besides witnessing the poor prostitute's accidental demise, I had every reason to be joyful. I was to be Walter's wife! So why did I feel troubled instead?

Once I reached Peirce Mill, one of the oldest gristmills still working, I stood on the footbridge above the tailrace, letting the steady turning of the waterwheel ease my palpitating heart. When I found I could take a deep, steady breath, I pulled out my notebook and made a list of all the questions that were distressing me.

1. Why was Jasper Neely at Senator Smith's home this morning?
2. Who was the man who left Annie Wilcox to her deadly fate?
3. Why was there animosity between Simeon Harper and Chester Smith?
4. Why was there animosity between the Smiths and Senator Abbott?
5. What had Chester Smith done that could cost his father the election?
6. What will Sir Arthur say when I tell him of my engagement?

And there it was. Sir Arthur. I wasn't dismayed by Jasper Neely; who was he to me? I pitied the dead girl and regretted her death, but again, she was no acquaintance of mine. And as for Simeon Harper, Senator Smith, or Chester, they could argue and fight all they wanted as far as I was concerned. It was Sir Arthur who was worrying me. I had yet to gain a private audience with him, and the longer it went, the more anxiety I felt. I despaired at the thought that Sir Arthur would not give Walter and me his blessing, that he would see my involvement in the "fallen woman's" death as scandalous, that he would be cross when I failed to produce the property index he wanted today.

I glanced at my watch. Oh, no! It was already eight thirty, and I had much work to do before the march.

I hurried back the way I had come, nearly running to the trolley stop, the brisk exercise and the focus on what I needed to do doing more for my troubled thoughts than anything I'd tried so far. I alighted from the trolley in front of the Metropolitan Club and walked past the Corcoran Art Gallery as a man was unlocking the doors. Knowing the Treasury Building would be locked until after the march, I headed straight across the street and into the State, War and Navy Department building. Not far from the entrance, several distinguished and well-dressed men stood about in discussion. And they all wore black lasting buttons on their vests.

"And I, for one, believe that if tramps and vagabonds can be kept out of the procession and a respectable lot of men gathered together, as I think will be the case, the demonstration will have a wholesome effect," a man wearing the collar of a clergyman said.

"I disagree. This march is the work of a man, who, if not a knave, is crazy, and who does not represent any of the principles of our party," another man said. "I for one am glad the police and the army are on hand."

"But they come under the guise of doing Christ's work," the clergyman said.

"Have you seen this morning's headline? They stole a train!" another man declared, holding up the newspaper he had held rolled under his arm. In letters large enough for me to see, it read:

GOVERNMENT WILL STOP THE STEALING OF RAILROAD TRAINS

ATTORNEY GENERAL OLNEY TAKES
ACTION AGAINST THE COXEY
MEN WHO HAVE SEIZED A TRAIN

BELONGING TO THE NORTHERN PACIFIC,
AND ARE NOW FLYING THROUGH MONTANA

That's terrible, I thought. Having been to their camp and having met Jacob Coxey, Carl Browne, and some of the marchers, I'd dismissed the talk of the destruction and danger Coxey and his army posed. But stealing a train. That did sound serious.

And then I saw him again! Jasper Neely was standing no more than fifteen feet away from me. He was speaking to someone, with their backs to me. The two men's heads were close, and I couldn't hear a word they were saying. I continued on my way, but slowly, hoping to catch a glimpse of the man Neely seemed to be conspiring with. As several others traversed the hall, including a woman pushing a cart with squeaky wheels filled with file folders, Neely never noticed me. And then I was rewarded. With the nodding of heads, the two men parted. Neely disappeared almost immediately into an alcove behind him. The other man turned and strode confidently across the hall toward the front entrance. It was Senator Abbott.

What a coincidence, I thought, knowing full well I didn't believe in such coincidences. Jasper Neely had prearranged to meet someone in Senator Smith's home in the early hours only to meet with Senator Smith's rival a few hours later, all on the morning of the much-anticipated march. I watched Senator Abbott push through the tall, heavy doors, before heading toward the Record and Pension Office in the War Department and the work I needed to do, but I couldn't shake the dread I felt.

What was Jasper Neely up to?

Chapter 15

"The march is finally here! Isn't this exciting?" Sarah Clayworth said.

After working for several hours in the War Department, I'd returned to Senator Smith's house. I'd explained to Sir Arthur about the Treasury closure and gave him the Civil War pension records I'd compiled. Luckily he was satisfied. Neither one of us mentioned the drowning incident or Simeon Harper's article about it. I was relieved. And then Walter, his sister, and brother-in-law arrived. We'd planned to all meet and go to the Capitol together. Sir Arthur, Senator and Mrs. Smith, Chester Smith, and Claude Morris opted to squeeze into their cabriolet phaeton, which bore the golden *MLS* monogram on its dash, while Walter, Sarah, Daniel, and I decided to walk, hoping to join the marchers as they passed.

"It is exciting!" I heartily agreed with Sarah.

Walking arm in arm with Walter while his sister did the same with her husband, we made our way down Pennsylvania Avenue, along with a throng of tens of thousands of others lining the streets, who had come out for the arrival of Coxey's

Army. Despite being elbowed in the back and having my foot stepped on, we were lucky to squeeze through the crowd and find a spot on the curb to see the approaching procession. With the carriages of the Public Comfort Committee of Washington, D.C., for escort, the "Goddess of Peace" Mamie, Coxey's seventeen-year-old daughter, dressed in an all-white riding habit and a red, white, and blue cap, led the way on her white stallion. Behind her was Coxey himself, in a phaeton with his wife and infant son. In a crowd, the architect of this entire enterprise, this unremarkable, bespectacled man, would never had stood out. Marshal Browne, on the other hand, in his buckskins and a formal necktie, on a gray Percheron stallion flanking Coxey's carriage, was unmistakable.

Other characters I'd read about came to life before our eyes: the cowboy "Oklahoma Sam," who showed off by riding his pony backward; Jesse Coxey, the eighteen-year-old son of Coxey, who wore blue and gray symbolizing the Civil War; and Christopher Columbus Jones, the wrinkled old leader of the Philadelphia contingency, who wore a suit of shiny broadcloth and an oversized stovepipe hat. And behind them came the faithful, dust-covered, road-weary men who had marched in dilapidated shoes and threadbare suits all the way from Ohio. They carried American flags and banners that read: PEACE ON EARTH, GOOD WILL TOWARD MEN, BUT DEATH TO INTEREST ON BONDS and CO-OPERATION, THE CEREBELLUM OF THE COMMONWEAL and THE MEDULLA OBLONGATA AND ALL OTHER PARTS OF THE REINCARNATED CHRIST IN THE WHOLE PEOPLE. A small band, mostly of brass drums and cymbals, accompanied the men with a rendition of "Marching Through Georgia," an old Civil War song.

Adding to the carnival atmosphere were spectators cheering and chanting "Coxey, Coxey, Coxey!" Some overenthusiastic admirers even attempted to climb into Coxey's carriage. As the procession passed us, the streets and the sidewalks grew

more and more crowded. It was soon impossible to say where
the men who had marched from Ohio began and the spectators who had joined them ended. I clung to Walter tightly,
afraid to be separated from him in the melee as we pushed
through the crowd up the hill toward the House of Represen-
tatives entrance, hoping to reach the Capitol steps in time to
see Coxey speak. And we weren't the only ones. Along with
thousands of onlookers, Coxey and his men had three or four
hundred policemen waiting for them.

"We're so close, we'll be able to see everything," Sarah said
gleefully. I smiled at her enthusiasm.

And then I saw him again. Jasper Neely! He was leaning on
the low stone wall, talking to a woman next to him. It was
Lottie Fox, the madam. Unlike most of the revelers, her face
was somber. She nodded her head several times in response to
whatever Mr. Neely was saying.

"Hattie, is something wrong?" Walter asked.

"No, it's just that—"

"Daniel Clayworth, I will have a word with you!"

We all turned at the shout above the din of the crowd
around us to see the man I knew only as Billy pushing his way
toward us. Daniel was scowling.

"Daniel?" Sarah asked, concern on her face.

"Let's go," Daniel said, grabbing Sarah's hand and pulling
her in the opposite direction.

"But, Daniel, stop! We'll miss everything!" Sarah's desperate pleas were ignored. As the two disappeared into the crowd,
Walter stepped in front of the approaching stranger.

"Can I help you?" he said, blocking Billy's forward progress.

"No," Billy said, with a resigned sigh. From Daniel's anger, I'd
expected Billy to be combative or try to force his way past, but
instead he sadly shook his head, turned away, and disappeared
into the crowd.

"That was odd," Walter said. "Wasn't that the same man Daniel argued with at the camp yesterday? The same one you met after the carriage accident?" I nodded. "But what does he have to do with Daniel?"

"Something upsetting or Daniel wouldn't have left so abruptly. Poor Sarah, she'll miss everything."

"But you haven't missed a thing," a voice said behind me. Walter and I turned to find Simeon Harper beaming from ear to ear. "And it looks like you found a prime viewing spot."

"How did you find us?" I asked, looking out at the crowd, a teeming sea of hats stretching in all directions.

"Sir Arthur told me where you all were to meet. Speaking of . . ." I studied the mass of people Simeon Harper pointed to and found Sir Arthur, Senator Smith, Mrs. Smith, Chester Smith, and Claude Morris slowly making their way toward us.

"What happened?" I asked when the Smiths and Sir Arthur arrived.

The once oversized puffy sleeves on Mrs. Smith's dress were crushed against her shoulders, and she clutched Spencer as if he'd leap from her arms at any moment. She wasn't smiling. The senator and his son, whose pant legs were splattered with dirt, wore the same identical scowl.

"It seems you were right to walk, Hattie," Sir Arthur said, brushing dust from his jacket. "We had to abandon the Smiths' phaeton at Sixth Street."

"It's ludicrous!" Senator Smith said. "Arrangements should've been made; an escort should've been supplied. I'm appalled we were forced from our carriage to walk among the common throng in the street!"

"If we hadn't, we'd never had made it," Claude Morris said.

"Yes, but the filth. Just look at my suit." Senator Smith brushed his vest and the lapels of his coat.

"Maybe we shouldn't have come, Father," Chester said. "What's the point anyway? No one is going to let any of these riffraff speak from the Capitol steps."

Senator Smith shook his head in disappointment. "You were right to go into banking, son," was all his father could say.

"Well, you see, Mr. Smith," Claude Morris began explaining, "it is important that your father be here to do exactly that, prevent the riffraff, as you call them, from gaining the steps. His constituents will expect him to witness firsthand Coxey's arrest."

"Arrest?" Mrs. Smith said with some alarm. "I didn't know they were going to be arrested. Is it proper for us to be here?" She gestured toward me as she said it. "By the way, dear girl, where is Congressman and Mrs. Clayworth?" She made the effort of glancing about her. "Weren't they to meet us here as well?"

"Yes, my sister and her husband were here, but that's a strange story," Walter said. Mrs. Smith searched my face, hoping to learn the meaning of Walter's cryptic comment without outright asking.

"A man approached Congressman Clayworth who the congressman didn't want to see," I said. Mrs. Smith nodded and smiled, as if accepting the explanation, but I could tell she wanted to know more. The senator, his aide, and his son didn't even appear to have heard a word of what we'd said.

"So, Harper," Chester Smith was saying, a sneer on his face, "this is where they kill the goose that laid the golden eggs. Once these cranks are locked up and the rest of the rabble go home, you won't have an easy story to write."

"I could always write about you," the journalist said, unwrapping a piece of chewing gum. Chester's face reddened and he curled his hands into fists at his sides. His mother stepped between the two men.

"That's enough. You'd think you were schoolboys again!" Chester shot one last angry glance at Simeon, who simply popped the gum into his mouth and smiled, before storming off into the crowd. "Chester! You'll miss all the excitement," Mildred Smith called to her son.

"You knew the senator's son in school?" Sir Arthur asked the journalist.

"We both went to Emerson before he was kicked out for cheating."

"Explains quite a bit," Sir Arthur said. Simeon nodded and opened his mouth to reply.

"Attention, Commonweal! Halt!" Marshal Browne's voice boomed above the din of the crowd, cutting off Simeon Harper's reply.

The procession had reached its destination and stopped before the waiting line of police. The journalist motioned for us to follow, and we hurriedly got as close as possible to Coxey's phaeton. After escorting Mamie Coxey, the "Goddess of Peace," to the safety and shade under a maple at the curb, Browne returned to the phaeton.

"Are you ready?" he said to Coxey.

Coxey nodded, bent to kiss his wife, which brought cheers from the crowd, and then jumped to the ground. To my relief, he wore white agate buttons on his vest. With Browne carrying a banner and Coxey carrying his speech, the two men headed for the steps.

Chapter 16

"You can't pass here with that flag," a mounted policeman said, blocking their way.

"Why can't I pass?" Browne asked.

"Jump over the wall," an onlooker shouted before the policeman could reply.

In a flash, Coxey and Browne cleared the low stone wall
that encircled the Capitol grounds and disappeared into the
crowd already gathered on the hillside lawns. Well-wishers and
members of the Commonweal of Christ rushed the steps; arms,
shoulders, and hands pushing and shoving their way through
our group, separating us from one another. The mounted police
were quick to follow in pursuit.

"Walter!" I called out as I was swept away by a throng of
mounted police, onlookers, and marchers.

With my hat slipping off my head, I stumbled along, jostled by the mob racing by, as I desperately tried to keep my
feet beneath me. The small trees, bushes, and flower beds that
were flattened by the onslaught of mounted police in pursuit
of Coxey and Browne were proof of what would happen

should I fall. Ahead of me, Christopher Columbus Jones, the old Coxeyite from Philadelphia, dodged the pressing crowd, hoping to join his leaders, but was grabbed by several policemen, who jammed his stovepipe hat over his eyes and dragged him to a nearby patrol wagon. Suddenly Marshal Browne was not far in front of me. Coxey was nowhere to be seen.

"I am an American citizen. I stand on my constitutional rights!" Browne yelled as a dozen policemen tackled him.

But as they led him to a patrol wagon, Marshal Browne twisted around suddenly, freeing himself from their grasp, and attempted to run back into the crowd. As the onlookers stared in horror, myself included, a policeman launched himself onto Browne's back while others beat him upon the head and face, tearing his shirt from the collar to the trousers and ripping from his neck a string of amber beads, given to him by his deceased wife.

Browne struggled to free himself again as the police forced him toward the nearest patrol wagon. As they attempted to get Browne into the wagon, Lottie Fox, the madam, shouting, "He's alive! The Cerebellum of Christ—He's alive!" forced her way against the patrol wagon door. She wouldn't budge. As one officer grabbed Lottie Fox by the arm and yanked her free of the patrol wagon, several of the marshal's other well-wishers grabbed the bridles of the policemen's horses. The policemen and horses together were forced against a low wall with several officers tumbling violently to the ground. Provoked by such defiance, the police charged into the crowd, their clubs held high, and beat anyone within range. Lottie Fox was the first woman I saw fall, collapsing to her knees in a daze. Screams erupted as I twisted about in an attempt to flee. But as I ran, a woman frantically pushing a baby buggy crossed my path. While trying to avoid the baby, I toppled onto one knee, landing on the sharp edge of a rock. Stifling a cry, I glanced back as the ground trembled with the trampling and pounding of hundreds of feet, horses' among them. Then a man, bare-headed and wearing no coat, turned as I had at the sound of the approaching police and stepped on my skirt, pinning me in place. I yanked at my skirt, freeing myself, but the man's boot left a muddy footprint on my skirt's field of yellow flowers. I looked back again. They were coming! Elbows, knees, loose bags, and boot tips bashed into me as I scrambled in a vain attempt to rise. And then a mounted policeman was upon me. I could feel the breath of the horse on my face and smell the shoe polish on the officer's boot as he leaned toward me.

"No!" I screamed, throwing up my hands to protect my head as he swung the thick wooden club toward me.

Crunch!

As the club made impact, I cringed at the sickening sound I heard the instant before intense pain exploded in my arm. I crumpled to the ground, cradling my shattered arm. The officer and his horse skidded around me in his haste to attack the next person unfortunate enough to be close at hand. I sat swaying, the heel of my shoe stabbing my hip, the taste of salt in my mouth as tears streamed down my face. And then the pandemonium was over almost as soon as it had begun. But instead of cheers and applause, the grounds were filled with wailing, crying, and angry shouts.

"Oh my God, Hattie!" Walter shouted as he raced toward me, dropping to his knees before me. Tears blurred my vision, but I knew it was him.

"My arm, Walter. My arm," I sobbed, collapsing into his embrace.

"What do you want to do here?" Simeon Harper said, performing his best impersonation of a police officer by frowning and sternly folding his arms across his chest.

"I wish to make an address," Harper continued, now trying to copy Jacob Coxey's voice.

"But you can't do that." Again Harper was using the stern police officer's voice.

"Then can I read a protest?" Harper said, imitating Coxey's response.

"And you know what Coxey did then?" Harper asked, in his own voice. He waited for my response. "Miss Davish, do you know what Coxey did then?"

He was trying to distract me from Walter's ministrations with the tale of Coxey's moments on the steps that I had missed. But I could do little else but focus on Walter as he bent my arm at the elbow and at the wrist, so that my fingers were turned upward toward the front of my arm.

"Forgive me," Walter whispered. Before I could ask for what, he yanked slightly but forcefully on my arm.

"Ah!" I gasped as a sharp pain sliced through my arm.

"I'm sorry, my love, but I had to realign the bone. It should heal properly now," Walter said, as he tightened one of the marchers' white peace banners, which he had found fluttering on the ground, around my neck to create a sling.

"Don't worry. I'm fine," I whispered, tears of pain still welling up in my eyes. He smiled at my attempt at a jest.

"What did Coxey do then?" Sarah said, with eager anticipation.

She knelt next to me opposite Walter, with her hand on my good arm for comfort. She had been distraught when she'd rejoined our group and had heard what had happened. But now, as she too had missed the climactic moment on the steps, she listened in rapt attention. After leaving with her husband to avoid Billy, she had insisted on returning alone. Unfortunately, she arrived only in time to see Coxey drive by her in his carriage as the crowd around her chanted "Speech, speech!" Of our group, only she, Walter, Simeon Harper, and Sir Arthur had gathered where I lay.

"Coxey pulled a typewritten manuscript from his pocket

and unfolded it," Harper said. "But before he could utter a word, the policemen pushed him firmly back down the steps."

"So he never got a chance to say a word of what he walked hundreds of miles to say?" Sarah said disbelievingly.

"Not a word. Even when the crowd shouted for a speech as he left in his carriage, his words were lost in the clamor." Sarah was nodding her head, having seen that firsthand.

"Astonishing!" Sir Arthur said.

"Disappointing, is what I'd call it," Sarah said.

"Ah, but, fine lady, that's not the end of the story," Harper said cryptically.

"It isn't?" I said, my curiosity overcoming how dreadful I felt.

"No," the journalist said, "for as he was pushed, Coxey, the champion of the poor and oppressed, tossed the manuscript into the crowd and said, 'That is for the press.' And behold!" Harper yanked a folded piece of paper from inside his vest pocket and brandished it about as the prize that it was.

"Is that it?" Walter asked, astonished enough to look up from checking the tightness of my sling for the third time. Even I was captivated by the possibility that Harper held the forbidden speech in his hand.

"It is and I'll be the first to print it!"

"Jolly good show, my boy!" Sir Arthur said, proud of his ambitious friend. "Give it here." Harper handed the speech to Sir Arthur, who immediately started reading.

"Have you read it?" Sarah asked.

"Of course," Harper said.

"But what about Marshal Browne and . . ." I couldn't bring myself to voice Lottie Fox's name. "And the others who were arrested or injured?"

"Only Browne, Christopher Columbus Jones, and Miss Lottie Fox, a fervent follower of Marshal Browne, were arrested," Simeon Harper said. "Coxey was allowed to leave with his family."

"Of the injured, all but you have already walked away of their own accord." I still wasn't sure how well I would do on my own two feet again.

"Yes, the crowd is dispersing peacefully now that Browne and Coxey are gone," Sir Arthur said, looking about us.

"Where are the Smiths?" Sarah asked.

"Senator Smith and his wife left right after Coxey did. I assume Morris went with them," Sir Arthur said. "Chester left some time before that."

Sir Arthur diplomatically avoided mentioning the row between the senator's son and the journalist, but Sarah's interest was piqued when Simeon Harper grinned smugly.

"Mr. Harper, you didn't—?" Sarah began.

"*Aaaaaaaahhhhhhh!!!!*" someone screamed, interrupting Sarah's question. We all snapped our attention toward the source of the scream.

"What the devil?" Sir Arthur said.

The scream came again. "*Aaaaaaaahhhhhhh!!!!*"

Sarah, Sir Arthur, and Simeon Harper leaped to their feet and dashed toward the sound. I struggled to stand. Instead of insisting I stay where I was, Walter knew better and simply helped me, wrapping his arm around me for support. My arm throbbed, but I wasn't going to be left behind. We followed, though more slowly than I would have liked, the small crowd now heading in the direction of the scream to a stretch of the low stone wall that encircled the entire Capitol grounds. The woman's screaming had been replaced by a multitude of exclamations murmured through the crowd.

"Oh my God!"

"What happened?"

"Who is he?"

"Stay back. Give him room!"

"Bloody hell!"

Walter and I easily pushed our way through, the onlookers standing back when they saw my sling. We stopped at the front of the crowd. Sarah was crying, her head turned into Sir Arthur's shoulder, shielding her eyes from the scene at her feet. Simeon Harper, with his back to us, knelt beside a prone figure on the ground next to the wall. With Harper partially blocking our view, I could see two legs in dusty brown trousers, bent awkwardly, one on top of the other, as if they had crumpled beneath the man, sending him sprawling to his side. On his feet were boots cracked and worn so thin, a brown stocking could be seen through the hole in the bottom of the left boot.

One of Coxey's marchers, I thought, staring at the well-worn boots.

Walter eased himself away from me and joined Harper. He bent over the man, and although I couldn't see, I knew he was checking the man's wrist and neck, hoping for even a faint sign of a pulse. When Walter sat back on his heels and I saw the look on his face, I knew the man was dead.

"Can someone find a police officer? There were plenty about earlier," Walter said, uncharacteristically bitter.

"I will," a man called from the back of the crowd.

"Poor soul," said a lady next to me in a purple braided straw hat with a plethora of green leaves and lavender silk flowers. "Must have walked himself to death."

"I heard they never had enough to eat," another one said.

"If Cleveland would only find work for these men, it wouldn't have come to this," someone else added.

As the speculation grew in grumbles around me, Walter stood and said sharply, "Don't blame the march on this man's demise."

"What? Why?" someone asked.

Simeon Harper stood and faced the crowd. "Because this man's been murdered."

"Oh!" Sarah cried as a collective gasp arose from the on-lookers.

Sir Arthur escorted her away through the crowd, which had instinctively stepped several feet backward. I alone seemed rooted to the ground and remained where I was, two or three feet from the dead man. With Walter and Harper standing, the man and the scene of his death were laid out in full before me.

His eyes were closed, but there was nothing peaceful about him. His face, with his mouth frozen in an open grimace, still held the surprise and subsequent pain of his attack. A thin trail of blood from a hole on one side of the man's neck streaked across to the other and pooled on the ground beneath him. In his hand, his fingers stained by his own blood, the dead man gripped a penknife, the tip of which was also darkened with blood. No one could doubt what had happened. And I had no doubt who the "poor soul" was.

It was Jasper Neely.

CHAPTER 17

"How long has he been dead?" Sir Arthur asked.

"Not long. The man's body is still warm, his lips and fingernails still have color, and lividity hasn't set in yet," Walter said. Sir Arthur stared at Walter, anticipating a more precise answer. "I'd say less than fifteen minutes, no more than thirty."

Satisfied, Sir Arthur nodded and turned toward Simeon Harper when high-pitched whistles marked the approach of the police.

Several policemen arrived, mostly in uniform but three wore dark brown sack suits with derby hats to match. It was the bespectacled man in a suit, with dark wavy hair and mustache and a pronounced dimple in his chin, who took charge.

"Secure the area," he said to the uniformed officers, who immediately began yelling and pushing the bystanders back from the dead man.

"Back away!" one of the uniformed officers yelled at us, grabbing Walter forcibly by the arm. Walter went peacefully until the second policeman grabbed my arm and yanked me backward.

"*Aaahhh!*" I cried as pain from the jarring shot through my body. Walter shook off the policeman's hold and raced to my side.

"Unhand her. Can't you see this lady has been injured? And by the likes of you, I might add."

"What happened to her?" the bespectacled man asked Walter as if I wasn't there.

"She was beaten by police with clubs, unprovoked. She's very likely broken the ulna in her arm."

"If she's injured, what are you two doing looking at the body of dead man?" the bespectacled man said.

"I'm a doctor. As I was tending to Miss Davish, I heard another needed my assistance. So I came."

"But why are you here?" the policeman said, looking at me for the first time. He squinted at me despite his spectacles.

Before I could respond, Walter said, "I couldn't leave her unattended, so I asked her to accompany me."

"Yeah, okay. But I will need a statement from you, Doctor—?"

"Dr. Grice."

"And everyone in your party."

"Of course."

"Rhodes, take statements from those in the crowd," the man in charge said, pointing to one of the men in suits. And then he pointed to the other. "Gallaher, I want you to take statements from Dr. Grice and his companions. Don't let anyone leave until you do."

"I beg your pardon," Sir Arthur declared. "I am Sir Arthur Windom-Greene, and this"—he indicated Sarah, who was still using his arm for support while she dabbed her eyes with a handkerchief—"is the wife of Congressman Daniel Clayworth." The bespectacled policeman raised an eyebrow.

"And?"

"If you will not allow us to leave, then at the very least we deserve your full attention, as the detective in charge, Mr.——?"

"Lieutenant Whittmeyer, of the Detective Corps, Metropolitan Police," the detective said. "My men are all special officers in the Corps, Sir Windom-Greene, but if you prefer waiting while I conduct a full investigation of the body and the area, then I will be happy to oblige." He tipped his hat, almost mockingly, and turned away before Sir Arthur could respond.

"Damn cheek!" Sir Arthur said. "Forgive my language, Mrs. Clayworth."

"Forgiven, Sir Arthur. The man was inexplicably rude."

"Are you all right, Hattie?" Walter said.

"Did that ghastly policeman hurt you?" Sarah asked.

"I'm fine," I said, smiling at Walter. He'd heard me say this too many times to count and usually I wasn't fine at all. "My arm does throb a bit, though."

Walter frowned. If I admitted to any pain, he knew I was in trouble. "I need to get my bag. Come with me."

As Detective Gallaher approached, hoping to convince Sir Arthur to speak to him instead of waiting, Walter led me gently toward the detective who was kneeling beside Jasper Neely's dead body. He removed the penknife from the man's grip and stood examining it.

"Lieutenant Whittmeyer?" Walter said, stopping several feet from the body and the detective. The man didn't look up but instead lifted the penknife to his nose. "Lieutenant Whittmeyer?" Walter repeated, now urging me forward.

The detective still didn't acknowledge us. We took a few more steps, but this time, in my state, I was unsteady and tripped on a rent I hadn't noticed before in the hem of my skirt. I stumbled slightly, my good arm reaching for some purchase. Walter steadied me, but not before the detective reached out to my aide. I immediately detected a strong scent about him.

"Coconut oil," I said, without thinking. He released his grip on me.

"That's right," the detective said, sniffing the penknife again. "I couldn't place it, but you're right." He looked at me again as if seeing me for the first time. "I don't think I got your name." I steadied myself, with Walter's help, straightened my hat, and took a step back from the policeman and the body.

"Miss Hattie Davish."

The detective nodded. He handed the penknife to a uniformed policeman and then looked sharply back at me. "Hattie Davish, did you say?"

"Yes, I'm Sir Arthur's secretary."

"I know you."

"I'm sorry, but I don't think we've ever met."

"No, but I've heard that name before. I can't place it, though. Were you the one who got in the way of my men's arrest of Marshal Browne?"

"I beg your pardon?" I said, indignant. "As Dr. Grice explained, I was an innocent bystander who was beaten without provocation by your men. Like many other innocent people who were attacked. As Marshal Browne, Mr. Jones, and . . ."— I still couldn't bring myself to name the madam—"the others were well within your custody, there was no reason for such violence against women and children."

"If you were innocent . . ." he said, and before I could argue added, "I agree with you, Miss Davish. The incident will be investigated. And I will remember where I've heard your name before. But right now, I'm more interested in how you knew this was coconut oil."

"I'm an amateur botanist. I collect plants and flowers and know many of their scents by heart. Besides, it's commonly found in ladies' toilet soap." I looked at the penknife in the detective's hand. In addition to the blood, a clear, oily sheen was on it. "But that looks like pure coconut oil. It probably helped

Mr. Neely pull the penknife out of his neck after being stabbed. But how did it get on the penknife?"

The detective stared at me for a moment as if not knowing how to respond. In the end, he decided to ignore my question and ask one of his own.

"Familiar with penknifes are you, Miss Davish?"

"Yes, I have one much like that one. A tool of the trade, you might say." The detective squinted his eyes as he regarded me.

"So you knew the victim?"

"In a way. I saw him at Coxey's camp yesterday, though we were never formally introduced." I wasn't about to mention I'd met Jasper Neely for the first time at the scene of another death.

"Lieutenant Whittmeyer," Walter said impatiently. "If you wouldn't mind?"

Without taking his eyes off me, he said over his shoulder, "What was it that you wanted, Dr. Grice? I'm assuming you have a good reason for interrupting my investigation?"

"Yes, Miss Davish is in pain, and I need to get to my medical bag."

"Very well, you may go, but I want your statement first. Gallaher!" he yelled. "Stop what you're doing and come get a statement from Dr. Grice."

"Thank you," Walter said, gently urging me toward the approaching detective.

"I didn't say Miss Davish could leave, now did I?"

"You have no cause to keep her," Walter said, again supporting me as we walked away.

"Wait a minute!" Lieutenant Whittmeyer shouted. Walter and I stopped and turned to see him pointing at me. "What is that?" We followed his gaze to the mess that was my skirt.

"A muddy footprint," I said.

"No, there," he said, pointing to a dark brown splotch on my dress. He bent down and, without warning, pinched part of the fabric of my skirt between his fingers, bringing it close to his face. I leaned back in an effort to distance myself from this affront.

"Blood, I would think," Walter said, gently removing the detective's hand from my skirt.

"Yes, that's what I was thinking too," the detective said. "Stay right where you are, Miss Davish." As if to prevent me from fleeing, the detective firmly gripped my good arm. I hissed through gritted teeth at the pain the jarring caused in my other.

"Whittmeyer, what are you doing?" Walter said. "This is ridiculous."

"What in the devil's name is going on here?" Sir Arthur said, ignoring the protests of Detective Gallaher, as he came to my side. "Why are you manhandling my secretary? Release your hold immediately, or I will speak to your superior."

"And you may do that, sir, if you find cause to complain of my conduct toward you, Mrs. Clayworth, or your companions," the detective said, but didn't release his hold on me.

"Then release my secretary this instant."

"I'm sorry, sir. I can't do that."

"But she needs medicine," Walter said. "She needs treatment."

"Once you've given your statement, you are free to retrieve your bag, Doctor. But I'd advise you to bring it to the Fifth Precinct station. This lady is coming with me."

"On what grounds?" Sir Arthur demanded.

"On suspicion of the murder of Jasper Neely."

Who killed Jasper Neely? I thought, trying to distract myself from the pain in my arm every time the patrol wagon hit a bump in the road. *And why?*

As I jostled about in the back of the wagon, the first time I'd ever been inside such a vehicle, the fear of why the police had taken me into custody far outweighed the pain in my arm or the curiosity that drove me to wonder about Jasper Neely. The question I really wanted answered was, Why me? Why were they taking me to the police station for questioning? Why wouldn't they allow me to meet them at the station accompanied by Walter or Sir Arthur as both had insisted? Thinking about Jasper Neely's murder was easier to contemplate, the questions easier to answer: Who had a disagreement with Neely? Who had the opportunity?

Not being able to use my arm to write a list, I made a mental list of suspects instead and counted them off on my fingers. A futile exercise, but it provided the distraction I needed.

1. Lottie Fox
2. Senator Abbott
3. Chester Smith
4. If not Chester, whoever met Neely at Smith's house: Senator Smith? Mildred? Claude Morris? One of the staff?
5. Any one of hundreds of men from Coxey's Army

"*Ouch!*" I cried as we passed through a particularly deep rut that sent me several inches into the air before landing hard again on the wooden bench that lined the inside of the wagon.

"All right, miss?" the police officer driving shouted back to me.

"Yes, I'm fine."

I wasn't. I was in a great deal of pain and I was frightened. I cradled my arm, which did nothing the sling wasn't already doing, but it made me feel like I was in control of something. Because I wasn't. A few hours ago, I was contentedly digging through old war pension records for Sir Arthur, and now I was tied up in yet another murder. And this time they thought I did it.

When the wagon stopped, a uniformed officer helped me disembark through the back, carefully holding my good arm with one hand and putting his other hand around my shoulders for support.

"Careful now, miss." He was the first policeman of the day who had shown me any compassion.

"Thank you."

He led me into the station, an undistinguished three-story limestone building, down an unadorned hall, and into a small, windowless, whitewashed room furnished only with a simple wooden table and three plain wooden chairs, two on one side of the table and one on the other. He sat me in the single chair and told me to wait.

"I'm going to see if I can get something for that." He indicated my arm with a jut of his chin. "We should have something around to ease the pain."

"Thank you. May I also have a glass of water?"

"Of course, miss," he said before closing the door behind him. I heard the bolt of the lock click.

I let my forehead drop to the table and allowed myself a moment of despair. Tears welled up in my eyes, tears of pain, tears of fear and insecurity, and tears of self-pity. I was innocent, but would anyone believe me? I'd seen Sir Arthur's countenance cloud over when they lifted me into the wagon. When this was all over, would I still have his support? Would I still have a job? Sir Arthur would not abide any scandal in his household or among his friends. I could easily imagine that the moment the police insisted I accompany them to the station, Sir Arthur was already contemplating how quickly he could acquire a new secretary.

Sarah's face too, as the patrol wagon hauled me away, had

clearly showed her mortification. But why? Because she believed I was being mistreated or because she believed the false
allegations against me? Or did she believe me innocent, but as
a congressman's wife she could ill afford to show me any support without jeopardizing her husband's career in Washington?
At one time I would have thought the latter, but now I didn't
know.

Thank goodness for Walter. Thinking of his consternation
at not being able to join me in the wagon or give me relief
from my pain gave me the strength to lift my head and wipe
away the tears. A wave of shame swept through me. It did neither him nor me any credit to indulge my self-pity and doubts.
I knew Walter would support me regardless of what was to
come. I knew I could rely on his faith, his love, and his support. We weren't married yet, but from the moment I saw the
look on his face as the patrol wagon rumbled away from the
Capitol, I knew he'd already taken the marriage vows to heart.
Now I must prove worthy of such a man. I pulled back my
shoulders, tucked in the stray curls under my hat, and wiped
away all remains of my tears.

It can't be all that bad. Can it?

CHAPTER 18

Click! Despite my newly found courage, I flinched when the door unlocked.

Buck up, Davish! That won't do, I admonished myself silently as the policeman entered carrying a plain white china cup with a chip on the rim and a small bottle of reddish-brown liquid.

"Here you go, miss." The policeman set the cup, filled with water, before me. "And your doctor friend brought you this." He held out the bottle. "He said to drink it all."

"Dr. Grice is here?" I said, reaching for the bottle. It tasted terribly bitter, but I drank every drop without hesitation. Once, not long ago, I would've avoided such medicine, even when racked with pain, not trusting the prescribing physician to treat me. But after learning the truth behind my father's death and knowing Walter, I'd come to trust again. At least to trust Walter unequivocally.

"Yeah, can you believe it? Must have followed us here pretty fast." I nodded, almost smiling, thinking of Walter's reckless driving. This time I was grateful for it. I drank the water then.

"Thank you, Officer—?"

"It's Lynch, miss."

"Thank you, Officer Lynch. You've been most kind."

"You remind me of my wife. I can't imagine you're mixed up in all this nasty business. Besides, it doesn't do any harm to treat everyone with a little respect."

"And everyone does get treated with respect here, Lynch," Lieutenant Whittmeyer said, entering the room without warning.

"Of course, sir. Sorry, sir."

"You're dismissed."

"Yes, sir." Officer Lynch cast a quick glance at me. Was that pity I saw? If so, it didn't last as he left the room as fast as he could, shutting the door behind him. I was now alone with the detective.

"So, Miss Hattie Davish, can you explain the blood on your dress?" he said without preamble. I looked at the dark splotch spread across my skirt.

"Yes, I can. When I was running from your officers during the melee that occurred after the arrest of Marshal Browne, I tripped and met with the sharp edge of a stone. It scraped my knee and I bled."

"I don't see a cut in your skirt."

"There is a slight rent in the fabric, here." I pointed to the spot. He leaned down and examined the fabric, and to my surprise, poked his finger through the tear. I instinctively sat farther back in the chair, trying to distance my skirt from his inspection.

"It doesn't go through. You could've easily torn your dress in any number of ways." He stood straight but continued to stare at me. "It doesn't explain the blood. I'll have to see your knee."

"Excuse me?" I was shocked. He expected me to show him my leg?

When I didn't move, he said, "Right now, without convincing evidence indicating otherwise, I have to assume that the blood on your skirt is from the neck of the murdered man."

"But there were plenty of people bleeding after your officers took clubs to their heads," I said, sounding more confident than I felt.

"That may be, but none of them was standing next to the dead man. Only you, of all those who discovered the body, had blood on them."

"But—"

"Show me the knee," he said, folding his arms across his chest.

"If suffering this indignity is the only way to clear me of suspicion, I will have to endure it."

"Yes, you will."

We sat staring at one another in silence for several moments. He was obviously not going to change his mind.

"Well, Miss Davish? Shall I show you to a cell or are you going to show me your knee?"

What choice did I have? So I took a deep breath, silently counted in French to five, and then slowly pulled up my skirt, revealing my fine cotton hose an inch above my knee. The stone had ripped a hole in my stocking. My bare pale skin, marred by an irregular dark red gash, was easily seen through the rent. I lifted my head and stared at a thin, meandering crack in the wall near the ceiling as the man had the indignity of examining the area, his face mere inches from my leg.

"So I see," he said, stepping back. I immediately dropped my skirt, shielding my leg from his eyes. I smoothed the skirt across my lap as he took a seat across from me at the table. "Your own blood then."

"Yes, as I told you it was. There was no reason to subject me to such indignity."

"But you could've lied now, couldn't you?"

"Why would I lie?"

"To hide the fact that you killed Jasper Neely." I knew he had suspected me, but to hear him say it out loud silenced the indignant reply on the tip of my tongue.

"And now?" I asked. He stared at me in silence while my heart raced. I could feel every heartbeat against my stays.

"Tell me what you know of Jasper Neely," he said slowly.

"I've already told you."

"Tell me *everything* you know about Jasper Neely."

"Why do you think I know anything more than I told you?"

"Don't be coy with me, Miss Davish. I know who you are."

"So you said before."

"Yes, but now I remember where I heard your name before. You are no ordinary bystander, are you, Miss Davish?"

"What do you mean?"

"I mean, I know all about your involvement in several high-profile murder cases in the past two years, and I'm not just talking about the well-publicized case of Mrs. Edwina Trevelyan, the temperance leader."

"But—"

He leaned forward across the table. "I even know about Newport." I was speechless.

Due to her celebrity, Mrs. Trevelyan's death and my involvement in aiding the police in discovering her killer was in all the national papers. Several of the other crimes I'd helped solve were widely known as well, but none outside of Newport knew about the murder there. Or so I thought.

"How do you know about Newport?"

"You are in Washington, D.C., now, Miss Davish," he said, as if that explained everything.

If he knew about Newport, did he know as well that I was the secretary mentioned in the newspaper who had witnessed the death of Annie Wilcox?

As if in response to my thought, he said, "Oh, yes, I know all about your involvement with violent deaths. So I don't believe for a moment that it was a coincidence you were on hand for this one."

"But—" I started to argue that of course it was a coincidence but stopped myself.

"Don't deny it."

"You're right. I don't believe in that type of coincidence either." He was a bit surprised by my sudden capitulation. He relaxed back into his chair.

"Okay then, tell me everything you know about Jasper Neely."

So I did, almost. I told him about seeing Mr. Neely at the camp the day before, spouting his views that were detested by Senator Smith and his son but that had the ear of half of the camp. I retold how Chester Smith and Neely came to blows. I described how I'd seen Neely slip into the senator's house before dawn this morning and his smugness upon leaving.

"And what were you doing outside before dawn this morning?"

"I don't sleep well, Lieutenant, and often hike in the early-morning hours before I must attend to my duties." He nodded and waved for me to continue.

I then told him how I'd seen Jasper Neely conspiring with Senator Abbott in the State, War and Navy building later in the morning.

"But everyone in Washington knows Smith and Abbott are political enemies," the detective said. "Why would the victim be conspiring with both? What do they have in common?" He stared at the blank ceiling, thinking. His questions were rhetorical so I waited for him to finish, watching a moth, having gotten into the room somehow, batter itself against the electric lightbulb.

"I can't possibly think of anything those two men have in common," the detective said. He rubbed his cleft chin thoughtfully for several moments before saying, "Go on."

I hesitated. This was the part of my story I felt the most awkward about. "I saw him again right before the marchers arrived at the Capitol."

"Of course, he was marching with the rest of them."

"No, he wasn't."

I hadn't thought that odd before, but thinking about it now it did seem strange. Simeon Harper had said that Neely had been one of Coxey's original followers, marching with him all the way from Massillon, Ohio. Why would he not want to be a part of the climactic finale?

"So what was he doing?" Whittmeyer asked me. I hesitated again. "What was Neely doing instead of joining Coxey and Browne at the Capitol steps, Miss Davish?"

I took a deep breath. "He was speaking with Miss Lottie Fox." There, I'd said it. I'd said her name out loud.

"You mean the madam from the Apple House on C Street?" I'd surprised the policeman. I nodded, holding back the urge to chuckle.

I hadn't noticed the name of the establishment the two times I'd been there, my focus being diverted elsewhere, but it was clever. Apple in the language of flowers meant temptation. As I'd once speculated, the name truly was an advertisement in itself. What better description than "Temptation House"?

"I should ask how you, a respectable lady, know Lottie Fox by sight. But in this one case, I'll take your word for it. I know she's been following the marchers for a while, and it's reasonable she would know Neely." I blushed at his remark but said nothing. "Is that all? Have you told me everything?"

"Yes." But that wasn't all. When had I acquired the ability to lie to the police? I wondered, not really wanting to know.

"Very well, you're free to go."

"I am?"

"Of course. I never thought you had anything to do with this. In fact, before I came in here, I read several statements of witnesses that prove you hadn't the opportunity to kill Neely, being part of the commotion involving the arrest of Carl Browne. And I can't imagine your motive."

Whether the medicine Walter gave me had lessened the pain or my fear had turned to anger, I don't know, but it took all the training I'd ever had working with demanding employers not to lash out at this man. I'd felt guilty for holding back information from him but not anymore.

"*Un, deux, trois,*" I counted beneath my breath, trying to calm myself down. When I was calm enough, I said slowly, "So you scared me to death, while possibly tarnishing my reputation by bringing me here under a cloud of suspicion for murder, merely to learn what I know? Couldn't you have simply asked?"

"I've learned witnesses are more honest when they are under duress." He stood, walked to the door, and held it open as he waited for me to leave.

"You made me lift my skirt, sir!" I said, astonished I'd been mistreated so.

"It had to be done."

"I see," I said, already imagining Sir Arthur's reaction when I told him the truth. "Then you wouldn't mind if I ask you a question." I rose from the table and approached the door.

"Not if it's reasonable, no."

"The carriage accident in the carp pond by the Washington Monument yesterday morning. Have there been any further developments?" He raised an eyebrow and frowned.

"Read about that in the paper, did you?"

"Actually, I witnessed that too." The man chuckled under his breath. So he didn't know, after all.

"So you're the secretary the article mentioned? I knew I was right to bring you in."

"A woman died. Have you learned who was driving the carriage?"

"A prostitute died, you mean."

"But the man left the woman to die."

"It doesn't matter. Even if it hadn't been an accident, in this city, considering the victim, we have far more important cases to pursue." I was mortified by his callousness. She might have been a fallen woman, but she was a person after all.

"Would it make a difference if I told you Jasper Neely was among the men who tried to save her?" I said.

"And you are just telling me this now?"

"Will you investigate further now?" I said, ignoring his question.

"Not unless Neely was the driver. Was he?"

"No, of course not. He arrived after the fact and besides, his clothes were dry."

"Then good day, Miss Davish. Let's hope I don't need to bring you in again."

"Yes, let's," I said sincerely, slipping by him, grateful to be out of that room. I had no intention of coming back.

CHAPTER 19

But I was slower leaving than I anticipated, and not from any physical constraints. As I passed the next room, with its door wide-open, I slowed my steps, keeping my head facing forward but glancing into the room from the corner of my eye. Five men, in rumpled shirts and knee-stained pants, faced Officer Lynch across a table. I recognized all the disheveled men as marchers in Coxey's Army, and they were talking about Jasper Neely. When I'd cleared the door, I stopped to listen.

"But he was as loyal as they come," one man said, answering a question I hadn't heard. "Walked every step of the way from Massillon to the Capitol steps."

"I can't imagine who would want to kill him," another added.

"But who were his enemies?" Officer Lynch asked.

Silence reigned until one man said, "It had to have been one of them damn politicians who wouldn't lift a finger to help out the common man."

Grunts of assent filled the room. "Now, now," the policeman said. "We won't be having you accuse anyone without just cause. Think now. Back at the camp, were there any quarrels between Neely and any of the others?"

"The only quarrel Jasper had was with those hoity-toity men who came to gawk but refused to consider sponsoring the bill that Coxey and Browne and everyone was proposing. 'Where's the respect?' Jasper would ask. 'We aren't animals in a zoo, we're men who only want to work, to put food on our tables, and take care of our families proper.' That's what Jasper said, and those 'gentlemen' didn't like it."

Could they be referring to Senator Smith? Or were there others? Many "gentlemen" had come to the camp those last two days before the march, even members of the Chinese legation.

As if to answer my silent question, one of the men added, "One of them even punched Jasper in the nose."

Chester! He was an obvious suspect. He could easily have been who Neely was meeting with this morning. But why? I still couldn't imagine any reason, good or bad, why Jasper Neely had business at the Smith House. Another suspect was Senator Abbott. I'd seen Senator Abbott speaking with Mr. Neely twice— at the camp and at the State, War and Navy building. But they seemed more like conspirators than enemies. Could the conspiracy have gone sour? At one time I would've been mortified even considering the possibility that a United States senator was a murderer, but I'd learned the hard way that, given the right motive, anyone was suspect.

So what could the motive be? I wondered.

As if he'd heard my thoughts, Officer Lynch asked, "But what motive would any respectable gentleman have for killing Neely? Surely not a wallop in the nose?" Again, silence. I leaned back slightly to hear what was said next.

"What are you doing, Miss Davish?"

"Oh!"

Lieutenant Whittmeyer startled me as he emerged from

the room next door. When he noticed the door to the interview room was open, he closed it, and I could no longer hear
if the men offered an answer to the question of motive.

"Can't find your way out?"

"I was feeling a bit faint and was resting against the wall."
The lie came out effortlessly. Inwardly I cringed at deceiving
the policeman, and yet I had no regrets.

"Do you need me to escort you?"

"No, thank you. There's no need. I'm feeling much better."

"Good day then, Miss Davish."

"By the way, Lieutenant, since I am still here, would it be
possible to speak with Marshal Browne?"

"No."

"But I—"

"I know what you're thinking, but you're not in Podunk,
Miss Davish. You're in the seat of the U.S. government. If I
find that you are in any way meddling in police business, I will
not hesitate to arrest you. And unlike this time, I can guarantee
it will not be pleasant."

Pleasant? This had been far from pleasant. I blinked in astonishment and felt my heart skip a beat or two. I had met
with resistance from police before, but I'd never been threatened with incarceration.

"Surely you don't mean if I—"

"In any way," the detective said, enunciating "any" with
particular force. "Do I make myself clear?"

None of this had anything to do with me, I reminded myself. I was simply indulging in the curiosity that had gotten me
into too many bad predicaments already. The man was right.
This was none of my business.

"Yes," I said.

"The door is that way." He pointed down the hall. Then he
tipped his head, satisfied that he would never have to deal with me

again, and strolled away. Without hesitation, I hurried toward the exit, knowing my freedom depended upon leaving as quickly as I could.

"Miss!" someone called in a loud whisper. Despite my hurry, I slowed to look about. I was alone in the hallway. "Please, miss, I need to talk to you," the voice pleaded.

Could they be talking to me? I wondered. Why would they be? Besides, I needed to get out of there. I picked up my pace.

And then Lottie Fox stepped out from the shadows of a darkened intersecting hallway, blocking my way. I stopped at once. I looked about again. Luckily we were still alone in the hallway. But what was I to do? How could I possibly speak to a woman like her in public and not risk my reputation? But how could I ignore her plea? Did I simply act as if she didn't exist, push past her, and keep walking? Did I return with her into the dark hall where no one could see us?

"Miss Fox?" was all I could muster, before realizing my mistake.

I shouldn't know her name. A respectable woman wouldn't know her name. But our paths had crossed several times over the past few days. Did that say more about her or me? I stood rooted to the spot, tongue-tied and not knowing what to do.

Sensing my predicament, the madam said, "Please, miss, I know you don't want to be seen with me, but I have to talk to you. If you'll stand next to the wall where you can hear me, I'll go back there." She pointed toward the darkened hallway.

As if in a dream, I nodded and stood close to the corner of the wall as she slipped back into the dark. I glanced around me, to see if anyone could have seen us together, but only a few policemen were about and none seemed interested in anything other than his own affairs.

"Were you hurt?" I finally gathered up the courage to ask.

I could still picture her staggering to her knees after being hit by a policeman's club.

"I'm fine, miss. Thank you."

"Weren't you arrested?"

"Yes, but I know the police superintendent." She said no more, and I was grateful. "You don't need to know any more about me, but aren't you the one that witnessed my Annie drowning in the carp pond yesterday morning?"

I was stunned into silence. This wasn't what I'd expected. For some reason I'd assumed she wanted to talk about Jasper Neely. And then the reality of what she'd said seeped into my muddled mind. She knew me. She knew I'd witnessed the carriage accident.

"Simeon Harper," I hissed beneath my breath. How else would she know I was the secretary mentioned in the newspaper?

"Yes, Simeon told me," she said, unaware of my anger. "Please, Miss Davish, can you tell me anything? Annie was like a daughter to me."

He had told her my name! I seethed as I immediately glanced both ways along the hall to make sure no one heard her. How dare Mr. Harper compromise me in such a way? How dare he betray my confidences and to a . . . a madam, of all people? How dare he!

"Please, miss, I don't know what else to do," Lottie Fox was saying.

Focused solely on my anger and the choice words I had for Simeon Harper if I ever saw him again, I'd barely heard another word of what she'd said. Her pathetic pleading brought me back. I couldn't see her face, but grief and remorse was obvious in her voice. The woman was wretched; she was stifling tears. Not for Jasper Neely, however she was connected to him, but for a girl who sold her body for money.

"I'm not sure I can ease your sorrow," I said, moved by her grief, "but I can tell you what I saw and what I know."

I'd never considered that a madam would care for the women who worked for her. I'd never considered that those types of women would have feelings like any other woman, but she did. So I told her what I knew, including a description of the carriage driver's horrendous behavior.

"But I'm sorry to say that when I asked, the police indicated they weren't going to investigate further. They have other cases that take precedence over an accident."

"You actually asked about it? To the police?" Miss Fox's voice betrayed her disbelief.

"Of course I did."

"But Annie was a harlot." I flinched at her vulgarity, but in different words that is what the police had said. "Why would you care?"

I wonder myself sometimes, I thought, and then told her the truth.

"It was a tragedy. A woman died and she deserves justice. I still have hope they'll find the man who did it." A stifled sob escaped from the dark hall that hid the madam. I almost turned to face her but cowardly held my back against the wall as a policeman, roughly escorting a disheveled man reeking of whiskey, passed by.

"I didn't expect such kindness," she whispered through her tears. "God bless you."

I felt ill at ease. I'd done nothing but express my desire to see justice for that poor dead girl. I wished I had done something worthy of her gratitude.

"If you want to thank anyone, thank the man, the Coxeyite, you know as Billy. Along with Jasper Neely, he stopped and tried to save Annie."

"I will. I didn't know Billy and Jasper had been there. Poor Jasper. I told him . . ." She hesitated. Told him what? I waited in anticipation, but she never finished the sentence. Instead she said, "Please tell Mrs. Smith and Mrs. Clayworth that I'm sorry."

"What?" I nearly spit out the word in surprise.

What on earth did Jasper Neely have to do with Mrs. Smith and Sarah? Was Mrs. Smith the one who had met Neely this morning? I couldn't imagine why. And Sarah, had she even met Neely? How could she possibly have anything to do with him? And how did Lottie Fox know Mrs. Smith and Sarah? Was Simeon Harper to blame for that as well?

"I thought . . . but how was I to know?"

Know what? Before I could ask, she added, barely above a whisper, "Please tell them I regret it now. Oh, how I regret it."

"Regret what?"

Disregarding my own sense of caution, I turned the corner into the adjacent hallway. But the madam, her heels clicking sharply on the linoleum floor, was running away from me as fast as she could, shoving open a door at the end of the dark hall, and disappearing behind it. I flattened myself back against the wall, my mind racing. Another policeman walked by, eyeing me with suspicion, but said nothing when I smiled.

"Regret what?" I said again out loud to myself the moment he was gone. My fingers shaking, I rummaged through my bag for my pencil and notepad. Using my injured arm to support the notepad, I scribbled a quick list.

1. What did Miss Fox regret?
2. What was Miss Fox sorry about?
3. What didn't she know?
4. What had she told Jasper Neely?
5. Could she know something about his murder?
6. What did Mrs. Smith and Sarah have to do with it?

How could they? I reread the last thing I'd written. Perhaps Mrs. Smith was mixed up with all this, but Sarah? No. I couldn't accept that my future sister-in-law had anything to do with Jasper

Neely's death. I stared at the words I'd written one last time before crumpling the paper and stuffing it deep into my bag.

"Say hello to Daniel Clayworth for me, ma'am," someone called when I arrived in the lobby, jammed from wall to wall with people. From their worn, sun-bleached clothes and the strong scent of unwashed bodies, Coxey's men made up the majority, with a handful of others I recognized as witnesses at the scene of Jasper Neely's dead body. I looked about to see who had called out. The man I knew as Billy pushed back the new wool cowboy hat that had covered his face, and rose from the bench he'd been sharing with several others.

"Billy McBain's the name," he said, holding out his hand. "We weren't formally introduced when we met before." He glanced around. "Also under unusual circumstances." He smiled.

Knowing now that he was no friend of Daniel Clayworth's, I didn't know what to do. I hesitated. Would I offend the Clayworths if I was friendly toward Mr. McBain? But then again, I reasoned, he had attempted to rescue the life of the drowned woman, and for that alone I took his hand, however reluctantly. Rough and calloused as a man's who spends most of his time outdoors would be, his hand was also missing the tip of his middle finger. I could only wonder what had happened to it.

"Yes, both unfortunate circumstances," I said. He nodded. "I'm Miss Davish."

"How are you, by the way, Miss Davish? It's not every day a lady like yourself bears witness to two deaths in so many days," he asked, appearing genuinely concerned.

"I'm fine, Mr. McBain, but thank you for asking."

"I'm glad to hear it, and please, still call me Billy, will you?" he said, before leaning in and whispering, "Have you learned anything more about Annie's death?"

"I did ask, but they told me nothing. In fact, they might not be investigating the accident at all."

"If it was an accident," he said cryptically.

I'd seen the carriage careening toward the pond. I'd seen the horse rear up and bolt. I had no doubt what had happened. "A tragic accident and nothing more," I said.

"Was it an accident that the driver fled and left Annie to die?"

I sighed. Having witnessed another dead body and escaped the accusations of participating in the poor man's demise, I wasn't prepared to ponder such a thought. Instead I changed the subject.

"How do you know Congressman Clayworth, Billy?"

"No need to bother yourself with details. Just tell him Billy says hello. And that I saw Doggie Miller hit a home run against Cleveland. He'll love that!"

"I'm sorry, Billy, but—"

"Just tell him. He knows who I am. We go way back." The man grinned, as if he'd told a joke I was supposed to find funny.

So there is a connection between him and Daniel Clayworth, after all, I thought.

Originally I'd presumed Billy was a stranger, possibly a disgruntled constituent taking advantage of the chance meeting with his representative in Washington. It didn't seem possible a member of Coxey's Army could have any other connection to Walter's brother-in-law, a congressman no less. But I'd seen Daniel interact with Billy McBain, twice. I'd seen the anger Billy aroused in him, and the disappointment in Billy's manner. And how would Billy know Daniel loved St. Louis Browns baseball, Doggie Miller being one of their players? No, I had no doubt Daniel Clayworth knew Billy McBain. And yet neither Sarah nor anyone else seemed to recognize him.

Before I could inquire further, a policeman called out,

"Alexander, McBain, Pfrimmer, and Schwantes. If you would follow me, please."

Billy McBain tipped his hat and joined the other men who had been called. "Just tell him Billy said hello," he said again before following the policeman back down the hall I'd left minutes ago.

I've been given the second behest by a relative stranger in less than ten minutes, I thought, watching the men disappear down the hall. *What am I to do now?*

Was I to convey the message and possibly incur Daniel's ire or forget the encounter ever happened? I couldn't help feel a bit of sympathy for a man who risked his life for a fallen woman. And yet? And what about the message Lottie Fox wanted me to convey? Would Mrs. Smith and Sarah understand the cryptic apology, or would they be appalled when I mentioned Miss Fox's name in their presence? Banishing the indecision and conflicting emotions from my mind, I navigated my way across the crowded lobby, pushed open the police station door, and stepped out into the fading evening sunshine.

CHAPTER 20

"Miss Davish! Miss Davish!"

A group of men, all wearing brown derby hats, rushed at me, some waving their hands and notebooks closer than a foot from my face. I backed away until I was flat against the station door.

"Why did the police question you?"

"Did you know the murdered man?"

"Has the killer of Annie Wilcox come forward yet?"

"Why are you wearing a sling?"

"Was the madam Lottie Fox arrested?"

"Did you speak to Carl Browne? Does he know one of his men has been murdered?"

"I don't know," I said, putting my free hand up to shield my face from their intense questioning.

"Hattie!" Walter said, shoving his way through the men. "Leave her alone. She doesn't know anything."

"She witnessed Annie Wilcox's death, and now she's being questioned by the police after another murder," one of the men said. "How can she not know anything?"

"Go away. Find someone else to harass." Walter put his arm around me. "How are you? How's the pain? Did you take the laudanum?"

"Much better, thanks to you," I said, patting the hand he'd placed on my good arm.

"Let's get out of here." He led me through the throng of journalists toward a four-passenger phaeton across the street, the horse looking vaguely familiar.

"Are you a suspect in the murder, Miss Davish?" a journalist shouted at our backs.

Not wanting to encourage them, I ignored the question. But as I approached the phaeton, a head peeked around the side and said, "Well, are you?"

"Harper!" Walter said. "You know she's not."

"Then why did the police take you in?" he said, holding out his hand to help me into the phaeton. I reluctantly took his hand but said nothing until Walter was settled beside me.

"Miss Davish has been through an ordeal and needs medical attention. Can't this wait?"

"Sure, she can tell me all about it on the way back to Senator Smith's house." I groaned as his horse, Swift, with a little urging from Harper, slowly clomped away from the curb.

At this pace, I'll have time to tell him my life story, I thought. But I had no intention of telling this journalist any more than I'd told the reporters at the police station. Walter had the same idea.

"I'm so sorry you had to go through that," he said quietly.

"I was worried you'd think I had something to do with it," I said.

"Never," Walter said, frowning. "How could you think such a thing?" I indicated Harper's back, in the driver's seat in front of us, as he guided Swift through a right turn.

"He did. Sir Arthur might."

"I am not Sir Arthur," Walter whispered, sensing my concern. "When we are married, you will not be gaining another demanding master. You and I are a team, are we not?" I nodded, too relieved for words.

"Now, if you two lovers are through, I suggest you start from the beginning and tell me everything that happened, Miss Davish," Simeon Harper said. But before I could say a word, he asked, "Did you see Browne? Why did the detective think you knew anything about Jasper Neely? Where did the blood come from that was on your dress?" I ignored all of his questions and snuggled closer to Walter. "Well?" I remained silent several moments more. I was enjoying his distress. "Well, Miss Davish, aren't you going to tell me what happened?"

"No, but you are going to answer a question of mine."

"What?"

"Why did you mention me in your article as a witness to Annie Wilcox's drowning, after promising you wouldn't?"

"I didn't mention your name," the journalist said. "I merely mentioned the secretary to a reputable historian visiting the city."

"A very thin veil, Mr. Harper. Why do you think those journalists were waiting for me outside the police station? They figured out who I was. Even Lottie Fox figured it out. She called me by name, Mr. Harper."

"Yes, well . . ." He had no defense for himself. "What? Wait. Lottie Fox spoke to you personally? Where? At the police station? Do they know anything more about the Annie Wilcox case? Have the police figured out who fled the scene yet?" I said nothing.

"Aren't you going to tell me anything about Jasper Neely's murder? About what the police questioned you about?"

"I wouldn't," Walter said. "You're a scoundrel, Harper. Why should Miss Davish tell you anything?"

"Sure, I'm a scoundrel. But I too have read all those news-paper articles about you, Miss Davish. I even wrote one of them. I know you want justice done."

"And telling you will help?" Walter said.

"Yes."

"That may be so—" I said.

"So you're going to tell me?" Harper interrupted.

"I would, but I'm too tired to tell this tale twice."

"Twice?"

"I have to tell Sir Arthur. So come with us to Senator Smith's house and you can learn everything I know."

"*Aaaggh,*" the journalist groaned. "You know they won't let me back into Smith's house."

"Yes, I do know," I said, feeling pleased with myself. Walter smiled and Harper fussed as Swift slowly plodded toward Lafayette Square.

"Sir?"

After parting with Walter and Simeon Harper, I'd headed straight for Senator Smith's study. My head pounded, my arm was beginning to hurt again, and all I wanted to do was go to my room, but I had to explain what had happened to Sir Arthur first. I stood outside the open study room door, not having been invited to enter. A haze of smoke filled the air as Sir Arthur, Senator Smith, and Chester lounged about puffing on cigars. Claude Morris, with his back to me, was hunched over a stack of papers at the secretary desk against the opposite wall. He glanced up for a moment, saw that it was only me, and then returned to his work.

"Ah, Hattie. You just getting back then?" Sir Arthur said.

"Yes."

"Did you have a chance to get the records I wanted this morning?"

"I did," I said, trying to keep the sigh out of my voice.

"Good. Have those typed up for me by morning." And then, as if an afterthought, he glanced at my arm bound in the new, proper sling Walter had rewrapped it in during the carriage ride back. "That is, if you can manage."

"It will take me a bit longer, only having one hand to type, but it will be done by morning, sir."

"Good. I knew I could count on you. Now, tell me what happened at the station."

Before I could answer, Spencer came scampering into the room, a tattered rag white with flour and smelling of sour milk and yeast hanging from his mouth. He'd been in the kitchen wastebaskets again.

"Mildred!" Senator Smith shouted. "Mildred! Come get your goddamn dog!"

I consciously maintained my composure, not because of the senator's use of such a vulgarity, but because of my own urge to smile at the senator's growing annoyance as he rose from his chair and attempted to kick the dog from the room. The dog easily avoided his master's foot and instead ran behind the overstuffed leather armchair the senator had been sitting on. As Mrs. Smith was not forthcoming, the senator shouted again while Spencer attempted to bury the filthy rag behind the chair.

"Mildred, come get your blasted dog!" Senator Smith's face was beet red with anger as he muttered more obscenities under his breath. "If she doesn't do something about this dog . . ." he threatened.

"Don't worry, sir," Claude Morris said, springing from his chair. "I'll take care of it." With great ease, he knelt behind the armchair and scooped the dog into his arms. Spencer attempted to wriggle from Claude Morris's grip, but dog, rag, and clerk quickly disappeared through the door and down the hall.

"I swear if that dog . . ." the senator muttered again.

"Mother does indulge it, doesn't she?" Chester said, smirking. His father merely glared at him as he collapsed back into his chair.

"As I was saying before we were interrupted," Sir Arthur said calmly, as if the butler had delivered the post, "what happened, Hattie?"

"I'm not sure we can trust what the girl has to say," Senator Smith said, as if I wasn't standing a few feet from him. "In fact, I'm wondering if she should even be in this house anymore." His mood was fouled by the incident with the dog.

"And why is that?" Sir Arthur said, a current of tension in his tone.

"You saw the article in the paper mentioning her in connection with the death of that strumpet."

"Yes, I was indirectly mentioned as well. Are you asking me to leave?"

"No, no, of course not."

"Did you see the headlines this afternoon?" Chester said. "The police are calling for the unidentified man to come forward. He'll never do it, of course."

How would you know? I wondered, still suspicious of Chester's late-night stroll.

"Never mind that," Smith said, grumbling. "The girl was witness to it, not you."

"And how is that her fault?" Sir Arthur said. Silently I sighed in relief. Until now, I had no idea how Sir Arthur felt about my involvement in Annie Wilcox's drowning and the subsequent mention in the newspaper.

"The girl was also brought to the police station for questioning, Sir Arthur. I can't be associated with a woman questioned by the police. It's not proper."

"But she's my secretary, not yours."

"Thank God!" Senator Smith said, ignorant of the sting of

insult evident on Sir Arthur's face. "Morris would never do any-thing to bring scandal into this house. He is as loyal as a bee."

"And Hattie would never do anything to discredit me ei-ther, Senator," Sir Arthur said, crushing his cigar forcefully into the tray. "What are you bloody implying?"

"That she's a liability," Chester said. "I should know all about that." He glared at his father, who ignored him.

"I am a guest in your house, Senator," Sir Arthur said. "I resent your accusations. My word that she is above reproach should be enough."

"It's nothing personal, Sir Arthur, but I'm a politician, man," Senator Smith said, trying to defuse Sir Arthur's anger. "I can't have anyone think I condone this march or its mes-sage. What will people think when they learn a woman staying at my house was arrested at the march and was associated with such depraved men, let alone a murder? With elections com-ing up, I can't afford to be tainted by scandal." He pulled a handkerchief from his vest pocket and wiped his spectacles.

But you went to the camp! I wanted to shout, but wisely said nothing to point out his hypocrisy.

"She wasn't arrested," Sir Arthur said, quietly seething be-fore I had a chance to defend myself. "She was merely brought in to aid the police in their murder inquiry. Nor was she ever associated with Coxey's men, any more than you or I were. Isn't that right, Hattie?" He said it without looking away from the senator.

"Yes, sir. That's right."

"The police lieutenant who escorted her to the station probably knew how she had been a boon to other police de-partments during their murder investigations and thought she could aid him in this one," Sir Arthur said. I nodded. That was only partially true, but I knew better than to enlighten them.

"Well, then tell us exactly what happened, to put Father's mind at ease," Chester said.

"As I'd asked her to do before she was interrupted," Sir Arthur said, still annoyed. "Hattie?"

"Yes, sir."

I wasn't asked to sit nor was I even looked at as I described the interview with Lieutenant Whittmeyer. The two Smith men puffed on their cigars and stared purposely at the bookshelves filled with volume after volume of the *United States Statutes at Large*. Sir Arthur glowered as he lit himself another cigar. I related my tale with as little emotion and as little embellishment as possible. I could feel the tension in the room and didn't want to add to it. None of the men interrupted me, but Chester Smith yawned loudly several times.

"Is that it?" Chester asked when I'd stopped talking.

"Yes." I'd briefly mentioned Lottie Fox's inquiries about the drowning, but said nothing of her mention of Mrs. Smith or Sarah or her cryptic message, nor did I mention Billy McBain. That was between him and Daniel Clayworth.

"Very well. It doesn't seem I have much to fear from the girl after all. Will you accept my apologies, Sir Arthur?"

"Of course," Sir Arthur said, having regained his composure. "Thank you, Hattie. You're excused."

"May I have a private word with you, sir?" I said, reminding him he'd promised me a moment alone.

"Tomorrow. By the looks of you, you need a good night's rest."

I nodded as I retreated from the doorway. Disappointment and frustration were all that kept me from stumbling, as the pain in my arm and the final humiliation of the day had sapped my strength. Yet again I'd been denied my private interview with Sir Arthur, but he was right. I didn't even have the strength for it. I wanted only to go to my bed.

"I have to say, Sir Arthur," Senator Smith said as I slowly made my way toward the stairs. "I was surprised when you first arrived, what with all the scandal she's been mixed up in, that you still employed that girl. Now look what happened today. Sure, she might not have been arrested this time, but I'd discharge her if I were you."

Too tired and frightened to hear Sir Arthur's reply, I scrambled up the stairs as fast as my aching body allowed.

CHAPTER 21

To my delight and surprise, a package and a telegram waited for me in my room. With renewed strength, in part due to drinking more of Walter's medicine, I read the telegram. It was from Miss Lizzie and Miss Lucy, the elderly sisters who had befriended me after my first foray into solving a murder. Having last seen them in Newport last summer, we wrote often. This was their response to the telegram I had sent them on Saturday. Both being in good health and good spirits, they were overjoyed with the news of my engagement and hoped for an invitation to the wedding. I smiled. And then I opened the package. It wasn't my trousseau purchases from Hutchinson's as I assumed, for the simple card was signed: *LOVE, WALTER.*

What could he be sending me?

I carefully lifted the light pink tissue paper and gasped. Inside was the most beautiful dress I'd ever seen. For several moments my fingers hovered over the ivory silk satin fabric, afraid to touch it. And then, with my free hand, I lifted it out of the box, first the bodice and then the skirt, and laid it out on the bed. With stylishly puffy gigot sleeves, it had pale pink silk chiffon decoration at the neck and bodice. The long skirt had an asymmetrical sunbeam-and-cloud pattern of pale pink silk tulle and bead embroidery. I'd never seen anything like it. I peeked at the label. It read: *HOUSE OF WORTH*. Exhausted but happy beyond words, I climbed onto the bed next to my dress.

My wedding dress, I thought, smoothing the skirt beneath my hand until I fell asleep.

And I slept better than I had in weeks. I woke early but refreshed and typed the pension records Sir Arthur had requested last night. Even my arm felt better, though having to wear the sling created an awkward situation when I tried to type, let alone undress and dress by myself. I'd slept in my clothes. That morning, after realizing I was unable to undo the buttons of my dress, I had to ask Mrs. Smith for the help of a maid. As I awkwardly stood while the maid helped me out of my dirty, torn dress and stockings and then into a clean shirtwaist and skirt, I reflected on ladies like Mrs. Mayhew, my employer in Newport last summer, who had ladies' maids assist them every day. But then I thought of women like Lottie Fox and Annie, who spent most of the day in various stages of undress. I was grateful and relieved when the maid was finished. I thanked her for her help while at the same moment vowing to dress myself from now on, even if it was a struggle to do so.

Once I determined I was presentable, tucking a stray curl back under a pin and smoothing my skirt with my good hand, I took another peek at my House of Worth dress, carefully packed back in its box, and then picked up the typing I'd finished and headed for the senator's study.

"Come!" Sir Arthur said from inside when I knocked.

"The pages you requested," I said, holding out the typed pension records.

Sir Arthur was sitting behind the senator's desk, breakfast on a tray and several newspapers spread out before him. He took a sip of his tea with one hand and took the pages with the other.

"You managed despite your arm. Jolly good, Hattie."

"Thank you, sir."

"Today, I'd like a copy of that index to the property destroyed by the Confederates and by the Union. With the march behind us, the Treasury should be open."

"Of course, sir."

When planning this trip to Washington, Sir Arthur had acquired several invitations to stay with friends; even Simeon Harper had offered his house on Vermont Avenue near Iowa Circle. When Sir Arthur had accepted Senator Smith's invitation, I'd been surprised, as he knew the senator only by association and had therefore to refuse offers from much closer friends. But when we approached Lafayette Square for the first time, I discovered how clever Sir Arthur was. The senator's house was a block from the Treasury, the White House, and the State, War and Navy building: all the places we knew for certain we would need to access for his research. Granted, I'd discovered boxes of Civil War records and photographs stored in basements, storage rooms, and attics of other buildings scattered around the city, but the bulk of his work, my work, would be done mere steps from Senator Smith's house. I could easily fulfill Sir Arthur's requests in a fraction of the time.

I turned to leave but stopped, appreciating for the first time that he was alone in the room. "Sir Arthur, would you have a minute to discuss that personal matter I spoke of?"

Sir Arthur pulled out his pocket watch. "Yes, I have a few minutes." He clicked the watch closed. "Sit, Hattie."

He indicated the armchair I'd often seen the senator occupy. I had no intention of sitting, I was too nervous, but I knew Sir Arthur wasn't making a request. So I slipped onto the edge of the armchair, smoothed out my skirt, and waited for him to speak.

"Now, what is this personal matter you need to discuss with me?" He lathered marmalade on his toast and took a bite. "I don't think you've ever required my advice or opinion regarding your personal life before."

Because I did what I was told and had no personal life before, I thought but wisely left unsaid.

"It is something that concerns you as well, sir, or I would never have bothered you with it."

He set down his toast. "Oh, yes? I see. What is it?" He frowned as he raised his teacup, light blue with gold trim on the rim and handle, to his lips.

"Dr. Grice has asked me to marry him and—"

"What?" Sir Arthur, lunging forward, sputtered between several coughs. "What?"

Thinking he hadn't heard me, I repeated myself.

"I heard you the first time, damn it," he snapped. He stabbed a sausage on his plate and then another and then another. He lifted them to his mouth. After a moment's hesitation, he thought better of it and hurled the fork, sausages and all, against the wall. They smacked against a row of books and dropped to the floor. With no more warning than the slight clicking of nails on the parquet hall floor, Spencer bounded into the room, pounced on the sausages, and darted back out the door.

"How dare he!"

"Oh," I said, taken aback by his sudden irritability. I was used to his brusque manner, but had never seen him like this about something as minor as a dog's frisky behavior.

"What a scoundrel," Sir Arthur muttered. He leaped out of his chair and began pacing. "And to think I admired him."

"Sausage was bound to be a temptation for Spencer, sir," I said, trying to placate Sir Arthur without contradicting him. "Dogs are said to have a strong sense of smell." Sir Arthur stared at me, his eyebrows pinched.

"I'm not concerned with the dog, Hattie."

"But then who?"

"How dare Dr. Grice try to steal my secretary? Bloody hell! How does he expect me to find someone as competent, obedient, and discreet?" He spoke as if I wasn't in the room. It rankled me to hear him speak of Walter, or me for that matter, in such a way, but the fear of his disapproval was deeply embedded and I remained silent. "Damn him! What does he think he's doing?"

Was that a rhetorical question or not? I wondered. And then he swiveled on one foot to face me. He pinned his eyes on me. I couldn't have looked away if I'd wanted to.

"As always you did the prudent thing, coming to me, Hattie. You must not worry one moment more about this. Leave it to me. I will speak to Dr. Grice and put an end to it all."

As he spoke, my toes tingled and my body began to shake with anger. This was not what I had expected. This was not anything I had prepared for. In one thoughtless sentence, Sir Arthur had revealed his plan to destroy my future. With the pain in my arm throbbing, the strain of the last few days, and now this, I couldn't take anymore. I'd been a loyal, discreet, and efficient worker. I'd done nothing without considering Sir Arthur's opinion. I'd done everything, everything this man had ever told me to do. But I couldn't do this. I couldn't sit there in silence and let him do this. So instead, I did something I had never done before.

"No," I said.

"What did you say?" Sir Arthur said, taken aback by my defiance. Luckily, by then I had regained my senses.

"I'm truly sorry, Sir Arthur. I don't mean any disrespect and I appreciate your concern, but you have misunderstood me. I love Dr. Grice, and it is my sincere wish to marry him. I had hoped to get your approval."

"You've accepted him?" I'd never seen surprise on Sir Arthur's face before. He was genuinely astonished.

"I have."

"I can hardly believe it of you. You of all people, Hattie. You obviously have not thought this through. How is it that you don't see why you cannot marry?" He waited for my response. I said nothing, so he continued. "Your marrying would leave me without a secretary, Hattie."

"Sir?"

"If you married, you wouldn't be able to work. You do realize you couldn't work for me or anyone anymore, don't you?"

"Yes, sir."

"Isn't that enough to dissuade you?"

How many times had I let my behavior be guided by what Sir Arthur would think? I knew he would be disappointed and inconvenienced by having to replace me, but I never thought he would suggest that as a reason for my not marrying. I knew Sir Arthur to be selfish, but I never thought he was heartless as well.

"I'm sorry, sir, but no. I love my work, but I love Dr. Grice more."

Despite the early hour, Sir Arthur clipped the end off a new cigar, lit it, and puffed vigorously while shaking his head.

"You'll be bored, Hattie. You were not meant for the life of a housewife. You need challenge, purpose. I can't condone this. I can't stop you from doing this, but I won't give you my blessing either. Besides losing the best secretary I have ever had or will ever be likely to get, I don't think you'll be happy."

It was the first time I'd ever heard Sir Arthur consider my feelings. I was touched and flattered by his praise while at the same time annoyed by his presumption. Had he always believed he knew me better than I did?

"I'm sorry to hear that, sir."

"Think carefully before making such a commitment, before destroying everything we've worked for."

"I thank you for your concern, but I have already made the commitment. I will be marrying Dr. Grice."

"Very well," Sir Arthur said, uncomfortably conceding. "When will you give notice?"

"I will stay on until you can find my replacement."

"Damn it, Hattie! Haven't you heard a word I've said? You're irreplaceable!"

He turned his face away from me and dismissed me with a wave of his hand. Speechless, I rose and headed to the door.

"I want that property index as soon as possible," he said, closing the blind on the window, as if nothing had happened. Despite the brilliant sunshine seeping around the edges of the blind, the room was instantly dim. I turned on the gas lamp nearest the desk. When I looked at him, his back was to me and he was staring out the darkened window, his reflection (and mine) staring back at him. Were his eyes glazed with tears or was that only a trick of the gaslight?

"Of course, sir," I said, my voice shaking.

When I closed the door behind me, I took a deep breath and then ran as fast as I could out into the sunshine, not even pausing to pin on my hat. I'd never argued with Sir Arthur, and I felt the blow as much as if he'd punched me in the stomach. We'd always respected one another, relished the work, and even, dare I presume, enjoyed each other's company. He was the mentor, the benefactor who possibly separated me from Annie, Lottie, or any of those women of the streets. And he refused to condone my engagement.

"Miss Davish! Miss Davish!" cried the men waiting outside the senator's door. More reporters. "What can you tell us about—?"

"Leave me alone!" I yelled with a vehemence that surprised even me. The men backed away and didn't follow as I hurried by them and ran down the street.

Even as I entered the Treasury and plunged into copying the property index Sir Arthur had requested, I found no solace in the work. I loved Walter and I was going to marry him. I was more than willing to give up my work, but until that moment, I hadn't realized I was going to have to give up Sir Arthur too.

"Damn," I said, cursing for the first time in my life as my tears splattered my notes beyond recognition. *What am I going to do now?*

CHAPTER 22

"What good timing," Sarah said, as she saw me coming out of the Treasury. "They told me at the Smiths you were working here. I was prepared to roam the halls looking for you." She laughed.

"I finished early."

"Lucky for me then," Sarah said, as she leaned in to hug me. And then she saw my face up close. She held me by the shoulders to look me in the eyes. "What's wrong, Hattie? Have you been crying? Is it your arm?"

I shook my head vehemently. How did I tell Sarah that Sir Arthur was against my marrying her brother or anyone, for that matter? It would be a relief to discuss my predicament with a sympathetic ear—I hadn't had the luxury of a close female friend in a long time. But not Sarah, not yet.

"No, my arm's fine. Were the reporters still there, outside the senator's house?"

"Reporters? No, why?"

"Good."

"Have they been hounding you? Is that what's made you upset?"

"I'm fine," I said, self-consciously wiping my eyes with the back of my free hand. She pouted at me but didn't question my reply.

"So your arm is feeling better? You're still wearing the sling, though. My, that must make things difficult."

"Yes, it does. I can type with one hand, albeit much slower, but I needed the help of a maid to get dressed this morning."

"My maid helps me every day and my arms are perfectly fine," Sarah said, laughing. "You could get used to it, I'm certain."

"I don't think so."

"Can you take the sling off soon?"

"Walter insists I wear it until he's certain I'm well healed."

"Well, he's the doctor, and besides, it's certain to cause a stir," she said without further explanation.

"A stir?"

"Didn't I tell you? It's the reason I came to track you down. I'd like you to accompany me somewhere this morning." And before I could ask where, she said, "Good, there's Wallace." We crossed the street to Lafayette Park as the Clayworths' driver brought the Victoria around the corner to meet us.

"Isn't Walter coming?" I asked, when I climbed into the Victoria with the driver's help. Sarah climbed in next to me.

"No, he's at the Medical Museum on the Mall. Besides, he wasn't invited." She giggled as she wrapped her hands around my good arm. "I think you'll find this interesting."

"Where are we going?"

"We're settled. We can go now, Wallace," Sarah told the driver.

"Very good, madame." Wallace snapped the reins. We pulled away from the curb and headed up Pennsylvania Avenue.

"Where are we going?" I asked again. I wasn't in the mood for surprises.

"We're going to a meeting of the Washington Wives Club."

"Oh?" I said, not able to hide my disappointment.

"Now, now, Hattie, don't judge us yet. I know after that nasty business with that women's temperance club, you were put off women's clubs forever. But we're different."

"How is the Washington Wives Club different?"

"We use our positions as wives of the Washington elite to do good works. I'm proud of what we've accomplished for the poor and needy of this city."

Most members of the American Women's Temperance Coalition would have said the same thing about their cause, but what had I to lose? I wasn't getting any work done. I might as well do something to distract me.

"Then of course, I'll be happy to attend and help if I can," I said.

"I knew you'd say that," Sarah said, smiling and giving my good arm a squeeze. "Any wife of Walter's would say nothing less." After a few moments of silence, Sarah added cryptically, "And of course this particular meeting is special."

"Why? What's different about today's meeting?"

"That I can't tell you." Sarah indicated Wallace with a slight tip of her head. What couldn't she say in front of the driver? What kind of meeting was this? My first instincts were right. The Washington Wives Club wasn't any different from the temperance club after all. Why did I agree to come?

"But—"

"You'll see when we get there. You do love surprises, don't you?"

I detested surprises. Very few of them ever turned out to my liking. But I didn't tell Sarah this. Instead I smiled weakly and said nothing.

* * *

When we arrived at the clubhouse of the Washington Wives Club, a three-story redbrick row house on the south side of James Monroe Park, we disembarked, climbed the narrow stair to the second floor, and entered a simple room with a high ceiling, filled with several rows of chairs and a table under the windows laden with refreshments. A portrait of Frances Cleveland, hung behind the podium, was all that adorned the pale yellow walls.

"Let me introduce you around," Sarah said.

She grabbed my hand and guided me through the crowd of women, mingling about in groups chatting. She introduced me to wives of politicians, bankers, naval officers, college professors, and even a few women who were powerful in their own right. Mrs. Smith was there, surprisingly without Spencer, and happy that I'd come. Everyone was welcoming. Everyone except the woman who blatantly pointed at me and whispered to her companion, disrupting my introduction to one of the Mrs. Willards of the Willard hotel fame.

Was it because I was wearing a sling? I wondered. Is that what Sarah had meant when she said it would cause a stir? If I had known where we were going, I would have risked Walter's wrath and come here without it.

As I wondered how I could remove it unobtrusively, the woman's companion, standing near enough for me to hear her loud whisper, said, "I believe, Mrs. Abbott, that the woman with Mrs. Clayworth was beaten by police during the march and then taken to the police station for questioning. If I'm right, she's the same one who was mentioned in the papers in connection with a drowned 'fallen girl.' "

She might not gossip about me if she knew Mrs. Abbott's husband had been speaking with Jasper Neely not long before the man was murdered. He might even be a suspect.

"Her? How could Mrs. Clayworth bring her here?" Mrs. Abbott whispered back, in a drawl similar to her husband's. "But then again the congressman never could control his wife, bless his heart."

Had Sarah heard her? Had anyone else? Of course, if I had heard her at that distance, so had a great many other people. I glanced at Sarah. She wore a scowl, the likes of which I'd only seen once before, when her husband dragged her away from the march. I had little doubt she'd heard the comment as well.

"Ah, Mrs. Clayworth," Mrs. Abbott said, when Sarah made her excuses to Mrs. Willard and led me over to the Populist senator's wife. Her companion, obviously not a courageous woman, had slipped away without being introduced. "So charming to see you again."

"And you, Mrs. Abbott," Sarah said, smiling and congenial as if she hadn't heard the whispered comments.

"And you brought a friend to our little meeting today," Mrs. Abbott said.

"Mrs. Abbott, may I present Miss Hattie Davish, my soon-to-be sister-in-law. I do believe your husband already met Miss Davish at Coxey's camp on Monday."

"How nice," Mrs. Abbott said, obviously not meaning a word. "You've been injured, Miss Davish?" Sarah winked at me, as Walter is wont to do to reassure me in difficult times, before answering the senator's wife for me.

"As you may well know, Mrs. Abbot, Miss Davish, a completely innocent bystander, was brutally attacked during the riot that occurred when the police arrested the Coxeyites yesterday at the march." Mrs. Abbott's face reddened in embarrassment. "Luckily, my brother, who is currently visiting, is an excellent doctor. Miss Davish shall soon be herself again."

"I'm so glad to hear it," Mrs. Abbott said, only attempting to sound polite.

"If she was innocent, why was she taken into police custody?" someone nearby whispered.

"And why was she all alone early enough in the morning to witness that girl's drowning?" someone else said behind their hand.

"Now if you'll excuse us, I see someone I would like to introduce Miss Davish to before the meeting starts," Sarah said, ignoring the whispered accusations and quickly guiding me away.

"I'm so sorry, Hattie," Sarah said as we made our way toward the table laden with various sliced fruits, breakfast puffs, muffins, coffee, tea, and chocolate. "Ignore Mrs. Abbott. Her husband and Daniel are always at odds."

"It's all right, Sarah, though I'm learning that what these politicians, and their wives, say and do are often very different things."

Not unlike the society ladies in Newport, I thought.

"Welcome to Washington," Mrs. Smith said, smiling as she joined us. I'd no doubt she had witnessed the entire exchange.

We helped ourselves to the refreshments and then took a seat among the rows of chairs. As we nibbled on our muffins and drank coffee, a buxom woman in the chair next to Mrs. Smith, with a large mole on her cheek, leaned over and said to me, "Is it true you saw the dead man after the march yesterday?"

Before I could answer, Sarah leaned toward the woman and said, "We were both there, Mrs. Horton." The woman's hand flew to her ample chest in dismay.

"Oh, my, Mrs. Clayworth, that must have been truly ghastly. How did you sleep last night after seeing such a horror?"

"Yes, it was upsetting. Thank you for your concern." Sarah sat back and took a sip of coffee, but Mrs. Horton wasn't finished.

"Is it true you were beaten by the police?" Mrs. Horton

indelicately pointed to my arm in the sling. I thought she was going to touch me.

Again, Sarah spoke before I could. "Yes, my poor future sister-in-law, a completely innocent bystander, was brutally beaten by the police, along with many other women and children."

"Children!" Mrs. Horton exclaimed, again resting her hand upon her large bosom. "I had no idea. Are you in great pain, my dear? Did you say future sister-in-law, Mrs. Clayworth?"

"Yes, my dearest brother proposed when he arrived in town on Saturday."

"Well, congratulations are in order." I wasn't sure if Mrs. Horton was directing them at me or Sarah.

I'd remained silent during this exchange as the two women spoke of me, but never to me, as I sat between them. It reminded me of so many similar conversations I'd endured over the years, most recently the night before between Senator Smith and Sir Arthur. So when Mrs. Horton paused, I wasn't sure if I was expected to respond or not. But Sarah looked at me, with a slight nod to her head, so I said, "Thank you."

"But I'd heard you were taken to the police station after you'd seen the dead man. Did you go as well, Mrs. Clayworth?" Again, neither woman let me answer the questions directed at me.

"No, Mrs. Horton, I wish I could've been of use to the police, but only Miss Davish was given that privilege. It was most kind of Miss Davish to help, don't you think?"

"Yes, Mrs. Clayworth. I myself wouldn't be able to keep my head enough to help in such a situation. And you saw the death of poor fallen Annie Wilcox as well. It's a credit to you, dear, that the police thought you could help."

Several other women, who had been listening as the conversation continued, nodded their heads. I sat there, amazed at how Sarah had turned a scandalous situation into something to admire, almost to be envious of. Clearly the men were not the only politicians in this town.

"Thank you," I said.

"By the way, Mrs. Clayworth, have you heard . . ."

We sat there for another ten minutes, listening to the other gossip Mrs. Horton spread, before Sarah leaned over and whispered to me.

"I think that went well, don't you?"

"I don't know what to think."

"Well, at least, you can rest assured that Congressman Clayworth's future sister-in-law and her adventures will not be the first topic of discussion again, unless in praise of your levelheadedness and keen wits."

"Is that why you brought me here? To deflect scandal from Daniel?"

"Not the only reason. I truly think you'll enjoy the meeting, which should start any moment now." She glanced at the watch dangling from the gold chatelaine at her waist. "You're not cross with me, are you?"

"No, of course not." I was cross, just not with Sarah.

"Then it's already been a productive morning and the meeting hasn't even started."

Sarah patted my knee and turned her head toward the podium set up at the front of the room. I glanced at her once more, both admiring and deploring her political savvy, before following her gaze. A tall, pale woman with copious freckles on her face was taking her place behind the podium. But I wasn't anticipating the start to the meeting. Instead, all I could think about was Madam Lottie Fox's message: *Please tell Mrs. Smith and Mrs. Clayworth that I'm sorry. Please tell them I regret it now.*

How was I possibly going to protect Sarah from the scandal of it as well as she had protected me?

"I call to order the Washington Wives Club," the woman at the podium said. I shifted in my seat. Despite Sarah's assurances, I was still anticipating something like the American Women's Temperance Coalition I'd encountered in Eureka Springs. I'd had my fill of zealots. But when the president of the club read the agenda from the last meeting for votes to approve, the items seemed harmless enough: quilting bees, fund-raisers to benefit widows with children, and preparations for Decoration Day.

"Why all the secrecy?" I whispered to Sarah. "What couldn't you talk about in front of your driver? What's surprising about placing flags on soldiers' graves on Decoration Day?"

"Nothing is surprising about it. But this is a special meeting. I couldn't possibly have Wallace hear what we're doing here." Before I could ask for an explanation, she said, "You'll see what I mean."

But I saw and heard nothing in the next hour that was special. The women discussed which committee should organize a clothing drive, who was going to deliver the baked goods the women had their cooks make to the local orphanage, among other things. Bored, I was concentrating on the lace curtains billowing in and out of the window in the breeze when the president of the club indicated that they were about to discuss the final item on the agenda.

"But you won't find it on the official agenda today or any day," the president said. I immediately took note. "If any woman here feels that she cannot participate in, sanction, or has reservations about our proposal, she may leave now with no recrimination."

Several women stood, apologizing that it was a risk they couldn't take, and left.

"What's so risky?" I asked.

Mrs. Horton, the buxom woman beside Mrs. Smith, put her finger to her lips. "*Shhhh!*"

"Borrowing from my husband's field, I've named this 'Operation Saving Sisters.' All in favor say aye." Every remaining woman besides me said aye.

"All opposing, say nay."

Several women stared at me, daring me with their eyes to oppose them. I remained silent. I wasn't a member of this group. It wasn't right that I vote one way or another. Besides, I had no idea what they were talking about.

"Very well, the ayes have it. Operation Saving Sisters, it is. Now, I have made the initial contact and was met cordially by the . . . proprietor, who introduced me to several . . . workers wishing to avail themselves of our help. I was encouraged. There seemed to be sincere interest in meeting us halfway. Now I would like to open it up to the floor for suggestions as to how to proceed."

The women discussed "Operation Saving Sisters" for a quarter of an hour and not once did I learn what they were proposing to do or who they were trying to help. With the terms *proprietor* and *workers* thrown about, I could only guess it was a labor issue. So many across the country were suffering from unemployment, hence Coxey's March. Perhaps these women were proposing to find jobs for these unfortunates as well. But why was doing so risky? Why the need for secrecy? Was my presence the reason that they felt they needed to speak in code? Regardless of the reasons, they did, to my complete bafflement. When they concluded their discussion and asked for volunteers to complete the next step of the "operation," all eyes looked at me.

Did they expect me to volunteer? I didn't even know what they were talking about. But I'd misunderstood.

Mrs. Smith leaned toward me. "Would you mind waiting in the hall, Miss Davish?"

"But—" Sarah started to object.

"Please, Miss Davish?" Mrs. Smith asked again.

I looked around me. Every eye was still on me, expecting me to leave. Still confused, I could only guess that they didn't want me to learn who was volunteering for a task, though I had no idea what it was.

"Of course." I gladly retired to the hall, busying myself while I waited by studying the portraits of former First Ladies on the wall.

I didn't have to wait long. Having started chronologically with Martha Washington, I was admiring the exquisite bonnet worn by Louisa Adams, John Quincy Adams's lovely wife, when the women came pouring out of the room, expressing their farewells as they went. Sarah and Mrs. Smith rejoined me.

"Now wasn't that more interesting than typing, Miss Davish?" Mrs. Smith smiled while she put on her gloves.

What was I to say? That I enjoyed typing, it being a soothing and satisfying task? That since I'd come to the meeting, instead of doing my work for Sir Arthur, I would have a great deal of typing yet to do today? Or, more to the truth, that I had no idea what she was talking about, that I was still in the dark about what the club was doing?

"It was . . . interesting," I said, trying to be both truthful and diplomatic.

"I'm sorry you had to leave the room, Hattie," Sarah said. "I thought they trusted me enough not to bring someone to the meeting who would run and tell their husbands on them, but obviously not."

"May I ask what that was all about? Operation Saving Sisters?"

"*Shhhh!*" Mrs. Smith chided me. "You mustn't repeat a

single thing you heard in there. Promise me, you won't tell a soul."

"Not even Walter," Sarah said, frowning. "I think he'd understand, but I'm not sure Daniel would."

"I know Meriwether wouldn't approve," Mrs. Smith said. "Besides, our husbands' careers could be affected if this got out."

Still not knowing in the slightest to what they were referring, I asked, "Then why risk it in the first place? Is it that important?"

Both women nodded. "Yes, it is, Hattie," Sarah said. "And not just for obvious reasons either." Since I didn't know what she was talking about, no reasons were obvious to me. "This is Washington, and we women deserve to have our own secrets."

Mrs. Smith's smile widened. "Yes, we do."

"But what about all the good works you spoke about publicly? Aren't they enough?" I asked.

"Yes and no. Everything this club does is important, but there are some things no one else is going to do if we don't. Do you understand?" Of course I didn't understand. I had no clue what they were talking about. But I didn't want to disappoint my future sister-in-law, so I took a deep breath to curb my frustration, and then half smiled and lied.

"I think so."

"Good," Mrs. Smith said, smiling at me with approval. "I knew you'd get something out of coming today. You'll have to come again. If you're here long enough, you could join."

"Yes, that would be lovely," Sarah said, hooking her arm in mine as we descended to the street and the waiting carriages. "I'm so happy to finally have a sister, Hattie. Think of all that we can do."

I smiled genuinely this time, happy too to have a sister. But if her idea of things we could do together was anything like this morning, I couldn't leave Washington soon enough.

Chapter 23

After having Sarah bring me back to the Treasury, I spent several hours diligently copying the property damage index Sir Arthur had requested. The straightforward work was a welcome respite from the morning's arguments, secrets, and veiled discussions. In fact, for several hours all the questions that haunted me were kept at bay. And then I came to an entry in the index, the burning of apple orchards in Arkansas, which reminded me of the proprietor of Apple House and her words of regret.

I might never learn the truth, having been barred from any form of investigation, but I could still ask myself the questions. Sitting in the windowless room, I put aside my work and made a list.

1. Why had Jasper Neely visited Senator Smith's house that morning?
2. Who was he visiting?
3. What had he come to say?

4. Did that visit have anything to do with his conversations with Senator Abbott and Lottie Fox?
5. What did Lottie Fox do that she needed to apologize for?
6. Why did she regret it?
7. Will Annie Wilcox's companion step forward?
8. Is Sir Arthur's refusal to bless my marriage insurmountable?

Unable to face the personal heartbreak of my last thought, I reread the others. There had to be a connection. But then that meant that someone in the senator's household was in some way connected to the madam.

You already knew that, I reminded myself silently.

But I didn't want to believe it. Lottie Fox had mentioned Mrs. Smith, after all. But I couldn't believe Mrs. Smith had anything to do with Jasper Neely's death. She was with her husband when Jasper Neely was killed. Wasn't she? But then what was the connection? And how did any of this involve Sarah? Lottie Fox had mentioned her as well. But I remembered Sarah's reaction to finding Jasper Neely. She had been genuinely distressed by the man's death. Hadn't she? I envisioned Sarah at the Washington Wives Club meeting, adeptly transforming my visit to the police station from a scandal into something heroic. Could she be that crafty in the face of a dead man? Or did the connection have nothing to do with Jasper Neely? Could Lottie Fox know more about Annie Wilcox's death than she was admitting to? Could Sarah and Mrs. Smith have a connection to Annie?

These were the thoughts I couldn't fathom but couldn't shake. Having work to do was the only remedy. And a remedy it was, for when I completed my task, my only thoughts were of the satisfaction of a job well done and my upcoming rendezvous with Walter.

And then I saw Chester Smith. He had cornered a man, most likely a bank clerk or accountant based on the green celluloid eyeshade he wore on his brow, between the wrought-iron railing and the ornate Corinthian column at the bottom of one of the massive spiral stairwells. The two men stood close, whispering so that I couldn't hear what they were saying, but the clerk shook his head vigorously several times. Something in their manner suggested they didn't want to be interrupted or overheard, reminding me of the conversation I'd witnessed between Senator Abbott and Jasper Neely. I stopped and stepped behind another column. But as I stayed hidden, several people simply passed by, ignoring the two men as they went.

Was this the usual way of having a private conversation in this town? I wondered.

I was gathering my courage to walk past myself, hoping my casual manner would not draw Chester's attention, when he pulled a thick envelope out of his pocket. He thrust it toward the clerk. The clerk glanced around, to make sure no one was about. I ducked back behind the column for a moment and then peered around it again. The clerk opened the envelope, pulled out the edges of a stack of dollar bills, and nodded. There had to be over a hundred dollars in the envelope—more than a month's wages! The clerk slipped the envelope into the pocket of his vest.

Chester Smith, his shoulders now relaxed, nodded and said in a regular voice, "Remember, the National Bank of the Potomac."

"*Shhhhh!*" The clerk looked about him furtively and then dashed away without another glance at Chester.

Chester, on the other hand, took his time. He straightened

his tie, pulled at his vest, and allowed a smile to slowly spread across his face. Then casually he strolled down the hall in the opposite direction. I waited until he disappeared around a corner before stepping out of my hiding place. I was stunned. The National Bank of the Potomac. That was the same bank Simeon Harper was inquiring about. Could that be the contention between the two men? But what did Chester Smith have to do with the National Bank of the Potomac? Why would he bribe a clerk in the Treasury Department? But to do what? Could any of this be connected to Jasper Neely's death? Could Chester Smith have been the one Jasper Neely was visiting yesterday morning?

I blew away a loose curl that tickled my forehead. *What do I do now? Do I tell the police what I witnessed?* Lieutenant Whittmeyer had made it clear that he was not going to tolerate my intrusion into their investigation in any way. And perhaps bribing officials is commonplace in this city of politicians and bankers, and bringing it to the attention of the police would only be borrowing trouble. Who was I kidding? I was making excuses for not reporting the incident and I knew it.

It has nothing to do with me.

I was eager to leave the building and its intrigues behind but knew full well it wasn't as simple as that.

Despite the sunshine, the blossoming trees, the fat squirrels scurrying about, and the anticipation of meeting Walter, my mood deteriorated as I meandered ever more slowly along the winding paths of the Mall. For the first time since I'd met him, I was dreading facing Walter. And why? Because I had vowed not to keep secrets from him and yet failed to tell him about Lottie Fox's message to his sister? Or was it having to describe Sir Arthur's reaction to our engagement that made my feet feel leaden and slow?

What's wrong with you? I asked myself. *I've never shied away from the truth before. Why now? Besides, it's Walter. He'll forgive and understand anything I say. Won't he?*

"What's wrong, Hattie?"

Walter was waiting for me outside the expansive three-story brick building that housed the Army Medical Museum, the Library of the Surgeon General's Office, and the Army Medical School. When he spotted me he smiled, and most of my worry vanished in an instant. He took my hand and led me down the path toward the famed National Museum, a fairy-tale building of geometric patterns of polychrome brick, pavilions three stories tall, rotundas encircled with skylights and windows, which dwarfed the Smithsonian Castle next to it with its 80,000 square feet of exhibit space.

Room after room, and mahogany case after mahogany case, it was a world of wonders: relics belonging to several presidents including George Washington and Andrew Jackson; animal specimens of fish, birds, and reptiles; geological specimens; precious stones; extraordinary examples of printing, painting, embroidery, engraving, and weaving; exhibits on agriculture, transportation, and history; and, as the *Altograph of Washington City, or stranger's guide* I'd picked up at a newsstand claimed, "thousands of curios from every part of the globe." And yet no matter how hard I tried, I was too distracted by the events of the past few days to enjoy it. And Walter knew it.

"Didn't you enjoy Sarah's surprise? Where did she take you?"

"I enjoyed your surprise immensely," I said, smiling as I pictured my new House of Worth dress. "It's the most beautiful thing I've ever seen."

Walter leaned in close and whispered, his breath tickling my ear, "You're the most beautiful thing I've ever seen." I blushed, and couldn't help but smile in delight.

"Did Sarah help you with the measurements?"

"It fits perfectly," I said.

"I'm glad you like it. But you didn't answer my question."

"Sarah took me to a meeting of the Washington Wives Club."

"Now I see why Sarah insisted the two of you go without me." He laughed. "Didn't you enjoy it?"

"It was kind of Sarah to take me," I said, trying to avoid having to explain the meeting and all its secrecy. Walter frowned.

"That's not what I asked you. What happened?"

"It's complicated. It's more than what happened at the meeting." Walter led me to a bench beneath the enormous skeleton of a whale suspended from the ceiling.

"Tell me."

I put my free hand in my lap and stared at it. Walter put his hand on top of mine.

"We are soon to be husband and wife. You can tell me anything." I looked at him, into his eyes, and found nothing but love and concern reflected back at me.

"Walter, I finally spoke to Sir Arthur."

He looked at me expectantly. When I wasn't forthcoming he said, "And?"

I remained calm, but sadness swelled up through my chest until it hurt.

"He won't give us his blessing."

Walter looked away but continued to hold my hand. We sat in silence for several moments as a rotund woman with pinched lips, clutching a child with each hand, ineffectively attempted to herd a group of children between the collection cases by shouting, "Children. Now, children," as the little ones ran hither and thither to their delight.

"Did he say why?"

"He doesn't believe I was meant to be a housewife, that I'll be unhappy and bored. He thinks I'll be giving up my purpose in life if I don't use my talents and work."

"And what do you think?"

"I love you, and if I must give up my profession to be your wife, then I'm happy to do so."

"You don't have to give up anything for me. We've discussed this before. You can work in my office if that is what you want, or you can find something else worthwhile to do. I never once expected you to spend your days simply managing our home."

"Simeon Harper insists I'd make an excellent reporter." I laughed at my jest.

"It's true. You would, if that's what you wanted."

"So you wouldn't mind if your wife wanted to follow in Nellie Bly's footsteps?" I was teasing but eager for an honest answer.

"I'd be nothing but proud."

"Perhaps if you spoke to Sir Arthur," I said, more hopeful than I'd been since the argument this morning, "he might reconsider?"

"Consider it done," Walter said, raising my hand to his lips. I smiled back until a pang of guilt made me look away. "Is something else bothering you?"

"I already told you about my visit to the police."

"Yes?" Concern clouded his countenance.

"What I didn't tell you, or anyone else, was that I was approached by two separate people before I left the station."

"Who?"

The first one was easy. "A man named Billy McBain. We've seen him on several other occasions. He's one of Coxey's marchers."

"What did he want?"

"He wanted me to tell Daniel that he said hello."

"That's it?"

"Yes."

"But why?"

"I don't know except he's the one that we've seen argue with Daniel on two separate occasions."

"Him?" Walter furrowed his brows. "He didn't threaten you, did he?"

"No, no. He simply wanted me to relay his greeting."

"And did you?"

"Not yet."

"Well, I wouldn't bother. Whatever is between Mr. McBain and Daniel is better left between them."

"Good. That was my feeling as well."

"Who was the other person?"

I hesitated and took a deep breath. I looked at Walter but had to look away before I said, "Miss Lottie Fox."

"The madam of the girl who drowned in the carriage accident?"

"How did you know that?" I looked back at Walter in surprise.

"Harper told a group of us when he pointed her out at Coxey's camp. Said she was a follower of Carl Browne's 'Theosophy.' Supposedly Browne told her she was born with a drop of the soul of Jesus. Of course, he claims to have far more than that," Walter scoffed. "Browne probably said that to get her to donate money or . . ." Walter stopped, realizing what he had almost said in my company.

"Yes, her," I said, trying in vain not to blush. "If you remember, she was arrested for trying to stop the police from arresting Carl Browne."

"What did she say? Why did she speak to you at all?"

"She knew I was witness to the girl's death and simply wanted to know what I saw. She was genuinely upset about it all."

Walter frowned.

"I don't like the idea of a woman like that imposing herself on you. I hope she was discreet."

"She was, and I couldn't deny her what little I knew."

"You are a kind soul, Hattie. Is that it? Is that what you hesitated to tell me?"

"No, though that would have been enough to give me pause. No, Walter, it's much worse."

"What is it?"

"She also asked me to convey a message for her."

"The presumption!" Walter's voice echoed off walls and the vaulted ceiling.

"Walter," I said, purposefully almost at a whisper, as two ladies—in straw hats ironically decorated with songbirds similar to those in one of the museum's cases—stared over at us before moving to the next room. "She wanted me to relay the message that she was sorry. 'Please tell them I regret it now. Oh, how I regret it.'"

"Regret what? Sorry for what?" Walter said, his voice lowered again.

"I don't know. She didn't tell me."

"So who are you supposed to relay this message to?"

"To Mrs. Mildred Smith and—"

"The senator's wife?" I nodded. "How would a madam know the senator's wife? What would she have to regret or feel sorry about that would concern Mildred Smith?"

"I don't know."

"Well, I can see why you didn't know what to do, why this is weighing on your mind. Any hint of this could endanger not only Mrs. Smith's reputation but the senator's career."

"I know." I looked at him, wondering how I was possibly going to continue, to finish what I had to say.

Maybe he doesn't need to know everything, I thought. And then he made the decision for me.

"You said *them.* 'Tell them I regret it.' Who else did she name, Hattie?"

"Sarah." At first I wondered if Walter had heard me. He didn't gasp, he didn't shout, he didn't move. I'd spoken his sister's name so quietly I barely heard myself. But then he surprised me, reaching out his arms and engulfing me in his embrace.

"I love you, Hattie Davish," he whispered in my ear. "Thank you." When he released me, I was still bewildered, and although I relished each and every embrace, I had no idea why he'd responded so ardently.

"What do you have to thank me for? I've told you that your sister's name passed the lips of a . . ."

"And you told no one."

"Of course not."

"Your reputation for being trustworthy and highly discreet is well deserved."

"You don't need to thank me, Walter. It's an essential part of my job."

"But you weren't doing this as part of your job. You did this out of your love for me." He was right. If Mrs. Smith's name alone had been mentioned, I would've told Sir Arthur as I planned to tell him about Chester Smith's activities. But everything changed when I heard Sarah's name. "Hence the thank-you."

"You are more than welcome. But do we tell Sarah?"

"Yes, but first things first." Walter smiled at me again, as he had the first time we'd met, his teeth brilliantly white. "We have a man's mind to change."

"Yes, let's." We stood to go and Walter offered me his arm. As we strolled past a case filled with seashells from all over the world, polished and gleaming beneath the glass, I added, "You'll never guess what I saw Chester Smith doing this afternoon."

"What?"

"Bribing a clerk at the Treasury Building."

Walter tilted his head back and laughed, his laughter echoing off the high ceilings. "Hattie Davish, or should I call you Nellie Bly, whatever am I going to do with you?"

"You could kiss me?" And, to my delight and surprise, he did.

CHAPTER 24

"Why are you still up, Meriwether?" Mrs. Smith's voice reached me from the hall.

Thinking everyone was in bed at this late hour, I'd brought my work to the library. I couldn't sleep. Walter and I had met with Sir Arthur earlier. After telling Sir Arthur about Chester Smith's bribery, trusting he would know how best to handle the information, Walter and I had appealed to him, explaining our plans and Walter's support of any work I wished to pursue, but Sir Arthur had listened in silence and made no promises to reconsider. When he finally did speak, he'd said, "I'll need you at the trial of Coxey's men tomorrow. I'll trust you will be prepared?" He'd been smoking his cigar and scowling when we'd left dispirited and disappointed. Hence my sleeplessness.

Engrossed in transcribing the section of the index of property damage I'd copied earlier, I hadn't heard the front door open, but the annoyed inflection in Mrs. Smith's voice as the door closed behind her grabbed my attention.

"I've been waiting for you," her husband replied, the annoyance in his voice outmatching his wife's. "It's late. Where have you been?"

"You know I was at a club meeting."

Could there have been a second club meeting tonight? Could their need for secrecy be so great that they met again after dark? What could their secret possibly be?

"I'm going to ask you one more time, Mildred. Where have you been?"

"Don't be childish, Meriwether. Now let me pass so I can go to bed."

As their voices raised, uninhibited by any concern for waking the rest of the house, I slipped from behind the desk and went to the library door. It was slightly ajar from when I'd arrived, and as I peered out, Mildred was attempting to step past the senator. The couple was only a few feet away, in the middle of the entrance hall. Above their heads, the porcelain lamp painted with white cherry blossoms was dimmed, per the hour, casting their shadows across the gleaming parquet floor. He wouldn't let her by. Her normally cheerful countenance was clouded with irritation. As she shoved him aside, he grabbed his wife's wrist and held her tightly in his grasp.

"Meriwether, you're hurting me." He released his grip but gave no apology. "What is this all about?" Mrs. Smith rubbed her wrist.

"This!" Her husband produced a piece of paper from inside his vest pocket and waved it inches from his wife's face. Her eyes widened as she caught the meaning of the paper.

"Oh, dear."

"Well?"

"Where did you get it? Were you going through my desk?"

"Where have you been?" her husband asked again, ignoring her questions.

"I was at the Club today, I promise you, and that"—she

pointed to the paper her husband was now crumpling in his fist—"is not what you think."

"It is exactly what I think. And in addition to everything else, this . . . this . . . woman has the audacity to mention my name in connection with Coxey's cockeyed Good Roads Bill." He shook the fist with the paper in it.

"It came several days ago. I didn't bother you with it, did I?"

"You always go too far, Mildred. Too far."

"But—"

"What if this got out? What if someone from the press . . . that Harper fellow has been snooping around here enough lately; what if this made it into the papers? I would be ruined, Mildred, ruined! And for what? One of your charity cases? One of your causes?"

"But, Meriwether, isn't that what I'm supposed to do?"

"Only when it is a credit to me, Mildred. When will you ever learn that? You only do what is good for me. I am the one who is important, my career, not you or your silly causes."

As the senator spoke, he deliberately tore the paper, letting the pieces drift to the floor.

"And from this day forward, I forbid you to attend another meeting of that damn club of yours. I want a woman who is going to be home day and night!"

"But you're never here," Mildred said, in her defense. Suddenly Spencer came scampering down the stairs, snatching one of the pieces of paper littering the floor, and ran, jumping into Mildred's outstretched arms.

"That damn dog! If he gets in my way again, I'm getting rid of him."

"Oh, no, Meriwether. Even you wouldn't be so cruel."

"Don't tempt me. Now go to bed." Before his wife could comply, the senator strutted into his study and slammed the door.

Carrying Spencer in her arms, Mildred slowly climbed the

stairs. The moment she was out of sight, I stepped into the hall and picked up the remaining pieces of paper, scattered about on the floor. I glanced at each one as I collected it, but most of the pieces were too small to provide any useful information. A few, however, were large enough to reveal that it had been a letter addressed to Mrs. Smith from Madam Lottie Fox.

No wonder the senator was livid. If only I knew what the letter said. Did it mention Sarah?

As I tried to read more, I heard a creak on the stair and looked up, alarmed that Mildred or Senator Smith might catch me with the paper fragments. I hastily shoved the papers into the pocket of my dressing gown, several escaping and flutter-ing back to the floor. I didn't have time to retrieve them.

It was Claude Morris. He was frowning at me.

How long had he been there? Had he overheard the argu-ment? I'd be surprised if the whole house hadn't overheard the argument. It was most likely what drew the secretary from his bed in the first place. But had he seen me with the papers? Luckily neither Senator Smith nor Mildred had mentioned the nature of the letter. If he had overheard, let Claude think the Washington Wives Club was at fault.

"What on earth are you doing up at this time of night, Miss Davish?"

"I could ask the same of you, Mr. Morris." I glanced at the paper fragments on the floor out of the corner of my eye as I passed the secretary on the stairs. I couldn't retrieve them now. Hopefully he wouldn't notice them and they'd be swept up by the maid in the morning.

"It's good night then, Miss Davish?" Claude said to my back as I ascended the rest of the stairs.

"Good night, Mr. Morris."

"What do you mean it's lost?" a man demanded.

After a long night of wondering where Mrs. Smith had really

been the night before, a quick, refreshing stroll to the Washington Monument and back along the Mall this morning was what I needed to clear my head. Two reporters loitered outside the house, but I ignored them. Then I headed to the Treasury Building again, where I spent many productive hours copying the entire Confederate half of the property damage index. I felt clearheaded and satisfied when it was time to go. But my peace of mind fled the moment I heard a familiar voice shout outside in the hall. I peeked around the open door.

It was Simeon Harper. His face was red and he was clenching his jaw. "It can't be all lost!"

He was speaking to the same clerk I'd seen with Chester Smith. The man stared at his feet and mumbled something I couldn't understand. And then I caught, "National Bank of the Potomac." That same bank seemed to come up again and again.

"Everything?" Harper said, disbelieving. The man nodded, still looking at his feet. "How incompetent must someone be to lose everything pertaining to a particular bank? It's not like the Coxeyites stormed the building and all the bank records were destroyed." Before Harper could say more, the clerk dashed past, making a wide berth of the journalist.

"Fool!" Simeon Harper exclaimed through clenched teeth, staring at the retreating clerk.

I stepped back behind the door to avoid being seen. I was torn. Did I reveal myself and tell Simeon Harper that I'd seen Chester Smith hand the same clerk at least $100 while mentioning the National Bank of the Potomac? And that it might not have been simple incompetence that led to the disappearance of the bank records?

What would Sir Arthur want me to do? I wondered, inwardly cringing as I recalled his aloof behavior toward Walter and me yesterday.

On one hand, Sir Arthur might appreciate me confiding in a man who was his known friend. But on the other, I'd be committing an indiscretion that might compromise the son of the man hosting Sir Arthur. I'd been quick to confide in Simeon Harper before.

And look where that got me. No, the man's very occupation was defined by indiscretion. Even I had been the subject of his wagging tongue and his careless pen.

Even as I decided that I wanted no part of whatever Simeon Harper was planning, I heard footsteps pass by the door. And when the journalist muttered, "I'll get you somehow, Chester," I knew for certain I'd chosen right.

CHAPTER 25

The police court was crowded. With the disappointing climax to Coxey's March behind us, the city was clamoring for one last dramatic episode in the saga of the Commonweal of Christ. The fate of the men who were arrested would soon be determined, and no one wanted to miss it. I pulled out my pencil and notebook, as Sir Arthur wanted the entire trial recorded for his perusal later, and waited with the rest.

The marchers, still dirty and disgruntled, shared the room with the likes of Elizabeth Haines, an owner of a dry goods store, and Emily Edson Briggs, one of the major landholders on Capitol Hill, who between them, everyone now knew, had put up Marshal Carl Browne's bail. Along with the journalists who had followed Coxey's Army for months, dozens of witnesses, men and women from every class and every walk of life who had followed the accounts, rubbed elbows as we waited for the trial to begin. I even spied Lieutenant Whittmeyer leaning against a wall. And like so many other women, I held a handkerchief to my nose, hoping to ward off the scent of so many unwashed bodies tightly packed into the gallery of the small courtroom. It did little good.

Judge Thomas F. Miller sat high on his bench. The jury fidgeted in their wooden chairs, while U.S. District Attorney Birney and Assistant District Attorney Mullowney conversed with heads bent toward each other, not even bothering to look up when Carl Browne, in his usual buckskin clothes, and Christopher Columbus Jones, looking haggard having been the only one to spend time in jail, entered the room. Half a dozen Populist congressmen, who had volunteered their services as defense attorneys, accompanied them. Both cheers and jeers arose as the progression headed toward the defendants' table. Neither the madam Lottie Fox, despite having been arrested, nor Jacob Coxey were among them.

Lottie Fox was sincere about knowing the police superintendent, I thought. But what did she do to persuade him to drop the charges against her? Did I really want to know?

"Do you know any of those men, Sarah?" Walter asked, leaning over toward his sister as Browne, Jones, and the congressmen got settled. I sat on the other side of her with Sir Arthur and Simeon Harper on my right.

"I've met Mr. Pence of Colorado and Mr. Thomas Jefferson Hudson of Kansas, but the others I know only by sight and reputation. They aren't from Daniel's party."

"I wondered because—"

Walter's comment was cut off when the murmur of "Coxey" rose in volume as it spread through the court.

"I was worried he wasn't going to appear," Simeon Harper said. "They need him as a witness."

I craned my head and saw Jacob Coxey come into view as he approached the front of the courtroom, trying to find a seat near his companions. Judge Miller peered over the bench and saw him as well.

"I have been informed that a man named Jacob S. Coxey is in the court," the judge said.

The judge explained that after a police investigation, he had decided to secure a warrant for Coxey's arrest. Shouts of protest boomed from the gallery. The judge put his hand up, demanding silence with that simple gesture.

"I have made out a warrant, but if he is willing to submit, I do not care to have it served upon him."

"I am ready," Coxey said, before any more supporters could disrupt the court with their objections.

The court proceeded smoothly as all three defendants were charged with violating the act of July 1, 1882, that regulated the use of the Capitol grounds. Specifically, they were accused of carrying banners—the inconspicuous insignias that the men wore on their lapels—and trampling the shrubs and turf of the grounds. Murmurs rose again, in overwhelming support of the Commonwealers. All around me I heard the criticisms.

"Doesn't Congress have better things to do than to arrest men for treading on the grass?"

"This is an outrage! Such trivial charges demean us all."

"What about the police? Didn't they bash some bushes while they were clubbing women and children? We should arrest them."

"What did Coxey and Browne do but want to give a speech? So they stepped on the lawn?"

"Shrubs? Turf? Lapel badges? Why aren't we talking about murder?"

I glanced around quickly to see if I could learn the identity of the speaker of the last comment, but it was impossible to tell who had said it.

Again the judge insisted on silence, this time banging his gavel and demanding it. Once the room settled into a quiet murmur of discontent, witnesses were called in the three men's defense: Journalists, who Browne had once called "argus-eyed demons of Hell," spoke on their behalf, including several who testified that not only had the police themselves been standing on the grass but that they had purposefully driven citizens onto it.

They're absolutely right, I thought. I still can't get the grass stains out of the dress I was wearing that day.

Several witnesses raised doubts as to whether Coxey himself had stepped on the Capitol grass. On cross-examination of one witness, asking of the thousands of people cheering when Coxey arrived at the Capitol, the prosecutor asked, "Disorderly, were they not?"

"Oh, no," the journalist said. "They had a right to cheer. They were American citizens." It elicited subsequent cheers from the gallery that were quickly squelched by Judge Miller.

And then a black man, Edward Johnson, who had already received a thirty-day sentence for disorderly conduct, took the stand and swore that he saw billy clubs flying and that he'd been clubbed over the head by a police officer.

"Is that what happened, Hattie?" Sir Arthur whispered to me, a look of unexpected sympathy in his eyes.

"Yes, sir. That is what happened."

"Inexcusable." I agreed but kept any comments to myself.

During the man's riveting account, I kept my head down and focused on taking my notes. Sir Arthur would not appreciate my showing the tumult I felt as I relived the riot through Mr. Johnson's words. Nor would it do to notice the many eyes that strayed in my direction, as if my sling were a flag, when Mr. Johnson spoke of defenseless women being clubbed down in the grass. Walter and Sarah both watched me, concern on their faces, but I gave them no reason to suspect anything was wrong. Or at least that's what I hoped.

When Mr. Johnson stepped down, Judge Miller announced that he would refuse to hear any other witnesses who might speak of the policemen's conduct. Coxey, Browne, and Jones were on trial, not the Washington, D.C., Metropolitan Police Department.

That too is inexcusable, I thought, but again kept it to myself. And then a movement caught my eye.

"Daniel?"

"What was that, Hattie?" Sarah said, engrossed in the next witness's story. I'd said it out loud? I hadn't meant to. But it was too late. Sarah's attention was fully on me. "What did you say about Daniel?"

"I was wondering why he didn't come."

"He wanted to avoid any misunderstandings. He doesn't want anyone mistaking him for a Populist. So he thought it was better if he stayed away."

"I see."

And I had seen, literally. As I'd tried to keep my gaze from the witness box, I'd caught a glimpse of someone moving stealthily along the wall. He had only been in my sight for a few moments, but I couldn't mistake him for anyone else. It was Daniel Clayworth.

Was that why he was sneaking along the wall, hoping not to be seen? Then why come at all? And why lie to your wife about it? Had he simply changed his mind? I hoped so.

The trial went on until finally the prosecutors delivered their summations. Assistant District Attorney Mullowney condemned Jacob Coxey as a self-aggrandizing hypocrite, citing that the leader of the Commonweal of Christ stayed at hotels while his "army" camped in the rough, that he secured the best legal representation for himself while supplying less competent representation for Browne and Jones.

District Attorney Birney was worse. During his speech, hoping to ridicule the idea that these men could possibly represent workingmen, he pointed toward Browne and said, "That man, a working man? A man who looks as though he never did a day's work in his life! Save the world! A fakir, a charlatan, and a mountebank who dresses in ridiculous garments and exhibits himself to the curious multitudes at ten cents a head!"

And then Mr. Birney turned to Coxey. "The other man a laboring man! A wealthy man, who owns a stock farm and stone quarries, who admits that he has received all the money contributions for the movement bearing his name, and has never made an accounting."

Little was said about the three men trespassing on the Capitol grass until Judge Miller gave the jury their instructions. "The people have the perfect right to ventilate their views, but they must do it in a proper way, and within the law."

Marshal Browne took the opportunity to tell the court that he fully expected to be convicted on a technicality. "Christ was convicted on a technicality!"

And then the jury was dismissed. We waited but two hours before the jury returned a guilty verdict. The three men, free on bond, were to be sentenced later.

The verdict had not been a surprise, though I was dismayed nonetheless. Jacob Coxey, Marshal Browne, and their marching army simply wanted to give a speech, illuminating all the sorrow and suffering in this country. Despite all the rumors and fears, hundreds of men marched into the nation's capital peaceably and, for all their efforts, were arrested for walking on the grass. But knowing men like Senator Smith, it didn't come as a surprise. Like Daniel, the senator wanted to stay clear of the trial and any assumed association with "those indigent crack-brains."

How quickly he forgot his visit to Coxey's camp, I thought.

But what was a surprise were the mumblings, the complaints, and the criticisms I heard as I followed Sir Arthur and Walter out of the crowded courtroom. They weren't only about the verdict. Everyone was talking about Jasper Neely and Annie's deaths.

"Sure, Coxey trespassed, but did he kill one of his own?"

"Not one word was uttered about the dead man or woman."

"What is this country coming to? A woman is drowned, a man is stabbed in broad daylight, and no one cares. But heaven forbid you walk on the grass!"

"Maybe one of the police killed that man. That's why the judge wouldn't hear anything more about the riot."

"No one in the Commonweal killed Jasper or drowned that woman. They are innocent, I swear to you."

The last voice was familiar. I stopped and looked around me. A few feet away, surrounded by journalists and other spectators, was Billy McBain.

I started toward the group surrounding Billy, when Lieutenant Whittmeyer stepped out of the crowd directly in front of me.

"Staying out of my investigations, right, Miss Davish?" he said, a smirk on his face, as if daring me to ignore his warnings.

"Yes, I have no desire to cross you, Lieutenant."

"Good, just checking." The man slipped back into the crowd. I shuddered. Never having to speak to him again was reason enough to stay out of his investigation.

But that didn't mean I couldn't listen like everyone else, I thought, as I proceeded again toward Billy McBain. I was surprised to see Senator Abbott, his planter's hat tipped back on his forehead, standing next to Billy.

"But, Billy," one the reporters said, "how can you be so sure? Neely was one of you. And he was witness to the prostitute's drowning. Don't you think that's quite a coincidence?"

"First, Jasper arrived after the girl drowned in the carp pond. I've always been clear on that. And second, as you say, he was one of us. You've heard Jasper preach. You've heard Marshal Browne preach. You know what General Coxey stands for. Our march was inspired by the soul of Christ to cast the light on the plight of the unemployed worker, to gain support for the Good Roads project. No one supported this goal more than Jasper Neely. Why would General Coxey or Marshal Browne have any cause to kill him?"

I wondered that as well. But did Mr. McBain know about the secret meetings Jasper Neely conducted the morning of the march? The morning he died? And one of them being with the man standing next to him?

"But what if they argued about the best way to accomplish their goal?" one of the journalists asked. "Look at what happened between Browne and the Great Unknown."

"But they didn't," Billy McBain said. "I spoke to Jasper myself a little while before they found him dead. He was more enthusiastic, more confident about the success of the Good Roads project then I'd ever seen him. Do you think he'd be that exuberant if he was at odds with the general?"

The reporters grumbled and shook their heads.

"But what about someone else in the camp?" someone else shouted.

"We're brothers. We bonded like only those who have marched halfway across this country for a cause could. I can't believe anyone in the Commonweal of Christ could've done this." Senator Abbott leaned over and whispered something in Billy McBain's ear. "That's all I have to say."

"Then who did?" someone shouted, as McBain, with Senator Abbott at his side, tried to push his way through the crowd.

That's what I'd like to know, I thought as I watched Billy McBain disappear among the multitude outside the courthouse.

"Miss Davish!"

With Billy McBain gone, as one, the reporters swiveled on their heels and turned on me. With notebooks and pencils held high, they vied for a spot closest to me. As I stepped back to put distance between us, they moved in closer. Soon I was surrounded by reporters shouting their questions at me.

"Do you have anything to add to what Mr. McBain said?"

"Have you had any further contact with Coxey, Browne, or the other Coxeyites?"

"I saw you talking to Lieutenant Whittmeyer; are you helping in the investigations?"

"No, no, and no!" I said, before they could ask me another question. Heaven forbid the reporters insinuate that I was in any way aiding Lieutenant Whittmeyer in his investigation. One word of such an accusation in the newspaper, whether true or not, and the detective would probably arrest me.

"Leave Miss Davish alone." Walter, having finally pushed through the mob around me, put his arm around my shoulder. "Isn't Coxey's story enough?"

"No," one of the reporters said. "That's old news."

"Just ignore them," Walter whispered to me.

As he steered me away from the reporters, one shouted, "But surely, Miss Davish, you know something you can tell us about Jasper Neely's murder or Annie Wilcox's drowning?"

If only I did, I thought, keeping my head down and my back to them. *If only I did.*

CHAPTER 26

"So how was the trial?" Daniel Clayworth took a sip of his red wine, as the footman placed a tray of fillet of beef with mushrooms in front of me. Having little appetite, I waved him away.

Why would you need to ask? I wondered. *You were there.*

To escape the press of the reporters after General Coxey and Marshal Browne were convicted at police court, Sarah had invited us to ride in her Victoria and join her for dinner. I'd wanted nothing more than to go back to my room at the Smith home and type the notes I'd taken this morning at the Treasury. But she'd insisted. She and Walter had chatted about the trial while I'd watched the city go by, yet again ruminating on the same unanswered questions. Who killed Jasper Neely? Who left Annie Wilcox to drown? Was Billy McBain sincere in his belief that no one in Coxey's Army had been involved? If only I could . . . I'd stopped the thought right there. Lieutenant Whittmeyer had been abundantly clear that I was not to question anyone, look for anything, or to appear in any way to be seeking out Jasper Neely's killer.

And he's right, I'd thought. *It has nothing to do with me.*

After almost a half hour drive, we'd arrived at one of the fashionable four-story redbrick row houses a few blocks from Dupont Circle, a wide circular thoroughfare transected by four avenues and encircling a park lavishly ornamented with flowering trees, exotic flowers, and a statue of Rear Admiral Samuel Du Pont at its center. Dinner was waiting.

"The trial was very exciting," Sarah said. "I'm disappointed that they found the men guilty, but of course it was expected. A little ridiculous but expected."

"The men violated the law and were found guilty."

"Of what, treading on the grass?" She rolled her eyes before she too took a drink from her wineglass.

"They didn't have to come to Washington and break the law."

"How else would they be heard? What about their cause?"

"As John Sherman put it the other day from the Senate floor, 'Nobody is denied the right to petition.' Whatever they might think, whatever causes they stand for, whatever hardships they may have suffered, any member of the Senate would offer the petition. It's their right and Coxey knew that." She rolled her eyes again.

"Yes, Daniel dear, but—"

"What I found ridiculous," Walter said, interrupting his sister in an attempt to defuse the argument brewing between husband and wife, "was how the judge refused to consider the police's misconduct. Jones and Browne were both in custody when they started clubbing innocent people." Walter gazed at me sympathetically.

"The judge was only doing his job," Daniel said. "Coxey, Browne, and Jones were on trial, not the Washington Metropolitan Police."

That's exactly what the judge had said. How would Daniel know that? How would he know that Lottie Fox hadn't been on trial as well? Unless he was there. Or did he know of the police superintendent's proclivity for Lottie Fox's charms?

"But Hattie was seriously hurt, Daniel," Sarah said. "It's not right that the police can do such a thing and not suffer consequences. It makes one feel in danger from the very people who are supposed to enforce the law, not break it."

"I'm truly sorry for what happened to you, Hattie," Daniel said. "I do hope you are feeling well again."

"I'm fine."

Stifling a laugh, Walter nearly spit out the bite of beef he had put in his mouth and then began choking from the attempt. How many times had he heard me say those words when we both knew them to be untrue? So many it had become a jest between us.

"Walter, are you all right?" Sarah said.

He held up his hand to ease her concern. "I'm fine," he finally said. If he hadn't had me worried as well that he was choking, I would have laughed. Instead I gave him a shake of my head.

"And to answer you, Daniel, Hattie's arm is healing nicely, if she doesn't do anything foolish, like take her sling off to type." He mockingly wagged his finger at me. We both smiled.

"I'm glad you are both well," Daniel said, unaware of any humor in the situation. "And I want to assure you both that justice will be done. Even now, in the House, we are debating resolutions calling for a congressional investigation into whether the police used excessive force."

"Well, I for one am glad to hear it," Sarah said. "As justice was certainly not done today."

"They broke the law, Sarah," Daniel said, annoyed.

"A woman drowned and a man was murdered. That's horrible. That's breaking the law. General Coxey walked on the grass, Daniel. The grass!"

"Have you ever heard of the National Bank of the Potomac, Daniel?" I asked, hoping to change the subject again. My arm was beginning to ache, and I was losing patience with Daniel's heavy-handed opinions about Coxey.

"Yes, in fact, I have. Why do you ask?"

"Simeon Harper, the journalist Sir Arthur knows, is investigating the bank. Do you know why that would be?"

"Not particularly." Daniel took another sip of his wine. "What was he investigating?"

"Mr. Harper mentioned the bank may have redeemed their federal notes for gold before the Sherman Silver Purchase Act was repealed."

Daniel set down his wine. "You know of the Sherman Purchase Act?" He sounded more astonished than I cared for.

"Miss Davish is full of surprises," Walter said, smiling at me. "Though I'm not surprised she knows about the Sherman Purchase Act. She enjoys reading the newspapers, don't you, Hattie?"

"Of course. How else does one know what is going on in the world?" I said. Sarah laughed nervously. "Why do you laugh, Sarah?"

"Because to quote a man I met at a dinner party not too long ago, 'Women don't need to know what is going on in the world. That is what men are for.' "

Walter chuckled, assuming his sister was joking, but Daniel Clayworth wasn't smiling.

"I would agree with that," Daniel said. "News, politics, and business affairs all needlessly confuse women. Why distract them from what they really need to know?"

Walter's mouth gaped open in astonishment. I was glad he disagreed. And then I noticed Sarah's cheeks burning red. She had either drunk too much wine or wholeheartedly disagreed too. She opened her mouth to speak.

To defuse the moment and change the subject yet again, I said, "Could you explain to me then, Congressman, why Mr.

Harper would find fault in what the National Bank of the Potomac did?"

"What? Oh, yes, of course, Hattie. If you are as well read as you seem, then you know that the U.S. Treasury was almost depleted of its gold reserves because banks and individuals, having purchased federal notes, redeemed them for gold instead of silver before Congress could stop them and repeal the Sherman Purchase Act."

"Yes, but if hundreds, if not thousands, were doing this, why would one bank be suspect?"

"If I'm correct, it would be in the timing."

"Timing?" Walter asked, finding interest in the subject. Sarah tried to stifle a yawn.

"Few banks, let alone individuals, knew the dire straits the Treasury was in. But there were a few, with what some would call 'inside' knowledge of the fact, which should have stopped their demand for gold. But since they continued to demand gold for their notes, some considered it traitorous."

"Could that be what the National Bank of the Potomac did?"

"Absolutely, as the president of the bank was the son of a senator who was on the Senate Finance Committee."

"But you're not going to say who?" Sarah asked, suddenly interested.

"No, it is not my place to name the alleged traitor. There was a call for an investigation at the time, but the senator in question was . . . is powerful enough to persuade his colleagues to stop any debate, let alone an investigation."

"But why would Simeon Harper investigate this now?" Walter asked. "They repealed the Sherman Purchase Act last year."

"Last October, to be exact," Daniel said. "I have no idea why he would want to drag this all up again. This country has enough problems."

"Yes, isn't that what Mr. Coxey and his army were marching for in the first place? To shine light on so many of the problems workingmen are facing?" Sarah said. She wouldn't leave it alone.

Having warmed to his subject, Daniel frowned again. He obviously didn't approve of Coxey's Army or Sarah's obvious sympathy for them.

I'm grateful Walter doesn't mind me stating my opinions, I thought.

"At least that's what they say," Daniel said. "I personally think, by them coming here, they merely distracted us from getting any real work done."

"Could Harper's investigation into the National Bank of the Potomac be connected to Coxey's appearance in town?" Walter said, still wanting an answer or at least a consensus on his question.

"I don't see how. As far as I know, neither Coxey nor any of his compatriots have any connection with the National Bank of the Potomac. It must be a coincidence."

"You don't believe it's a coincidence, do you, Hattie?" Walter said, who was studying my expression. How well he knew me.

"No, I don't."

"Why? Do you know something, Hattie?" Sarah said, nearly rising from her chair in excitement.

"I know the names of the senator and his son who escaped investigation."

"You do? How?" Daniel said, nearly demanding with the force of his question.

I suppressed the reflex to answer him. He sounded very much like Sir Arthur, but I wasn't his employee, and I didn't have to tell him anything. So I ignored his question.

"And I think I know why Mr. Harper is investigating the bank now after all this time."

"Why?" Daniel demanded again. Walter's eyes lit up as realization came to him.

"Chester," Walter said. I nodded.

"Chester Smith?" Sarah said. "It couldn't be. Senator Smith wouldn't abide traitorous behavior from his son, even if he was acting unknowingly."

"But he would send him away while at the same time squelching any possible investigation into his son's business affairs," I said. Sarah's eyes widened. "And now the son has returned to witness Coxey's arrival. Why else would Harper be interested after all this time?"

"Oh my God, Daniel, is this true? Did Meriwether Smith use his political power to subvert an investigation into his son's bank dealings? Isn't that illegal? Immoral? Could he even do that? How could such a secret have been kept in this town?"

Daniel wiped his mouth before slowly putting his napkin on the table. He frowned at me.

"I cannot comment and will not have any more of this discussed at my dinner table." It was as much of an admission as we were going to get. "Now, if you ladies will leave Walter and me, we will join you later in the parlor."

Sarah, still shaking her head in disbelief, stood automatically and strode toward the door without another word. I couldn't be so complaisant.

"You asked us how the trial was." I rose from the table.

"Yes?" His displeasure that I wasn't following his wife's example of obedient silence was obvious in his tone.

"Why?"

"What is it, Hattie? Why do you ask?" Walter, sensing the rising annoyance of his brother-in-law, hoped to quickly put an end to yet another quarrel.

"Why would you ask when you were there?" I looked straight at Daniel, trying to ignore the startled expressions on both brother and sister.

"I was not."

"I saw you. You were trying to go unseen, but I saw you. Why?"

"I was not there. And how dare you interrogate me at my own table? Walter, if you would please escort your—"

"I apologize, Congressman Clayworth. It was not at all my intention to anger you. I was mistaken in my informality, seeing as we are to be family. I was curious, and as Walter can tell you, it has been my undoing more than once."

I lied as Daniel had lied to me. I wasn't simply curious. I knew exactly what I was doing. Daniel Clayworth was hiding something, and after being beaten and questioned by the police for a man's murder, I was willing to incur the man's outrage to find out if his secret had anything to do with it.

My words seemed to defuse the tension; behind me, Sarah sighed out loud. Daniel took several deep breaths before reaching for his glass. He took a sip of wine before answering.

"Your apology is accepted."

"Thank you."

"We will see you ladies in the parlor, then?" Walter said. Daniel nodded as did Sarah when I joined her by the door.

"I'm afraid I must say good night," I said. Walter's eyebrow arched in surprise. I waited a moment, but no one voiced an objection. Was that even a look of relief on the congressman's face? "Walter, will you escort me to the door?"

"Of course." Walter rose from the table, offered me his arm with questions in his eyes, and we headed to the door. Sarah left the room ahead of us. Before we could follow, I stopped, forcing Walter to stop as well, and turned back to the politician at the head of the table already preparing his cigar.

"I forgot, Mr. Clayworth," I said, having made up my mind the moment he'd lied to me. "When I was at the police station being interrogated for my role in Jasper Neely's death, I met a man who had a message for you. I've been debating whether to relay it to you or not. It may cause you some alarm."

"Don't concern yourself, Miss Davish," Daniel said with a tightness to his voice that negated his words. "As a member of Congress, I get messages from my constituents and members of the general public all the time. Some are unpleasant, but I am well used to dealing with them. What was the message?"

Don't say I didn't warn you, I thought.

"The man said, 'Tell Daniel that Billy McBain says hello.' "

Daniel's face went white. He sat motionless for a moment or two before Walter, taking on the role of physician, inquired, "Daniel, are you all right?"

"Yes, yes, I'm fine."

"And Mr. McBain also said to tell you that he saw Doggie Miller hit a home run against Cleveland."

"He did?" Was that a slight smile on his face? If so, it was gone as quickly as it came. "Good night, Miss Davish."

"Good night, Mr. Clayworth. Thank you for inviting me to dinner." It would most likely be the last invitation I would receive.

Me and Simeon Harper, I thought, *the unwanted dinner guests. Maybe I could be a journalist after all.* It was an amusing thought.

Daniel nodded, but he had clearly already dismissed me and everyone around him from his mind.

"I thought we'd decided you weren't going to tell Daniel about Mr. McBain's message," Walter said as he escorted me toward the Clayworths' Victoria, which Sarah had arranged to take me home, albeit not so early.

"I'm sorry, Walter, we did. But then he lied to me about not being at court today. I thought giving him the message might prompt him to give us some answers."

"But we still don't know anything more, do we?"

"No, but there's something between them for certain. Billy McBain knew Daniel would react that way. He laughed after he gave me the message."

"Do you think it has anything to do with that Lottie Fox?"

"I don't know. I'm worried it's worse than that."

"Worse? How can it be worse?"

"Billy McBain was a member of Coxey's inner circle, along with Jasper Neely and he—"

"Oh my God, Hattie," Walter said, interrupting me. "Are you saying you suspect Daniel might be involved in . . ." He couldn't bring himself to voice the thought out loud. "But why?"

"I don't know, Walter. I truly don't know."

I didn't want to suspect him any more than Walter did, but why else would Daniel Clayworth become as white as a sheet at the mention of Billy McBain's name? Why did he deny being in the courtroom? If he didn't have secrets, then why?

CHAPTER 27

"I'm so sorry, Hattie," Sarah said, as I placed a foot onto the carriage step. "Daniel is in a foul mood about Coxey tonight." She had appeared in the front door suddenly and had joined Walter by the road. "You shouldn't have to leave."

"That's all right, Sarah. I have work to get back to." How many times had I been grateful to do something productive with my hands when my mind was upset?

Too many, of late, I thought as I sat in the back of the Victoria.

The horse shifted its feet, and for a moment I feared the driver would encourage the horse to leave before I got a chance to say good night, but Walter grabbed the horse's bridle.

"May we be alone, Wallace?" he said to the Clayworths' driver. "Five, ten minutes should be enough."

"Of course, Dr. Grice." The driver clambered from his seat and strolled down the sidewalk toward Dupont Circle.

Sarah stared at Walter, nervously tapping her nails against her teeth, waiting impatiently for Wallace to be away.

"What is this, Walter? Why did you send Wallace away?"

"We have something to ask you, Sarah, and I couldn't miss this opportunity of you being alone."

Her eyes went wide in fear. "What is it?"

"Would you tell her, Hattie?" Sarah shifted her gaze from Walter to me but never blinked. I told her about my encounter with Lottie Fox at the police station.

"Her message was meant for you, Sarah," I said. Her cheeks were red, but her shoulders were straight. "Does she have cause to know you?"

"Yes, she does."

"Sarah! I thought it must be a mistake. How on earth does a woman like that—?"

"Please listen, Walter." Sarah put her hand on her brother's chest and looked at him intently. "Listen."

"I'm listening."

She stepped back so she could address us both.

"First, I want to thank both of you for not mentioning this in front of Daniel. He would never understand." That I could believe, even without knowing the circumstances. "Second, I want you to listen to my whole story before you make any judgment."

"Of course," I said.

Walter hesitated before answering. "Very well, but you must be quick because Wallace will be back soon."

Sarah glanced down the street toward Dupont Circle and, not seeing Wallace returning yet, glanced at the house. What was she looking for, someone watching us from a window? Daniel didn't strike me as the lurking type. He'd more likely confront her from the doorway if he had a mind to.

But then again, he had been sneaking along the wall at the trial, hoping to remain unseen, I thought. I too glanced up at the window. No one was there.

"I met Lottie, Miss Fox, through my club, the Washington

Wives Club. As a group, we are attempting to try to help her and some of her 'girls' reform and find new lives. Miss Fox approached one of our members and has been an eager partner ever since she met Carl Browne. She's become religious, in her own manner, and wants to leave her old ways behind. 'Like Mary Magdalene,' she said. However, this part of the club's charity work is controversial, even among our members."

"Is that what you were discussing yesterday at the meeting?" I asked.

"Yes. We have tried to keep it secret. We're afraid to even tell our husbands."

"Daniel doesn't know?" Walter said.

"No, and I beg you not to tell him, Walter. He wouldn't understand."

"No, he wouldn't, because I still don't understand. Why would you risk your reputation for a . . . ?"

"A woman who has made mistakes, who has not had the advantages we take for granted, but who wants to make her life better?" Again I was struck by the idea that, with but a twist of fate, I could've been a woman like that. "Besides, I'm not risking my reputation by aiding a fellow human being. But the politics of this town might not be so kind to Daniel."

"Or Senator Smith," I said.

"Of course," Walter said. "Mrs. Smith is involved in this as well."

"I'm afraid I have bad news, Sarah," I said.

"What?"

"Senator Smith knows."

"What? No!" Sarah glanced around her again.

"What makes you think so, Hattie?" Walter said.

"I was working late and overheard the senator and his wife arguing last night about a letter Miss Fox sent to Mildred. Was Mrs. Smith at another club meeting last night?"

"She was. It was called at the last minute. Lottie Fox was

supposed to meet us, but she never showed. Oh, Lottie!" Sarah exclaimed. "How could you be so stupid?"

"It may not be as bad as you think," Walter said. "Meriwether Smith isn't going to tell anyone. He wouldn't risk anyone knowing of his wife's involvement."

"He did ban her from attending any more meetings of the club, though," I said.

"And Daniel will ban me too if Meriwether tells him," Sarah said. "And then how are we going to help these women?"

"You truly believe you're doing those women any good?" her brother asked.

"Yes. Without our help, these women are destined to be . . ." She hesitated, searching for the right word. "To be the way they are forever. It's mortifying to me, Walter. What if I were destitute in this way? Wouldn't you want someone to help me?"

"But you never would be, Sarah."

"Then what about me?" I said quietly. Sarah gasped at the thought. Walter frowned.

"This is not a conversation we should be having," Walter said, avoiding the question. Sarah, after her initial shock, seized the opportunity to enlighten her brother.

"She's right, though. Hattie, orphaned at a young age, with no money, no protector. I don't like to contemplate the idea any more than you do, but it is girls like our Hattie who end up this way. Don't you think they deserve a second chance?"

Walter couldn't look me in the eye while Sarah spoke, but instead stroked the white star on the horse's forehead.

"Now do you see why what we are doing is so important?" Sarah said. "Why we are willing to risk doing it behind our husbands' backs? If a person was ill, would you not want to make them better? These women are morally sick and they need to be saved."

We stood in silence for several moments before nearby steps on the pavement alerted us to Wallace's return. Walter looked at the approaching driver, stole a brief glance at me, before meeting his sister's inquiring eyes.

"I think I understand now."

Sarah smiled and took Walter's hand. "Thank you, dear brother. I knew you would."

"But, Sarah, what was it that Miss Fox regrets, what did she wish she hadn't done?" I said. The madam had been clear on that point but hadn't enlightened me as to what she meant.

"All ready for me to take the lady home, Dr. Grice?" the driver said as he arrived next to the Victoria.

"Yes, thank you for your indulgence, Wallace. Good night, my love," Walter whispered before releasing his grip on the bridle.

"Good night." I wished I didn't have to leave. Now I'd have to wait for my answer.

The driver climbed into his seat and raised the leather whip. The horse stomped its feet a time or two before heading forward.

"Good night, Hattie!" Sarah called, waving.

Walter said something to his sister I couldn't hear, but as the carriage rode away, I caught Sarah saying, "What Lottie Fox regretted? Walter, I honestly don't know what Hattie was talking about."

When had everything gone wrong?

A few days before, when Walter had proposed, I was the happiest woman in the world. Since then, I'd seen a woman drown, had seen a man lying dead from a penknife that had been stuck in his neck, had been beaten, questioned, and warned off by the police, had been hounded by reporters looking for answers I didn't have, had suspected my future sister-in-law of cavorting with prostitutes, and had quarreled with Sir Arthur. And after a dream, where I saw myself in a cracked mirror wearing the garish crimson, yellow, and lavender dress Annie Wilcox had drowned in, I'd barely slept. Now, though it was not yet dawn and still too dark to hike, I was in great need of fresh air. So I glanced about for any sign of reporters, and seeing none, I sat on the front steps, in a simple shirtwaist and skirt, brooding.

So what am I going to do about it?

About what? About the dead girl's drowning, the Coxeyite's murder? With the police prohibiting me from any involvement in the investigation of their deaths, I couldn't even tell the police what I did know without risk. About the unwanted attention from the press? I could only ignore them and hope they lost interest. About Sir Arthur? Yes, that was still disconcerting. I had every intention of marrying Walter, but I couldn't imagine parting ways with Sir Arthur like this. Would Sir Arthur listen to my reasoning if we spoke again? Could I get him to understand? Could I get him to change his mind? Had Sir Arthur ever changed his mind? I grew more despondent as I reflected on the answer.

"*Pssst,* Hattie," someone called from across the street.

My instinct was to blow out the lamp I'd brought out and set beside me. But the person had called my name. Who could it be? I held up the lamp and glanced about warily until I saw Sarah peek out from behind one of the trees in the park. She was dressed in a simple, woolen black dress. Thinking only something terrible would bring her here at this hour, I leaped to my feet and rushed across the street to her.

"Walter said you like to hike in the morning before you work, but it isn't even light out," Sarah said when I reached her.

"What's wrong, Sarah? Why are you here? Has something happened to Walter?"

"No, no, it isn't anything like that."

"If all is well, why are you out here in the dark?"

"I was waiting for you. Like I said, Walter told me you hike in the morning. I came early hoping to catch you before you left."

"But why?"

"Because of this." She held a small white piece of paper that appeared to glow in the lamplight. "It was slipped beneath my front door after you left last night. It's from Lottie Fox."

"Like the one Mrs. Smith received?"

"I don't know. Maybe. She might have contacted Mildred first, but then Senator Smith discovered the note, so she wrote to me. I'm grateful I saw it before Daniel did."

"What does it say?"

"Here, you can read it for yourself." I took the note she held out to me and read,

> Now that Mr. Neely is dead, my conscience dictates I
> must give you something. I know it is a great risk to
> you, but I beg you to meet me early tomorrow morning
> at the Apple House. I have no one else to turn to.

It was signed *L. F.*

"Will you go with me?"

"You're going?" I was astonished that she would even consider it.

"How can you, of all people, ask that? You've done this sort of thing many times, haven't you?"

"I—"

"Walter told me all about how you helped solve several murders, Hattie."

"Yes, but—"

"Who knows, Lottie Fox may have something that may help the police catch Mr. Neely's killer."

She was right. If I'd found that note slipped under the door, I would've pinned on my hat, slipped on my gloves, and headed straight for C Street. So why was I hesitating now? I was already at odds with Sir Arthur over my engagement. Was I concerned about what he would say if I went lurking about Hooker's Division in the dark in a quest to uncover yet another murderer? Was it because of what Walter might say, if he knew? What if Lieutenant Whittmeyer found out? Was it worth the risk? Was it because I'd already been involved in several murders? Had I had enough? Yes, I had. At least that was what I told myself.

"She didn't say she had something that indicated who killed Mr. Neely, just something that she no longer wants in her possession. Perhaps something belonging to the dead man." I was hedging, and Sarah knew it.

"I feel compelled to meet her, regardless. I once told her I'd help her, and I don't intend to break my promise. So, are you coming with me or not?"

"Why me? Wouldn't Walter or Daniel be a better escort to meet her in that place?" I remembered the warnings Claude Morris had issued the day of Mrs. Cleveland's reception. I remembered what I'd seen of Hooker's Division and the Apple House in the daylight. I wasn't eager to find out what such a place was like in the dark.

"Daniel? You know he'd never let me go, let alone accompany me. No, Daniel can never find out."

"Walter, then."

"My brother is a wonderful man, but I don't think he'd approve of his sister going to Hooker's Division before dawn to meet a madam any more than Daniel would."

"I don't think he'd approve of his fiancée accompanying his sister there either."

"That's why we don't tell him."

But I tell Walter everything, I thought.

Seeing my hesitation, Sarah, still trying to persuade me, added, "You might help solve Mr. Neely's murder and come to the aid of a fallen woman all in one fell swoop." She was persuasive but not enough.

"It's too dangerous, Sarah. Why not give the note to the police and let them handle it?"

You're a hypocrite, Davish. How many times had I risked my reputation, position, and even my life, because my curiosity and sense of duty drove me to meddle in police affairs?

"I'm going with or without you, Hattie." Her statement startled me. I held up the lamp to see her face more clearly. Her countenance was full of determination.

"No, Sarah, you can't go alone."

"Then come with me."

I looked back at the house, half expecting to see someone at the window, curtain pulled back, but all was silent and dark.

Maybe Sir Arthur would never find out, but if I did accompany Sarah, I was determined to tell Walter afterward. I didn't keep secrets from Walter. He would be dismayed, perhaps even angry, but he would understand and forgive me. Sir Arthur, I knew, would not.

But after our argument and his aloof treatment of me of late, maybe it didn't matter. I shivered at the thought of no longer being in Sir Arthur's good graces. For the second time today, I pictured myself wearing the dead girl, Annie Wilcox's, garish dress. And then I remembered her pale, lifeless face covered in algae.

That could've been me without Sir Arthur's protection, I thought, not for the first time.

But no, my father was my protector—having supplied me with a typewriter and the education to best use it to my advantage. I was already a competent secretary when Sir Arthur met me, otherwise he would never had taken me on. I would never have been in a predicament like that. But did that give me the right to ignore the plight of these women? Sarah was determined not to. I looked into Sarah's eyes again. She was more resolved than ever.

Setting aside for the moment what Walter would think of me going to Hooker's Division, I considered what he would say if he knew I had let his sister go there alone.

"Well, are you coming or not?" Did I have a choice?

"Yes, I can't let you go alone."

Sarah wrapped her arm through mine and smiled. "I was hoping you'd say that."

CHAPTER 28

"Let me get my hat," I said.

"There's no time," Sarah said. "We have to go before it gets too light."

She was right. In the park, the darkness clung to the trees, but in the empty street, the first signs of dawn could be seen. I nodded as I touched my hair self-consciously. I'd never spent any time out-of-doors without a hat on. It was disconcerting.

Not any more than visiting a bawdy house in the dark, I thought.

"Besides, you might wake someone," Sarah said.

"You're right. Let's go." To Sarah's surprise, I took the lead, waving off her offer of Lottie Fox's letter with the address on it. I knew exactly where I was going.

On Pennsylvania Avenue, the buildings, their windows still dark, loomed high above the quiet streets. I kept up a brisk pace and a keen eye out for any of the reporters. Luckily I saw no one. Sarah kept up, though barely, as she nervously searched the street for signs of danger. She started and grabbed my arm when a dairy wagon, its milk cans rattling against each other, passed us on the street. She obviously had never been out at this hour before. And then we came to Thirteenth Street. Unlike Pennsylvania Avenue, this street was alive with lights and music. I slowed and stepped into the shadows on the east side of the street. As we passed the second building on the block, with light blazing into the street from its open second-story windows, revealing silhouettes of half-naked women singing a slurred version of the old drinking song "Vive la Compagnie," Sarah grabbed my free hand and held on tight. She walked behind me, but so close that her breath, smelling of tooth powder, tickled the back of my neck. For all her bravado, she was more nervous than I was.

We walked nearly a block, past several more bagnios and saloons still filled with boisterous patrons, even as dawn seeped across the city, when a well-dressed man in a top hat stumbled out of an alleyway. A light, wet stain blotching the front of his jacket, he nearly careened into Sarah's shoulder as he wiped his mouth with the back of his gloved hand. He smelled of liquor and stomach sickness. He reached out to steady her, or himself, I couldn't tell, and began coughing violently the moment their eyes met.

"Congressman Tignor?" Sarah whispered, stunned. Without a word, the man let his hands drop, lurched backward a few steps, before turning on his well-polished boot heels and staggering away as fast as he could.

Could he have been the man who left Annie Wilcox to drown? He was a visitor to Hooker's Division. He was wearing pearl buttons. But like the policeman had said, this city was rife with powerful, rich men. It could've been almost anyone. Besides, Congressman Tignor must weigh three hundred pounds.

Definitely not a strong swimmer, I thought.

"I can't believe it," Sarah said, still shocked at seeing someone she knew. "You don't think he'll tell Daniel, do you?"

"I wouldn't worry. He probably won't even remember seeing you."

"Is it all like this?" Sarah stood rooted to the ground, staring at a woman wearing rouge, a corset, a half-open yellow-and-blue-striped dressing gown, and little else, leaning against an alley wall. A man in a gray derby, his hand on the wall beside her, kissed her neck as she giggled.

"Quick, in here!" I ignored her question and pulled her with me into the shadows of a doorway.

"Ew!" Sarah groaned at the smell of urine beneath our feet. "My goodness, Hattie, this is disgusting. Why—?"

"*Shhh!*"

Ambling down the middle of the street was a group of men, five or six in number, and these men were no journalists. A glint of metal caught my eye as one man tossed a knife up and snatched it out of the air by the handle. Two of the others were arguing loudly in such slurred voices, I understood little beyond "horse," "bet," and "cheat." Another man, wearing only dirty trousers and a shirt with rolled-up sleeves, drank from a whiskey bottle. When it was empty, he tossed it carelessly away. Shards of glass glimmered in the streetlight as the bottle smashed against the side of a building. He staggered toward one of his cohorts and snatched that man's whiskey bottle. The victim, his arms flopping about, plunged forward and threw an aimless punch. As the thief cackled with glee, his victim nearly crashed down when he missed his target. Yet they moved closer and closer.

As they approached our hiding place, the man who'd lost his whiskey bottle, a lopsided smile spreading across his face, pointed toward us. Sarah whimpered. I put my arm across her and pushed us both flat against the wall. And then, as one, the men looked up.

"Hey, girls!" the man with the knife shouted, as he pushed his cap back. A line of grime crossed his forehead.

"Hey there!" came several high, trilling voices from above. Unable to look up without stepping out of the shadows, I could only guess who the women were.

"Why don't you come on down here and say a proper hello?" another of the men said, smiling. He was missing two bottom teeth.

"Yeah, come on down," the man with the stolen whiskey bottle said. He puckered his lips in mock kisses.

I guessed right, I thought, silently praying the men would soon be on their way.

"There's a party at Celia's," one of the girls above us said. "We'll catch up to you there."

"See that you do," the man with the knife said, tossing it up and catching it again. I could feel Sarah trembling beside me.

"Ta-ta," one of the girls said. A window banged closed above, and with a few chuckles, the men sauntered away.

"Oh, Hattie," Sarah whispered, tears glistening in her eyes. "If this is what your adventures are like, next time I'll pass."

Next time? I hoped there never was a next time. I gave her hand a squeeze. I'd been as frightened as she was, but I wasn't going to let her know.

"Let's go. It's not far now."

Sarah nodded and managed a slight smile as we, hand in hand, crept out of the shadows toward the Apple House.

When we passed the respectable Galvanized Iron Cornice Works, loud clanking noises emanating from within as their work-day began, Sarah let go of my hand and sighed in relief. But then I stopped in front of the Apple House.

"Is this it?"

I nodded.

Sarah's eyes widened as she studied the place, which was surprisingly dark and silent. In contrast, a "house" a few doors down blazed with electric light pouring out of its downstairs windows and a few bars of "Take Your Time, Gentlemen," playing on a phonograph, escaped into the street. Why was Lottie's place so quiet?

"Welcome to the Apple House," I said.

Third time's a charm, I thought, staring at the empty balcony. *Poor Annie's dead, but maybe we'll finally learn something useful.*

"The letter says to go to the back door," Sarah whispered.

We circled the building and found the alley I'd hidden in before. A scrawny orange cat, balancing on the rim of a barrel, had its head buried in the refuse. It looked up, a torn scrap of stocking draped across its head, and hissed at us, but stayed clinging to its perch as we passed. A fat gray rat, its nose skimming the ground, scurried across our path. I cringed as it crawled over the toe of my shoe. Stifling a cry, Sarah put her hand over her mouth and hurriedly followed me to the door in the back.

Before we had the opportunity to knock, the door flew open, light spilling into the dark alley around us. A young black-haired woman, barely into her late teens, dressed only in a plain white nightgown with several cloth buttons undone at the neck, stood holding the door. A purple bruise tinged with green, circling her eye, marred her otherwise pretty face. That and the scowl she wore.

"Who's this?" she asked Sarah, pointing at me. "I was told only a blond lady was coming, not a brunette."

"This is Miss Davish," Sarah said, in her best parlor voice. "My brother's fiancée. You can trust her as you trust me." The girl huffed at that, obviously not trusting Sarah much either. "I'm Mrs. Clayworth."

"I know who you are, the congressman's wife. Lottie told me."

"Yes, that's right."

"And you are?"

The girl frowned, surprised I'd asked.

"Fanny."

I'd heard that name here before. Wasn't that who Chester Smith agreed to "see" the day Annie drowned? I was sure it was.

The girl waited, as if expecting us to challenge her on her name, but when we remained silent she said, "You're to follow me."

We fell into step behind the girl. To Sarah's relief, evident by her reassuring smile, we were spared the lurid display of the "fallen women" vying for men's attention. For Fanny led us, not through a room filled with overstuffed chaise longues and closed, dark, heavy drapes where half-dressed women drank whiskey while laughing at their male companions' jokes, as I imagined, but along an austere whitewashed hallway and up narrow back stairs. So why was I disappointed? Was it my curiosity taking hold again? Or was it something more?

I've come this close, I thought, *and will never get the chance again.* But did I truly want to see the vulgar scene? I looked at the bare legs and feet of the girl ahead of me. No, not really. But I couldn't help but ask her questions.

"How long have you lived here, Fanny?"

"Miss Lottie took me in after I ran away from my pa. He used to beat me terrible." Oddly, she chuckled. "Funny, ain't it?" She pointed to her bruised eye.

"Not particularly, no," I said. Fanny dismissed me with a wave of her hand.

"What do you know?"

"Who did that to you?" Sarah asked. "I can't imagine Miss Fox allowing violence in her establishment."

"You're right. Miss Lottie is real protective of us girls. Any customer who gets nasty never steps inside here again."

"What happened to you?" I said.

"Someone got nasty."

"I'll say," Sarah said.

"You might even know him," Fanny said slyly. Sarah's shoulders tensed. No woman wanted to learn that a man she knew or loved visited one of these places. "He's the son of a senator."

"Chester? Chester Smith did this to you?" I said, aghast. What would Mildred Smith say if she knew her son not only frequented a place like this but purposely beat the girl?

"Yeah. How did you know?" The girl eyed me suspiciously.

"When did he do that, Fanny?" I said. "Was it the day Annie drowned?"

"Poor Annie. Thought she'd found herself a rich man. Thought she was getting out of here. She should've known better. None of us are getting out of here."

"That's not true," Sarah said. "I belong to an organization of influential ladies who can help any girl who wants to leave here and start over."

"Yeah, Lottie told us about you."

"When did Chester do this to you, Fanny?" I asked again. I'd seen Chester take a swing at more than one man and now Fanny. With such a temper, it wasn't hard to imagine Chester abandoning Annie and then attacking Fanny later that morning.

"There's the rub. I was with Lottie and a bunch of the other girls at the edge of the Capitol grounds the morning of the march." When Sarah grimaced, her eyes wide with dismay, Fanny stuck out her chin and added, "We have a right to see Marshal Browne and General Coxey and their men as much as the rest of you."

"Of course you do," I said, trying to placate Fanny before she decided not to tell us any more. "Miss Fox is a friend of Marshal Browne's, isn't she?"

"Yes, that's right," Fanny said, again surprised by what I'd said. "And Marshal Browne isn't ashamed to be seen with her either." She glared at Sarah. Poor Sarah hadn't said anything disparaging, but even as she was determined to help these women, she still couldn't help react the way most would at the thought of a gathering of fallen women at a public event.

"No, I'm sorry to imply otherwise," Sarah said. Fanny appeared satisfied.

"So you were at the march and then what happened?" I asked.

"And then Chester Smith happened, is what. He spied me in the crowd and dragged me back here. He used to be one of my regulars, generous too, until he left town all of a sudden. But that was months ago. I couldn't say no, I needed the money, but he made me miss seeing Coxey and Marshal Browne. With all the talk from Lottie about them having part of Jesus's soul, I was sorely disappointed about that."

"Exactly when did Chester hit you?"

"Afterward, when he was dressing. I asked him where he'd gone, why he left town. He'd been in a foul mood since the moment I laid eyes on him so he growled at me, told me to shut up and stop asking questions. He'd always been testy, but he was so generous, I didn't care. I never thought he'd hit me, though. But then again, it was my fault. I should've stopped asking him questions."

"It was not your fault," I said.

"He does seem an irascible sort, but that's inexcusable," Sarah said.

"Ah, I don't know. At least he had a reason. Pa used to hit me for the fun of it. These are Lottie's rooms." Fanny stopped

in front of a highly polished wooden door with an open tran-
som window.

"How long was he here, Fanny?" I asked.

"Like I said, long enough for me to miss the whole thing.
He left when the girls came back telling me Lottie had been
arrested."

Long enough to have an alibi for Jasper Neely's murder, I thought.

CHAPTER 29

"No, I'm sorry. My mind is made up," a woman's voice declared from behind the closed door. It was Lottie Fox.

"You were willing to give it to an unbalanced radical but not to me?" a man said, his Southern drawl vaguely familiar. "What could he do, use it to get one bill passed? I could change this whole darn country!"

"My answer is no."

"You know where I am if you change your mind."

"I won't. Please go."

"Dang it, woman!" The door flung open, and Senator Clarence Abbott stood on the threshold, Lottie Fox in the room behind him. His planter's hat in his hands, he grimaced when he saw us. Lacking his characteristic charm, the Populist senator shoved past us without a word and stormed down the stairs. We all stood in silence until we heard the back door slam.

"That will be all, Fanny," the madam said. Fanny dropped her gaze and scampered away like a scolded puppy. "Please, Mrs. Clayworth, bring your friend and come in."

The parlor, which could have been in any respectable

home, was richly furnished in plush green velvet, highly polished oak furniture, and green-and-gold Brussels carpets. A half-packed travel trunk sat open next to the unlit fireplace.

"Was that . . . ?" Sarah, dumbfounded to see someone she knew coming out of a madam's room, didn't want to believe her eyes.

"Mr. Abbott, the junior senator from North Carolina?" the madam said. "Yes, it was."

"My," was all Sarah could say on the subject. Recovering quickly, she added, "Miss Fox, this is Miss Davish, my brother's fiancée. I believe you met on a previous occasion?" Sarah was diplomatically referring to our encounter in the police station.

"Yes, Miss Davish and I have met."

"I hope you don't mind that I brought her with me. She is known for her discretion."

"I don't mind at all. It is prudent of you not to have come alone. Mrs. Smith couldn't come?"

"No," was all Sarah said.

"Well, thank you, Mrs. Clayworth and Miss Davish, for coming. I know you both took a risk coming here, and at this hour, but you are doing me a great service. I'd hoped to do this at the club meeting the other night but . . . it didn't work out." She said no more on the subject and we didn't pry. "I hope what I show you will compensate for your efforts." She walked over to the oak secretary and lifted a thick, black, leather-bound ledger. "As you can see, I'm packing. I've decided to use some of the resources your club, Mrs. Clayworth, has provided for me and leave Washington. I'm going to live with my sister in Fabius, in upstate New York. She runs a general store there, and I'm going to help her. I'm leaving tonight."

"That's wonderful, Miss Fox," Sarah said, clapping her hands together. "I wish you all the best."

"Thank you, Mrs. Clayworth."

"But that's not why you asked Mrs. Clayworth here, is it?" I said. The madam held out the leather book.

"This is my register. It goes back to 1883 when I took the business over from Sally Jones."

She needn't say more. Both Sarah and I stared at the book containing the names of all the men who had frequented Lottie Fox's "establishment" in the past eleven years. Sarah reached out slowly to touch it, but pulled her hand back as if the book had bitten her.

"Is that what Senator Abbott wanted?" I asked.

"Yes, but I wouldn't give it to him."

"But why show us?" Sarah asked.

"Because I believe I can trust you."

"But why show anyone?" I said.

"I'm afraid a man may have been killed over it."

"Jasper Neely," I said. Sarah turned to me wide-eyed, but Lottie merely nodded.

"Yes. I once agreed to let Mr. Neely have it. He was to approach Senator Meriwether Smith, the chairman of the Finance Committee, and 'convince' him to support the Good Roads project that Marshal Browne and Jacob Coxey championed. It was to put thousands of men back to work. After Marshal Browne brought clarity, peace, and purpose to my life, after he showed me how I too have a part of Christ's soul in me, it was the least I could do."

"And what if Senator Smith refused to sponsor the bill?" Sarah asked.

"Mr. Neely was to threaten to put the register into the hands of Senator Abbott."

"Senator Abbott?" Sarah asked. "But you denied him it."

"Yes, I changed my mind."

"Why not give it to Simeon Harper or someone else from the press?" I said.

"At the time, Mr. Neely too mentioned Mr. Harper, but that was going too far. I have helped Mr. Harper before, when I could, since he is a decent fellow and always kept my name out of the papers as he promised. But even he wouldn't be able to resist publishing all of these names. No, this was supposed to help get the Good Roads Bill introduced, not target men who had nothing to do with it."

"So why Senator Abbott?" I asked.

"He is Smith's political rival," Sarah said. "He would be judicious in his use of the book, only targeting his rivals and keeping all his allies, including the Populists, who supported Coxey, Browne, and the Good Roads Bill, out of it."

"Exactly."

"So why not give it to Abbott now?"

"I changed my mind."

"Did Smith refuse?" Sarah asked.

"He did, and now Mr. Neely is dead," she said.

So that's what Jasper Neely was doing at the Smith house the morning of the march, blackmailing Smith into supporting the Good Roads Bill. And why Neely was talking to Senator Abbott not long after, and then Lottie not long after that. But something wasn't right.

"But you still have the book," I said. "And Abbott is still trying to get it from you. Why?"

"I changed my mind."

"Why?"

Lottie put her hand on the simple gold cross hanging from her neck.

"When Mr. Neely approached me before the march, telling me that Senator Smith wouldn't support the bill and that he was going to give Abbott the register, I had a change of heart. I listened to the part of Christ in me. Besides, Marshal Browne never approved of the scheme in the first place."

"What would Senator Abbott have done with the register

if Jasper Neely gave it to him? Do you think he'd expose the contents, as Sarah says?" I asked. "Or at least threaten to?"

"I don't know what Senator Abbott would've done or will do. That's partially why I changed my mind. I don't know that man. I was going on Mr. Neely's word that he could be trusted not to misuse the information. A great many people's careers and lives could be damaged or destroyed if the complete contents of the register were revealed. I wanted to help the cause. I wanted Senator Smith to support General Coxey's Good Roads project, but it was too much of a risk in the end."

"So you refused to give Neely, and thus Abbott, the register," Sarah said.

"And less than half an hour later, Neely was dead," I said.

"Yes," the madam said sadly.

"Do you think Senator Abbott killed Neely, Miss Fox?" I asked.

"Like I said, I don't know that man."

"He couldn't have," Sarah said. "When I was making my way back to Walter and everyone at the Capitol, I saw Abbott with several of his Populist colleagues. He was nowhere near the site where Neely was killed."

"Did you kill him, Miss Fox?" I said. Unlike Sarah, who stood gaping at me for my audacity, Lottie barely blinked at my accusation.

"No, Miss Davish. I didn't. Mr. Neely and I believed in the same cause. I wouldn't have destroyed an instrument of Christ, a man who stood for positive change."

"What did he do when you refused to give him the register?"

"Told me to talk to Marshal Browne after the march. That maybe he'd be able to convince me to change my mind."

"And that's how you left it? That was the last time you saw him?"

"Yes, Miss Davish. He was determined to change my mind, but he was very much alive." She shook her head. "Yet I can't help feeling that if I'd never agreed to his plan in the first place, he'd still be alive."

"So you think he was killed because he threatened to expose the contents of the register?"

"I think he died because he was attempting to blackmail powerful people."

"Is Senator Smith in your register, Miss Fox?" Sarah gasped again when Lottie nodded her head. "So you think he might've killed Jasper Neely to protect his secret?"

"I do."

"No!" Sarah said. "I can't believe that."

"What about Senator Abbott? Is he in the register?" I asked, ignoring Sarah's declaration.

"No, until this morning, I'd never met Mr. Abbott."

"Could there be others in your book who had reason to kill Jasper Neely?"

"If you are asking if other powerful men might be destroyed if the contents of the register were released, I would say yes—many. But I don't know of any one of them, besides Smith, who had direct contact with Mr. Neely."

"But that doesn't mean they didn't at some point, without your knowledge. Many people visited the camp before the march. I personally saw Jasper Neely speaking to several members of Congress. It could be anyone listed in your book."

"Yes, but as far as I know, only Senator Smith was directly threatened by Mr. Neely."

"Or it could've been an internal dispute, someone from the Commonweal who had a falling out with Mr. Neely?" Sarah said. I'd only seen evidence that Jasper Neely was a vital member of the Commonweal of Christ, as well as a respected, well-liked one.

"Maybe," Miss Fox said slowly, as dubious of the idea as I was.

"But you're convinced it was Senator Smith?" I said.

"I am."

"I don't want to know," Sarah said, "but I have to ask . . ." She hesitated.

"Whether your husband's name is in my book or not?" the madam said, saving Sarah the humiliation of asking. Sarah nodded.

"No, he's not." Sarah let out a loud sigh of relief. "It's the reason I approached you with the truth. Of all the women in your Washington Wives Club who have offered me help instead of derision, only your husband's name wasn't in my book." Sarah's mouth dropped open and she gaped at Lottie.

"Oh my God," Sarah said. "I had no idea. Does Mildred know? Do anyone of the others know?"

"Not from me," the madam said.

"Thank you for your discretion," Sarah said.

"You don't need to thank me. I do it for my own selfish reasons. I can't make a new life for myself and have peace of mind knowing I'd helped ruin people's lives."

Again I was struck by the morality of a woman who most couldn't conceive had any at all.

"You wrote a letter to Mrs. Smith, Miss Fox," I said.

"Yes, I wrote to her before all of this, before Mr. Neely was killed. I wrote to Mrs. Smith urging her to convince her husband to support the bill. I mentioned nothing about the consequences if he didn't." That was consistent with what I'd overheard.

"So why are you telling us all of this?" Sarah asked.

"I regret ever being a part of this scheme. I wanted to confess to someone in hopes of undoing, at least in part, what I've done."

"You didn't give the register to Abbott," Sarah said. "What could we possibly do?"

"You want us to go to the police with this," I said, guessing what she'd say next. Sarah was shaking her head before I finished.

"I appreciate you wanting to clear your conscience, Miss Fox, to start anew, but you don't expect me or Miss Davish to take this information to the police, do you? No, I'm sorry. We're already risking too much by being here. The wives' club is risking more than you know by helping you and some of your girls start again."

"But they won't listen to me," the madam said, almost pleading. "And what I've told you might lead to Mr. Neely's killer."

"I'm sorry. Truly I am, but I can't possibly get involved in a murder," Sarah said.

"What about you, Miss Davish?" the madam said. I hesitated.

How many times had I been unwittingly involved in death and murder? Now I was being given a choice. And Lottie was right. If Senator Smith killed Jasper Neely, Lottie's information could make all the difference. But did I have a choice? Unlike on previous occasions, the police here in Washington had threatened me with imprisonment if I involved myself in any way. Would Lieutenant Whittmeyer regard giving him this evidence as tampering with his investigation? Yes, he would. He would question where I got the book, how I knew Lottie Fox, and why I was speaking to her at all. Without the connection of death between us, both Annie Wilcox's and Jasper Neely's, there would be no occasion for us to have ever met. And then there was the possibility of further scandal. I'd already been caught up in the scandal over Annie Wilcox's death and then again when I was questioned at the police station. Sarah had adeptly limited the effects, but would she be able to again? And what would Sir Arthur think, if I involved myself once again? What would Walter think? And as my future family, how would it affect Daniel and Sarah, who had to live there? Was giving evidence that might catch a killer worth the consequences? If it were only me, I might say yes. But thanks to dear Walter's proposal, I now had a family and their future to consider.

"No," I said. "I can't either." Sarah smiled in relief. Miss Fox frowned in disappointment. "But maybe we can think of a less risky way of revealing your information to the police than any of us telling them directly."

I'd approached Sir Arthur with more delicate complications than this before. Even if he still wasn't pleased with me, he was the one to deal with Lottie Fox's black book.

"Maybe," the madam said doubtfully.

"Speaking of the police," I said, as the two women reversed their expressions, Sarah now frowning as Miss Fox looked eager to hear what I had to say. Miss Fox was to be disappointed again. "Have you learned anything more about the accident that killed Annie?"

"No, nothing. You were right. Despite all the talk in the newspapers, the police are doing nothing to find the man who left Annie to die."

"I'm sorry," I said.

"All the more reason to not approach the police with this," Sarah said, pointing to the register in Lottie's hands. "There's been enough scandal and slander about of late."

"But it wouldn't be slander if it were true," Miss Fox said, opening the drawer of the secretary and putting the register away. She took a key off the ring hanging from her waist. She locked the drawer and then, to my surprise, grabbed my free hand. She put the key in my palm and folded my fingers over it. I'd come to know this woman too well to shy away from her touch. Sarah, on the other hand, grimaced. "And now you know where the register is if you come to need it as proof of the truth."

How could something so small have such a weight attached to it? I wondered, as I slipped the key between my glove and my skin and closed my hand. But then again, there were those pearl buttons.

"Senator Smith killed Mr. Neely, and nothing you can say will convince me otherwise," the madam said.

"I can't imagine Senator Smith being involved, even if he was being blackmailed," Sarah said, still staring at my hand. "He's got too much to lose."

"All the more reason to silence Mr. Neely before it was too late," the madam said.

"But you've held this register for years and no has ever harmed you. Why would Jasper Neely be any different?" Sarah asked.

"Because Miss Fox has never threatened to hand the key to Smith's destruction to his political rival, as Neely threatened to do," I said.

"Do you realize what you're saying, Hattie?" Sarah said, mortification written across her face.

"That I agree with Miss Fox that Senator Smith is a suspect in Jasper Neely's murder? Yes, unfortunately, I know exactly what I'm saying."

CHAPTER 30

After wishing Lottie Fox well in her new life in New York, Sarah and I slipped silently down the stairs, out the back door and, with dawn fully upon us, snuck back along the alley. To my relief there were no reporters lying in wait. I accompanied Sarah to the nearest trolley stop in silence, and after seeing her off walked the few blocks to the Mall. I slumped onto a wooden bench and leaned back against the trunk of an elm tree. I closed my eyes for a moment, my mind swirling with questions, suspicions, and concerns. After several minutes of reflection and still finding no peace, I pulled out my notepad. As I put pencil to paper, a nanny, in a dark blue cotton dress and white bonnet, pushed a baby carriage past. Her cooing did nothing to quiet the squalling baby inside. I watched the pair grow smaller as they made their way down the Mall until the only sounds I heard were the chattering of birds and the occasional distant clang of a trolley bell. Then I made my list.

1. Did Senator Smith kill Jasper Neely?
2. If not, who did? Someone from Coxey's camp?

Someone from Smith's house other than Smith? Someone other than Lottie at the Apple House? Someone who didn't want the Good Roads Bill passed? Someone I haven't considered yet? (It could be almost anyone.)

3. Who could not have killed Jasper Neely? Chester Smith, Senator Abbott, Marshal Browne, Lottie Fox.
4. Could Neely's death have nothing to do with Coxey or the Good Roads Bill?
5. Is there a connection between Jasper Neely's death and the National Bank of the Potomac?
6. Is there a connection between Jasper Neely's and Annie's deaths?
7. Will they ever discover who abandoned Annie Wilcox to drown?
8. Could the same man who abandoned Annie be the man who killed Jasper Neely?
9. What will happen to Coxey, Browne, and the marchers now?
10. What should I do with Lottie Fox's key?
11. Will Sir Arthur change his mind and give Walter and me his blessing?
12. Will Walter and I be happy?

I looked at my list. The only question I could answer unequivocally was the last.

"Yes," I said out loud, smiling at the image of Walter teetering nervously on the edge of the wall surrounding the Bartholdi Fountain, the mist glistening on his hat, before proposing.

I looked at my list again. I had no more answers. What could I do? What should I do? Without another thought, I slipped the key from my glove and held it up to the rays of the rising sun.

"As Lottie Fox said, it's the least I can do."

Resolute, I stood and brushed off the back of my skirt. As

I moved to straighten my hat, I laughed as my fingers brushed my hair instead. In all of the excitement and revelation, I'd forgotten that I still wasn't wearing a hat.

Well, that at least is a simple enough problem to resolve, I thought as I walked purposely across the gardens toward Lafayette Square.

"Coxey, Browne Sentenced to Twenty Days in Prison!" a boy on the street, holding a *Washington Times* newspaper above his head, shouted. "Browne calls Judge Miller 'Pontius Pilate'!" I handed the boy a coin, took a paper from the stack beside him, and read:

TO JAIL FOR TWENTY DAYS

Coxey, Browne, and Jones Sentenced to Imprisonment

SPEECHES MADE IN COURT

Some three days ago Messrs. Jacob Coxey, Carl Browne, and Christopher Columbus Jones entered the Capitol grounds bearing banners, and yesterday in police court they were sentenced to twenty days' imprisonment for this action. In addition, a fine of $5 or ten days' imprisonment was imposed upon Coxey and Browne for trespass on the Capitol grass. There was a large crowd about the courthouse anxiously waiting for the result. Mr. Hudson, of counsel, stated that thousands of people stepped on the grass on that May Day with impunity, and yet these defendants were selected as objects of prosecution. Carl Browne tried to make one of his florid roadside speeches but was called down by the judge. Instead Browne quickly dispatched a message to the Commonwealers at the camp, announcing that, "President Cleveland, the Czar of the United States, from his throne has finally issued orders to Pontius Pilate Miller, who has carried out his edict." After denying Coxey's request to be driven to jail in an open carriage, the three men were compelled to go out to the old brownstone jail in the Black Maria police van along with a dozen vagrants and prisoners convicted of disorderly conduct.

How ridiculous! Fined and imprisoned for carrying banners and walking on the grass.

These were the same men who had aroused fear and derision, and had the city preparing for possible anarchy and bloodshed. At least now I knew what had become of Coxey and Marshal Browne.

What a regrettable, inane ending to an unprecedented march to Washington all in the name of bringing hope and jobs to thousands of desperate people. I'd miss reading about them, and I wished them well.

"Miss Davish, Miss Davish," several men, who had been loitering in the park across the street from Senator Smith's house, called the moment they saw me. They rushed to meet me, forestalling my progress to the house.

I won't miss the reporters when they find someone besides me to bother, I thought.

"Have any comment on Coxey's sentencing?" one of the men asked. His pencil had numerous chew marks on it. I ignored him and attempted to push my way past.

"Do you think Annie Wilcox's killer is now behind bars?" another asked.

"You think Coxey, Browne, or Christopher Columbus Jones was with Annie that morning?" I said, in spite of my vow not to speak to these men. Although I'd considered it, even examining the men's buttons, I'd never heard anyone else voice the accusation. It took me by surprise.

"Don't you?"

I didn't. But I wasn't going to tell them that. "Excuse me," was my reply as I shoved my way to the front steps.

"Who killed Jasper Neely, Miss Davish? Readers want to know. You know something you're not telling us."

I don't, I thought, clutching the key tightly in my palm. *At least I hope I don't.*

"Walter!" I said, as he stepped out of the dining room into the hall in front of me.

"Surprised to see me?" he said, before kissing me on the cheek.

"Yes, most pleasantly."

"Well, I had a little business to take care of while you were out hiking." I inwardly cringed. I hadn't been hiking and wasn't looking forward to telling Walter and Sir Arthur where I had been.

"What business?"

"A little man-to-man chat with Sir Arthur." Walter winked.

"What did you say? Did Sir Arthur change his mind? Will he give us his blessing?"

"He's considering it," Walter said, smiling. "He even offered me a cigar." That was enough for me. Overjoyed to know that the two most important men in my life where being congenial again, I threw my arms around him. "Oh, and Mrs. Smith informed me that a certain lady's trousseau arrived while she was out."

"I'm so glad you spoke to Sir Arthur. Thank you," I whispered. "It will make what I have to do next easier."

"What's that?" I took his hand in mine and led him back toward the dining room. I knocked on the door frame.

"I wasn't hiking this morning."

"But then where—?"

"Come," Sir Arthur called from within, cutting off Walter's question.

Sir Arthur was at the dining room table, reading his stack of morning newspapers. A cup of tea and a plate of buttered toast sat on the table in front of him. Luckily, he was alone.

"Have you seen these?" he asked, without preamble, holding up the *Washington Post.* The headline read:

LEADERS GO TO PRISON; HOW THE ARMY TOOK THE NEWS

THE MEN IN CAMP NEAR BLADENSBURG
REGARD THE SENTENCES AS UNNECESSARILY
SEVERE AND DECLARE THEIR INTENTION
OF HOLDING TOGETHER—STILL
LOYAL TO THEIR CAUSE

And then he held up his copy of the *New York Times,* which read:

COXEY IN THE "BLACK MARIA," CLOSING SCENE OF HIS FAMOUS MARCH ON WASHINGTON

HANDCUFFED LIKE COMMON CONVICTS
DURING THEIR RIDE TO THE PRISON

"Yes, I have."

"It's bloody ridiculous, but that's the end of Coxey's Army and their Good Roads Bill," Sir Arthur said.

"Do you think so?" Walter asked.

"Yes, nothing will come of it now. Do you have the index for me, Hattie?"

"I do." I handed him the completed *Index to Property Destroyed by Confederate Authorities and that which was Destroyed by the Enemy.* He flipped through it, exclaiming with the occasional "Well, I'll be damned," or "Bloody hell."

"Brilliant. This is better than I thought it would be."

"Sir?"

"Yes?" He continued studying the index.

"I need to speak to you." Sir Arthur looked up.

"Now, Hattie, Dr. Grice and I have been talking and—" Anxious to say what I must, I did something else I'd never done before. I interrupted him.

"Sir, this has to do with Senator Smith and Jasper Neely, the Coxeyite who was murdered."

Knowing my past history with murder, Sir Arthur said nothing of the interruption. Instead he put the index down and indicated for Walter and me to sit.

"What do you know, Hattie?"

So I told him.

CHAPTER 31

"And this is the key to the drawer containing the register?" Sir Arthur said, holding the key before him. I'd
finished my tale of my visit to Lottie Fox's Apple House that
morning.

"Yes." I glanced over at Walter, not for the first time since
I began my disclosure. Instead of frowning in disapproval as
one would expect, he was stifling a chuckle.

How I love that man.

"You were right to come to me instead of the police, Hattie," Sir Arthur said. "I'm astounded that you went to Hooker's
Division, but, as always, your judgment is impeccable. If you
hadn't . . ." He stared at the key again. "Well, there seems to
be nothing left to do but to confront Smith." Sir Arthur
pushed back from the table. "I believe he took breakfast in his
study."

Sir Arthur strolled across the hall, and without knocking,
opened the study door and went in. Walter and I followed. The
senator was sitting at his desk, a tray of coffee, orange juice,
toast, and two fried eggs untouched beside him. Claude Mor-

ris stood bent over beside the desk. They were both studying a bound set of papers before them.

"Smith," Sir Arthur said, "I'm afraid I must interrupt your work."

Both men looked up and immediately glanced at Walter and me. Senator Smith frowned. Claude Morris, like any good secretary, held a neutral expression on his face.

"What is it, Sir Arthur?" Smith said.

"It's best we speak in private," Sir Arthur said, looking at Claude Morris.

"Of course," Claude Morris said, picking up the papers the men had been studying. I noticed he had an ink spot on his sleeve. Then I glanced at the buttons on his vest—plain bone.

Will they ever find who abandoned Annie Wilcox? I wondered. *Then I can stop looking at every man's vest buttons!*

"I will work on these and consult you later, Senator."

"Thank you, Morris," Senator Smith said. Claude quickly left, but not before I caught a flash of concern mixed with curiosity on his face. It was so brief I almost doubted I saw it at all. "And what about those two?" The senator jutted out his chin toward Walter and me.

"It is 'those two' who need to speak to you," Sir Arthur said. "Go on, Hattie. Tell the senator what you told me."

So I did, keeping my emotions at bay by reciting my tale with the same neutral tone I used to read back Sir Arthur's dictations. To his credit, the senator sat in silence until I had finished. His face grew flushed, and he took off his spectacles to wipe them when I mentioned his name in Lottie Fox's register, but he didn't deny it or try to stop me from saying what I'd come to say.

When I finished, Sir Arthur said, "Well, Smith? Is any of this true?"

"Yes, unfortunately, a great deal of what your secretary says is true, though I deny now and always that I played any part in that miscreant's death. Granted, I benefited from it, but I had nothing to do with it."

"So Neely was blackmailing you?" Sir Arthur said.

"As she says, he came here early the morning of the march. He'd given me a note at the camp warning me of his arrival. Luckily I was able to meet him at the door before anyone else knew of our appointment."

But someone else did know. Someone had been looking out the window. I said nothing, though, and let the senator continue.

"And yes, he pressed me to introduce some preposterous bill that would use federal money to employ men to build new roads and bridges. It was ludicrous! Do you know how much money that would cost the United States government?"

"But then he told you about this madam's book?" Sir Arthur said. I was content to let Sir Arthur question the senator. I had learned from experience that a man of power would be more forthcoming with his peer than with someone he saw as beneath him, and we all needed the senator to be forthcoming.

"Yes, the weasel threatened to deliver this book, with mine and many others' names in it, to Senator Abbott, who wouldn't hesitate to use it against every Democrat in the register."

"But you refused to support the bill?" Sir Arthur said.

"Not outright."

"What?" I couldn't help from speaking out at my surprise. "But Miss Fox led us to believe that you had refused to sponsor the bill. That was why Neely was going to carry out his threat."

"No, the madam was wrong. In fact, I considered quite seriously giving in to his demands. I'm up for reelection soon, and if the truth about my visits to the Apple House got out, it would tarnish my image. I'm a family man, after all." How could he say that without a trace of irony? Could he truly be oblivious to his hypocrisy or did he know very well what he said? "So I told him I would consider it and would speak to him after the march."

Then why would Miss Fox have us believe that Smith had refused outright? Was she hoping to implicate Smith for her own unknown reasons or was she telling us the truth as she knew it? Could it have been Jasper Neely who had lied to her? Or was Senator Smith more duplicitous than I'd imagined? With one dead and the other on her way to New York State, we might never know.

"But sponsoring such a bill would also have been politically damaging, would it not?" Sir Arthur asked.

"Yes, but whether it was worse than having Abbott disclose my indiscretions, I didn't know. I wanted time to consult a few of my most trusted colleagues and get their advice. It was repugnant to think of having to do either."

"But then Neely turned up dead," Walter said. He'd been silent throughout but now couldn't help but add to the discussion.

"That's right," Smith said. "With the man dead, I wouldn't have to make that terrible decision."

"It was convenient for you that he died then?" I couldn't keep a hint of contempt from my voice.

"Yes, it was more than convenient," Smith responded sincerely, oblivious of my disdain. "I have to say it was good timing as well. I hadn't even broached the subject to anyone. But still there's Abbott to deal with. He won't say anything without evidence, of course, but I'll have to put up with more of his smug grins than usual."

"Do you have any idea who could've killed Neely? Do you think Abbott capable?" Sir Arthur asked.

"Abbott? No, no. The man's a snake, but he'd never do anything that threatened his Populist image. He's too smart and too crafty for that."

"Anyone else then?"

"I can only imagine that some other wayward, misguided follower of Coxey had a disagreement with Neely and acted out the only way short-sighted, ignorant men do."

"Well, thank you for being so honest, Meriwether. Speaking for all of us"—Sir Arthur didn't bother to even look at us, assuming it was his right to do so—"consider this the end of the matter. We won't speak of it again."

My objection was on the tip of my tongue when Walter touched me lightly on the shoulder and put his finger to his lips. He was right. Questioning Senator Smith further wouldn't help. For now, at least.

"We will let you get back to your work," Sir Arthur said. "As I believe Hattie needs to do as well."

"Yes, sir," I said. "But what will you do with the key?"

"I know a carp pond you can throw it in," Sir Arthur said. Was Sir Arthur joking with me? What had Walter said to make Sir Arthur so congenial?

"You've gone too far this time, Chester!" someone yelled from the other side of the door.

Sir Arthur pulled the door open to reveal Simeon Harper shoving Chester Smith in the hall. Senator Smith leaped from behind his desk and joined us in the doorway.

"Leave me alone, Harper," Chester said. Senator Smith pushed his way past us.

"What is going on here?"

"Yes, Simeon. What is going on?" Sir Arthur said.

"He got in past the maid and started harassing me when I'd come in for breakfast," Chester said.

"You've been an invited guest in my home. Why would you come to harass my son?"

"Because your son defrauded the government and attempted to cover it up," the journalist said.

"I don't know what he's talking about," Chester said.

"Does the National Bank of the Potomac jog your memory?"

"Now, now, Harper," Senator Smith said. "We faced accusations before and nothing was proven. That's all behind us
now, and I'd like to keep it that way."

"I'd have to agree with the senator," Sir Arthur said. "It's
indecent of you to bring up such a controversial topic. Let the
matter drop."

"But I can prove it," Simeon Harper said.

"And how can you do that?" Chester said snidely. "From
what I hear, all the records at the Treasury have been misplaced
or destroyed."

"Because you had them destroyed," Harper said, stepping
aggressively toward Chester again. Chester took a step back.
"But I went directly to the bank where a pretty little secretary
was more than willing to show me the original records. And all
I had to do was promise to take her to dinner tonight." Chester
went white.

"I will not have you accusing my son of any wrongdoing,"
Senator Smith said. "You will leave this house at once."

"But don't you want to hear the story they're going to run
in tonight's *Evening Star*?"

"Okay, okay," Chester said. "I admit it, just don't print it in
the paper."

"Chester!" Senator Smith exclaimed. "According to the
law, you did nothing wrong."

"So you knew about this?" Sir Arthur said.

"I found out after the fact that he'd used information I'd
discussed with him privately to have his bank buy the treasury
notes with silver and redeem them for gold. I sent the boy
away so that the uproar could die down. But like I said, he did
nothing wrong."

"Legally," Harper said. "But I'd be willing to bet that my
readers might think he was acting less than morally. And isn't
that what you want your voters to believe, Senator? That you
and your family are moral, upstanding citizens?"

"Get out of my house!" Senator Smith said.

"Let me tell you the headline before I go: Senator's son defrauds government with insider information: Good Business or Treason?"

"What do you want from us?" Senator Smith said. "You are supposed to be a friend of Sir Arthur's. Why are you doing this?"

"I received anonymous tips I couldn't ignore."

"From Senator Abbott, no doubt. Who else would go to such lengths to ruin me? It wouldn't be the first time."

"What else has Senator Abbott done?" Harper asked.

"If I tell you, will you retract your story about Chester? Will you promise, with Sir Arthur as witness, that you will leave my name and my son's name out of anything you ever print again?"

"I promise I'll drop the fraud story. But I can't guarantee not to mention you or Chester ever again."

"But you will leave my name out of what I'm about to tell you, or I won't tell you," the senator said. "Is it agreed?"

"Very well. It's agreed."

"Tell him what you told me, Miss Davish," the senator demanded without even looking at me. I hesitated, taken by surprise. I looked to Sir Arthur for guidance. He nodded his head.

"Hattie? This involves you?" Harper said.

"Yes and no," I said, and then told him about Lottie Fox, Jasper Neely, and Senator Abbott's plan to blackmail Senator Smith with humiliation if he didn't support Coxey's bill.

"So Miss Fox thinks you killed Jasper Neely?" Harper said smugly to the senator when I'd finished.

"But of course I had nothing to do with it."

"What about Chester?" Harper said. "His name is in the book too." The senator turned to his son.

"Is this true?" Chester shrugged. "But how did you know?" the senator asked Harper. The reporter exaggerated a shrug in imitation of Chester. Chester glared at the reporter.

"So it could've been Chester who killed Neely to prevent his name from getting out. Sounds like an awfully good story to me," Harper said.

"You wouldn't!" Senator Smith said. "You promised—"

"I promised to keep your name out of it, not Chester's."

"Harper, that's low," Sir Arthur said.

"And untruthful," I said. Everyone looked at me. "Chester Smith didn't kill Jasper Neely."

"And how do you know that, Hattie?" Sir Arthur asked. Walter's eyebrow was raised in surprise too.

"Do you have proof?" Harper said.

"Yes."

"By God, Miss Davish, I was right about you," Simeon Harper said, smiling and shaking his head. "If you were a man, you'd be one of the best journalists in town." It took all of my professional composure not to blush at the compliment.

"Of course I didn't kill anyone," Chester said, sneering.

"But you did punch an innocent woman in the face," I said.

"What?" Senator Smith said, jerking his head around to face his son. "How could you?"

"She wasn't an innocent woman, Father," Chester said. "She was one of Lottie's girls."

"Her name is Fanny," I said.

"Whatever," Chester said. "She was asking me too many questions. She wouldn't stop. I was already in a foul temper. She had it coming."

"Very well," his father said. "Let's not mention it again. I understand, but I doubt your mother would if she found out."

I stood dumbstruck. It was acceptable to punch a woman in the face simply because she was a fallen woman? What else was acceptable? I shuddered to think, but I wisely kept my contempt of both men to myself.

"I won't ask how you know about Fanny, Hattie," Harper

said. "Or I might be compelled to put your name in the papers." I blanched at the thought.

"I should hope not," Sir Arthur said.

"Rest assured, Sir Arthur," Harper said, pulling out a packet of gum. "But, Hattie, you never said how you knew Chester couldn't have killed Jasper Neely."

"He couldn't have killed Jasper Neely because he was with Fanny at the time of the murder."

"So the woman you punched in the face is your alibi, Chester." Harper sneered. He popped a stick of gum in his mouth. "Aren't you lucky?"

"Get out, Harper," Chester said.

"I'm going. I have a story to write."

"And you will abide by your promise, to leave our names out of it?" Senator Smith said.

"I will. But I'd stay clean from now on, Senator. That promise doesn't extend to the next story I uncover about you and your family."

And with that, Simeon Harper, whistling "The Laughing Song," strolled down the hall toward the front door.

"I expect an apology for Harper," Chester said, glaring first at Sir Arthur and then quickly at me. "Father invited him in because of you."

"Yes, but it was your own behavior that gave him fodder for his paper," Sir Arthur said.

"Well, that's insulting. I'm leaving, Father. I won't stay here and be insulted. I'm going back to Philadelphia."

"That's a good idea, boy. It's better for all of us."

"Better for you, you mean." Chester glowered at his father before swiveling on his heels in disgust.

We watched Chester storm away in the opposite direction from where Simeon Harper had gone. Then the senator turned to me.

"I thank you and my wife thanks you, Miss Davish, for

clearing my son's name in the murder. Even I wondered, knowing Chester's temper and knowing he'd disappeared before Coxey arrived. I couldn't fathom why he would do such a thing, but we all saw the altercation between the two that day at the camp." They were the first kind words he'd said to me.

"You're welcome, Senator."

"But then who did kill Jasper Neely?" Walter said.

"Some worthless miscreant from Coxey's Army, I dare say. Nothing to do with us, thank God," Senator Smith said.

"Yes, I'm sure it has nothing more to do with you," Sir Arthur said.

I wished I could be so sure.

"By the way, Sir Arthur," the senator said, taking off his spectacles and wiping them with his handkerchief again. "I appreciate you coming to me first with the business we discussed."

"Of course," Sir Arthur said.

"Why involve others unnecessarily? That's my thinking as well. See you at tea."

"Will do. Ah, what good timing, Morris," Sir Arthur said, watching as Claude Morris returned carrying a larger stack of papers than he had left with. I noticed the ink stain was gone.

"Yes, Morris often anticipates my needs," the senator said. "I don't know what I'd do without him."

"I can appreciate that," Sir Arthur said. I expected him to glance at me, but he didn't.

Claude Morris shuffled by quickly, his cheeks red with embarrassment at overhearing such praise.

"How did you remove the ink stain on your sleeve so quickly, Mr. Morris?" I asked as he passed me. Claude glanced at the damp spot on his sleeve.

"It's quite simple, Miss Davish. I'm surprised you haven't figured it out for yourself." I sighed at his patronizing tone but said nothing. "A little soap and water, is all. I find Kirk's Castile works best. It cleans pen nibs as well as fabric. And heated up a

bit, it's an excellent lubricant for penknifes and letter openers."
I was stunned. I would never had guessed.

Claude Morris, waiting for the senator to join him, set the
stack of papers on the desk and a pen on top of the stack for
the senator to sign.

"You anticipate all of the senator's needs?" I said, turning
my head slowly to face him.

"I try," he said meekly but smiling at me. I took a deep
breath and silently counted to five in French: *un, deux, trois,
quatre, cinq.*

"Is that why you killed Jasper Neely?" Claude Morris's
eyes widened in surprise.

"Hattie!" Sir Arthur and Walter said simultaneously.

"Miss Davish!" the senator exclaimed. "How dare you!"

"But it's true, isn't it, Mr. Morris?" The eyes that had been
glaring at me for my accusation shifted to stare at the senator's
secretary.

"It is," Claude said quietly.

"Morris, how could you?"

"How could I not? The man was blackmailing you, Senator," Claude said, growing more confident with each word. "I
overheard everything. The gall! You are Senator Meriwether
Lewis Smith. Who was he but a disgruntled, devious little man?
How a good-for-nothing like that had the audacity to come
into your very home and give you an ultimatum, to threaten
you, the man pivotal to this government, and all the important
work you have yet to do for this country, is beyond my comprehension. And as it was beneath you, it was up to me to confront him."

"But you killed the man!" Sir Arthur said, in disbelief.

"I didn't plan to kill him. I didn't go to the march thinking
I was about to kill the man. But when I saw him with that har-
lot and overheard him scheming to expose you, Senator, to
Senator Abbott, even before you'd given him your answer, I

knew he had to be stopped. And the sooner the better. While you, and everyone else, were preoccupied during the confusion with Coxey and the police, I saw him standing alone by the wall. I seized the opportunity to put an end to this nonsense. I approached him and was met with derision. When I tried to reason with him, convince him it was for the greater good that he abandon his plans, he wouldn't listen. I pulled out my penknife, thinking threats and violence were all this man understood. But all he did was laugh. He laughed in my face, his crooked nose less than a foot away, as he pronounced his intentions to follow through on his threat. He gave me no choice. So I stabbed him. He staggered, grasping at the penknife. I couldn't stand to see the agony on his face, so I hurried away into the crowd and rushed back to my place at your side."

When the senator, stunned into silence, said nothing in response, Claude said, "You would've been ruined, sir."

"Quite so, Morris," Senator Smith said quietly. "Quite so."

"I'm afraid we can't avoid involving the police now, Meriwether," Sir Arthur said.

"No, you're right, Sir Arthur. This must be done right. I must appear beyond reproach." Sir Arthur rang the bell for the butler. "You understand, don't you, Morris?"

"Of course, sir. I'm only sorry I was found out. But better this than you having to give in to that blackmailer." The senator nodded slowly.

"Though I don't approve of what you've done, for it will cast a shadow on me for a time, it does pain me to lose you." After all his service, this is what the man says to whom Claude devoted his every waking hour? I was speechless but unfortunately not surprised.

"Thank you, sir. It's been an honor to serve," the secretary said, straightening the stack of papers on the desk before taking a seat to wait for the police to arrive.

CHAPTER 32

"How did you know, Hattie?" Walter asked. Pratt, the butler, with the help of two tall footmen, led Claude Morris away, to be watched in the servants' hall until the police arrived.

Whether Senator Smith's insistence that Claude wait downstairs was due to his fear that Claude would attempt to run away or whether the sight of his secretary made him feel guilty, I wasn't sure. But I could guess.

"I didn't, for certain. But when Mr. Morris mentioned Kirk's Castile soap, I thought it might be him."

"I don't understand. What was it about the soap that made you suspect him?"

"Kirk's Castile is a coconut oil soap. Coconut oil was on the penknife that killed Jasper Neely."

"But coconut oil is commonly found in toilet soap. My mother will use nothing else. How could you link the oil on the penknife to Morris?"

"Because Mr. Morris admitted to using Kirk's Castile to not only clean ink spots out of fabric but to lubricate penknifes."

"You're right. That's not the usual use of coconut oil soap." We sat in silence for several moments before Walter added, "I can't get over how calm Morris was, how matter-of-fact he was about the whole thing."

"Unfortunately, I can. He's a secretary and is extremely loyal. His whole life revolved around Senator Smith. A perceived threat to the senator was a threat to him as well. He saw killing Jasper Neely as one more task to perform in the service of his employer. I know because I'm not much different."

"But you would never kill someone to protect Sir Arthur's reputation."

"She would if she were as loyal as Morris," Senator Smith said, his first words in several minutes. I was speechless. Luckily Sir Arthur wasn't.

"Forgive me, but killing anyone outside of war is crossing a line," Sir Arthur said. "I demand loyalty of all my staff, but I would never condone anyone doing such a heinous thing."

"I didn't say I condone it," the senator clarified, "but I'm neither surprised nor dismayed by it. A loyal servant should be willing to do anything."

"I disagree," Sir Arthur said. "I've required Hattie to do a great deal outside of typing and taking dictation, including help investigate murders, but no one could possibly have the right to expect their servants to kill for them. It's beyond comprehension."

"*Suum cuique,*" the senator said, shrugging. "To each his own."

"The Latin phrase can also be translated as 'to each what he deserves,'" Walter said. Though I shouldn't have been surprised, knowing many medical terms are written in Latin, I was. Yet another facet of Walter I didn't know.

And I get to spend the rest of my life learning every facet of him, I thought, inwardly smiling.

Suddenly Spencer sprinted into the room, yet again dragging something in his mouth.

"Mildred, come get your damn dog." The senator was furious. Mrs. Smith scampered into the room behind him and picked up the growing puppy. "If that filthy dog ever comes into my study again . . ."

"You'll do what?" Mrs. Smith said, snuggling the dog to her breast.

"I'll—" The senator, glancing from his wife to the Chessie, stopped mid-sentence. "Give me that!" He strode over to the dog and yanked a large piece of silk cloth from its mouth. He wadded it up in his hand and tossed it into the wastebasket. But not before I'd seen what it was. Or more important, what was sewn on to it.

"Sir, the police," Pratt announced as Lieutenant Whittmeyer, accompanied by two uniformed officers, stepped into the room. With the senator focused on the arrival of the police, I retrieved the dog's treasure from the wastebasket and slipped it into my skirt pocket.

"What are you—?" the senator said, seeing me out of the corner of his eye. "Give me that." He lunged toward me. I dodged his grasp and slipped to the other side of the room next to Walter. Walter questioned me with a glance.

"I'm sorry to intrude on you, Senator," Lieutenant Whittmeyer said, raising an eyebrow when he spotted me, "but you requested our aid?"

"Yes, yes," the senator sputtered, frustrated at being distracted.

"Is that woman giving you trouble, sir?" the detective said, pointing his long finger at me. "I've warned her, more than once."

For a brief moment I saw hope light up in the senator's eyes. But before he could respond, Sir Arthur said, "Of course not. It's his man, Morris. He's confessed to killing that Coxeyite Neely during the march."

The senator glowered, the opportunity to retrieve the object in my pocket thwarted. The policemen regarded the senator, now slumped in a chair with his chin on his chest. "Is that true, Senator Smith?" Lieutenant Whittmeyer asked.

"Yes, unfortunately."

"Where is the man now?"

"He is in the servants' hall," Sir Arthur said.

"Have him brought up," the detective said. The senator gave no indication that he had heard or was going to cooperate. Sir Arthur pushed the call button.

Only a minute or two of awkward silence passed before Pratt arrived. "You rang, sir?"

Again, the senator stayed sullen and silent in his chair. "Bring Morris up, will you?" Sir Arthur said.

"Very good, sir."

When Morris arrived, each arm held by a footman, the lieutenant looked at me, and then at Walter, and then at Mrs. Smith, Spencer wiggling in her arms, but directed his request to Sir Arthur. "I need all unaffected parties to leave."

"Yes, of course," Sir Arthur said, leading the way.

As soon as the policeman closed the door, I retrieved the object from my pocket and held it out for Mrs. Smith to examine. It was filthy, ripped in several places, and coated in slobber.

"Is this your husband's, Mrs. Smith?"

"Yes."

"What is it, Hattie?" Sir Arthur said.

"All that's left of a man's vest with several of its fancy etched-pearl buttons missing."

"What are you saying?" Mildred Smith said, her usual smile gone.

"That it was your husband Hattie saw running away from the carriage accident that morning," Walter said. I nodded. The remaining buttons matched exactly. Now knowing that Senator Smith was a regular customer of Lottie Fox's establishment, I realized it had been the senator, and not his son,

Chester, who Spencer had barked at as the senator left late the night before the accident.

"Oh my God," Mildred said. "If this gets out, it will ruin him."

I shouldn't have been shocked by Mildred's instinct to first protect the senator's career over concern that her husband not only was with a "fallen woman" but by his negligence had cost the woman her life. But I wasn't.

I could never be a politician's wife, I thought. I glanced at Walter, concern written on his face. I never thought I could be a doctor's wife either.

"So that's why he's so sullen," Sir Arthur said. "I thought it was because of his man, Morris."

"What are you going to do?" Mildred said. "You can't tell the police."

"And she's not going to," Sir Arthur said to my dismay. Again, the rich and powerful looking out for their own.

"But, Sir Arthur," Walter protested. "The man left a woman to drown."

"It was an accident," Mildred Smith said.

"Regardless, a person died," I said.

"What was that?" Lieutenant Whittmeyer, opening the door as I spoke, asked.

"We were discussing the murder," Sir Arthur said. It was his way of forbidding us from speaking to the police about the carriage incident. I was used to holding my tongue when told to, and I knew Mrs. Smith wouldn't say anything, but would Walter abide? He frowned but stayed silent.

"We'll take it from here," Lieutenant Whittmeyer said. "No need to bother yourselves any more about it."

The detective stepped aside and let the uniformed officers, pushing Claude Morris, handcuffed, in front of them, through the door. After years of loyal service, this was what Morris was reduced to. I almost felt sorry for him. Almost.

As soon as Whittmeyer followed his men down the hall, Walter said, "I must insist this matter be brought to the appropriate authorities."

"And if the senator is guilty, as Hattie thinks, it will be," Sir Arthur said. "Now if you would all join me?" He indicated Senator Smith's study.

"What is it now?" The senator's face showed a fatigue that hadn't been there a few minutes before. "Morris is gone, and I'd like to be left alone, if you all don't mind."

"Show him, Hattie," Sir Arthur said. I held out the vest. "Is this yours, Smith?" The senator snatched it from my hand. He threw it into the fire.

"But it was yours, wasn't it?" Sir Arthur said.

"Yes, it was," Mildred Smith said.

"It was trash and nothing more," her husband mumbled.

I couldn't stay silent anymore. "I found buttons on the ground next to the carp pond after the carriage, *your* carriage, crashed, Senator. Those buttons came from that vest. It was you I saw rushing away that morning. You left that girl to die."

"It was an accident. The horse bolted, and I lost control."

"But why did you run away?" I asked.

"I panicked. I couldn't have my name associated with her."

"She bragged about you. She claimed you promised to make her respectable. You could've saved her, but instead you left her to die."

"Meriwether?" Mildred Smith said. "Is this true?"

"She was a whore."

A chill ran down my spine, and not because of the senator's vulgarity. How many times had I compared my fate to that of girls like Annie? Who could believe any life was worth less than another's?

"You said if he admitted to it, you would tell the appropriate authorities," Walter said, reminding Sir Arthur of his promise.

"Yes," Sir Arthur said, shaking his head. "I gave you the benefit of the doubt, Smith, but you freely admitted your guilt."

"You're not going to tell the police, surely?" The senator furrowed his brow in anger. "You understand, Sir Arthur. I have my constituents to consider, my committees, my colleagues. I have much work left to do before I retire. I can't risk tainting my name for the sake of a strumpet. Morris's mistake will be difficult enough to endure."

"Please, Sir Arthur," Mrs. Smith said. "Don't tell the police. What Meriwether did was wrong, but he doesn't deserve to go to jail."

How could his wife defend him? He admitted not only breaking his wedding vows and visiting a girl like Annie for "certain entertainments," but being indirectly the cause of the girl's death.

"I won't go to the police," Sir Arthur said. "You won't be going to jail."

"Sir Arthur!" Walter exclaimed. "You can't let him—"

"But I do know a friend of mine who will be very interested in learning about this," Sir Arthur said, interrupting Walter.

"How could you?" Mrs. Smith said, before bursting into tears and fleeing the room, Spencer clutched in her arms. Was she referring to Sir Arthur's threat to tell the journalist or her husband's despicable actions? I truly had no idea.

"You're going to tell that snake Harper that I was the one with the dead harlot that morning?" Senator Smith said, aghast.

Sir Arthur nodded somberly. "Then your constituents and your colleagues can decide for themselves if you did wrong."

CHAPTER 33

After Sir Arthur telephoned Simeon Harper and revealed Senator Smith's involvement in the early-morning carriage accident, he instructed me to pack my belongings. We left the Smith home within the hour, the senator locking himself in his study, and only Mrs. Smith and Spencer there to see us off. I sympathized with Mildred Smith, her fate tied to her husband's unknown future through no fault of her own.

"I'm sorry to have brought this upon you, Mrs. Smith. You have been nothing but a gracious and generous hostess," Sir Arthur said, kissing the matron's hand.

"It is of his own doing, Sir Arthur," she said before giving him a flash of her smile. "Do not trouble yourself about it. This too shall pass."

And maybe she was right.

As we left the Smith house for the last time, an onslaught of reporters, more numerous than earlier that morning, blocked our exit while shouting questions about the arrival of the police. Sir Arthur and Walter shielded me as they pushed through the men, who were waving their notebooks in their hands and shouting my name.

"Ask Simeon Harper," was all Sir Arthur said as Walter helped me into our hired barouche. "That will keep them busy for some time," he said, chuckling.

"Aren't you coming with us?" I asked Walter, when he didn't climb in beside me.

"No, but I'll see you soon." He tipped his hat and smiled.

"But—"

"The Willard hotel," Sir Arthur told the driver, and before I could say more to Walter, the barouche was rumbling away.

I wasn't happy. After the events of the morning, I wanted Walter there, beside me. We hadn't had time to properly discuss everything. Why hadn't he accompanied us? When would I see him again? What was I going to do until then? Work, of course. I'd finished the property index Sir Arthur had requested, but I was certain Sir Arthur had plenty more in mind for me to do.

As if to confirm my suspicions, Sir Arthur said, "There are a few manuscript pages I'd like you to finish, but you'll have to work quickly. We won't have much time once we get settled at the hotel."

"Of course." I wanted to ask why I had to work quickly but knew better. Luckily I didn't have to.

"When you're finished typing, we're going out. And you have Dr. Grice's permission to leave that behind," Sir Arthur said, pointing to my sling.

When had Walter said that? When the two men had met that morning before I arrived? What else had they discussed? Would Walter be where we were going?

"You'll need to wear your absolute best," Sir Arthur said.

I immediately pictured the new House of Worth dress Walter had bought me. That was to be my wedding dress. I hadn't imagined I'd be wearing it so soon. I couldn't imagine where we were going that required the loveliest dress I'd ever owned.

Were we going to meet the President?

"May I ask where we are going?"

Less than two hours later, after finishing my typing and un-packing, I stood beside Sir Arthur outside the famous hotel in my new dress. I brushed my hand down the soft silk of the skirt. It was so lovely I couldn't keep from touching it.

"It is a surprise, is all Mrs. Clayworth told me," Sir Arthur said, wearing his finest evening attire. I cringed. Not another one of Sarah's surprises. I hate surprises. "By the way, Hattie, you look lovely."

I was dumbfounded. Sir Arthur rarely complimented me on my work, and in all the years I'd worked for him, he'd only once commented on my appearance, and that wasn't to com-pliment me.

"Thank you," I said, as the Clayworths' Victoria arrived. Daniel and Sarah were inside, but Walter was missing.

"Isn't Walter coming?" I asked as I settled in beside Sarah.

"He went on ahead," she said, smiling. "What a lovely gown." She was dressed in an exquisite sea green silk gown with lace at the neck, cuffs, and bodice.

"Thank you." I ran my hand down the skirt again. "Walter gave it to me."

"My brother has good taste," she said, winking at me. As Wallace, the driver, coaxed the horse forward, Sarah looped her arm through mine. "Now tell me everything." I glanced at Sir Arthur. He nodded his consent, so I told Sarah what had oc-curred this morning.

After I'd finished, she said, "How despicable of Smith. Visit-ing the Apple House and then leaving that poor girl to drown. Poor Mildred. They are in for a rough ride."

"I wouldn't worry too much," Daniel said. "I agree with Smith; the voters will forget all about it by Election Day."

Are voters so forgetful, so forgiving? *Serves him right if they aren't.*

"And Claude Morris killing Jasper Neely? I still can't believe it," Sarah said, as the carriage stopped. "He seems so, I don't know, so ordinary, not at all like a killer."

I glanced out the window. We were parked in front of the White House. I was right. We were going to meet President Cleveland!

"What is a killer supposed to look like?" Daniel asked as he reached for the door handle.

"*Ahhh!* Like that!" Sarah screamed. She was pointing to the window. A man's face, sun-burned and with a scruffy mustache, peered in at us.

"Oh my God," Daniel said, more disgusted than afraid. "I'll take care of this."

"Daniel, who is he? Haven't I seen you arguing with him before?"

Daniel ignored his wife's questions as he clambered out of the carriage and stormed toward the man now waiting patiently with his hat in his hand. Sir Arthur followed.

"Who is that?" Sarah asked, not expecting an answer.

"It's Billy McBain," I said.

"You know him?" Sarah, surprised, turned back to look at me.

"He was one of Coxey's men. I've met him on several occasions. He tried to help rescue Annie Wilcox."

"But why was he staring into our window?" Sarah asked, as she alighted from the Victoria with Wallace's help. To my surprise, Sir Arthur, who had been silent throughout the carriage ride, offered me his hand.

"Because he's my brother," Daniel said, approaching the carriage, with Billy McBain following close behind.

"Your brother?" Sarah exclaimed. "You never told me you had a brother!"

"Hiya, sis," Billy said, tipping his brown derby. It looked new.

"We are only half brothers," Daniel said. "He didn't want Father's fortune, so he went out West to find his own when we were still in our teens. Obviously a fortune wasn't to be had." Daniel regarded his brother's road-worn clothes. "I haven't seen him in years."

That would explain the expensive pocket watch he'd had. A going-away present perhaps?

"And didn't wish to see me now, apparently," Billy said, smiling, unfazed by his brother's repeated rejections.

"I wouldn't have minded if you didn't look like a tramp—"

"I'm wearing the best I own." Billy's suit was worn but a definite improvement over the ragged clothes I'd first seen him in.

"—Or that you were known to have followed Coxey halfway across the country," his brother continued as if Billy had never spoken.

"Or that you were keeping company with Senator Abbott," I added.

"Him?" Billy said. "I thought he wanted to help Coxey, but he just wanted something Jasper promised him. I couldn't help him. I didn't even know what he was talking about."

Abbott will never get what Jasper Neely promised him, I thought. *Sir Arthur will see to that.*

"What would the voters say if they knew you were my brother?" Daniel said. "I couldn't have anyone thinking I supported Coxey or the Populists' ideas in any way."

"And now?" Billy asked. "Now that the march is over? Now that General Coxey and Marshal Browne are in jail?"

"You are welcome in our family," Sarah said, stepping up and embracing him.

"Thank you, Sarah," Billy said.

"Is that why you were at the police court?" I whispered to Daniel. "You were keeping an eye on your brother?"

"Yes. Ever since I discovered he was in town, I've been watching out for him but didn't want anyone to know, especially him. I'm truly sorry I was cross with you when you found me out."

"Apology accepted," I said. Daniel smiled and turned to his brother.

"Did you really see Doggie Miller hit a homer?" Daniel asked. Billy beamed and nodded.

"Jealous, aren't you?"

"I have to ask though, Billy," Sarah said, obviously not one bit interested in baseball. "How did you know we would be here?"

"Your brother, Dr. Grice, invited me, after I explained who I was."

"And where did you see my brother?"

"I saw him yesterday coming out of Saltztstein Jewelers."

"Oh, umm . . ." Sarah said, suddenly discombobulated. "Well, then, Daniel? Are you not going to welcome your brother?"

"Yes, well, it is good to have you back." Daniel held out his hand. The two brothers shook hands, and then Billy pulled his brother into an embrace. Daniel pushed away quickly, but smiled.

"Let's go in now, shall we? I believe we are expected," Sarah said, taking her husband's arm. "And no politics today, either of you." She looked knowingly at her husband.

"Of course," Billy said, chuckling. "It's gotten me into too much trouble already."

"I'd say," his brother said.

As the Clayworths gained the steps of the portico and headed for the door, Sir Arthur offered his arm to me. I was anxious as I took it. Would he scold me again for my foolishness? Would he speak of the work I had yet to finish because of the incident with Senator Smith and Claude Morris? Worse yet, would he simply escort me in complete silence? After several moments I'd concluded the latter, so when he spoke, I nearly jumped in surprise.

"I would like to apologize, Hattie," he said, quietly so only I could hear.

I nearly stopped to gape at him in my astonishment—Sir Arthur never apologized, not to me or anyone. But what was he apologizing for? I didn't dare hope he'd changed his mind about my engagement. But Walter thought it was a possibility, so what else could it be? My heart fluttered beneath my stays, but this was Sir Arthur after all. I'd spent countless hours in his company guarding my thoughts and feelings. He would get no inappropriate reaction from me. We continued on, as if he'd said nothing. But he wasn't finished.

"I was wrong to doubt your judgment, as yet again evidenced by this morning's events. You have served me unfailingly. I have never had cause to doubt you before. That, I'm afraid, is why I insisted you reconsider your engagement. As you know, I expect to get what I want, and I do not want to lose you. So I never fathomed for a moment that I would. But you are your own woman, and Walter is a good man. I regret your leaving, you're the best damn secretary I know, and to be honest, I'm going to miss you. But I give you my blessing and wish nothing for you but happiness."

It took me a moment longer than I would've liked to gain complete control over the emotions that were swirling throughout my body, but I did it. "Thank you, sir."

"And if you'd like, you having no father to do it, I would be proud to give you away."

"Thank you, sir. I would like that." How I managed to say anything was beyond me, for his kindness had proven too much. Tears unbidden welled up in my eyes as we reached the vestibule.

Sarah turned to say something to me and frowned, having noticed my tears. She glanced at Sir Arthur, who had joined Daniel and Billy, before whispering "Are you all right, Hattie?"

"Yes," I said, a smile spreading across my face as every obstacle to my happiness was now cleared. I looked at Sir Arthur and smiled. "He's given us his blessing."

"I know." Sarah smiled. Before I could ask her how she knew when he'd just told me, she patted my arm and said, "Shall we go in?"

We were escorted to the Blue Room, the distinctive oval-shaped parlor, luxuriously furnished in gilded blue Empire-style chairs and settees scattered about the room, blue wallpaper adorned with silver, thick blue drapes, and a glittering six-tier chandelier. No wonder it was the traditional place for presidents to meet guests. It was enchanting. Like the last time I was there, Mrs. Frances Cleveland, who had married the President in this room, stood near the door to greet us. Unlike the last time, the room felt intimate, warm and quiet, the only guests being our carriage party, Billy McBain, and two others. For standing between two five-foot vases filled with intertwining wisteria, honeysuckle, grapevine, Indian jasmine, and ivy, framing the window that looked out onto the South Lawn, was Walter, beaming in a new top hat, and Monsignor Thomas Sim Lee from St. Matthew's church.

"Why is . . . ?" It was all I could muster as Sarah led me toward Mrs. Cleveland.

"Congratulations, my dear, and thank you," Mrs. Cleveland said, leaning forward and kissing my cheek. "You make a most becoming bride."

"Bride?" Unchecked tears ran down my face. "Walter?"

Sarah pressed a posy of blooming red roses, ranunculus, lily of the valley, and baby's breath into my hand, as I looked again across the room at Walter. He hadn't taken his eyes off me.

"Surprise," Sarah whispered.

Maybe I'll have to reconsider my opinion of surprises.

"May I have the honor?" Sir Arthur said, offering his arm. I nodded.

It was like a dream. With the scent of roses mixing with that of the wisteria, the wide smiles on everyone's faces, the soft, fading sunlight reflecting off the gilded mirrors, I floated toward the only man I had eyes for.

When we stopped next to Walter, the priest, Monsignor Lee, said, "Who gives this woman to this man?"

"I do." Sir Arthur kissed my forehead and stepped away. Tears welled again in my eyes. Walter offered his arm and I took it.

"You are so beautiful," he whispered.

"But how?" I looked at Monsignor Lee as he continued with the marriage service. Normally a priest would not perform a wedding outside of the church.

"You don't deny a special request from the First Lady," Walter said.

"But why would she, for me?"

"Because she too is a member of the Washington Wives Club. I asked Sarah, and Sarah and Mildred asked her for this favor. She was touched by all your efforts in pursuing truth and justice over the past two years. Even before she knew about this morning, before she learned that you helped catch a killer in this city and found justice for a less fortunate soul, she was more than happy to oblige."

"And Sir Arthur?" I glanced in his direction. He stood next to the First Lady.

"What do you think we were talking about this morning? He too put in a word with the President and Monsignor, confirming everything this afternoon."

And Sir Arthur gets what Sir Arthur wants, I thought, never so happy for him to be obliged.

"You don't mind, do you? All of this, now? I couldn't bear

waiting one more day. But I had no idea what kind of day this would turn out to be."

"Mind? Walter, this is the most . . ." I couldn't find the words to express my joy.

As Monsignor Lee spoke, his words washing over me, I tried to imagine what Walter had said to change Sir Arthur's mind. I tried to conceive how Walter conjured up the elaborate idea of convincing Mrs. Cleveland to allow us to be wed in the Blue Room of the White House. I tried to comprehend how Monsignor Lee would have been persuaded to perform the ceremony. But it didn't matter. Walter had done it, and he had done it for me.

"Thank you," I whispered.

"You don't need to thank me. Just say 'I do.'"

I glanced about. Monsignor Lee, and everyone else in the room, was waiting for me to speak.

"Oh," I said, embarrassed. Walter squeezed my hand reassuringly.

"I will say it again, child," Monsignor Lee said patiently. "Will you, Hattie Maria Davish, take Walter Kenneth Grice to be your husband? Do you promise to be true to him in good times and in bad, in sickness and in health, to love him and honor him all the days of your life?"

I looked into Walter's eyes, knowing that the peace, love, and happiness that overflowed in my heart at that moment, regardless of what the future held, would ever be found there.

"I do."

AUTHOR'S NOTE

This book is a work of fiction. However, the story is centered around the very real, often overlooked, first-ever protest "march" on Washington.

Inspired to help those suffering from The Panic of 1893, considered by many to be the worst economic depression in U.S. history excluding only "the Great Depression" of the 1930s, businessman Jacob Coxey, partnering with eccentric showman Carl Browne, led a group of several hundred unemployed men from Massillon, Ohio, on March 25, 1894, toward Washington, D.C. Ahead of their time, their intent was to present a "petition in boots" for government-financed jobs and roadway improvements, all of which would one day become part of the New Deal. With journalists following the group outnumbering the members of "Coxey's Army," it was one of the most publicized events in American history. Every day new accounts would appear in the nation's newspapers. Readers were able to follow the "Army," or, as they called themselves, the "Commonweal of Christ's" progression, and the melodrama that ensued, in detail, every step of the way. When the men finally arrived in Washington on May Day, also known as International Workers' Day, the government was prepared for an invading army and for bloodshed. As nothing like it had been attempted before, there was no precedent to guide the government's reaction to it. Anything could happen. Luckily, the marchers arrived in peace and the only bloodshed was caused by the police melee described in the story. Jacob Coxey was denied permission to give his address. He and Carl Browne were arrested and sentenced to time in jail for trespassing on the grass of the Capitol grounds. Others, inspired by Coxey's message, attempted to follow, including a then unknown Jack London. Groups from as far away as California and Oregon set out to join Coxey's men in Washington, some even hijacking trains in the attempt, but few made it so far and none in time to see Coxey escorted by police off the Capitol steps. Although the "march" was all but forgotten and his compatriots spread across the country, Coxey never forgot his mission or his message. He tried to influence the government's policies for decades to come, with varying success. And on May 1, 1944, Jacob Coxey finally read his original speech from the Capitol steps from which he had been denied exactly fifty years before.

While incorporating this historic event into Hattie's fictional adventure, I have endeavored to be as historically accurate as possible. Luckily, this was not in any way difficult. I was able to read firsthand accounts, newspaper articles from the exact day or time I was researching, and speeches given by a particular character in the real story, including Coxey's original address. Photographs of the real-life players, their camps, their journey east, and more were readily available. I also relied on scholarly works published in the years after the event, particularly Benjamin Alexander's *Coxey's Army: Popular Protest in the Gilded Age* and Carlos Schwantes's *Coxey's Army: An American Odyssey*. I highly recommend both if you are interested in reading further about this first-ever protest march.

In trying to be as accurate and authentic as possible, I have, with very few exceptions, used only known quotes of a real, historical person when giving that character spoken dialogue. For example, all of the outrageous words spouting from Carl Browne in the story are true, word for word. Only in the timing of the trial have I consciously changed the facts to fit the story. All other major errors or inconsistencies were unintentional.

I thoroughly enjoyed bringing to life a forgotten moment in our nation's history, as seen through Hattie's eyes. I hope you enjoy it too.